The CURSED TOUCH

A novel by

RAASHIDA KHAN

ISBN: 978-1-77605-656-9
e-book: 978-1-77605-655-2

Cover Photograph by Remi Yuan (Unsplash.com)

Typesetting and layout by Janet Von Kleist

www.kwartspublishers.co.za

Please follow Raashi at:

🌐 www.raashisreflections.com

f www.facebook.com/raashisreflections/

🐦 @Raashisreflect

📷 @Raashisreflect

CONTENTS

Also by Raashida Khan

Happy Birthday, Raashi (poetry anthology)
Mirror Cracked
Fragrance of Forgiveness
My Voice, Your Strength and Other Stories
(short story anthology)

FOREWORD

The Cursed Touch is a compelling story that is beautifully written. This is not Raashida Khan's first rodeo at writing fiction, and it shows in the depth of the writing and the gripping story. Khan put her soul into this story, as is evidenced by the addition of deep, soulful poetry, which is a delightful surprise for me, but then again, this book is not typical in any way. This story can be described as the intersection of power, identity, loss, and redemption. At the same time, it is also a journey of self-discovery and self-acceptance.

As a political journalist who has dabbled a little into fiction writing, I have come to fully appreciate the craft that is writing fiction of this nature. Khan very effectively weaves together difficult topics – like the long-lasting effects of family trauma and the consequences of a history of bad decisions – into a work of fiction that is engrossing. The South African context makes it all seem familiar, with characters that are complex, layered, and most importantly, real.

Sondra Carim-Edwards is a Johannesburg-based powerful financial executive who has put work at the centre of her life over everything else – including her husband, David, and son, Michael. You hate her and love her at the same time. While you root for a happy ending, you are deeply satisfied by where her journey takes her. Reckless decisions send Sondra's life into a spiral, forcing her to realise the consequences of her actions. A powerful thread throughout the book is that Sondra is not a victim. Khan created a character in the firm grasp of power and navigates themes of accountability and regret. But by the end of Sondra's journey, you can't help but empathise with her as she tries to pick up the pieces of her life.

The Cursed Touch is not only Sondra's story. You meet characters like Hannah Bennett, David, and Michael, who are all dealing with their own emotions in the wake of Sondra's actions. Glimpses into Sondra's past – with her Coloured mother, Beryl, and Muslim father, Abdul – only enrich the story. Sondra's background, which is seated in this mixed race and multi-religious upbringing, gives the story a rich tapestry of depth to her character. But every single character is layered, compelling, and unique.

While this adds to the completeness of the story, it also is a step forward in the discussion around the portrayal of characters that are different, diverse, and refreshing. This impressed me as a reader because I have long agonised about the portrayal of women of colour in fictional literature. Recently, we have overcome the debate about why it is important to have more stories with female characters who are not simply blonde and blue-eyed. I think the two main reasons why we need to have more stories such as *The Cursed Touch* is inclusivity and perception. It reinforces that stories of women of colour matter and that we can see ourselves in and relate in some ways to such characters. This is a South African story, with all of the country's complexities and flavours.

The more you get to know about the protagonist, Sondra, the more you want to know about her. You feel what she feels: the visceral betrayal, the evocation of being unloved, the resolve for redemption. *The Cursed Touch* is foremost a journey of self-love and the complexities of what that means. Through Sondra's story, you learn how forgiving yourself is liberating and how self-love leads to healing and acceptance.

Qaanitah Hunter
Political Editor for *News24*

1

SEXY SONDS

S ondra sultrily drew up the black silk stockings over her caramel-toned skin. Her leg was temptingly raised, and her fingers caressed her calves while she checked that the stockings were straight. She wondered for the briefest moment if David, her husband, would still enjoy such a show. When they were first married, passionate play and foreplay had been the order of the day. Nowadays, when they shared passion, it was over almost as soon as it had started. Wryly, she acknowledged that this situation was almost all her doing. Her obsessive nature over everything other than her family had slowly but surely pushed him away. For Sondra, work came first, second, and third.

The thoughts were gone the instant that she heard the soft snoring that came from under the tousled sheets. Playfully, she kicked Vic's bare foot that stuck out over the side of the bed. 'Hey! Don't sleep.'

She switched on the floor lamp that stood behind the chair next to her. She liked that hotels invariably placed chairs instead of stools at dressing tables – they were much more practical. She turned her naked back towards the bed and watched in the mirror as Vic rustled the crisp sheets. Slowly, she stepped into her black pencil skirt that she had carefully laid on the back of the chair. Pulling on her blouse, Sondra did not button it just yet and ran a comb through her thick, dark hair, then started fixing her make-up. She was blessed with naturally clear skin so required little make-up, but she had learnt to accentuate what she considered her strong features – her chocolate-brown almond-shaped eyes and her pert, plump lips.

'Vic?' she probed again, making sure that her voice held the right mix of strength and seductiveness. 'Are you awake?'

'I'm awake.' Vic was on his back and pushed himself up on both elbows. 'My eyes are wide open, and ... I like what I see.'

Sondra smiled at him in the mirror as she appreciated the charming grin that complemented the boyish features of the man she had spent the last hour with. She noticed that Vic was staring at her reflection in the mirror. Instinctively, she sucked in her stomach and tilted her head at an angle that she knew was complimentary. While she rose, she leisurely buttoned up her blouse, making sure to push her bosom out, as she sauntered to the side of the bed, looking down at her most recent acquisition. She held her smile steady.

Vic laughed and pulled her back onto the bed. 'Come here, silly girl. You're perfect, Sonds.' Vic nuzzled her neck. 'Every luscious inch of you.'

Sondra lightly brushed his sandy blond hair, secretly de-lighted to be called "girl" as she had been the older side of forty for a few years already. The years had been good to her; she looked great and worked hard to keep it that way. She gave a girlish giggle and pushed him away. 'I need to get back to work. This was nice.'

'"Nice". "*Nice*"?' His features pulled in on themselves. 'Wow! Don't try and sugar-coat it or anything.'

Sondra recognised that Vic was pretending that his ego had been bruised and recouped with what she had learnt all men wanted to hear. 'You know your business in bed, Mister D.' Sondra kissed Vic solidly on the mouth and stroked her hand across his firm, sculpted torso. She could feel his heart beat faster at her touch. 'Mmm, a man who takes care of himself *and* his lady.'

Vic looked appeased and squeezed her hand, which was still playing with the soft hairs on his chest. 'I looooove your touch.' He spoke slowly, emphasising each syllable with deliberate steaminess.

Sondra's eyes flickered to the electronic clock radio on the pedestal behind him. 'Look at the time. I have to go.'

'Do you really?' Vic was attempting a come-hither look with a raised eyebrow and his dreamy blue eyes.

'I don't *want* to, but I must. I have a meeting back at the office in thirty minutes.' She energetically jumped to her feet and gathered her bag and shoes. 'You'll make that call for me?'

'You're something else, Sonds. Sexy Sonds. Ooh, those *sssexy sssounds* you were making *just now* when you were in here with me. You love your body, don't you?' His lips curled into a smile before his tongue darted out to lick them. 'And with a bloody clever mind to match it. How did you even know I knew Cravat?' Vic was referring to his school buddy and now obscenely wealthy Nathaniel Cravat who had just returned from Canada after having lived there for fifteen years.

'Did my research. Arrange that meeting, and we can do this again.' She gave him one last taste of her lips – the kiss was strong but lasted less than a second – and then she was out the door. Always leave them wanting more, right?

If Sondra had loitered for a moment longer, she would have heard Vic's hopeful voice saying, 'Call me.'

In the elevator mirror, Sondra admired her reflection. She was pleased that it didn't reveal any traces of the passion she had partaken in. Her full lips were stained subtly, looking again like they had that morning. Her hair fell like sheets of black glass to below her shoulders. Regular Brazilian treatments ensured her wavy tresses stayed super-slick and soft, just like she liked it. The high cheekbones and delicate, pointed chin set in her oval face were complemented by her dark hair and naturally bronze skin. She worked hard to stay slim, toned, and in shape, which she pulled off well because she was tall for an Indian woman but average for a Coloured. She was happy to have received more of her physical characteristics from her Coloured mother, Beryl Jobman, and less from her Indian father, Abdul Carim.

She clipped her pearl studs back onto her ears. As Sondra slipped her wedding ring back on, she was, and not for the first time, struck by the simplicity of the gold band. A gentle tugging at her heart reminded her how much she should appreciate David, her husband of the past eighteen years. He knew her better than anyone else and had known that she would prefer a simple, classy band. She admired it as it rested snuggly on her ring finger. It was raised in the middle with a bevelled ridge along the edges. David had had the word "Forever" inscribed on the inside, together with their names and the date of their wedding. The years fly by when you're focused on other things.

David was a good man and did not deserve to be cheated on, but Sondra quickly dropped her hand and pushed such thoughts out of her mind. She did not spend time on feelings of guilt or regret; they were wasteful emotions. It wasn't really cheating anyway. She had no feelings for Vic, or for any of the others, and would have had no interest in him – romantic or otherwise – if he didn't have such a good network. She and David were good, she reminded herself. Neither this nor any other liaison was ever going to affect their relationship. They worked well as a couple.

As the elevator quietly whirred to the ground floor, Sondra decided that she would have to rehearse her presentation in her head while she drove back to the office in Illovo. She would have preferred to have her carefully prepared

PowerPoint on her laptop to rehearse with, but the day had turned out more eventful than she had expected. When Vic had returned her call that morning, she had immediately agreed to see him. Time was of the essence when it came to getting an introduction to Cravat. Sondra would be the first investment consultant to reach out to him. He would be impressed and quickly learn to trust her; she would make sure of that. She had targeted fifty per cent of his substantial portfolio but was actually hoping for sixty-five.

There was a subtle fragrance of mint and patchouli in the hotel lobby that she quickly walked through. It was easy not to make eye contact with any of the other guests with the lobby being as quiet as it was. Apart from the front desk staff, who she ignored too, there were only a few people sitting at the tables that dotted the reception area. She focused on the detail of the décor, which was subtle and tasteful. It was a pity that she avoided visiting the same establishment twice in a year; this new avant-garde hotel was positively delightful.

Her mind drifted again to the possibility of securing Cravat as a new client. Her plan was simple: Vic would invite Cravat to lunch, and Sondra would arrive ten minutes after they ordered drinks; Vic would "spy" her across the room and introduce them; Cravat would ask her to join them, and she would decline twice before graciously accepting his generous invitation. She had full confidence in this plan – none of her other plans had ever let her down.

* * *

Back at the office, Sondra tossed her car keys to Nobuhle, the receptionist. Nobuhle caught the keys smartly. Sondra gave her a cursory nod before she immediately dove in.

'Get one of the interns to bring my laptop from my *boot*. Get them to plug it in in the boardroom and get my presentation ready. It's on my desktop. They need to check that the video links work. Check it all. I'll be there in ten.' She gave Nobuhle a thumbs-up to indicate her thanks.

'On it,' Nobuhle answered with a nod. 'By the way,' she added quickly, 'Rodrick sent an e-mail saying they're running thirty minutes late.'

'Oh, good. I'll have time for a dry run then.'

Alone in the bathroom, Sondra breathed in and out slowly for a minute. Once she felt more composed, she checked her make-up again. All was still fine, so she made her way down the corridor. She took a few steps passed the water cooler, stopped, then walked back. She downed a glass of cold water dispensed from the machine and decided that she had some time to make an appearance in the bullring.

The smart clicking sound of her heels against the laminated wooden floors was the only sound that could be heard over the consistent hum of the computers that emanated from the bullring, so called because it was where fierce financial battles were fought. She loved high heels – the sexier the better. The only downside was that they did not allow her to move quietly down this passage. The dozen or so researchers, analysts, and junior investors would be prepared for her entry. That was fine. There were other ways of observing them unseen. It actually made them feel a mite more secure that they would have twenty seconds notice in preparation for answers that she may demand.

Each drone, as she called them, worked on their own portfolios, ensuring the company was solidly busy for eighteen hours every day. It was sometimes longer on days when international market movements were critical enough to warrant immediate reaction rather than waiting for their day to catch up with the East or responding later to the West.

Sondra relished the knowledge that each of their fates rested in her hands. She had interrogated their portfolios, tracking their investment activities and performances on complicated spreadsheets that allowed no error to be missed. Notorious for being a hard taskmaster, Sondra was unforgiving after the first misdemeanour. Misdemeanours were classified as deals or buys that did not make the company and shareholders money or, even worse, lost money.

She had been as ruthless as ever in their quarterly reviews. Two were to be fired immediately, and three others were going to be suspended for two weeks. It wasn't the first time she had made people quiver at the prospect of being evaluated by her stringent standards. It had been seven years before when she had first heard pleas for mercy. A hard-won promotion at the time had meant everyone except the two partners and head of HR answered to her. It was a surprise to realise how much she enjoyed the power she wielded. She was in awe of herself.

Sondra was living proof of the truth in the saying that power is intoxicating.

2

AT HOME AND IN PRIVATE

Sondra drove her silver *Audi A1* into the garage at her home in Lonehill and walked into the house. As was her custom, she dropped her bags on the floor in the entrance hall and walked into the kitchen. She called out a general 'hello,' but no one answered. She wondered if David and Michael, their sixteen-year-old only child, were upstairs. She was relieved to see that Cynthia – her lifesaver and the family's domestic worker – had supper prepared already.

Sondra flipped through the newspaper that lay on the granite countertop. The kitchen had finished being re-vamped when Michael was around ten years old – the last big project that they had completed. They had bought the house when Michael was two as David had wanted a garden for the "kids" to play in. Even then, Sondra had made up her mind about only having one child, but she knew that David had hoped for more.

Eventually, when Michael was six or seven years old, David had given up asking and had devoted himself to his only son. The house was on a large plot and was bought at a steal be-cause it was, as advertised, a "fixer-upper". Slowly, she and

David had renovated: bathrooms first, then bedrooms, then the study and living areas, and finally, the kitchen. Those were the best years for the family. Turning their house into a home that suited them all had brought them close.

Weekends had often been spent together, choosing and deciding on fixtures and fittings. Shopping expeditions would end somewhere they could have a relaxed late lunch at or at a park for Michael's entertainment. She would never have guessed the cute little boy would have grown up to be this dark and handsome young man that she would know less and less about. Secretly, she loved that his hair was dark brown and curly like his father's – like his father, it made him look youthful. His eyes were dark too and piercing; they suited his aristocratic features. She had always wondered where the strong, proud visage had come from. His face didn't really look like either of them, though there was defi-nitely some of David in Michael.

Nowadays, though, things were different from the young family they once were. Sondra was too busy, even over weekends, considering that her career had progressed exactly as she had envisioned and had come to consume most of her time. Michael was a typical teenager, enthusiastic when it suited him but often moody and grumpy, especially with his mother. He and his father shared their love of sports and would spend time together, watching TV or attending matches. Their relationship had always been solid and easily survived any little disagreement. Grudgingly Sondra acknowledged that David did make more of an effort than she did in the parenting department. She dismissed the notion quickly; it was pointless thinking about things that she had no intention of changing.

Sondra closed the newspaper and added it to the small stack on the open shelf underneath the counter. There was some mail too. She was surprised to receive an invitation to her high school reunion. She wondered who had managed to track her down, having avoided all groups or mailing lists from her past. She tossed the invitation, along with other unnecessary post, into the bin. Like everything else from her youth, growing up in Durban was something she would rather keep forgotten.

Sondra sighed as she retrieved her bags to go upstairs. She passed the entrance to the TV room and saw her son, lounging in front of the TV as usual. He had probably heard her come in but hadn't bothered to respond to her greeting. She knew better than to raise that with him.

'Hi, Michael. Good day at school?'

His response was standard, as were her next questions.

'Homework sorted? Do you need anything?'

This time, he didn't answer, and Sondra didn't pursue it. If he needed anything, or if there was something that required attention, she would hear about it eventually.

David was in their bedroom when she entered. David Edwards had grown up in the Durban Coloured township of Wentworth. He had been living in Johannesburg since he had secured a job at a respectable law firm soon after finishing his studies. David had been young and hungry as a newly qualified law graduate, which had served him well. He had been lucky. Many other graduates waited for years before being employed, but he had been open to taking a low-level job and working his way up.

Sondra had grown up in Durban too but didn't know Wentworth well. As a child, she had occasionally visited there until her maternal grandmother had passed on. Sondra had been eight years old at the time. Her grandmother had been a single mother too, and Beryl had had no siblings and not much contact with the extended family. After her granny passed away, Beryl and Sondra never returned to Wentworth.

David was handsome, and despite being older than Sondra by eight years, had aged well. His curly hair was soft and lightly speckled with grey, and his brown eyes lit up behind his glasses as he rose to hug her. She pecked his bearded cheek, simultaneously greeting him and asking about his day.

He started telling her about some issue he was having with a case. He was a confident and well-respected lawyer, specialising in labour law. His clients were mostly employees dismissed unfairly. It was not particularly lucrative work, but he made a comfortable living and was happy, which he valued more than money.

Sondra half-listened while she concentrated on removing her make-up and clothes. She changed into spandex running pants and a T-shirt. She turned to look at David, who had not stopped talking.

'... but I'm sure I'll get it sorted.' His eyes flickered over her warmly. 'You look young when you're not all power dressing. I like that. You're going for a run?'

'Yes. I'll be back in forty minutes.'

'I'll join you.'

'Nah. You can't keep up and will slow me down.' With her back to him, Sondra inserted her earphones so that, even if he tried to ask again, she wouldn't hear. He was actually as fit and as fast as she was, but Sondra preferred to run alone.

When she got back fifty minutes later, she found David and Michael in the TV room. David apologised because he and Michael had eaten dinner without her again. 'He was hungry, and you know I don't like him to eat alone.'

'Don't stress. I don't mind.' Sondra polished off the remainder of the salad directly from the platter and cut a slice of lasagne onto her plate, which she carried to the TV room.

Michael, sitting on his favourite – or was it preferred because no one could sit next to him? – single-seater armchair, tossed her the remote. 'You can change it. I'm not really watching.' He didn't look up from the cell phone in his other hand.

'Thanks. I'll just catch up on the news and markets.' She changed the channel and sat back in the middle of the three-seater couch in front of the TV. As she forked cold lasagne into her mouth, she texted Vic.

Today was great. See you soon?

Images of some disaster flashed onto the screen, so she turned up the volume. A second earthquake had hit Mexico – the death toll was nearly a hundred, but thousands were affected. Natural disasters and conflicts in even the remotest areas affected the markets. It was critical to stay in touch.

Suddenly, tiredness washed over her in a wave. She put her plate on the dark wood coffee table, kicked off her running shoes, and stretched out on the couch.

David looked up from the book he was buried in, sitting opposite Michael on the two-seater couch. 'You look tired. Why don't you have an early night, Sonds?'

'I wish. But work beckons. Was out of the office for a few hours today. Then there was the pitch to Rodrick's team. Now, I have to play catch-up.'

'Oh, yeah? That was the new pension scheme proposal, right? How did that go?' David lowered his book to his lap, showing her that she had his full attention.

'Well. *Very* well, I think. I'm sure they will adopt the solution I'm proposing. The trick would be to get HR to sell it to the staff. It would mean a higher percentage of staff contributions, but in the long run, they'll all benefit.'

David nodded and checked his wristwatch.

'Sorry I'm boring you. I'm going to bath, then I'll at least check my mails before I go to bed.'

'Mmm, okay. I'll be up after *Thrones*. I recorded it so that I can skip the ads – an hour tops.' David was an avid *Game of Thrones* fan, but it was not something that Sondra had cared to invest time in.

Upstairs, in the quiet of her bathroom, Sondra applied a treatment to her hair before checking her phone. There was a message from John. Young, sweet John Bennett had started as an intern at the firm five months before. He had been particularly eager, even for an intern, doing more than his share of research for his accounts, as well as general office admin and running around. He quickly became known as the gofer and had managed to attach himself to Sondra as an unofficial personal assistant.

It had become clear early on that his admiration for her was not just professional. Sondra had found the personal attention endearing and, against her better judgement, had allowed him closer.

Three weeks before, when he had stayed late to help with putting together a last-minute presentation, she'd ordered pizza and had invited him to share it with her. She had kicked off her heels and had relaxed on the couch in her office. When he had moved to sit at her feet and offered a foot massage, she had readily agreed. Sondra had repositioned herself and had shrugged off her jacket.

'Your feet are beautiful.' He had raised shy, pale-blue eyes to hers before they had darted away. He had clearly been self-conscious and in awe of her. It had been amusing but thrilling too. She had stretched her arms above her head and had moved her head from side to side, relaxing while his hands had worked.

'Your shoulders are tight? Here, let me.' In an instant, he had been standing behind her, expertly working away the knots.

'Mmm, that's good. You have good hands.' Sondra had unbuttoned the top buttons on her shirt and had pulled it down her upper arms to allow him better access. After a minute, he had slipped her bra strap off her left shoulder. She had felt his lips flutter above and plant a tentative kiss at her hairline.

'Hey, what're you doing?' But her protest had been half-hearted. His soft, full lips had played havoc with her insides in her relaxed state. 'Stop that, Jake ... uh, I mean, John.' She had known that she should have moved his hands away but couldn't bring herself to do so. 'What are you do-ing?'

'What I've wanted to do since the first moment I saw you.'

She had registered surprise. This boldness had been un-characteristic of the serious youth she had known him to be. His hands had hitched her shirt down further, and he had cupped her perky, round breast.

I should stop this, her internal voice had warned. *But damn, that is good.*

Sondra had leant forwards and had thrown her head back to allow his explorations to intensify. He hadn't needed much persuasion. The next second, he had pushed the coffee table away, had lain her down on the couch, and had fumbled a tad as he stripped her of her clothes and sensibilities.

The risk of being caught had heightened Sondra's pleasure, and she had heard herself moaning as he drove her to the heights of ecstasy that belied his young age.

You'll regret this, Sonds ...

Yet she had not stopped it. Her desire had risen. Her need to be fulfilled would not have been ignored. It had been her hands that had unbuckled his belt and had pushed down his pants and boxers. When she had felt his throbbing hardness, it had been her who had guided him into her, and it had been her who had taken control of his wild thrusting. John had lifted his head and tried to kiss her on the lips, but she had moved her face away from him. When she had felt his kiss deepen at her neck, she had pushed his head lower. A visible hickey would have been tough to hide and explain.

When they had finished, Sondra had gathered her clothes and phone, had dressed quickly, and had gone to the bath-room. Her reflection in the brightly lit mirror had been unfamiliar, a mixture of bewilderment and naivety etched into her delicate features.

Bloody hell, she had sworn silently. *This is crazy!*

She hadn't felt confident enough to face John after that, so she had texted him instead.

> Don't know what I was thinking.
> It was once-off stupidity, but I
> can't say I regret it. You're sweet.

> Nothing must change between us.
> We don't need rumours to affect
> our work. You can leave now. I'll
> finish up. Good work tonight.

His response had been immediate.

> That was wonderful
> Sondra. Don't worry. This
> is our precious secret. I'll
> see you tomorrow.

Sondra had expelled a loud breath in relief. She had counted on her authority to ensure this stupid mistake would be quickly forgotten and never repeated.

Later that night, her phone had buzzed, indicating the arrival of a message. The hairs on the back of her neck had stood up, and she had licked her suddenly dry lips. Even before reading the message, she had known it would be from John and that she would not like the content.

She had been right.

She had deleted it without responding and had switched off her phone. She would have to deal with him in person at the office. That night, her body and mind had been exhausted. In bed, she had set the alarm to allow her an hour in bed to finalise the presentation.

She shook her head now as she read his message once more before deleting it. So much for her initial resolve. John had been persistent, persuasive, and had kept his promise of being discreet. She had succumbed and had allowed him to drive away any feeble misgivings she had had. It was the first time Sondra had agreed to an interaction – Sondra never thought of it as a relationship or an affair – that was purely for her. There was no ulterior motive or benefit to be had apart from her sweet, secret pleasure and to bask in John's adoration.

She silenced her own niggling voice with the argument that he would be gone soon when his internship ended in a few weeks' time and that she would not have to see him again. The interactions were never again at the office, which would have made things more complicated. She resisted his attempts to meet for meals or on any other pretexts. While she loved the attention and his obvious reverence, she saw no need for such time-wasting activities.

'This is just about sex,' she had told him repeatedly. 'Pure and simple.'

He hadn't seemed to mind that. He had used his youthfulness and growing prowess in bed to help him find his voice. 'As you wish, my lady,' he had said. 'You like this young, fresh cock, don't you?'

The sexual banter extended to their private text chats too. Now, as she filled the tub, she responded to the earlier suggestive message while simultaneously checking e-mails. *Great.* There was nothing that could not wait until the morning. She could close her eyes as she soaked and relaxed.

3

THE PAST COMES FLOODING BACK

Sondra was running late for the meeting at Michael's school. She was lucky to find a spot that she managed to squeeze her small car into. It was not really a parking place, and the car jutted out into the road a bit. She ran quickly through the school gates, keeping her head down to avoid the waving hands of the security guard. She would leave sooner than most parents, and her car was not actually obstructing anyone else's, so there was no harm done.

She recognised the stock-standard speech from where she stood at the back of the hall. The principal was droning on about the importance of parental involvement, punctuality, and discipline. David caught her eye and waved her over, indicating that he had saved her a seat. She shook her head and gave him her customary thumbs-up sign. She was fine where she was. She searched the rows of heads on the right-hand side of the hall where the students were seated but could not make out which one belonged to Michael.

She joined in the applause from the audience, wondering if everyone else was as relieved as she was that the principal was done. Now, the heads of the various departments would talk about each of their subjects. These annual information mornings were a bloody waste of time. When the next teacher started, Sondra moved outside to make a call. Twenty minutes later, she walked back and was relieved to see that they were at the end. Parents were encouraged to stay for a cup of tea and to meet with the teachers.

Searching the mass of people, Sondra saw David was on his way to the garden. She caught up with him and pulled at his sleeve. 'I have to get going, David. You're staying to chat to the teachers?' She grimaced involuntarily.

David looked down to her hand that was still on his sleeve. 'Aren't you?'

She dropped her hand and answered hastily. 'No. I ... uh. If you're staying, there's no point in both of us being here. I have an appointment anyway.'

David's eyes narrowed, but he said nothing.

'I'll find Michael and explain. See you at home?' Sondra didn't wait for a response.

She pressed past the other parents walking in the opposite direction, calling, 'Michael. Michael.' She'd spotted him and wanted to grab him before he disappeared with his friends. He turned to face her, and her breath caught in her throat. She was eye-height with this handsome, strapping young man in his school blazer and tie, neatly knotted at his collar. Did he look like his father? She could never be sure. He didn't resemble *her* at all though, that was for sure.

'Hi, Mom. You made it.'

Sondra reached up to run her hand through his curly, neatly cut hair, but he ducked away from her touch, then quickly glanced over his shoulder at his friends.

'*Soooorry.*' Sondra grinned. 'Forgot your friends are here. I was a little late, and I've got to go now. I have a hair appointment.'

'You're leaving?'

'I have to. Dad's staying though. I'll get pizza for supper.' Sondra hoped that his favourite takeaway food would ease his disappointment.

Michael shrugged and started walking back to the group of kids hovering to the side. 'Whatever. Later.'

Sondra almost called after him but realised that there wasn't anything she could say to appease him. It would just make things worse. *Nothing to be done.* She really could not force herself to stay anyway.

At the car, she gave the security guard an extra big tip, hoping that that would forgive her inconvenient parking. She was glad she had managed to change her hair colour appointment to earlier. If she did not let them dry it, she could probably squeeze in a rendezvous with John.

* * *

As she sat down in the chair and the tent-like apron was draped over her shoulders, she texted John to check his availability. It was unusual for her to initiate a meeting, but then again, everything about her interaction with John was surprising. His response was immediate and positive, just as she had predicted. He would drop anything he had planned if she snapped her fingers.

> This must be telepathy. I was thinking about you. Who am I kidding? I'm always thinking about you. I was updating my diary – you've inspired me to start writing again.

> What? Don't be daft, John! You can't do that. We have to be careful. No one can find out about us.

31

Don't worry. No one will
ever see it. Our special
delicious relationship is
our sweet, sexy secret.

Sondra snapped her phone shut angrily. This boy was im-
mature and foolish. She'd have to get him to destroy any
trace of their liaison. Sondra narrowed her eyes as her nostrils
flared inadvertently.

Angie, her stylist, misunderstanding her irritation hastened to apologise. 'Sorry to keep you waiting. Saturdays are
always crazy.'

Sondra shrugged and forced herself to exhale slowly.
Angie checked on the dye in the plastic bowl and asked if
they were going to trim.

'Not today. I have to rush. After it's washed, I may just
towel dry and scoot off.'

As always, Angie tried to engage her in conversation as
she painted Sondra's hair with the dye, but after answering
one or two questions perfunctorily, Sondra buried her nose
in a magazine, hoping that Angie would take the hint.

'Sondra! Sondra Carim? I cannot believe it. It is you,
isn't it?'

Warily, Sondra raised her head to look in the direction of
the vaguely familiar voice. The smiling face was round, and
the cheeks were accentuated by dimples that were cute years
ago. Yes, this was definitely a face she knew from years
back. Sondra looked directly at the eyes that searched hers.

'It's me, Khadija. Khadija Seedat. Remember, from school?'
Khadija nodded enthusiastically. 'Wow! It's been years, man.
You're completely off the radar. Some of the girls even
thought maybe you'd died. But here you are, in the flesh.'

Angie had stopped to stare at the woman who had walked
in a minute earlier. Angie's applicator brush was held mid-
air; her mouth hung open. Sondra could only guess why. The
brightly coloured *abaya* and fake designer handbag perhaps?

The accent when she pronounced Sondra's surname – not Carim, but *Kareem*? – or was it the surprise at someone else knowing her client of seven years who had never spoken of any attachments, least of all friends?

'I'm sorry. Do we know each other?' Sondra's mouth felt parched, so she sipped some of the cooling tea the assistant had brought to her as she had arrived. 'From school, you say?'

'Yes. Yes. SHS for Girls. We were in the same standard and the same classes in standard six and seven. How've you been?'

'Well. I'm well, thanks. How are you? Mmm, you must forgive me. Your name again?'

The woman laughed throatily. 'Khadija. Don't worry. I've changed a lot. It's been more than twenty years, and I've picked up a couple of kilos. I used to have long hair in two pigtails.' She indicated the length with a palm facing upwards next to her plentiful waist. 'You look the same though. No fair.' Khadija feigned jealousy. Well, Sondra would not have minded if it was not pretence. She knew she looked good and would continue to work at keeping it that way.

Of course, Sondra remembered the woman. She forgot nothing. All efforts to obliterate her younger years had failed ... dismally. Wanting to steer the conversation away from herself, Sondra enquired, 'How've you been? Living here now?'

'Moved up last year. But so nice to see a frie—uh ... familiar face. Hubby was transferred – a promotion. One daughter, one son.' In a flash, Khadija whipped open her over-sized handbag and pulled out a folder of photographs encased in plastic sleeves. 'Ruxaana and Rashid.'

Sondra used the time that she took to view and murmur appreciation over the photos of the portly children as an opportunity to push aside harsh memories. *I need to find somewhere else to colour my hair*, she thought with an inward sigh. *That's good, Sonds. Focus on something else.* 'Are your children at school in the area?'

'Yes. Good school.' For the next five minutes, Khadija spoke animatedly about her children and their education. 'But here's me, prattling on. Tell me about *you*.'

Angie leant her upper body towards Sondra's head. She was done painting and was checking that all the roots were properly covered with the dye, as well as – more than likely – eavesdropping to learn something—anything about Sondra. Women, particularly nosey women, were irritatingly predictable.

'Married? Kids?' Khadija asked.

'Yes. One son. Sixteen. Michael.' Sondra closed the folder and passed it back. She turned in the chair to face the hairdresser and away from Khadija. 'Angie, please set the timer. How long? Thirty minutes?'

'Mmm, maybe forty. I want to make sure the few greys will catch the colour. Leave the timing to me please.' Was there a note of irritation at being told how to do her job? 'Come, Missus Farook.' She gestured towards the basins at the back and led Khadija in that direction.

'Please—' Khadija touched Angie's lower arm kindly as she followed. '—call me Khadija.'

Sondra breathed a sigh of relief. She turned her attention back to the magazine but took nothing in. After a minute, she gave up all pretext. She shut the magazine, closed her eyes, and let the past come flooding back. It was so real and tangible ... like it had never left her.

* * *

The citrusy scent caressed the edges of her subconscious accompanied by an image that drifted in her silent thoughts. The fragrance of her mother's hand cream was as vivid and as real from all those years ago as it had been for her when she was a young girl. Beryl had always squirted a little in Sondra's palm too.

She remembered sitting at the kitchen table at their home in Sydenham – a Coloured suburb close to the city centre of Durban – doing homework, while her mother cooked and chatted merrily. The first thirteen years of Sondra's life were happy and carefree. She was the illegitimate child of a businessman, Abdul Carim, and was raised by Beryl, who doted on her. Beryl had worked as a bookkeeper for Abdul. This had led to an affair that lasted all of Sondra's thirteen years, as well as the two before her birth.

Beryl was young and naïve. She became captivated by the good-looking, charming, rich man. When she fell pregnant, he asked what she wanted to do, though his feelings were made clear. If she was to have the child, the boy or girl would be raised Muslim. Beryl wanted the child but had resisted raising her child as Muslim, much to Abdul's chagrin. Beryl had eventually agreed and allowed Sondra to attend *madressah* to learn about and to practise the Islamic religion, but Beryl also taught Sondra about Christianity and took her to church upon occasion, particularly at Christmas and Easter. They had compromised and said that, when Sondra was ready, she could decide which faith she would choose.

When Abdul arrived for his weekly conjugal visits with Beryl, Sondra had to stay quietly in her room and not see him. Glimpses of his sports jacket or pullover jersey was all she saw of him through the keyhole as he passed her room before disappearing down the passage to her mother's room. A hollow *thud* as the door closed was all she heard until she fell asleep. When she woke in the mornings, he would be gone.

Abdul provided financially for Sondra, and he also gave her his last name, but was never a father to her. Her ever-attentive mother more than made up for the lack. Sondra hadn't needed more. Then tragedy struck. Beryl was hit by a minibus taxi while walking home one day and was killed instantly. And so, ended the first part of her life, the first thirteen happy years.

Beryl had no close family, and Abdul did what he thought he had to. He brought Sondra to live with his family, and she – a mere child – had no say in the matter. She was not asked or even told properly what was happening. Abdul swept into the house, got her to pack her clothes and school stuff in a bag and a box, and whisked her away from the home she'd been brought up in with love and care, away from any connection to her mother. After she'd moved in with the Carims, Abdul continued to keep his distance from her – his illegitimate daughter.

Sondra was witness to his tenderness when he interacted with his other children. Three of his four children were daughters, two of whom were older than Sondra, the third, Salma, was a year younger. The youngest was a son named Abdullah. While caring and kind to the girls, he was exuberant in his interactions with Abdullah, so named because "Abdullah" is the most-beloved name of Allah. Sondra wondered if the Almighty Himself could have loved AB – as he was called by all of his sisters – as much as Abdul did.

The younger two children were the only ones who treated Sondra like a sister. It was as though, because she existed before they did, Salma and Abdullah could have no objection to her. Hers was a presence that they were not aware of until their father marched her into the comfortable double-storey house and announced that she was their sister and would be living with them from then on.

The older sisters, Haniefa and Luthfia, mostly ignored her but were nasty to her on occasion. Sondra had not fully realised the implications of the name that the two used to call her – "*bushie*", a derogatory term that Indians often used for Coloured people – until her stepmother took the second-eldest daughter, Luthfia, to task for using the word. Luthfia was made to apologise to Sondra and was warned never to use the word again. If the relationship between her half-sisters was stilted and awkward before, it was positively strained after. Sondra did her best to avoid Luthfia after that. This meant that she hardly interacted with either of her elder siblings because the two, who were only a year apart in age, were inseparable.

When the news of Sondra living with the Carims was initially announced, Abdul's wife, Sarah, made a feeble attempt at protest, then quickly acquiesced when she saw Abdul's stony face. This was decided. Sarah had no say in the matter. Sondra ventured into the dimly lit hallway to go to the bathroom on the first night that she slept in the strange bed in the unknown house in Asherville, an area that was close to and similar to Sydenham in many ways. Sondra stopped outside their bedroom door when she heard Abdul talking at Sarah.

'This child must be a shock,' Abdul's deep voice echoed down the hall. It sounded authoritative, almost bossy – Sondra had only really heard that tone from her school principal and the *maulanas* at *madressah*. 'I'm sure you know I've had a mistress for years. You don't know her, but it doesn't matter now. She is dead. I have no intention of replacing her. I named the child "Saadiyah", but when her mother registered her, she changed that to "Sondra". We will call her Saadiyah and raise her as ours and as a Muslim. She is a clever girl and, apparently, helpful as well. Her school and *madressah* education have been sorted all these years; I made sure of it. She has my name. I don't expect you to love her or be a mother to her, but you will raise her as my own.'

He had spoken.

There was a charge to the air as though Sarah wanted to say something but was unable to verbalise the words. Sondra crept away quietly, fearful and confused.

And so, Sondra lived within the family but never became a part of it, continuing to feel like she did that first night she arrived, fearful and confused. She kept her head down, studied hard, and helped where she could. She quickly learnt to blend into the background. She remained Sondra everywhere else and never grew to identify with the name "Saadiyah". She prayed daily and fasted in *Ramadaan* with the family, even reading the Quran as she had been taught at *madressah*, but she did not feel Muslim.

When she passed *matric* – her results far surpassed her older sisters' – she was awarded a scholarship to study a BCom in Financial Management at the *University of Cape Town*. That was her ticket out of the house and family that oppressed her. She accepted the university placement and the scholarship without hesitation. She had to work over her holidays at the company that had awarded her the scholarship, and this helped her afford the other sundry expenses. But Sondra did not mind; the company was based in Cape Town, and so, she never needed to return to Durban.

The year before she qualified, Abdul died. She heard the news from his lawyer three weeks after the fact. The hardly sufficient monthly allowance Abdul transferred to her, which had supplemented her student income, was to be stopped immediately. There was a small amount in a trust, which she would receive when she turned twenty-five. Other than that, she was on her own. A silent mental calculation done while she passed on personal details to the lawyer suggested bleak prospects.

Boldly, she asked the attorney what her options were as she was dependent on the allowance for another year at least. He suggested that she apply for a bank loan. He would authorise that the trust fund proceeds would be used as surety. She assured him that the loan would be paid off even before the funds became available to her.

'I have no doubt it will. Send me the paperwork from the bank, and I will attend to it.' He gave her his contact details.

'Thanks very much, Mister Walters. I appreciate your help.'

'It's no problem. I trust my instincts, and I can tell you're going to be fine. Your father only spoke of you once about ten years ago, when he had me change the will to include you.

I wish the other children were as level-headed.' Mr Walters paused for a second. 'Sorry. How unprofessional of me.'

And that was that. Sondra never spoke to the lawyer again. When she turned twenty-five, she found out that the trust was set up from proceeds of the sale of her mother's home, not a bequest from her father. It didn't surprise her, so she shrugged off the knowledge just as she had the years that he had ignored her.

After qualifying, a lecturer gave her a glowing recommendation, citing her astuteness as an asset. She had the choice of internship offers and opted to move to Johannesburg, which was cosmopolitan enough for her to completely cut off ties with Abdul's family and remain anonymous.

Her talents were recognised, and Sondra's career reached heights rarely seen in one so young or without any connections. The only disadvantage – that of being a woman – she turned to an advantage, using her beauty, wiles, and charm as additional tools to achieve her goals. She had expected to be treated fairly but learnt quickly that it was a man's world. Often men were recognised or celebrated over her, even if her skills and talents were superior. Rather than lamenting the unfairness, it was easier and more prudent to make her femininity work for her.

* * *

'Sondra, come, please. It's time to wash your hair out.' The assistant interrupted her wayward reflections to guide her to the basin.

Sondra adjusted in the seat and nodded that the water temperature was fine. Reliving the past made Sondra simultaneously wistful and uneasy. She decided she didn't want to see John and sent him a message to cancel. He was disappointed, of course, but she ignored his pleading messages. She didn't need to explain anything to him.

4

FOLLY'S GIFT

On Monday morning, John came to see her as soon as he could, quietly closing the door to Sondra's office behind him.

'I missed you. All weekend long, I thought of you.' He sounded upset – a mixture of hurt and anger. The sulky attitude was not unlike what she sometimes experienced with Michael.

Sondra sighed. She really was not in the mood for this. 'Well, you know how hectic things get. I was busy with my family.' Sondra often made reference to David and Michael in her conversations with John, never complaining but intimating that she was happy and in a solid marriage. He needed to know that she was not available over weekends unless it suited her.

John squeezed his eyes shut for a second. 'I got you something.' His voice was a little cheerier as he held out a blue cardboard box tied with a red ribbon. 'Look.' An eager smile spread over his handsome features.

Sondra drew in a ragged breath. Exchanging gifts wasn't the kind of thing they should be doing. It wasn't that kind of relationship, and she needed him to understand that.

'You shouldn't have. It's not right.'

'Please. I want you to have it. It's just something small. I don't expect anything in return.'

'That's not what I mean. Just leave it on the desk there. You need to leave my office now. I'm busy preparing for status.'

'Not even a kiss hello?' John smiled a sexy, slow smile, one that she found hard to resist.

'No. It's too risky. It's Monday morning. Anyone can just walk in.'

He looked forlorn, almost lost. It was quite incredible how quickly and often his mood and manner had changed in the two minutes since he'd walked in. Young people can be so unnecessarily dramatic!

She softened her tone. 'Later, okay? I'm busy. You should be too. Please, let's be professional.'

'Right, my lady. Your wish is my command.' He bowed, turned slowly, and walked out. She grabbed the box to put it into the bottom drawer of her desk before it was seen by anyone. Sondra's office and desk had no personal items – not even a picture of Michael. She found this limited idle chatter from colleagues or clients and prevented anyone from trying to get too close. After a few minutes of staring at her computer screen, Sondra eyed the drawer and took the blue box out. She was careful not to lift it above the level of her desk. It contained a dainty, silver, heart-shaped pendant on a fine chain.

She smiled inadvertently. *Poor John.* He had no idea who she was. Sondra would never wear something delicate and petite. She hardly wore jewellery at all, apart from diamond or pearl studs in her ears and her wedding ring, but when she did, she preferred the piece to make a statement.

Sondra tossed the box back into the drawer and turned back to her screen. Unnecessary distractions were time wasters. She put her head down and got on with it.

* * *

Hours later, Sondra's cell phone screen lit up. Her eyes grew as she recognised the name.

'Well, this is a blast from the past.' Her voice became consciously husky. Enzo Vittone had been on the board of a company she'd worked at before this one. He was older and influential, and their short liaison had ensured her a promotion that had been deserved. Any of Enzo's detractors who had pushed for a male colleague to get to the post had been silenced because she had not disappointed.

The excited laugh on the other end of the line was instantly recognisable.

'Enzo Vittone. Enzo. Enzo. How *have* you been?'

'Well! I've been well. For months—years, I've wanted to get in touch. Today is my birthday, so I decided to gift myself: to hear your voice, or maybe if I'm lucky, you will join me for coffee? Or have you finally grown up and drink now?'

It was great to hear his soulful, honeyed tones. 'Aah, you know I love a man who gets straight to the point.'

'I'd like you to get to my point.' The suggestion in the loaded comment was all too clear.

'Well, if it's your birthday ... a gift *is* in order. I can only get out of here by six. Shall we meet for a drink at Carlo's.'

'You were never much of a drinker.'

Aah, so he remembered her well. Good. 'I still hardly drink, though. Especially if I'm driving, I stick to soft drinks. Boring, I know.'

'Of all the words I could use to describe you, "boring"? No!'

Sondra laughed as she graciously accepted the comment.

'Right then, six PM. I'll push my dinner for later, and I'll see you there.'

'Done.'

'And Sonds?' The sugar-coated notes became evocative, dripping in anticipation. '*Really* looking forward to seeing you.' The emphasis on "really" warmed her, igniting memories buried but not forgotten.

'I'll see you later. Loads to get through today. Bye now.'

As she ploughed through spreadsheets and live data from foreign markets, she wondered what prospect Enzo would bring to her. *He'd better not think that I'm giving him my time just because it's his birthday. There is no such thing as a free lunch.*

* * *

The drink date that evening was unsatisfying. In the past twelve years, Enzo had become a bohemian, swearing off conventional attitudes. He had become a philanthropist but one who would not give over-generously – he could still maintain a lavish lifestyle. She barely recognised him in his loudly printed shirt and sandals.

After two quick drinks, she excused herself and left. *What a waste of his talent*, she mused to herself while she waited for her car to be brought around. He had been a wheeler-dealer supreme, callous in his takeovers of companies, a force to behold. Alas, he was of no use to her anymore.

* * *

The next day, John was in her office as soon as she walked in – this was becoming a habit that she was increasingly irritated by. 'I need your approval on these reports.'

She ignored his petulant tone, indicating he should leave them on her desk and leave.

He turned to leave, then must have changed his mind. He whirled around. 'What happened? I waited for hours.' When she raised an eyebrow quizzically, he retorted, 'We were going to meet after work. How could you forget?'

'What? Oh, I guess it slipped my mind. I was really busy all day and then had to meet an old friend for a birthday drink.'

John's pained expression was pathetic, Sondra noticed, feeling her annoyance with him starting to creep up the back of her neck. 'Sorry. I forgot. Let's not make a big deal out of it, okay?'

'Who is he?'

Sondra removed her reading glasses and sat back in her chair. *Is he really questioning me?* 'That is hardly any of your business.' Her stony look matched her voice.

'But I thought we ... you ...' He stumbled and stopped speaking. His face contorted into a grimace of hurt.

'For God's sake.' Sondra could not mask her exasperation any longer. This was becoming tiresome. 'Listen. You will be leaving in two weeks, but we may as well end this now. I can't have these dramatics at the office any longer. I have work to do. And so do you.'

Sondra swivelled her chair away from him and buried her head in a file. She heard how he tried to control sobs that had started and, after a moment, unsteady footsteps, then her door closing with a quiet click.

Sondra sighed testily. It's a good thing that all of the interns were leaving soon. Then, she could close the chapter on her stupidity. She vowed never to get involved in a similarly sticky situation again. Men have their purpose and role. She should not confuse enjoying their attention with any-thing else.

5

THE END OF SOMETHING STUPID

Sondra was busy with month-end reports. She hoped to finish by Friday so that she could enjoy a rare work-free weekend. Today, Wednesday, was already crazy, even without the lunch for the departing interns, which had stolen a full hour of her day.

It was late, and most of the team had left already. Sondra kicked off her shoes and placed her stockinged feet onto an upturned bin under her desk. As she moved her head from side to side, stretching her tight neck muscles, she made a mental note to book a massage. Hopefully someone would be able to fit her in over the coming weekend.

There was a rap on her office door, quickly followed by John letting himself in. He closed the door and leant against it, watching her.

Sondra's nostrils flared. She struggled to keep her voice down. 'What do you want? I thought I'd seen the last of you.'

His hands were behind his back as he leant against the door. He looked casual and relaxed. His blue eyes looked sleepy; clearly, he had had more of the plonk that they had served with lunch than he should have.

'I'm busy and need to leave soon.' Her brow furrowed. She focused on her laptop screen, hoping that ignoring John would get him to leave.

Still, he said nothing. He just stood and stared at her. A minute passed. Her patience was wearing thin. 'John, what do you want?' This time, she didn't bother keeping her voice down.

'I ... want ... you.' He answered slowly, never once taking his eyes off of her.

Sondra was unnerved by his boldness, then quickly recovered. 'We don't always get what we want. Get used to it.'

'You want me too, Sondra. I know it. I can feel it. Why are you denying this?'

'Sure. I wanted you. Why not enjoy the flavour of the month?'

'Is that all I am to you?' His words were drawn out as his eyes swept over her searchingly. 'No. I don't believe that.' John moved into the office; his presence filled the room and her view. 'You like this, don't you?' He was behind her now and caressing her neck.

'Yes, very nice. But I can pay for way better massages.' Sondra hoped her voice sounded sure and shoved his hands away. 'It's over now, John. We have stopped these foolish games.' Sondra was annoyed to silently admit that she enjoyed the heat and pressure of his hands. His touch was intoxicating, and his hands were on her once more.

She slapped his hands off again, swivelled her chair around, and rose to face him. She had forgotten she was barefoot but was reminded when she had to raise her head to look at him directly. She was unnerved by his closeness and the solidness of his stature. She felt tiny. When he closed the centimetres between them and wrapped his arms around her, she caught her breath involuntarily and breathed in the scent of him – a mixture of man and the musk of his cologne, with the aftermath of the wine.

'Stop. John. This is—' Her voice was unsteady and then was arrested midsentence as he bent his head down to kiss her hard on the mouth.

His grip tightened, and she was raised off the ground. Her attempts to push him away were futile. He held on tight – his caresses and kisses persuasive. Her body was no longer in her control. Her head flew back to allow him to deepen the kiss and explore her neck. She stopped pretending.

This was the signal he was waiting for. He undressed her and laid her on the couch. She unbuttoned and unzipped his pants and pulled him on top of her.

'Now!' Sondra was equally aware of her rapidly beating heart and racing pulse as she was of the risk of someone walking in. Sondra increased the intensity of her movements, and on cue, John responded as enthusiastically.

'*Sondraaaa.*' John's voice was thick and raspy. 'Oh my god. This is so—'

Sondra silenced him with a hand clamped over his mouth. She wanted him, but she wanted him quickly and as quietly as possible.

'Don't worry, babe. We're alone. Everyone has left. I made sure.'

'Now!' she repeated. She didn't want this to be a lingering seduction. It was a "wham-bam-thank you, ma'am" episode, and he should know it as such.

When they were done, she gathered herself together and showed him the door. 'Look, John. Get yourself together and leave.'

He tried to pull her against him.

'Stop.' She walked back to her desk and dressed quickly.

'Sondra, I need you.' The pleading tone was pitiful, but when she turned to face him, she was thrown by the tears that shone in his baby blue eyes and the tortured look on his face. 'You're everything to me. This can't end.'

Sondra looked away as she smoothed her hair back in place. 'It has to.' He had to leave her alone. This was now totally out of hand. Her voice rose authoritatively. 'Consider this our farewell fuck, John. This was the last time. Your internship is over now, as are we. We will never see each other again.'

'Please, Sondra. I love you. I know you love me too. Who cares about age? We belong together. I want to make my life with you.'

Sondra felt hot and cold simultaneously. *What the hell is he saying?* She swallowed and tried to hydrate her mouth. She couldn't believe what she was hearing.

'We can get married. Your son can live with us. You don't want more kids, so we can raise him as ours.'

What the FUCK!! Sondra felt panicked. *Is he out of his bloody mind?*

Sondra laughed. It was a harsh, bitter sound, but she could hear a hidden note of terror too. 'Are you out of your bloody mind?' Her whole body was quivering, and it was not because of any afterglow. Any remnant of pleasure was completely obliterated by the nonsense that John was spouting.

John continued as though he hadn't heard her. 'Leave your husband. You don't love him. We can be together. This can work. We're good together, Sondra. I'll be happy and spend the rest of my life making you happy. That's all I need. You're my whole world. My first and only. I'll die without you.'

Sondra's dark eyes narrowed. She took a calming breath. 'Listen to me, and listen to me good.' She checked that he had stopped his blubbering and was giving her his full attention. 'I have no feelings for you. There is no way in hell that I would ever leave my family. My life is exactly where I want it to be. This ...' She waved her hand dismissively between them '... is over. *Over.* It was a bad idea from the start. I was stupid to get involved with you and to let things get out of control.'

'Please, Sondra. Don't say that. I love you.'

'Love? *Love?* What do you know about love? You haven't even lived your life yet. Go get a life. Go to your girlfriend.'

John looked dejected. 'Girlfriend? You mean Denise? I broke that off as soon as we started seeing each other.' He pointed to her and himself in turn. 'You're all that I want and need.'

Sondra's eyebrow raised. 'Well, that was foolish. Your behaviour is crazy. You shouldn't have done anything drastic on my account because we were never "seeing each other". Well, I hope you can get her back. Get another girlfriend. Get three. Whatever. Just stop this bullshit, and leave me the fuck alone.'

'How can you say that? I'll never look at another woman again. It's only you. I never knew what it was like to love—to truly love someone until I met you. Now, I know I will never love anyone else.'

Sondra's body shivered as her mind whirled at the possibility of him becoming obsessive. No! She would not allow him to infringe on her perfect life. She laughed, a harsh, cynical sound that failed to hide her terror. 'Silly boy. What were you thinking? Clearly, you weren't thinking at all. Here is the problem: you let your *dick* think for you. First mistake.' She switched off her laptop and gathered her things. 'You'll get over this, you'll see. It's not real.'

'It's the only real thing now. You and loving you – that's my whole world.'

'Oh, *please*.' Sondra drew out the last word to emphasise her incredulity and his lunacy. 'Right. I'm out of here. Pull the door shut when you leave. Leave now. Never come back. Goodbye.'

In the car, she rested her head on her hands, clasped tightly onto the steering wheel. Her breathing was heavy and laboured, rasping out of her as the fear and anxiety set in. Then she had a scary vision flash through her mind's eye of John running up to her car. She frantically looked around while she started the engine, then pulled out of her parking place at such a speed that her tyres screeched against the concrete.

How did I get myself into this mess? Thank god his internship is over now. I will never have to see him again.

By the time she got home, there were two voice messages and a bunch of texts from John. She deleted everything and blocked his number. He would grow tired and eventually forget about her. She too planned to forget him and this ridiculous phase immediately.

6

A MOTHER'S LOVE

Hannah Bennett tried to live as uncomplicated a life as possible. Since her husband, Eliot, had passed on four years back, her world had revolved around her only child, John. She had started a job as it had become necessary, but work was something that had to be done. She didn't think too much about it, nor did she become very involved in office socialisation. She was dependable and consistent, but colleagues would find it difficult to describe her in any further detail if they were ever asked.

Since Eliot's passing, she hadn't bothered to keep up with her in-laws either. Eliot's parents had long passed, and she made sure that John visited his only uncle around birthdays and Christmases, but neither encouraged nor discouraged anything more. She was loving, dutiful, and responsible to her ageing mother, Sylvia – her only other family commitment, but her devotion was to John alone.

She drove into the retirement village where Sylvia resided for her weekly visit. It was a time for her to drop off groceries and medication or other supplies, however, the true purpose of her visits was to spend an hour or two, having tea and a chat with Sylvia and Doris, the domestic-cum-companion.

For the hundredth time, Hannah was grateful that her mother was secure enough to be able to afford the accommodation. Sylvia was able to participate in activities and outings, and she always had someone to talk to about ailments and families. Hannah was grateful too that Sylvia was sprightly and alert, reaping the benefits of a tough but fulfilling life.

Hannah greeted her mother with a kiss and handed packages over to Doris. 'I'm putting the kettle on, Mother. Tea or coffee?'

'Thanks, Hannah. Tea, please. How are you, child?'

'Fine, Mother. How're you?'

'Okay. My shoulder has been acting up again. Aah, but what can you do? It's age and arthritis.'

Hannah nodded sympathetically as her mother continued.

'How's Eliot?' Her mother made the mistake of asking after Hannah's late husband but realised almost as soon as she said the words. 'Oh, dear. I'm sorry. I forgot again. Silly me. I meant John. How is my grandson?'

'Okay. We're well.' Hannah sniffed the milk before pouring a little in her mug and a little more in her mother's.

'His job going good?'

'Yes, I think so. It was an internship, but it's over now. He's looking for work, for something permanent.' Hannah didn't add that she had noticed that John had been quiet and despondent since the six-month position had come to an end. *Had he hoped for a permanent position there?* she wondered.

It had been made clear from the outset that there were no permanent positions available. The only thing promised was a recommendation letter based on performance. She had encouraged him to apply for his honours while job hunting, but heaven knew if he was considering that. Hannah sighed silently and pulled things out of the shopping bag.

'The batteries for your massager. I'll put them in.'

'Thanks, dear. And did you remember my *You* magazine? I love doing the crossword puzzle.'

'Of course. Do I ever forget?'

Sylvia tittered a light, tinkling laugh that sounded like it came from a woman decades younger. Hannah marvelled at her mother's resilience and love of life. It was in no small part because of her innate spirituality too, Hannah was sure of it. She loved visiting her mother and always left feeling refreshed and positive.

'I bought lemon creams,' Hannah said, pulling out a red and yellow package next.

'Lemon creams.' Sylvia's face darkened, and she cast her eyes down.

'Mother? What's the matter? I thought you liked them?'

'I do. They were a favourite of Gertie too. My aunt, who lived with us when I was growing up. Today would have been her birthday.' Sylvia pulled her mouth to one side. 'You remember her, Han?'

'Granny Gertie? Mmm, sort of. I knew her more through the photographs in your old family albums. She was an attractive woman.'

'Beautiful, yes ... but troubled.'

Hannah frowned. 'Troubled? How do you mean?'

'I guess you'd call it depression, but who knows? As children, we were kept in the dark – those kinds of things were never discussed or understood. She had a ... a heavy energy that she never managed to overcome. As she grew older, she became a recluse, hardly leaving her room. It was like facing the world was too much for her. It was easier to stay away from everyone.'

'I didn't know this.'

'Yes. The adults never spoke about it, so we children learnt not to either. Eventually, she just blended into the background, until she eventually passed away.' Sylvia's eyes misted over.

Hannah sorted out the hand massager and tried it. It whirred to life. She tried to gently steer the conversation away from her mother's glum recollections. Hannah spoke instead about how busy she had been at work, and fortunately, Sylvia took her lead and lightened with the change of topic.

The time passed too quickly – time with her mother always did. While she drove back home, she thought about John. She had been fretful for days now. He had changed overnight without any obvious explanation. He had become distant, withdrawn, and sullen – almost morose. His demeanour made any attempts to talk to him impossible. Hannah felt cut off, and this scared her.

She wondered if breaking up with Denise months earlier was the reason, but at the time, John had not seemed upset. If anything there'd been a spring in his step. He was never seriously involved with Denise anyway, seeming more like good buddies who had decided to try a romantic relationship, which hadn't really worked for either of them. Nothing in her mind justified him turning into this stranger overnight.

Could he be depressed? she questioned. *But what possible reason could there be for that?* She didn't know the scientific details of depression, but even if it was caused by some sort of chemical imbalance, what would bring it up now and all of a sudden? He'd long passed puberty and all those dramas.

John hadn't entertained any attempts that she had made to address her concerns. He brushed her off, and if she persisted, he just shut down. But if things did not improve soon, she would have to force him to talk.

Maybe I should have a word with Pastor Benjamin on Sunday? John did not always come with her to church, but if the Pastor called him to chat, he would surely not refuse. He was respectful of the church and believed, although he was not as religious as either of his parents. They had not pressured him – they believed he would find his own way when he was ready.

Hannah made a silent prayer. *Dear God, please guide me. Please help me to show my love and acceptance of my son. Let him be free to feel Your presence and be guided by You.*

Her reaching out and surrendering to God's will should have helped settle her uncertainty, yet she still couldn't understand the situation. They were the kind of mother and son that talked about anything and everything. They were close. Eliot had mentioned more than once that he had felt that their kind of closeness was dangerous. Eliot would often say, "If something were to happen to either of you, the other would not know how to survive alone." Mother and son would laughingly dismiss his fears and imply that he was simply jealous of them and what they shared. The thought of her living without John had worried her though. She had extracted a promise from him years before: 'Promise me that you won't die before me.'

'Don't be morbid, Ma. I'm going to live forever,' had been his reply. 'You're stuck with me.'

She silently gave thanks for having John in her life. She and Eliot had married young. They had met at church and had found that they had much in common. Eliot had insisted that they marry quickly because, as a devout Christian, he would not consider pre-marital sex. He was certain that his feelings for her would never change.

'If they change,' Eliot had said in answer to her concerned questions, 'they will only get more serious. Our love will grow with us. This is right, Hannah. I've prayed on it. My heart is settled.'

Against Sylvia's advice, they had married. Eliot had been right. Their relationship had grown stronger as their love had. It had seemed that people's misgivings at them marrying too young or for the wrong reasons were unfounded. Eliot and Hannah hadn't really discussed a family or even moving out of his parent's home because he had been the only one who had been working. At that time, he had been a junior bookkeeper, while studying part-time for his BCom degree, and Hannah had been studying a teaching degree full-time.

When she had fallen pregnant in her third year of university after a year of marriage, their parents had encouraged her to drop out of university.

'You would only have worked until children came along anyway. So, what's the point of finishing studying now,' was their argument. 'Focus on letting Eliot finish his degree, and once he is earning well, things will work out fine. We'll help out until then.'

Hannah had never regretted following that advice. Theirs had been a simple, contented life. Eliot had completed his degree but had been unable to pass the bar to become a chartered accountant. It hadn't mattered. They had needed little for they had had each other.

Hannah had run an efficient house, and she filled her days with volunteering at the church. Eliot had hoped for more children but had accepted their fate of only one as God's will. Hannah was so in love with John from the moment that he was born that she never needed anything more. Her life had been complete, and she had been fulfilled. It had only been when Eliot had died suddenly of a heart attack at the young age of forty-two that she had regretted not finishing her studies. It would have been easier for her to find employment at forty-one years of age if she had had some qualification.

But that too had worked out eventually. The pay-out from insurance policies had secured the house and John's educa-tion. After more than a year of job hunting and rejections, her current job of office administrator and receptionist at a real estate office came up. The pay was not great, but it was enough.

The whirlwind of nostalgia, arbitrary thoughts, and concern for John's current mood seemed to quicken the drive, and before she realised, she was home. She didn't immediately get out of the car, reluctant to face the gloominess that John's disposition seemed to pass to the house itself.

A few minutes passed, but there was no sign of John. Up until a few weeks before, he would always come to greet her or offer to help with her bags or parcels when he heard her car. Sighing deeply, she cradled the bunch of flowers like a baby, swung the strap of her handbag over her shoulder, and headed inside.

The house was cold and still. She walked towards the kitchen, then stopped dead in her tracks. With steps that were as heavy as her heart suddenly felt, she turned and walked along the short passage, passed the guest toilet, towards the stairs. Just below the doorframe that lead to the stairs, John's blue and white *takkie* hung, suspended. It was still on his foot.

The flowers and her bag dropped. She flew up the stairs before they hit the ground. She knelt down over the railing and stretched out her arm but could not reach her child's body that swung from the balustrade. She fumbled with the rope that was attached to his neck. It was impossible to see through tears that welled up in her eyes and rolled down her cheeks. Without thinking, she dashed into her bedroom and ran back with a pair of scissors that snapped ineffectually at the thick, sinewy rope.

NOOOOOO! her insides screamed. The thudding in her ears drowned out the hopeless, hapless word "heeeeelp!" *Who would hear? Who would care?*

Hannah brushed her hand against her cheek and raced to the kitchen. She yanked open a drawer so hard that it flew off its hinge and clattered to the floor. She found a serrated bread knife, then she was up the stairs even before she had exhaled, and cut the rope in a few too many sawing motions. The rope gave way, and John – her baby, her life, her hopes, her dreams, her yesterdays, todays, and tomorrows – landed with a dull thud.

Hannah was down the stairs in a flash and pulled the rope away from the bruised, swollen neck. He was dead. She ran her fingers over his face, then straightened his body, and pried his mouth open to perform CPR. There was nothing but a stale dank odour that came from his mouth; there was nothing but a soft surrendering of the chest as she pushed in short thrusts. It felt like a hundred lifetimes, but it was only two short minutes before she slumped back on her heels, held her heart, and stared.

His left eye was shut, but the right was slightly open to reveal that the whites of his eyes had turned red, his pupil nowhere to be seen. His full, red lips were tinged with grey at their outer edges. The lips were open, and the tips of his bottom teeth peeked out from behind. The healthy glow on John's cheeks that had been there that morning when she had last seen him had turned ashen. His body was limp, his hands cold. Droplets of moisture darkened the cotton of breast pocket on his shirt – they were her tears.

She reached for his head and cradled it in her arms. She clutched him to her bosom and sat, rocking him and herself as her mind processed thoughts so alien, so foreign that it was like she had been spirited away to another world, another life, one where she was unable to understand anything.

John is dead. John killed himself. My son! My beautiful boy. John tied a rope to the railing at the top of the stairs, tied the other end to his neck, and jumped. He suffocated. He was unable to breathe. How long was he alive for as he swung until the lack of oxygen shut his body down 'til it was dead?

He died. He is dead. He is gone. He stopped. She stopped.

* * *

When she rose, her knees buckled under her, and she fell over his body. It was cold and unyielding. She jerked up and raised herself onto her hands and knees. And like that, on all fours, she threw her head back and screamed. She screamed loud and beastly, the sound scraping her raw and dry throat. Hot tears wet her face, her neck, her chest. Like a rag doll, she dropped onto the floor next to him. She moulded her body against his. Her head lay against his shoulder, and she wept.

Hannah didn't know how long she cried for. Eventually, her wailing turned to sobs, then whimpers. She screwed her eyes closed, bit the inside of her bottom lip to stop it quivering, and forced herself to stop crying.

When she was able to stand and walk, she found her bag next to the flowers that had been crushed under her running feet as they had carried her to the kitchen and back – crushed like her heart. She called the police, who said that they would send an ambulance and a car.

As she cut the call, John's face lit up the screen, his lips curling into a smile, the edges of his sparkling, blue eyes creasing to highlight the light that shone from them, the dark brown hair, silky and curling at the ends, the tip of his strong, symmetrical nose turning up as he smiled. She brought the phone up to her face until all she could see were the eyes, blurry now but still bright and luminous.

My son, John Bennett – who lived and loved and laughed and longed and offered and received – has stopped. How is it possible that I have not stopped too?

A second passed, a moment, a day, a week. A month? Who knew? Who cared? What did it matter? Hannah was in limbo, in a daze, a zombie. One day, she found a poem scrawled onto a paper napkin. She must have written it unaware. The words were blurry, and the napkin was torn where she had pressed the pen too deeply.

Stop!

Stop!
Stop!!!
Stop!!!!!
Stop!!!!!!!

Your breath stopped
My heart ceased
Your eyes closed
My soul halted

Your life extinguished
as wet fingers snuff out a candle
The wick singeing, sizzling, a faint
flicker of smoke trails
as the flame that burned true and alive stops

I stop
as the dark, demonic sea swallowed
whole, swallowed all
I am stopped
I am stone

She read it and dispassionately threw it away.

7

FALLOUT OF A FOOLISH THING

Sondra was seated in the boardroom at eight-fifty for the Monday morning status meeting. It suited her to be first and so ensured that she was always there before anyone else. She stared for a moment at the neatly designed logo of Ross Maphumulo Investments that was printed on the side wall. A moment of fantasy about it someday reading "Carim-Edwards Investments" flashed through her mind. Idle fantasy didn't get things done, she reminded herself, and set her sights firmly on the meeting that lay ahead.

Her eyes narrowed as she peered at her watch when, fifteen minutes later, no one had arrived. She checked her e-mail and saw that no message had been sent in explanation or apology. She shut her laptop firmly and reached for a biscuit that had been laid out on a plate in the centre of the table but soon realised that chomping hard on it didn't ease her irritation.

Sondra brushed crumbs off of her chest, the unsatisfying biscuit having been consumed, and reached for another when she heard the sound of excited voices outside. Suddenly, the boardroom doors were thrown open and the partners, Aidan

Ross and Thabo Maphumulo, entered, the other managers in tow.

'Sondra.' It was senior partner Aidan Ross who spoke. 'We've just heard that one of the interns, John Bennett – you remember him? – he's died.'

'What?' Sondra breathed out in shock.

'It's terrible, isn't it?'

All at once, everyone was talking, expressing their shock, grief, and confusion.

Sondra placed the biscuit on the table and balled her hands into fists. She dropped them to her side under the table and looked at her colleagues, who were either repeating themselves or shaking their heads at each other.

Sondra was as shocked and as confused as any of them. John was dead? It was crazy to imagine. *Sweet John? Naïve John? Poor John.* She didn't trust herself to say anything, so she kept staring ahead with her ears alert to any information that might be forthcoming. None really was. She was trying to make sense of this news that got her heart beating at an alarming rate and was failing.

Sondra looked from colleague to colleague. Were any of them trying to gauge *her* reaction? No. No one seemed to single her out. Good, that meant that no one knew about what had happened between her and John. Their discretion had paid off. She breathed a small sigh of relief.

After a few minutes, the HR manager, Vicky Moodley, walked in. She would normally not attend status meetings.

Vicky greeted curtly. 'I apologise for the interruption, but I thought I should speak to you first before sending out a general e-mail to the staff. We don't want this sad news to be distorted with rumours and innuendo. John Bennett passed away this past weekend. He was an intern here for six months until a few weeks ago. He left us when all the others left too.'

'Do we know what happened?' Thabo Maphumulo asked, rubbing a hand on the back of his neck.

Vicky shifted her weight to her other foot. 'Details are sketchy, but it seems like he took his own life.'

'That's so sad. What a waste.' Thabo dropped his arm to his side.

'How stupid.' The remark was blurted before Sondra thought it through. All eyes turned to her in surprise. 'I mean, what a waste of talent.' She nodded, hoping that that would convey her shock and sadness too. 'He was a good intern. There were a few in the last bunch that were worth it, and he was in that small few.'

'I don't remember him.' Aidan's eyes screwed up as he spoke. 'You worked with him closely, Sondra?'

'Yes, with all the interns. It was my project.' That was true. Sondra had initiated the internship programme five years back as a way to assist new graduates, as well as to ease the stress levels in the bullring. Young and eager, the interns could do much of the legwork and research on potential investments.

'I'll get the details of the funeral. I'm sure you'll want to attend?' Vicky cocked her head towards Sondra.

'I don't think that's necessary. Perhaps we can send flowers and a card?' Sondra hoped her voice sounded even and professional.

'The interns were here for six months. They spent so much time here, sometimes eighteen hours, five or six days a week. Do we not consider them to be family?' Vicky frowned at each manager in turn as she spoke.

'Interns are not permanent employees, and anyway, they left two months ago. I don't think we should be setting any precedents?' Sondra squared her shoulders and raised an eyebrow in Aidan's direction.

Aidan nodded gravely. 'Yes, I think Sondra is right. Flowers and a sympathy card will be enough. You'll take care of it, Vicky?'

Sondra knew Aidan Ross well; he would always go for the professional option and the least difficult route.

'If that's settled, shall we get started on status. We've lost enough time this morning.' Sondra wanted to move the discussion away from John's death to anything else.

'Yes, yes. Agreed. Let's get started.' Aidan nodded at Vicky, who excused herself so that the meeting could proceed.

As the meeting moved along, Sondra was relieved that she was prepared, like she was for all status meetings. It was easy enough to read off her notes without having to concentrate. Her head was still reeling at this turn of events. John dying so soon after leaving the firm and in such a manner ... No, she would not think about the implications.

Sondra forced herself to listen to the discussions and even commented on others' presentations. Fortunately, the news had put a dampener on everyone's spirits and the meeting rounded up quickly. No one lingered over coffee or discussed any of the prospects or projects at length. Sondra was able to make a hasty exit and escaped to her office. She shut the door behind her and leant her forehead against it. She could hear the loud thudding of her heart against her ribcage.

John is dead ...?

She couldn't believe it. She hadn't thought about him since he'd left the company. That was not entirely true – every now and then, a thought of him or them together would cross her mind. Not in a nostalgic or longing way though; she didn't miss him. What was there to miss? Nothing that she couldn't get from anyone else if she wanted or tried. If she hadn't tried, it was because she didn't want to. Whatever she got from her ill-considered liaison with John was not worth the drama.

And now this! Just when she thought she'd put all his craziness behind her. She groaned out loud. *What the hell, John? What were you thinking? Such a foolish thing to do. You did this, John – all on your own. I don't know what your reason was, but if it was because of the way you felt about me, that is not my problem. Nothing to do with me. I cannot be held responsible for your decisions. I was clear from the beginning: what we had was just a fling. Temporary. Just a little distraction to pass the time, and you knew it. I made that very clear.*

Sondra felt the beginnings of a headache creeping up her neck. *No!* She could not afford that now. It was a busy day and a busy week. She needed to focus and could not deal with this John drama now. It was not her problem. She did not do anything to encourage him. In fact, she went out of her way to let him know that there was no future for them, that she had no feelings for him. If he had fallen for her, was unable to deal with the rejection, and had resorted to an unnecessary and foolish way out, that was his problem. Not hers. She, Sondra, had done nothing wrong and would not spend another moment on this. Enough time had already been wasted that morning, and she would not allow a second more.

Sondra flicked her head back and felt her thick, dark hair slip back into place. She ignored the pain in her temples, strode to her desk, and concentrated on work.

8

QUESTIONS WITH NO ANSWERS

H annah would have liked to think that she emerged from a fog of unconsciousness, of being unaware of the truth of John being gone. Had that been the case, she would not have had to face a world without John for every second of the past seven months.

The truth was etched in the new lines that had appeared around her eyes and lips and on her forehead. The lines were fresh and raw like the pain that seeped out of every pore, every molecule, every nerve ending until all she was, was an empty edifice, bathed in burning tears. Hannah had always been a petite woman but had lost weight since John's passing, and nowadays, her clothes hung on her.

Hannah had been given three weeks leave after it had happened, yet when she had not been ready at the end of that period to return, she had managed to negotiate another two on compassionate and unpaid grounds. When she had eventually gone back to work, she had hidden, not wanting to interact with anyone. She had asked to be moved into the file room, where only a student worked in the afternoons. She had moved her computer there and had continued with her administrative duties as efficiently as before but without talking to anyone unless she absolutely had to.

She stopped seeing friends and never went back to church after John's funeral. How could she praise or pray to a god that had destroyed all that was good and pure in her world? If God was all powerful and loving, why would He have allowed this to happen? A few church members and friends dropped by a few times, but she saw no one, turning people away at the door, if she answered at all, and rejected all telephonic attempts at communication too. Hannah did not want to hear about patience and acceptance and God's plan, especially when they were ineffectual platitudes dripping with pity.

She ate and drank nothing apart from a sandwich that she picked up at the petrol station on the way home and endless cups of coffee, with an occasional biscuit at the office. She didn't want anyone or anything; she only wanted John back.

* * *

The call from the retirement village was fortuitous, even though the news was bad. Hannah's mother had fallen and had broken her hip. This coincided with Doris resigning for family reasons before Hannah's mother came out of the hospital. Hannah had no option but to snap out of it; her mother needed care around the clock, and Hannah had to step up.

Hannah moved her mother into her house until she was better – 'five, maybe six months' was the doctor's estimate – or until a new permanent caregiver could be found. Hannah was forced into a routine that included weekly shopping, cooking, and talking. For the first few weeks, Sylvia was helpless, weak from the immobility after the operation and the effects of the pain killers that had to be taken regularly. Hannah did everything for her mother.

Both women were quiet: Hannah because she had lost one of the most basic attributes of humanness – communication; and Sylvia because she was too weak to try. But as Sylvia healed and slowly began to regain her mobility, she became her usual chatty self.

Patiently and lovingly, she helped her daughter. First, she started casually mentioning John in conversations. The first few times Sylvia did this, Hannah invented reasons to excuse herself or changed the subject. After a while though, Hannah didn't anymore. Hannah sensed that Sylvia was heartened by that.

One glorious Johannesburg spring afternoon, Hannah wheeled her mother into the sun.

'Look at this colour I bought.' Hannah held the nail polish against her mother's fair, spotted hands. 'I think it'll suit you.'

The two women sat united in their grief, Hannah painting the fingernails of her mother's hands a pearly pink. It reminded her of the colour that the milk turned in John's baby cereal. Her hand trembled ever so slightly, causing a tiny smudge, which she hastened to wipe away. The tissue then moved to dab at her eyes.

'You will never stop thinking about him or missing him or needing him, my child. Motherhood ... having a child, loving a child ... it becomes everything. My girl ...' The words were hoping to impart comfort, but were heavy and fell like rocks, sinking to the bottom of a deep, dark ocean. 'I wish I could take away your pain, but miracles like that don't happen.'

Hannah didn't say anything. She kept her head bowed and concentrated on her task.

'He was a good boy, a great boy. We were blessed. You did well as a mother. You must believe that. You must not blame yourself. We don't know why things happen, and we question ourselves and God, but the truth is that some things are not for us to know. We must simply accept.'

'There. First coat done. While it dries, I'll make us a cup of tea.' Hannah forced cheeriness into her voice.

She walked into the house but didn't go into the kitchen. Rather, without planning or realising it, she walked into John's room. The door had been closed by him, probably one of the last things he had done before killing himself. The only people who had been in the room since were the two police officers who had been unable to find a note. Now, she stood in the middle of his room and tried to feel his presence, his essence.

Her eyes closed tightly as the image of an alive, vibrant, whole John came into view. *Why? WHY?* The single-word question she had no answer to thundered in her head. Registering the ordered, neatened room that was deathly still, she marvelled at how she had never had to nag him to clean it. He was a finicky person and was particular about things like that. The bed was made, the drawers were closed, and no books or clothes were lying around. Without thinking, she lay on her back on the double bed, with her arms spread out like Christ on the cross.

The light fitting, a red and blue wooden aeroplane that had never been changed, hovered and swayed above her. John's blue *takkie* had swayed like that when she had found him. Silent tears rolled out of her eyes and wet the pillow on either side of her face, the wetness collecting and being absorbed. If only pain could be so easily absorbed and forgotten. *No. I don't want to forget. John will be with me forever.*

Why, John? Why, God? WHY?

Hannah sat bolt upright. She had to know. She rose and surveyed the room again. What if he *had* left a note, somewhere hidden for her to find? A frantic search began. She pulled open drawers and tossed things out. She shook out books. She looked in pockets of jackets and pants. Her search revealed nothing except for her anger, buried and locked away. Today, her anger was unlocked, unearthed. She railed against the injustice. *Damn you, God! Damn you, John! How could you do this? How could you do this to me?* Slowly, deliberately, with shaking hands and seeing through misty eyes, she straightened up the room, then remembered her mother.

Hannah dashed downstairs and brought her mother into the kitchen.

'Look, Hannah. I did the second coat. Not bad, hey?' The women admired her handiwork as Hannah made tea. 'I thought I heard you in John's room.'

Hannah nodded but turned away from Sylvia. Silent moments laden with sadness passed.

'I'm glad, Hannah. It's good you finally went into the room. It's a start. I'm afraid if you don't deal with this soon, it may be too late.' The words were gentle, laced with love and compassion. 'You have to talk about it, child. That's the only thing that will help: talking – the thing that is hardest for you to do. We must learn to grieve him and let him go so that we can start to remember the happy times ... times when he was with us.'

Let him go? I have no chance to do that, not even if I wanted to. He was stolen from me, snatched away in a moment. Hannah sipped her tea but said nothing. What could she say?

Her mother sounded wistful as she spoke again. 'Are you praying? Even if you are not ready to go back to church, you should pray.'

Pray to God? The God that she, Eliot, and the whole family had been devoted to? The God that had chosen to punish them instead of loving them?

Sylvia's nostalgic voice cut into her thoughts. 'I loved how he would pretend to be cross over silly things so that he could just laugh and hug us hard, how he got quiet when he was tired or boisterous when he was nervous. He felt life so deeply. He loved everything and everyone. Even when he was moody, he was never quiet, was he? Such an alive young man.'

Was he quiet when he was upset? Sometimes, I guess. He could be moody, but everyone can, right? Even the happiest of people can feel down sometimes. No one can be in a perfect mood all the time, can they? Hannah blinked rapidly while she too relived John's wholeness as a person – his complexities and individuality. *Why? Why, John?*

'I want to know why.' Sylvia's voice was emboldened by the need to understand, the need her daughter felt just as fiercely.

'There was no note, no explanation.' Hannah's voice was hoarse and gruff, a loud whisper that escaped the depths of imprisonment. The anger made her utterance sound foreign to her own ears. 'I don't know. I don't know.'

Sylvia reached her arms towards her daughter, and Hannah fell into her mother's embrace, crying.

'I miss him, Mother, every second of every day. I can only think, "He's gone. John is gone." My beautiful boy is ... dead.'

Sylvia held her close and stroked her hair.

'What could have made him do such an awful, terrible thing? Why didn't he talk to me? Or anyone? I wanted to do everything for him. My whole life was him – for *him*. He didn't trust me. He didn't share with me. What was it that he couldn't tell me? I would have forgiven him anything. I would have moved heaven and earth for his happiness. Didn't I love him enough?'

Hannah blew her nose and dabbed the tissue ineffectually at her eyes. Turning her head skywards, she whispered, 'He didn't trust me. I must not have been the mother that I thought I was. I failed him. I failed.' Her voice was thick with emotion and the effects of sobbing.

'No, child, you must not say that. Don't ever think it. It was not your fault. You were the most giving, kind, loving, caring parent that I've ever had the joy to witness. If anything, you did too much for him. You not only protected him as any mother would, but you went out of your way to make his life happy, to make his life easy.'

'Then why, Mother? *Why?*'

'I don't know.' Sylvia's voice was muffled, but then it became loud, her tone indignant. 'But I want to. Don't you?'

'Of course, I want to know. I can't make sense of this. If there was some reason, then I could try and understand.'

'Then we must find out!'

'Find out?' Hannah's face crumbled in on itself, not understanding.

'Yes, something or someone must have brought it about. Even if there was some underlying unhappiness – if his ... moods were caused by something else ... some event or incident would have triggered such a drastic reaction, don't you think?'

'His moods?'

Sylvia's voice was laced with compassion and sympathy. 'There *were* mood swings, Hannah. As a youngster – when he would get quiet sometimes. They were never severe and never lasted long. They weren't noticeable because he wasn't different; his behaviour didn't change. It was more subtle than that, more like a shift in energy. I guess we thought they were typical teenage stuff.'

Hannah frowned as she remembered the times that her mother was describing. Yes, there were subtle changes in John's manner – not so much his actions or behaviour, just in levels of enthusiasm and engagement. Sylvia was right. They were not common and never really lasted long, but in retrospect, she could not pretend them away.

Was that what she had been doing? Had she been pretending that John was the perfect son and person that she had ignored anything else? In trying to give him the perfect life, had she failed him by choosing not to see his quiet, dark side – a side that predisposed him to end his life if things didn't work out like he'd hoped? Why hadn't she done anything about this? Why hadn't she noticed?

'I can imagine what you're thinking, but don't do that to yourself. I don't think you were wrong never to address John's changing moods. They were hardly noticeable. The subtle changes in his attitude were very rare that they never warranted any big intervention – I don't think. He was a typical teenager, I thought. Especially as an only child, it was expected that he could be a loner.' Again, her mother spoke as though she were reading her daughter's mind. Hannah stared while the realisation of her mother's words dawned on her.

'Maybe there was something like depression then. Maybe there wasn't. Maybe it resurfaced just before ... We will never know for sure. Even so, I still think something must have happened to cause his actions. We must find out.'

'What do you mean?' Hannah sniffed. 'How can we ever know? He left no note.'

'Did any of his friends know?'

'No. They were as shocked as I was. They asked *me* for answers.'

'Someone would know. Maybe someone from his work? Or anyone he would have gone to for work? A university lecturer perhaps?'

Hannah nodded slowly. Yes, there were many people that John knew, and not all would have been close enough to come to the funeral or to try and see her afterwards. People had sent cards, flowers, and messages through others. Maybe one of them had some idea.

'Okay, Mother, I get it. I should try and find out why. It's a good idea. Even if we don't solve the mystery, at least we would know we tried. I'll try. I need to know. I *really do* need to know why.'

Hannah left her mother and her barely touched tea in the kitchen and walked to the cards and notes on the mantelpiece above the fireplace in the living room. They were not displayed like Christmas or birthday cards might have been. Rather, they were collected in a bleak, dishevelled pile at one end, several unopened. Hannah started sorting through them and came across a card that was indented like it had been clipped onto those plastic holders that were stuck into flowers. It was typed.

Deepest sympathy from team and interns.
Ross Maphumulo Investment Co.

That was the company that John had done his internship with. She did a search on the internet for their telephone number and called. 'Ross Maphumulo Investments. How may I direct your call?'

Hannah dropped the call. *What was she going to say? Who would she ask for?*

Five minutes later, when she dialled again, she was better prepared. 'Hello. My name is Hannah Bennett. I'm the mother of one of the interns you had last year. You may remember him? John. John Bennett.'

'Sorry, ma'am. I'm new, just started last month. How can I help you?'

'I needed to thank someone for the card and flowers that I received. Who would I speak to?' The silence at the other end of the line had to be filled. 'HR, maybe?'

'I'll put you through.'

The call was answered immediately. The woman, who identified herself as Vicky Moodley, sounded pleasant and like she was in her fifties. 'We were so sad to hear about your son. He fitted right in and was a hard worker. But there was no need to call and thank us, really.'

Hannah thought about how strange it must have been for Vicky to receive her call after so many months and so out of the blue. No matter. Hannah would forge on, even if time had passed and it was weird for her to ask her questions.

'Actually, I was wondering if there was anyone I could talk to about John. A co-worker or boss perhaps?'

'Uh, no, not really.' The voice sounded kind but confused. 'It was a long time ago. What is this about, Missus Bennett?'

'Please, call me Hannah. I'd hate to bother you, but do you know of the circumstances surrounding John's passing?'

'We have heard some things, yes.' The concern she heard in Vicky's voice was encouraging, even though the words were strained.

'I'm trying to understand what happened, why he would do something like that.'

There was an awkward silence. Hannah knew that the woman was wondering how to handle this. Did her training prepare her for this sort of situation?

'I'm trying to piece together the last few months of his life. Work was a big part of that time. He loved it and was learning so much.'

Vicky hesitated for a moment before speaking slowly and deliberately. 'There would be no harm in sharing his file with you. I should warn you though, there's not much personal, just application forms, targets, assessments, and the likes.'

'Was he friends with anyone?'

'Not really. The interns stuck together.'

'Maybe I could talk to them?'

'They're no longer here.'

'How can I reach them?'

'I can't give out personal info.'

'Please, Vicky. There must be some way ... without getting you mentioned.'

'No, I'm sorry, Missus Bennett.' A short pause. 'Hannah. Look, give me your number, and if I think of anything else, I'll call. I'm not promising anything though.'

Hannah thanked her and gave her details. Once the call was ended, she futilely went back to the cards. What was she hoping to learn? Frustrated, she gathered them up to put into the box with old cards from years back. She searched the neat piles tied with ribbon or banded together with rubber bands and found the ones from John: cards from when he was young and had just learnt to write, crayon pictures that were of happy families with blue skies and bright yellow suns, all scattered with red hearts and red lips indicating kisses. This child – who had been so giving and loving, so communicative, so available – had turned away from her. Why? What could have caused this?

Wading through memories, she relived happy and fun times. Sylvia had wheeled herself next to Hannah and began a running commentary of John's childhood. Sylvia's memory had not tarnished with her years. She was tender and teary but still managed to chuckle every time a precious recollection allowed.

Hannah felt lost ... like an intruder in her mother's mind. She wished she was able to remember happily as her mother did. What she felt was confusion – confusion to the point of bewilderment. Nothing made sense; nothing felt real.

'I'll get you a tissue, Mother.' Hannah pushed her hands against her thighs and raised herself up with effort. When she returned with tissues, she announced, 'I'm going to find out what happened, Mother. I need to know. If I am ever ... ever going to be able to make peace and ...' *and what?* she asked herself. '... and carry on, I guess, I must know the truth.'

Sylvia nodded gravely. 'I'm glad. It's right you know. We all need to know.'

Hannah's quest – her quest for answers, for the truth, for understanding – formed quickly in her mind. She planned on starting an intense and methodical search of John's room, then she would deal with his bathroom and the living areas, and lastly, the garage. The best time to tackle the task would be over the weekend, which seemed so far off. It was only Thursday, but any delay felt interminable. It would not have been right to do any searching at night after work or even early in the morning because her mother was a light and restless sleeper.

Saturday morning could not come soon enough.

9

THE TRUTH WILL OUT

A plain seventy-two-page exercise book with blocks faintly lined throughout, the kind John would have used for maths at school – that's what she found. It was a diary of the last six months of his life, a detailed account of his internship and the affair he had had with an older woman, his boss. From Hannah's point of view, she was most likely sophisticated and experienced but ruthless – a woman who takes what she wants without care of who she hurts or kills in the process. The words John used to describe her were unfathomable: goddess, perfect, stunning, grace-ful, exquisite and other flowery descriptors. They jarred her. How could he gush over this woman who caused his death? This woman! This woman!

Sondra Carim-Edwards was the Business Development Officer at Ross Maphumulo Investments based in Fricker Road, Illovo. Sondra was not on *Facebook* nor did she seem to have a personal profile anywhere really, except on LinkedIn. The information here was only about her professional life, didn't seem to be updated, and did not include a picture either.

Where would Hannah go from there? Where could she even start? Her head reeled with questions. She had searched for answers and instead was more confused. Hannah felt gobsmacked by this shocking disclosure. She put the diary in an A4 envelope and hid it in her handbag.

Who are you hiding it from, Hannah? she asked herself. She realised that she didn't want to know.

* * *

For days, Hannah ignored her mother's questions about what the search had unearthed until Sylvia stopped asking. The revelation shocked Hannah. It rocked her fundamental understanding of who John was. He was a child, indulged and protected. She had thought of him as a pre-adult, someone who still needed to be taken care of. And she thought she had done that – taking care of him had been her whole world. Her job was to be his doting mother, and his was to let her and enjoy the love she lavished on him.

He had lived at home, even when he was at university, and led a sheltered and conservative life. He had many friends and was a well-liked, well-adjusted child, easy-going and respected by his peers, encouraged by his elders, and adored by younger ones. That was the John she knew.

This John, the one who had an illicit affair with a married woman, could not possibly be the boy she had raised. The mood swings and periods of quiet were few and far between – they were easily cured by a bowl of ice-cream when he was younger, or a new toy or gadget as he grew older. She screwed her eyes, but she could see him only as a simple, uncomplicated child. Her mind reeled with the new view the diary had unearthed.

Her mother would have been just as confused. Anyone who knew John would have been incredulous. Hannah, who had had a few nights' sleep since she had resolved to find answers, had now stopped sleeping altogether. She was a zombie, catching thirty-minute naps in the *Uber* she now used daily to work and back. She was too terrified to drive, being so exhausted and unconscious.

* * *

A week after she found John's diary – or was it two? – Hannah received a call from a number that she recognised even though it was not saved. It was Ross Maphumulo Investments.

'Hello?' Her voice was too soft, she realised, just a whisper. Then, louder, 'Hannah speaking.'

'Missus Bennett? Hi. It's Vicky Moodley. We spoke a few weeks ago.'

'Yes. Hi, Vicky. And call me Hannah, please.'

'How are you keeping?'

'I'm okay ... I guess.' Her voice cracked, so she cleared her throat. 'But with time, people say.' She tried to sound convincing – she didn't think it worked.

'Yes. I imagine it must be tough.' Vicky paused for a second or two. 'Is this a good time? You're not busy, are you?'

'It's fine. Please ...'

'I wanted to chat with you about John, actually. One of the interns that was in his group called for a reference, and I asked her if she remembered your boy. She did. I told her you'd called, asking if anyone was willing to talk about him. Uh ... her name is Samantha, Samantha Mdlalose. Apparently, they were at the same varsity but in different years.'

'I see. Thanks. That's some news, at least. How kind of you to remember and mention it to her.'

'It was lucky, I guess, her calling so soon after we'd spoken.'

'Yes.' Hannah's face screwed into a frown. It was something; a place to start. 'Samantha, you say? No, I don't think he ever mentioned her.'

'Samantha said I should give you her number and that you could call any evening after seven.'

'Thanks.' Hannah concentrated on writing the number carefully. '*Sjoe!* What will I say?'

'Just be yourself. Speak honestly, like you did with me. People respond to that.' Vicky wished her luck.

'Thanks again, Vicky. It means so much.'

'Take care, Hannah. Goodbye.'

Hannah was sure she heard Vicky's voice quiver. *She must be a mother too,* Hannah thought. She disconnected the call and wondered what the night would reveal.

Her worst fears were realised. Samantha Mdlalose was soft-spoken but self-assured beyond her years. Hannah didn't need to ask any questions. Samantha, "Sam" as she wanted to be called, was forthright.

'I met John at varsity but didn't really know him 'cause I was a year ahead of him. At Ross Maphumulo, we gravitated towards each other. Well, all the interns became friends. I'm not sure how much you know about what happened at work.'

'Not much,' Hannah had to admit. 'He seemed to enjoy it. He said that he was learning lots and found it challenging.'

'Yes. Yes. They have a good programme.' Samantha took a deep breath. 'Did he ever mention our boss, Sondra Carim-Edwards?'

This girl didn't waste any time. 'No.' Hannah exhaled. She realised she'd been holding her breath. 'But I found a diary recently. She's all he wrote about.' It shocked her for a split second how she had fallen so easily into speaking about John in the past tense.

Samantha sighed and was quiet for a short time, maybe waiting to see if Hannah was going to volunteer anything further.

'She was a good boss – demanding but fair.'

'What happened between the two of them?' Hannah wondered how much Samantha knew.

'John fell in love with her, and there was an affair. It was difficult to watch. He was besotted, but it was obvious that she was just using him.'

'Using him?' Hannah screeched the words out.

'I'm sorry. This must be tough to hear.'

Hannah took a deep, calming breath. She must keep Samantha talking. 'No, no need for apologies. I would rather know, no matter how painful. I gathered as much from what I read in the diary anyway.'

'I don't think she realised the power she had over him. I think, to her, he was just a fling, a diversion from the ... you know ... everyday mundane stuff.'

'I see.' Hannah's lips disappeared into her mouth. She bit down hard and forced herself to keep the phone pressed to her ear.

'When she ended things, he was devastated. It was like his world stopped.'

Yes, Hannah thought. *I know how that feels.*

Samantha continued. 'I've wondered for a while about how desperate or hopeless he must have felt to ... you know ... Was there a history of depression?'

'No. Nothing like that.' The answer was automatic. Hannah swallowed – her mouth was suddenly dry. *There wasn't, was there?* She shuddered and then continued, even less sure of anything than when this conversation had started. 'He's a ... John was a happy person. He brought joy to people.' Hannah sighed self-consciously. 'I guess that sounds corny.'

'No, not at all. It's true. He would walk into a room, and people would lighten up. He had a presence but wasn't intimidating or dominating or anything like that. I admired that about him.'

A quickly stifled laugh escaped from Hannah. 'I thought it was only me who saw that.' Hannah squeezed her eyes tight, mimicking the way that her heart was being squeezed. 'That's why it's been so hard to figure out.'

'Yes, I can only imagine. I guess when someone like John – so full of life and energy – they do everything so completely ...'

'Sorry?' Hannah had lost the thread of the conversation, recalling images of John smiling, laughing, and being his usual, exuberant self. There were other images too, of John angry and crying as a child. But she'd always been able to calm him down or make him laugh again when he was younger.

'I mean, he's the kind of person that would love totally, give himself completely.'

Yes, that was true. He was an all-or-nothing person. Both women fell quiet, each lost in thought or wondering what the other was thinking.

'He loved Missus Carim-Edwards,' Samantha continued after a brief moment. 'He was head over heels. For him, it was the real thing.'

'Did he talk about her?'

'No. It was not discussed at all. A few of the interns knew, but I doubt any of the other staff did. No one said anything.' Samantha paused briefly. 'I figured it out, I guess, because we were *kinda* close. In those few months as interns, I worked closest with him because we had the same portfolio.' As Samantha spoke, her voice caught.

'From what I read in his diary, he did believe that this was the real thing. He was an idealist, thought that they'd be together forever.' Hannah's brow furrowed.

'Still, I wouldn't've guessed, not in a million years, that he'd do something so drastic.'

'So drastic ...' Hannah echoed Samantha's words. Hannah licked her lips. They felt like rough sandpaper. 'She must be something special.'

Samantha laughed cynically – a harsh, bitter sound. 'Hah! Hardly.'

'What do you mean?'

'Sorry. I'm letting my personal feelings about what happened interfere. She was—probably still is professional. I can't comment on her personally because she never let us see that side of her. John was besotted and would have seen no wrong, but she took advantage of him. She should've known better.'

Hannah felt an intense rage at this woman boil up from the pit of her stomach. This woman had used her son and, when she was done, tossed him aside like garbage. 'I should confront her.'

'Would she see you or entertain anything?' Samantha snorted as though incredulous at her own question. 'I doubt it. Missus Carim-Edwards is not approachable in the least. Maybe only to men or people who can further her agenda.'

'Her agenda?'

'I mean, like, everything is all about her and what she can get from anyone. She's successful because she is driven and, frankly, ruthless. You should've heard the stories that went around the bullring.'

Hannah tried to imagine John navigating the relationship. Was he completely out of his depth, swept away by his emotions? Samantha was right. He was the kind of person who loved completely and loved to be loved in return as vociferously. He'd learnt that from her, unconditional, uncompromising love – the only way she knew how to love her son.

'My poor boy. I wonder how he coped.' The wistful voice became stronger as she became angrier. 'She took advantage. She destroyed him. My beautiful, caring, devoted child.' Tears burned her eyes and spilt onto her cheeks. 'I could kill her.' The last sentence rasped out of her, spat out in disgust, rage, and excruciating pain.

'I'm sorry ... I wish there was something I could say that could help, Missus Bennett. It's awful. What a waste of a life. We weren't that close but had become buddies. I didn't feel I could say anything to him. He was so secretive, never sharing what happened. The rest of us could only guess and jump to conclusions.'

'Sorry. I shouldn't be upsetting you. I don't know ...' Hannah trailed off as she tried to catch her breath and retake control. 'I ... I want to thank you, Samantha, for ... for talking to me, for being his buddy. And for talking to me.' Hannah stumbled over her words. 'I ...' The voice scraped the insides of her throat. 'I ... Thanks again. Goodbye.' Hannah cut the call immediately.

She sat where she was, lost in thought, for hours. That was where her mother found her, slumped over in the chair, sleeping but not resting, the next morning.

10

RESENTFUL RESOLVE

With the address repeating in her mind, Hannah circled the block twice before she found a parking spot diagonally opposite 21 Centre Crescent, settled down in her seat, and pulled her peak cap low. For the briefest of moments, she imagined that she was a private investigator in a movie and that this was a stakeout.

Hannah leant her head back and closed her eyes. Instantly, the image of John burned the insides of her eyelids – her darling son dangling from the balustrade. The image had become her outlook ever since she had come home to find her beautiful boy swaying ... strapping, handsome John, swinging from the rope, his head at an awkward, unnatural angle. When she cut him down, he had fallen. He had become a dead weight that had landed with a muffled thud on the thick-pile carpet on the floor in front of the little table in their hallway. The image was as clear as it was since the day it happened. The image caused a gaping wound that had opened deep and long in her soul. This was torture. She had to make it stop.

Her eyes flew open. She sat bolt upright. Her seat belt pulled angrily against her collar bone; she had not unclipped it. She breathed slowly and practised the technique that Mary, her therapist, had taught her.

'The technique needs to be practised, Hannah.' Mary had handed her an A6-sized lined hardcover notebook. 'Record your thoughts. It helps when you are able to track improve-ments, even minor ones. Your panic attacks should reduce in intensity and frequency. If there's no significant change, we can try alternative methods.' Hannah liked the practi-cality of the therapy. If it was touchy-feely, she would have baulked and run a mile.

Hannah imagined Mary's reaction when she relayed this misadventure to her at their next session.

'What were you thinking, Hannah?' Hannah heard Mary's even tones questioning her motivation. 'What were you hoping to achieve?'

What, indeed? thought Hannah. The house was empty. That woman – the reason John killed himself – was not there. What could she possibly gain from sitting a few metres away, watching a lifeless structure? She hadn't planned on doing this when she had woken up that morning. All she had wanted to know was what Sondra thought. *What happened?* She wanted to talk to her but was terrified. *Did you love my John? I read what he wrote. He loved you.*

What felt like a lifetime had only been a few days – a few days since that call with Samantha had confirmed what she had read in John's diary. She had called Sondra Carim-Edwards's office the following day. She had wanted to speak with the woman who had destroyed her life. But her attempt had proved unsatisfactory, to say the least. The woman was first cold but professional, then realising who Hannah was, she became curt, bordering on cruel. She was eager to get Hannah off the phone but not before demanding that she never call again.

'I have no reason to speak to you. Leave me alone,' were Sondra's parting words before she unceremoniously ended the call.

Hannah did not know what she had expected. Understanding? Sympathy? Guilt? An apology? She certainly hadn't expected her to take responsibility for her son's death, but maybe a guilty intake of breath as realisation dawned or a slight crack in Sondra's voice may have appeased her. *Really, Hannah?* she chided herself. *Was there anything Sondra Carim-Edwards could say or do that would ease the piercing pain you feel with every breath you take? Is there anything that anyone can say or do that would bring beautiful John back?*

She angrily brushed hot tears from her cheeks, started her car, and pulled away. It was bloody pointless and futile. Like every other attempt to move past this hurt, it was ineffective.

"Sorry for your loss", people said. The words were impotent and hollow. *Loss.* Can it capture what anyone who has lost a child experiences? *Loss.* Like it was something that could be found again. People meant well but could never understand what a mother loses when she loses a child. Death is final. Death changes everything until nothing is recognisable.

* * *

Today ... today, she was going to force Sondra to hear her. Hannah had been watching Sondra's house for a month. She had become a stalker. Something different had to happen; otherwise, she would be in this limbo forever.

Sondra's times were erratic, but Hannah guessed she would return to her house around seven that evening. She had been waiting since six, and when the silver *Audi* drove onto the property, Hannah locked her car and strode purposefully up the driveway before the automatic gate closed.

She scrutinised Sondra's bent torso as it leant into the *boot* to collect her things. She was dressed in a stylish but understated dark suit. She looked formal and, even while peering into the *boot*, professional.

As Sondra turned to walk towards the house, she caught sight of Hannah. 'Can I help you?' Sondra's eyes narrowed as though she was trying to place the woman. Hannah wondered what Sondra was thinking seeing this plain, nondescript woman standing at her doorstep.

When Hannah didn't answer, Sondra gingerly placed her bags on the ground at her feet and took a few steps towards the stranger. She held her keys in her right hand, prepared for anything. 'How did you get in?' Her eyes flitted to the gate and back to the new arrival. 'Who are you?'

'Hannah. Hannah Bennett. I am John's mother.' The corner of Hannah's mouth twitched grimly as she noticed Sondra's eyes grow wide. *Not in confusion, no,* Hannah mused to herself. *In fear maybe?* Hannah watched and followed Sondra's eyes as she looked towards the house. There was no movement within.

Sondra took the few seconds to compose herself. 'Why are you here? I told you, we have nothing to talk about.'

'We do: John.' The last word hung suspended between them, connecting and dividing them.

'John?'

'My son, John. Your lover. Your toy boy.'

'I'm not sure what you think—'

'I don't think anything. I know everything. I know you had an affair with him, and when you were bored, you tossed him out like yesterday's newspaper.'

Sondra could not hold Hannah's gaze. Her eyes flickered over Hannah as she pushed her shoulders back, squaring herself, evidently preparing for battle. She was going to get one.

'John was besotted. You used him. Young and innocent, he was defenceless against you.' Hannah's voice was strong, despite her insides shaking like jelly.

'I didn't expect that he ... He was ...' Sondra could not hold Hannah's piercing glower and dropped her gaze to the ground between them.

'Didn't expect what? That a man twenty years younger than you could love you? Or that any man could?'

Hannah registered a glimmer of satisfaction as she noticed Sondra's hands shaking. Then Sondra crossed her arms over her chest.

'What do you want? What can you possibly get here? I ... I don't ... I can't help you.' Sondra's eyes narrowed. 'I'm sorry for your loss. John's actions were foolish. I promised him nothing. In fact, I made it clear to him. I was not interested in a relationship. He pursued me.'

'You didn't try very hard to dissuade him, did you? It must have been great for your ego. A young, handsome, talented man chasing you. You should have known better.'

'And you should leave. We have nothing more to say to each other.'

'I have lots to say to you, and you will listen.' Hannah took a firm step forwards and planted herself solidly on the ground. 'My child, my amazing boy is gone. He killed himself because he could not bear to live without you. When you got tired, you just moved on without blinking an eye.' Hannah placed her hand on her head, then on her chest while she relieved herself of words that were eating her up. 'I found a diary he left. He was always such an expressive, loving person. You were everything to him. If you were going to just discard him, you should never have gotten involved with him in the first place. You are older and should have known better. A married woman, carrying on with a boy half her age – you should be ashamed.'

'Ashamed?' Sondra's nostrils flared as she glared at Hannah. 'Why? I feel no shame. I am who I am. I answer to no one and make no excuses for who I am. I am not ashamed of who I am.'

Hannah sensed she had touched a nerve. 'You should be. If you had an ounce of decency, you would be mortified by your actions and what you have caused.'

'This is getting us nowhere. I'm asking you to leave. Leave now. This drama is unnecessary and pointless.' Sondra dug her fists into her sides, her elbows jutting outwards. Her feet were waist-width apart, and the stare she fixed on Hannah was piercing and cold.

'My God, you *are* heartless, a cold-hearted ice queen with no compassion. You're actually proud. What is there to be proud of?' Hannah put her arms out, her palms facing upwards questioningly. 'You think your beauty and power are some great achievements? You have no concept of what it is to be a human being. Life is not about a big house, a fancy car, or a high-flying career. Your quality as a person is not measured in material things but in how you relate to others. It's our humanity that makes us good, successful people.'

'Hmph!' Sondra snorted derisively. 'Listen, lady, I've been patient up 'til now. You really don't want to see me lose my temper. You can take your baseless accusations and last-century values and get off my property. I will not explain myself to you.' Sondra marched to Hannah's side, grabbed hold of her arm at the elbow, and started pushing her towards the gate.

Hannah threw off Sondra's hand violently, the woman's touch burning her. 'Don't touch me, you bitch.'

'Aah, isn't that bloody marvellous? You come to my house with your holier-than-thou attitude and have the gall to swear at me? I guess you're really not as virtuous as you claim to be after all.'

Hannah brushed unstoppable tears of anger away. 'You *are* a bitch. I'm calling it as I see it.'

Sondra raised her arms on either side of her face, her palms open. Hannah could not believe how measured she was. *It must be an act.*

'Listen,' Sondra said in a calm and collected manner. 'Let's not make this personal. I don't know you, nor do I want to. I'm not judging. I'm sure you are in pain. While I'm sorry for your loss, I cannot be blamed for your son's actions. His internship and our … our … we were over for months when he … when the news broke at the office.'

'Those months were hell for him, the hardest he'd ever lived through.' At least she wasn't denying the affair happened. Hannah's body felt heavy. She felt the torture John described in his neat handwriting as intensely as he had. 'You were cruel. He was a gentle soul, one who felt deeply and completely. You used him, and he took his own life because of it.' Hannah shuddered. She swayed and moved her feet to steady herself.

Sondra shrugged. 'Not my fault or my problem.'

'Did you feel nothing for him? All that he was to you was sex? An ego boost?' Hannah threw her head back. The world went dark. She felt weak and found it difficult to remain standing. *I must not break down in front of her. I won't give her the satisfaction.*

'Hannah.'

Hannah's eyes flew open, and she stared at Sondra. It was the first time that Sondra had addressed her by name.

'Leave. Please.' Her words were firm but not cruel.

Hannah knew a flood of tears was seconds away. 'I hate you,' she spluttered. 'I hope you rot in hell.'

Her last words floated behind her as she scrambled towards the opening gate. As soon as she was out of view behind the wall, Hannah ran to her car. She drove like a mad woman, not aware of how she made it home.

As soon as she switched off the engine, the tears that had been welling up for minutes, hours, days, weeks, months tumbled out of her shuddering body, racked with pain, hate, and longing – pain at her loss of John, hate at the awful woman, and longing for release.

'I hate you, Sondra Carim-Edwards! I hate you, God!' Hannah needed to blame someone; someone or something had to be responsible for John's death. She could not accept it could be John.

It didn't help though. Nothing did. The hollowness she felt persisted. The encounter with Sondra Carim-Edwards did nothing for her. Her pain did not diminish, nor did her hatred. In fact, she felt them more acutely. Her longing for her son and her need to know what happened would remain unfulfilled too. Relief was not on her horizon, not anytime soon ... maybe never.

11

DEATH AND DESTRUCTION

S ondra watched the small woman leave. David didn't like the gate to be interrupted, preferring it to open and close fully, but now, Sondra stopped it as soon as Hannah had exited, then quickly closed it.

She turned and walked to her bags on the floor. As she reached for them, she noticed her hands were shaking. She slowly straightened to gather herself together.

Could Hannah Bennett have such an effect on me to leave me shaking?

Sondra wrapped her arms around herself for a moment, then collected her stuff, and trudged towards the house. Before she reached the door though, it was wrenched open from inside. She was startled to see Michael scowling at her.

His lips were curled into a sneer, and his eyes were flashing angrily. *No, he couldn't have heard anything, surely?* The altercation was not loud and was a few metres away from the house.

'You scared me.' She tried to move past him and into the house, but he remained rooted to the spot, glaring at her. Did she miss another meeting or something at school?

She hoped it was something as innocent as that. 'Michael? What's the matter? Let me pass.'

No, his look isn't an angry one, it's one of disgust. As this registered, she knew that it was something way worse. Her legs felt as heavy as lead when she managed to push past him and walk into the house.

'You're a piece of work, *Mother*.' The sarcasm dripping from the last word was palpable.

'I don't know what's got you in a huff. Whatever it is, can we deal with it later? I've had a crappy day.'

'I heard everything. What kind of a woman are you?'

The hairs on the back of Sondra's neck stood up. She had to think of something, but her brain could not function.

'It's bad enough you had an affair with someone young enough to be my brother but to treat that poor woman, his mother, so bad! I can't believe you.' Michael stomped after her.

'You don't know what you are talking about, Michael.' Was it just her voice or her whole body that was quivering?

'I saw and heard everything. Don't even try and pretend. I know your tricks too well.'

'Tricks?' She shook her head, not feeling as certain as she was hoping to portray. She must get control of this situation before ... 'What has got you all worked up, Mikey?' She used the nickname David used, hoping to soothe him.

'Does Dad know?'

Sondra turned on her heel to face her son, having deposited her bags on the small entrance hall table. She sucked the inside of her bottom lip to stop it trembling. 'Know what?'

'I don't know how he puts up with you and your selfishness.'

Sondra realised that she had better tread carefully now. David and Michael shared a special bond. As a child, Michael had worshipped his father like a hero. David had showered love and attention on their only child. Sondra hadn't protested too much because it meant it left her with time to focus on other things. She hadn't ever played much of a role in Michael's life, and as the years passed, they had grown apart, neither really finding this too much of a problem – Sondra, because it meant that she didn't have to give too much time or attention, and Michael, because he didn't know any better. His father had been the constant in his life, and that had always been enough.

'Dad needs to know. I'm going to tell him. You can't treat him like a fool. He deserves so much better than that – than *you.*' Michael's voice was raised now as he followed his mother into the kitchen. Sondra's back was to him, but she could imagine his angry eyes and the way his arms would be flailing – that was how he reacted when he was agitated or upset.

'You need to calm down, please. Getting angry or judgemental is not going to help the situation.' Sondra spoke as calmly as she could, hoping the authoritative tone would get through to him.

'The situation? *The situation?* What situation? That you are a cheap whore who cares only about herself?'

He called me a whore. A whore! Oh my God! Sondra could not believe this was happening. An hour ago, her world and everything she touched was perfect. Now everything was unravelling. She drew a ragged breath; her mind a blank.

'Michael!' David's voice boomed as he walked into the kitchen behind them. 'What the hell is going on here? What are you two arguing about? I could hear you from upstairs.'

Sondra looked at them and raised her hands in appeal. She could handle each of them individually. But how could she calm Michael down, while trying to keep David placated? 'Listen. I've just gotten home, it's late, and I'm exhausted.'

'Well, that's unusual.' Michael didn't bother to hide his scorn.

Sondra ignored the comment and continued evenly, or as evenly as she could muster. 'I'm going to the bathroom, then we can have supper and discuss this properly like adults.'

'Have you been behaving like an adult? A responsible one?' Michael took a step towards Sondra, again trying to bar her way. She was shocked at his obvious rage. He had never been so angry or inflamed about anything. Normally, his attitude was more "don't care" or "whatever", either feigning or feeling disinterest.

David intervened by placing a hand on Michael's shoulder and drawing him to his side. 'It's okay, Mikey. It's okay. Here. Come here.' He led his son out of the kitchen. 'Mom will be down in a couple of minutes, then we'll sort this out.'

Sondra grabbed the opportunity and raced up to her room. In the bathroom, she splashed water on her face and breathed slowly, deeply. *Shit! Shit! Shit! Now what?* David had turned a blind eye to her previous liaisons. There was an unspoken agreement between them: provided that she was discreet and didn't rock the boat at home, he looked away. She was certain he had always known when she played around. The spring in her step, the additional care with her appearance, and the extra attention she gave him in bed had been signs. Only she knew that the thrill was all hers.

She loved being in illicit relationships. It was a way to manipulate men and get them to do what she wanted, but also for the sex, which was mostly great, she admitted. Moreover, there was the excitement; the thrill of being sur-reptitious made the trysts all the more rewarding. The care she lavished on herself was not for any lover. It was a silent salute to herself and her own prowess.

Damn! She kicked off her heels and stared at her reflection in the mirror. She had to be the one to tell David. If there was any hope for him to understand or forgive her, she had to explain. She dashed down the steps and into the kitchen. The atmosphere in the dimly lit space was strained. She switched on the main light above the table and walked to the stove, casting a sideways glance at both men who were sitting at the table. David's mouth was set in a thin line, and Michael was rubbing his eyes and nose. Neither looked at her.

'Right, I'm ravenous. I'm sure you guys are too.' She forced normality into her tone.

'No. We won't be eating, Sondra, not with you.' David rose abruptly from his chair. Father and son started for the door.

'David?'

But it was Michael who spoke. 'I've told Dad everything. He knows.'

Sondra's survival instincts kicked in. 'I don't know what you think you heard, Michael.' Her eyes scrunched up in a silent plea for understanding. 'You misunderstood.'

'It was crystal clear. I was on the balcony right above you. The sound travelled up *perfectly*. I saw how upset that woman was. She was sure, and you didn't deny anything.' Michael's face was dark – he looked older than his seventeen years. His eyes narrowed to slits, and his nostrils flared. Hers did the same when she was angry.

Sondra appealed to her husband. 'I don't know what he's told you, but listen to me, please. Whatever happened was a silly, little thing. It was nothing. It meant nothing. Just a few weeks, and it was over.'

'It was nothing to *you*.' David's voice was soft but laden with emotion. 'But that boy, that poor boy, he ... he was destroyed. You destroyed him.' He sounded shocked, sad, angry and hurt all at the same time. His contorted features conveyed the confused feelings.

Sondra started to feel desperate. This was not the way it should have gone. 'I can explain. He was foolish. I never promised him anything. I made it clear from the beginning—'

'You made it clear?' David interrupted. 'He was head over heels in love with you. You expected him to be as cold and callous as you?'

'I think you just need time to see things from my point of view.'

'Like always? Like I always do, right?' David's voice was not raised, but it was harsh. Sondra had never heard this tone from him before.

'What do you mean?'

'All it would take is a bat of your eyelids or a swing of your hips, and I would submit to you and your will. Me – a grown man who has known you for years – even I would not be able to resist your charms. What defence would that young man have? He was a young man in love, and when you spurned him, he ...' David shook his head and turned away from her. He slumped back into the chair and covered his eyes with his hand.

Sondra's heart beat loudly in her ears, but her voice was thin and weak as she spoke. 'It wasn't my fault. What he did was foolish. I can't be held responsible for any fool in love.'

David rose from the chair in a jerky movement. His eyes bulged out of their sockets, and he shook his pointed finger in Sondra's face. 'You disgust me. What kind of a person are you? Who did I marry? I can't even believe the person you've become.'

Sondra stared at her husband, not recognising him. He had been the perfect match for her based on his calm, collected, and considered manner, but that person had disappeared. That man had been replaced by one who could not bear to look at her.

'You're not the woman I fell in love with, the woman I married. I don't care to know this person.' He turned away from Sondra so quickly that it seemed as though looking at her was untenable.

'Come on, David. Just calm down. What are you saying? You know me.' She came to stand beside him and tried to look into his face. She placed a hand on his arm.

David unceremoniously threw Sondra's hand off. 'I do know you. I was besotted by you, Sondra. All I wanted was to build a full and happy life with you. It became clear early on that you didn't reciprocate my feelings. Ours was a convenient relationship for you. It worked once, but you soon lost interest as you became self-absorbed.' David drew a short breath. 'Calculated.'

Sondra had to stop this ranting. 'Listen! Please—'

Her enraged, livid husband cut her off again. 'When Michael was born, I'd hoped that that would get you to commit to me, to us, to our family, but it was always all about you.'

'You're crazy. You're talking crazy. I loved you. *I* love *you*. You know that.'

'Do I? You only love yourself. I was agreeable. Good-looking enough, professional, not too clever, but clever enough to be at your arm at your fancy highfalutin client functions. And you know what? I didn't even mind that, as long as we were together, and I had Mikey.' He stroked his beard, but his gaze – the wide-eyed, blazing look – was hard to cover. 'And Mikey is all mine. Your lack of interest ensured that.'

Sondra felt like she was falling from a dizzying height. She needed to clutch at a lifeline, to stop her eventual crash to the ground. She looked around her in desperation.

David's biting critique continued. 'Nothing else mattered then. Your lack of love, your disinterest, even your affairs, I ignored.'

Sondra was suddenly painfully aware of their son scrutinising them. What would he make of this? 'Please, listen. Not in front of ...' She sucked in her breath and turned to face Michael directly. The look of revulsion on his face burnt. 'Please leave your dad and I alone.'

'Don't worry. I'm out of here.' Michael looked at neither of them as he strode to the door. 'I don't want to be anywhere near you.'

'Mikey ...' Sondra reached out for him, but he moved away. 'We'll talk about this later.'

'Don't bother. I have nothing to say to you and couldn't be bothered to hear any of your lies.'

Sondra watched him swagger out of the kitchen arrogantly. She wondered if the bravado was to cover up the hurt she had caused him. David might be the more involved parent, the one that he felt close to, but she loved her son as much as his father did. Maybe he didn't expect much from her as a mother, but *this*?

Sondra felt a pang of regret but realised that she needed to put out one fire at a time. Her priority had to be David. She turned her gaze and attention to him again. All her attempts were futile. He had closed off his mind and heart to her.

He spoke firmly. 'I think you should move out. You made your decision about choosing yourself over us a long time ago. This house is our home – mine and Mikey's. You should leave.'

'You want me to move out?' Sondra's voice was high-pitched with shock at this sudden turn. Would he not even give her a chance to explain?

'Yes. The sooner the better. Where you go makes no difference to me.'

Was he being unnecessarily harsh? It was unlike David to be deliberately cruel ... to anyone.

'You're ... you're talking about a divorce?' Tears smarted her eyes. This was too much. Everything was unravelling, and she had no chance to stem this riptide that was relentlessly pulling her under. If she could just surface for a moment and catch her breath.

'Yes.'

'Just like that! After all these years?' Sondra couldn't believe what was happening. A tear escaped her lids. She brushed it away with the back of her hand. 'David, please.'

David collapsed into his chair again and heavily hung his head. When he lifted his gaze to meet her face, his features were set in a forced strong look. 'I love you, Sondra. I love you too much. Because of my love, I was able to overlook everything: your obsession with work, your lack of interest in family life, your ... your affairs.' The last word ground out of him so harshly that spittle flew in her direction. 'I guess I knew they were just another means to an end for you, just like everything and everyone in your life. I don't think it's possible for you to love anyone else more than you love yourself – not any of your men, not me ... not even your own son.

'As soon as I realised that, it was easy for me to accept the situation. Asking you to change would have been ridiculous, and leaving you was not an option. Marriage is forever. I'd rather have been with you like we have been these past years than not have you in my life at all. Most importantly, I didn't want our boy to grow up with estranged parents. I figured this—' David's hands moved haphazardly in the space in front of his face. '—relationship we shared, while not ideal and nowhere near perfect, was better for him. I think it was. He was in a stable home, and he was loved by both of us. Maybe you had an odd way of showing it or tried to hide how much you loved him, but it was there.'

David stopped and rubbed the back of his neck, visibly trying to ease the tension there. The tension in the room could not be eased with a massaging hand. It would take a hammer to break it down.

'You're not thinking right.' Sondra spoke quickly, fearing interruption again. 'This is a shock, I know. Let's not make any rash decisions now. I think we should catch our breath and talk when we're calmer in a day or two.' If she had some time, maybe she would be able to convince him to see things her way.

'No amount of time will make me change my mind. You know me.'

She did know him, that he made up his mind quickly, and that when he did, that was that. Was he not even going to allow her to try to talk? *He* had to *listen*.

'Listen to me. Listen. I've made a mistake.'

He looked at her with surprise or confusion glistening in his eyes.

She faltered, then caught herself. She had to make this right. 'A huge, terrible mistake. Let's not make another. We have to take some time and think first.'

'The mistake would be to give in to you again. I'm done with that mistake ... forever. It's *you* who's not listening. I want you out. If you refuse to go, Michael and I will leave.'

She could tell that he was serious. His body was stiff while he watched her, his eyes stony.

He carried on carefully, calmly. 'But it's best not to disrupt his routine.'

Sondra was at a loss. It was obvious anything she could try was futile. Anything she said would fall on deaf ears. 'You're right. Of course, you are right, and I cannot argue with your reasoning.' Sondra raised her hand like she was taking an oath and shook her head. 'I haven't been the best mother. That is true. Or wife.' Sondra studied her feet as she spoke. Things were slipping from her fingers. David had seen through her lies, resisted her attempts at trying to persuade him, and had clearly shut himself off from anything further now. It was rare for Sondra to feel defeated; normally, she would never give up. This time, though, she could sense that nothing would work. Not now. 'Maybe we do need time apart while we get a chance to cool off. But you can't be serious about a divorce. Why mess up the life we've built? If Michael is the reason that we have stayed together, then let's continue to do so, for his sake. Let's not rock the boat.'

'Didn't you see him *just now*? Hear him? For him, it's already over.'

'I'm sorry. I'm sorry. Believe me, please.'

'Sorry?' David's look was incredulous. 'You're only sorry that you got caught. It's not a sincere or real apology.'

Sondra dropped her gaze again. She could not deny that. He knew her too well.

'You don't get it! You can't see anything except from your own point of view.' He studied her intensely, his dark eyes darting around her face frantically. 'Take a long, hard look at yourself, Sondra. I have, and I don't like what I see. You're ...' David shuddered like the words he wanted to say were too difficult to verbalise. 'I can't ... I don't want to bother to explain to you. It's not worth it. *You're* not worth it.'

David's words stung. Her son called her a whore, her husband thinks she's not worth anything – people who should love her the most. Is this what they thought of her? Sondra blinked rapidly. Her whole body was in knots.

David watched her and sighed. 'Mikey ...' He shook his head as the thought of Michael etched concern in the frown that seemed no longer directed at her. Had he stopped thinking about her already? His focus was Mikey and only Mikey now. 'Neither of us can believe you would do this. With such a youngster? Man, Sonds, just think about it. He's—he was young enough to be your *son*.'

'It's over. It's been over for a few months now. It didn't mean anything.' Sondra knew she sounded frantic. She felt frantic.

'To *you*. To you, it meant nothing. He was a plaything to you. But he *killed* himself because he loved you so much. How can you be so insensitive?'

Sondra could not believe she had to explain John's craziness like it was her fault. She shouldn't be held responsible. 'I didn't think it would get to that. It was supposed to be fun and over when his internship ended.'

David looked at her as though he was seeing her for the first time, then his face dropped. When he spoke, he looked and sounded sad. 'I don't understand how you can be so ...' He shrugged in a gesture of exasperation. '... so cruel. You're heartless.' There was a long pause, and when David continued, he didn't look at her. It felt like he wasn't even addressing her. 'Fun! Did you enjoy your fun, Sondra?'

Sondra could not meet his gaze. She saw herself through his eyes – a selfish ice queen – and felt regret, regret that things turned out the way they did. If John had not been so foolish ... 'I *am* sorry. I'm not heartless.'

'You *are* heartless! You care about nothing else, not this young man whose life is over, not his mother whose life is destroyed by your actions, and not me or Mikey.' His tortured voice rose again.

'I didn't put the gun in his hand.'

'Is that how it happened? He shot himself?' David rubbed the fingers and thumb of his hand over his shut eyes. He shuddered.

Sondra realised that she didn't know. Did John shoot himself, or fly off a building, or gas himself in a closed garage? 'I ... I don't know.' Her quiet voice echoed in her head, unnerved, unsure, unrecognisable.

David opened his eyes warily. 'I don't believe you! You don't know? You don't even know? You haven't even bothered to find out?'

Sondra had nothing to respond with. What would she say? What could she say? That David was right about her? That she *was* cold and callous? *Is that so wrong? Look how far being cold and callous has taken me. Look where I am in life. I have everything, everything I've ever wanted or dreamt of.*

David shook his head. 'You don't get it. You just don't get it, do you?'

What wasn't she getting? The boy meant nothing. *It's you who isn't getting it, David!*

'Have you felt even a smidgen of sorrow? Someone *died*. And all you can think of is self-preservation.' His handsome features twisted until he was unrecognisable. Suddenly, he turned away. He didn't like what he saw. He had to look away.

Sondra rallied bravely, trying to reach him. 'I know how this must look. But what's done is done. There's no point in messing up our lives for something that can't be changed now. Please, don't overreact.'

'Overreact? *Overreact?*' David shot out of his chair so violently that it fell over behind him, clattering loudly onto the tiled floor. His eyes doubled in size as they met hers. His mouth twisted, baring his teeth. 'I don't get you, and you know what, it doesn't matter anymore. I don't want to understand you or know you. You can go off and live in your own world, do what you like, it doesn't matter anymore. We are over.'

'What?'

'You heard me loud and clear.'

'David. Please. Think about what you're saying.'

'I know exactly what I'm saying, and I mean this. Even if I could move past this, which I can't, but even if I could, Mikey never will. I could see it in his eyes, hear it in his voice. He is disgusted with you and your behaviour. You have fallen too far to ever be redeemed. He was very clear when he told me he wants nothing to do with you.'

Sondra felt lightheaded and reached out. He pushed her away so that she swayed and landed, leaning heavily against the table. 'Don't touch me! Don't ever touch me again!'

He was shouting. Was her touch poison? Acid that scorched?

Sondra stood motionless, not breathing, not thinking. Shock had momentarily turned her to stone.

David took a breath. 'The best thing is for you to move out. I'll stay here with Michael until the divorce is finalised and we decide what to do with the house and other assets.'

'Divorce?' Sondra clasped her hands in front of her in a gesture similar to praying. 'No. Please. Don't say that. We can work through this. We can work it out and get back to normal.' She was spinning, falling, reeling.

'Our normal is anything but. If you think this is a shock, can you imagine what Mikey and I are going through? For once, try to think about somebody other than yourself. Please just ... go. There's only one thing you can do now: leave. Today. Now. Check into a hotel or something because there's no way I can allow you to upset Michael any further. He's my priority – my only priority.'

'Just like that?' her voice was a weak whisper.

David's shoulders drooped, his eyes shone damply, and his voice dropped to a hoarse, tormented murmur. 'There's no point talking about this anymore. My mind will not change. Leave. Go.' And without another word or backwards glance, he strode out of the kitchen and out of her life.

12

ANCHORLESS AND ADRIFT

Sondra shuffled into the lift of the building that she had moved into. Her apartment was on the fourth floor of the eight-storey building in Hurlingham, about fifteen minutes away from her offices in off-peak time. As she walked into the apartment, she was immediately met by the silence that sat like a sour, fat, old lady and which had become her daily welcome.

Instinctively, she switched on the TV, even before slipping off her jacket and heels. She had found this rental soon after David had thrown her out of the house and family, but she didn't feel lucky. Even though it was light and airy, had great views of the Sandton skyline, and was close to work, she didn't like it. She avoided leaving the office until late into the evenings and hardly bothered to stay long enough to eat breakfast in the mornings. Most mornings, she grabbed a sandwich or muffin on her way in and had the office's coffee.

She felt off-centre and could not settle into any sort of routine. She had stopped running and going to the gym altogether and refused to attend work events unless she absolutely had to. She had even handed over the overseeing of the latest group of interns to Karabo last month, citing that Karabo needed the experience of running the training in order to advance in her skills development. It was a fabrication, of course; Sondra had just lost the resolve.

For the first time, she found that she had no interest in work. It had become routine and tedious. Sondra went through the motions but had lost her edge. Two of her portfolios had suffered – they had lost revenue, significantly. Fortunately, the overall percentage loss was not huge. Her acumen and ear to the ground meant that these accounts, like all in her portfolios, had grown in the earlier two quarters.

She did not pursue any new accounts or leads. She had become the kind of financial manager she would not have tolerated before – one who did the bare minimum and was satisfied.

It didn't matter, nothing did anymore. All she wanted was her old life back. *No, not that*, she realised. She wanted a new life, a better life, one with David and Michael wholly in it. One where she could be the wife and mother they wanted and deserved. Deep in her heart she knew that would never happen; they would never forgive her and take her back. They saw her as selfish, self-centred, and self-serving, and had made it abundantly clear that she had no place in their lives. Sondra sighed pathetically. She was self-pitying too.

* * *

After much begging, David had agreed to see her. It was three weeks after she been forced out. They met for coffee close to where he worked in Braamfontein.

Her carefully planned speech was futile. She had played the scene over and over again in her head, hopeful that she would be able to make him see her point of view. But her words seemed completely useless – he was not interested.

'Let's try, please. I could move back, and we could give it a few weeks. Don't you think we should try ... for Mikey's sake?'

'If you were really thinking about what was best for Mikey, we wouldn't be where we are today.' His face was set, his eyes unblinking.

She sensed she was getting nowhere and felt the desperation clawing at the edges of her mind – this was a new feeling that she didn't want to get used to. 'Oh, come on. Don't be so dramatic.' As soon as she said the words, she regretted them.

'Dramatic?' David scowled – it made him appear older and unattractive. 'Damn! You still aren't getting it. This *is* a big deal. Just because *you* can sweep it all under the carpet doesn't mean that we can. I can't. I don't even want to. I don't like you.' For a brief moment, David buried his face in his hands. When he emerged he sighed deeply. 'You're not a good person, Sonds. You've lost your humanity. I wonder, did you ever really have any?'

David had shot down all her arguments. He was adamant that she could not return, that he and Michael were better off without her. 'We want nothing to do with you.'

'Please. You have to give me another chance.'

'Forget it. It's over. I'm done. The divorce papers will be sent to you. Please, just sign and let this all happen as quickly as possible. The sooner we can put this behind us and move on, the better.'

'"This"? You mean our marriage? Twenty years of our lives? Just like that?' A snap of her fingers emphasised her point.

David sighed and ran his hand over his thick hair. There seemed to be more salt than pepper in the waves. He looked like he'd aged. 'I knew it was a bad idea to meet. But you need to hear this face to face. Look at me, Sondra. Hear me clearly. I'm done, okay? *No* more marriage, *no* more mister nice guy, *no* more forgive-and-forget sucker. I'm done. I'm done with you.'

'You can't be serious?'

'Why not? You've used and abused me for all of those years, for all of our *marriage*. I pretended it was okay because I loved you and Mikey. I thought bringing him up in a stable home was the best thing for him. Now, I'm not so sure that we've done right by him.'

'He's a good person. He's happy and well-adjusted. You did a great job with him.'

'I have, yes, that's true. You had little to do with it. You always kept him at arm's length. So busy and so wrapped up in your own life and work that you had no time for him.'

'I can change. I *have* changed. I know I made mistakes, but I realise I can be the kind of wife and mother you need and deserve. Please, let me try. Give me a chance.'

He stared at her and then passed her while he pursed his lips together. He did that when he was worried or concentrating. Watching him now, Sondra realised how much she missed that gesture, how much she missed so much about him: his easy-going, relaxed nature that sometimes irked her; his dry, surprising sense of humour; his ability to make taking care of Michael and their home seem effortless; his ever-ready smile; and his eyes, particularly his eyes when he looked at Michael or her. She had taken it all for granted – especially his love.

She felt afloat, drifting aimlessly, an anchorless boat tossed around at the mercy of the currents. It was an unusual feeling. She usually felt in control, specifically when it came to getting her way with her husband. Not today, not now, not since that evening almost a month before. It was like talking to a brick wall. When did David become so stubborn? She tried another tactic.

'What about Michael? Surely, he needs to be in a stable, secure, loving home?'

'He is. Michael is a good kid. This thing that's happened has been tough, but he's been amazing about it. He's been worried about me and how I'm handling it. He keeps re-assuring me that he's fine, and I think he is. There's no pretence or show.'

'I want to see him. I need to. You can't stop me.'

'I can't, and I won't. Every child needs his mother. But this is his decision.'

'I can't believe he would not want to see me again. What have you said?'

David's eyes narrowed, and his nostrils flared as he exhaled noisily. 'I haven't said or done anything. You know me better than that. In fact, I've encouraged him to see you and listen to your side of the story. I even suggested he join me today or make another arrangement with you. He is adamant, and honestly, I don't think he will change his mind.' David sucked in his top lip pensively again and added, 'Not in the foreseeable future.'

Sondra could see that David was as sincere and upfront as always. 'This isn't right. If he would just listen, just one time. That's all I'm asking.'

'I know what you're thinking, and because of your history with us – with all the men in your life – you probably think you'll be able to persuade him to forgive you. Any other circumstance, and I would be inclined to agree with you. But not this time. My suggestion is to leave it. This *is* a huge deal.'

He keeps saying that, Sondra thought fretfully. The waves battered her this way and that again. 'You really think so? I don't know. I feel the longer I leave this, the worse it's gonna get.'

David leant his elbow on the table and rested his chin on his fist. His dark eyes searched hers.

'What? Tell me. You know him better than me.' The corners of Sondra's eyes crinkled. It was not easy to admit, but she needed his help. 'What should I do?'

David pulled his mouth to one side. He did that when he was unsure. Once more, the clawing dejection scraped nails on the chalkboard in Sondra's whirling mind. *What is he thinking? What is he hiding?* It was rare that the tables were turned in their relationship. Typically, she was in control, the one who had the power. This time, it was David who had the upper hand, or at least, he was the key to reaching Michael, and he seemed reluctant to help her.

She reached over and placed her hand lightly on his. 'Please, David.'

He raised an eyebrow quizzically, probably assessing if she was trying to manipulate him. Casually, he slid his hand away. He sat upright in his chair. 'Mikey was shattered when he heard what happened,' he said firmly. 'John killed himself. What was worse was how you treated his mother. He witnessed it all. Maybe he'll never want to see you again. He didn't want to believe you could be so calculating. Now, the truth is unavoidable.'

The words were blunt. Sondra bit the inside of her cheek, forced to acknowledge their veracity. *He knows Mikey well, better than I do.* Another truth that could not be avoided. Waiting was all she could do. Since she had moved out, Michael had not taken any of her calls or responded to any of her messages. 'I guess I have no choice then?'

'He'll come around eventually. Maybe. You'll just have to learn to practise patience.' A small smile crept over his features. 'Patience. Not your forte, is it?'

That was true too. David knew her as well as he knew Michael.

David breathed out audibly. 'I guess that's that.' He steepled his long, tapering fingers in front of his face. 'I've asked my lawyer to be fair. She'll be in touch with the papers. Please sign. Let's make this easy on all of us.'

Sondra realised David was resolute. Their marriage was over. Her vision blurred, and she blinked tears away. She busied herself with gathering her bag. 'I should get back to the office.'

'Yes, yes. I must get back too.' He glanced at his watch. 'How's work?'

'Fine. Same old, same old.' She inhaled through pinched nostrils at the thought of returning to the office. Work had become unbearable. She hated it, just like she hated everything in her life. And herself. She nodded a curt goodbye and left hurriedly.

13

THE HAUNTED FUNERAL

Hannah sat in her car in the carpark of West Park Cemetery. All the mourners had left, and some would make their way to her house for the small wake that she had arranged. There would be some family and friends and people from the old age home, some who did not feel that they would manage to attend the burial at the cemetery but who still wanted to pay their respects.

Flashes of the day that she had sat in front of Sondra Carim-Edwards's house and confronted her played on her mind. The encounter had been unsatisfying, to say the least. If anything, she was more enraged and frustrated than before. Her head dropped to her chest, and she imagined what her mother would advise her. "There is nothing you can do except pray – pray for yourself, pray that God puts love, acceptance, and forgiveness in your heart." Hannah's hands balled into fists. It had been months since she'd even thought of praying. If God could forget her, surely, she could forget Him and how to pray.

With difficulty, she relaxed her fingers. Her hands moved slowly as she started the car and put it into gear. The sooner she received her mother's mourners, the sooner this day would end. As she pulled out of her parking spot, she wondered why she wanted this day to be over. It wasn't like the next day would be any better. Her tomorrows stretched into a long, dark passage of sorrow and emptiness.

She had not recovered from John's death and accepted that she never would. At least having her mother to take care of had meant that she had had a reason to carry on. The prospect of pretending to live and function when all she wanted to do was crawl into a hole and wait for death herself was horrifying. Tears flowed unabated. She cried for her dead son, for her dead mother, and for herself, who may as well have been dead too. It was unchristianly to wish for death, she knew, but that didn't matter. Nothing mattered.

As she drove up to her house, there was no way she could get into her usual parking place – the minibus from the old age home had parked across her driveway to allow easy access for the wheelchairs. The sun shone gaily in sharp contrast to the doom and gloom she felt. She steeled herself and walked past the cars into her house. This was the last time she would be in the house with people.

Maybe I should sell and move, she thought. *Maybe I should run away? But where would I go?* There wasn't a place on this planet where she would not suffer the loss of her baby. That reality was not something she could escape.

Hannah pulled her shoulders back and set her features stoically. *Right. You can do this,* she encouraged herself. *If you've survived without John this long, this afternoon will be a piece of cake.*

Hannah stepped into the house and became the grieving daughter she was expected to be, greeting people she knew and some that she didn't, accepting condolences as graciously as she could, and ensuring pots of tea and plates of snacks were sufficient.

At four o'clock, the minibus from the old age home left, but by five o'clock, a few more neighbours arrived, and

Hannah forced herself through the routine again. She wanted the day to be over, but she also wanted it to continue forever. After this, she would be forced to face her unavoidable reality: living without John, learning to be alone – all alone – without the support of her loving mother or the distraction of caring for someone else.

'Hannah?' A familiar voice was trying to get her attention.

Hannah's stomach muscles tightened involuntarily when she turned to face her neighbour. 'Muriel. Hi.' Muriel had been a good friend of Sylvia's, often coming to spend an afternoon with her since Sylvia had moved in.

She reached out automatically to shake Muriel's hand, but the heavy-set woman wrapped Hannah in a bear hug. Hannah was taken aback. She didn't think that they were that close. Muriel rubbed her back in small circular movements, releasing a hint of a floral fragrance. It was subtle and not from a perfume, maybe from a scented hand lotion? The woman's touch was soothing, and Hannah found herself relaxing into the embrace.

When they moved apart, Muriel clasped Hannah's hand in her own and held her gaze. Her eyes were green – Hannah had not really noticed before – and kind. It was the kind of sympathetic look Hannah usually avoided, yet she found herself relaxing a little more.

'I'm so sorry about your mother, Hannah.' There was genuine sincerity in Muriel's words.

'Thank you.' Hannah replied softly but as sincerely.

'How are you doing?'

Hannah shrugged and managed a weak smile. *How does one answer that?*

'I'm sure it's very difficult, and so soon after your son.' Muriel shook her greying head like it was impossible to imagine.

Hannah felt her back straighten and her head rise up a notch. She hadn't counted on hearing about John today.

Vividly imagining him every second of the day, like all of her days, was all she could handle.

'Please, help yourself.' Hannah pointed vaguely towards the table where tea and eats were set up. 'Excuse me, Muriel. I just want to check on the kitchen.'

'Of course.' Muriel squeezed her hands briefly before releasing.

Hannah dashed towards the kitchen but was stopped by a distant aunt who also offered sympathy. Thankfully, she was saying her farewell too. 'Please,' she cooed, 'don't hesitate to call if there is anything we can do.'

Hannah simply nodded. Could anyone bring her John back? That was all she needed now. Nothing else.

14

A CHANGE IN COURSE

A soft knock on her office door jolted Sondra out of her reverie. The door remained closed. Did she imagine it? Another knock, more audible, followed.

'Come in.'

The handle turned, and the door was pushed open. Vicky Moodley smiled and greeted her in a friendly manner.

Now what? HR never visited unannounced. *Come to think of it, HR never visits ... The last time she saw Vicky was when John ...*

'Hi, Vicky.' Sondra walked around her desk and held out her hand. The woman had a dark complexion and fine features. Sondra guessed she was in her late forties or early fifties, but maybe she was even older. Indian women often looked younger than their age. 'What can I do for you?'

'Yes. Hi, Sondra. How are you?'

'Well. Well, thanks.' Sondra didn't repay the courteous question. She wanted this woman to say what she had to say and leave.

The woman patted the hair on top of her head, even though nothing was out of place, and cleared her throat. 'May I sit?'

'Yes, yes. Sure. Where are my manners?' Sondra gestured towards the chair at her desk and walked around to take her seat again. 'Sorry, I'm not thinking. My out-of-office meeting took longer than expected, so I'm just trying to make up the time. Busy as always.'

It was Vicky's turn to speak, but she didn't.

'Is this about the interns?' Sondra inquired, trying to get Vicky to her point. 'I've been monitoring their progress, and Karabo's been doing a great job.'

'Yes. That's fine. There's no problem with the internship programme. That's all on track and working well.'

'Good. That's great.'

Another pregnant pause.

Vicky examined her neatly manicured fingers that gripped an A4 envelope. 'I need to discuss your performance.' She straightened in her chair. 'There have been some significant losses. The DMD account in particular. Maiter and Maiter too. I have the figures here.' She flicked her hand to indicate the envelope's contents. 'Other issues too that cannot be ignored.'

Does she mean my fling with John? That must be it!

'What are you referring to?' Sondra's firm voice belied the nervousness she felt.

'An official written warning signed by Mister Ross and Mister Maphumulo. I didn't want to send it without speaking to you.'

'A warning?'

'Yes. It had to be done. Ross wanted you to be dismissed immediately. Your contract states that immediate dismissal with three months' salary is legal. I persuaded them to give you a chance.'

'You were pleading *my* case?' Sondra cocked her head as she examined the well-dressed woman. Vicky's shirt was white and very crisp. It was tucked neatly into the waistband of her dark skirt. Stocking-clad feet sat in sensible, expensive-looking leather court shoes. She may have been well dressed, but Sondra thought that her look was outdated and scoffed inwardly. Then she caught herself. She should remain professional.

'This is serious, Sondra.' Vicky met Sondra's eyes evenly. 'As head of HR, I look after employees and the bosses' interests. Where these collide, I am obliged to put the company's interests first.' Now that Vicky had started talking, she seemed to be on a roll. 'It was not an easy thing for me to negotiate. They want to ensure that if you're afforded another chance, the risk is managed. I've suggested you would benefit from an intervention.'

'An intervention?' Sondra suppressed a laugh that sounded strained and cynical. *An intervention! Like for an addict?*

'You need to go for an independent assessment – a psychological one. This will probably report that you need counselling. You need to do this, Sondra.'

'I will do no such thing.' Sondra rose and folded her arms against her chest. Her voice was not raised, but the tone was angry.

'You don't have a choice. If you don't agree to this, you *will* be fired.'

Sondra walked around her desk and stood next to Vicky's chair. 'I'm not crazy.' Sondra began pacing the short distance in front of her desk. 'I can't believe this. After everything I've done for this company, the hours I've worked, the millions I've earned over the years. Do you know how much?' Sondra spun round to face Vicky head on.

'Your record up until a few months ago spoke for itself,' Vicky replied in that same even tone. 'But this is how it goes, Sondra, you know that. You're only as good as your last deal.'

'I should've been offered equity. I deserve it.'

'Yes. That was all on track for the end of the financial year, three months ago.'

'What happened?'

'Do I need to spell it out for you? Your ... indiscretion ... the affair with an intern.'

'You know?'

'I found out recently.' Vicky shook her head. Her tone softened. 'You should've known better. Did you really think no one would find out?'

Sondra's heartbeat thundered in her ears. Her face felt hot; her mouth went dry. 'Is ... is that why?'

Vicky nodded.

Sondra looked at her hands, and she spoke softer, less assured. 'I didn't think anyone knew.'

'I only found out after the last group of interns left. One of them – Donovan Fisher – you remember him?'

Sondra nodded – she knew all the interns of the last group – John's group. They had reported to her.

'He mentioned something to me at his exit interview. I didn't pay much attention to it at the time. I hate indulging in gossip. I can't if I need to be professional. He was leaving – all the interns were leaving, so I put it out of my mind and forgot about it.'

Vicky stopped talking, but Sondra couldn't wait for her to continue. 'And then? What happened?'

'I had a call from John's mother.'

'What? When?' Sondra's fingernails dug into her palms. *John's mother called work? What the fuck?* Everything was unravelling, and she had no way of stopping the waves that were threatening to drag her under.

'A couple of months ago. She sounded ... it was an unusual call, and it got me thinking about the circumstances of his death.' Vicky shook her head. 'I made some discreet enquiries, and it wasn't difficult to confirm.'

'Oh.'

'Anyway, it was over, and I didn't think it warranted an investigation or even to be raised with you or management. But when the equity discussion surfaced a couple of months back, I dissuaded the partners. I didn't mention the affair. I suggested that all shareholding discussions be put on hold for a year. I referred to the proposed change in labour legislation, saying we should wait until there was clarity in the law and its impact.'

'But ... you're saying the reason was because of ... John?'

'Yes, truthfully, yes. But that wasn't the reason I gave the partners.'

'You kept it quiet? Why?'

'I ... maybe it wasn't the right thing to do ... but I was—I *am* keen for you to succeed. You're so ... you were so driven. The firm would've benefitted from a female partner. I thought that it was one silly mistake, and your whole career shouldn't be about that one thing. Men get away with much more and much worse.'

'You're rooting for me?'

'I'm always trying to help ... uh, maybe that's the wrong word. It's not like I play favourites with the women here. I encourage and try to give a woman the benefit of the doubt. It's not anything more than men enjoy every day in this corporate world. It's harder for us.'

Sondra understood what Vicky was saying. She had lived the reality of it for years.

'I ... I don't know what to say.'

'There's nothing to say. The partners were glad that we hadn't decided on equity. The last couple of months, your performance has suffered. That's why you're getting the warning. It's about the collective loss of almost a million. That cannot be ignored.'

'I see.' Sondra leant against her desk and held herself. She couldn't believe it. *A million? Big deal!* She had made the company hundreds of millions over the years. The company just acted like they always did. It was business first and foremost. It was a philosophy she shared, right? *Right.* At least, up until the moment when she had to be on the receiving end.

Vicky stood up and placed her hand on Sondra's arm. 'This must be hard to assimilate. I wish there was something more positive I could say.' Her arm dropped back to her side, and the professional voice returned. 'I suggest not reacting immediately. You have until close of business tomorrow to respond.'

'Can I fight this?'

'Don't, Sondra. For your sake, don't take Ross Maphumulo on. Think about your options. You know how small this town is. Everyone knows everyone in this industry. If you leave under a cloud, it'll be difficult to find something else.'

Sondra knew Vicky was right. 'Thanks, Vicky. Thanks for telling me to my face. Tell me, should I seek legal counsel?'

'That is your right. Don't be too hasty though. That's all I recommend. We'll talk tomorrow. I'll send a meeting request for the afternoon. Mister Maphumulo will be in attendance.'

Sondra's head snapped back. 'Is it a hearing?'

'No, just procedure. The terms of the warning will be read, and you'll be required to sign acknowledgement without prejudice. You don't have any option though.'

'Except to resign?'

'No, Sondra, don't. You need to get back on track. That's all. I imagine things – you know, your personal life, I mean – things are tough. This warning should be seen as a wake-up call. If you do as recommended, you can salvage the situation. Provided no other issues arise, things'll settle. A couple of big wins, and you'll be redeemed.'

'Hmph.' Sondra cracked the knuckles of her hands. 'I guess that's it then?'

Vicky's brow creased and her voice dropped to a softer, almost wistful tone. 'I used to think of you as an ideal female manager – firm with an understanding of the way things worked in a man's world, an example of a woman being professional—as professional as any man, who is supposed to be less emotional.'

Sondra lowered her eyelids. She had let her company down ... and herself.

'I'm confident that this is temporary. Whatever it is you need to sort out, you can. I've thought about this carefully, and from your point of view too. This is the best course for you.'

Sondra stared at Vicky. She saw only sincere concern and encouragement. 'I'll ... I'm ... Vicky, I'm sure it must be. Thank you.'

'You'll be okay, I'm sure. It'll work out.' Vicky rose and offered her hand to Sondra. Her grip was strong but warm. 'Goodbye.'

As soon as the door closed behind Vicky, Sondra tore open the envelope but found it hard to concentrate on the two-page warning. It was official. She'd screwed up – screwed up her life, one disaster after another. It was like everything she touched became malignant. She had thought she had led a charmed life, but now, it felt like she was cursed. She wondered what else was in store for her.

* * *

The next day, Sondra strode into the meeting and shook hands with Vicky and Thabo Maphumulo.

Before either proceeded with reading out the warning, Sondra presented her signed copy. 'I have read and signed acknowledgement of the contents. I have decided that I will take leave from the end of the week. I have several weeks due, and I think this will be the best course of action. On my return, I will respond officially to the warning. I will round off what I'm working on in the next two days and hand over my accounts and responsibilities.'

Thabo and Vicky eyed her cautiously. Was that a glint of admiration she saw in Vicky's face? Or just surprise at having her meeting being taken over? It didn't matter. Sondra could tell that they were not expecting her proposal. There was no way they could refuse a reasonable request that would appease all parties, in the short-term at least.

Their lack of reaction helped to quell the queasiness in her stomach, and Sondra felt bolder than when she had walked in. Her plan to speak first had worked, and it looked like she had bought herself some time.

Thabo and Vicky looked at each other, perhaps each hoping the other would react first. Vicky spoke. 'Give us a few minutes to confer. Please excuse us.'

'Sure. I'll be in my office.' She exited before either suggested she wait outside the small boardroom.

She closed her office door and leant against it. *Oh, please, let this work out!* She wasn't asking anyone in particular, certainly not God or Allah ... maybe the universe. She cracked the knuckles of her hands. This was a childhood habit she had outgrown years ago, or so she had thought.

She figured they didn't have much choice but to accept her proposal but would have to run it by Aidan Ross too. Realising that it would be some time before she heard anything, Sondra decided that she may as well get on with some work. But her concentration was shot.

After a while, she swivelled in her chair and turned away from her desk. She would be positive. They would accept her proposal for leave. She had to believe that they would. So, in preparation for her leave, she started making three separate piles of her files. One for Karabo, one for Thabo, and one for Aidan. This activity helped take her mind off the people metres away, discussing and deciding her fate.

She focused on her laptop again and started a spreadsheet with the names of the files and accounts that she would hand to the three individuals. She grimaced as she recalled how she hated doing this in the past on the rare occasion that she took more than a week's leave. Holidays had never been her thing. Others felt they needed to rest to energise them to tackle the challenges at work. Not her. She sighed, pushing the scatty, nostalgic thoughts away. *No point, Sonds. Focus on the here and now.*

By the time the e-mail from Vicky arrived, she had completed aligning her coded spreadsheet to the physical files on her desk. The communication from Vicky was brief and to the point – asking for an application form to confirm her leave and a reminder that the terms of the warning were still in place, to be revisited upon her return.

Relief washed over Sondra – a reprieve. She felt encouraged by her ability to turn the situation, if not to her advantage, at least in her favour, for now.

If only she was able to fix her personal life as easily.

15

A RETURN TO HER ROOTS

No sooner had Sondra entered the apartment that never felt like home than she started throwing stuff into a small suitcase. She forced herself to think about the handover she had just made back at the office. She was officially on leave now for three weeks. Apart from Thabo, Karabo and Vicky were present at the meeting. It went as well as could be expected. However, as she went over everything in her mind, she wondered what they had discussed after she had left. She was certain she hadn't missed anything in the handover, but because her confidence had taken a pretty big knock, she found that she had started second-guessing herself.

With the hastily packed bag in one hand and her handbag and laptop bag in the other, she surveyed the apartment. It was so far removed from anything she could consider as home. There was nothing in the fridge to get rid of. She had switched off the geyser, had her comfortable *takkies* on, and so, she locked up, went to the garage, and got into her car.

She drove to the petrol station on Jan Smuts Avenue where she bought two large coffees, which she decanted into a thermos, filled her tank, and made sure that the attendant checked the oil and water levels and the tyre pressure. Once she got onto the freeway, she consciously slowed down. A slow, steady pace would get her to destination in six hours and would minimise the need for a fuel stop. Durban! Of all places – Durban. That's where she was headed.

* * *

Eight hours after she had walked into the apartment, she could tell that she was getting close. She had driven through the night. Sondra rolled the window down to allow the smell of Durban – the humidity in the air, the whiff of the salt that blew in from the sea – to permeate her car and her senses. The prospect of staying in her rented apartment, alone, for three weeks was daunting. No, it was terrifying! Having all day and all night in the deathly still space with only the TV for company for twenty-one days was horrifying.

Her out-of-the-blue decision was bizarre. She had resisted going to Durban since she had left it twenty-five years before. Even if there were meetings she had to attend in Durban, she always ensured that she never stayed over – flying in early and flying back the same night. A return to her hometown now after so many years seemed contrary to everything she thought she knew about herself. Deep down though, she sensed that it was something that had to be done if she was ever going to be able to make sense of her futile life and existence. One thing that she had not completely lost faith in yet was her instinct.

The last time she had been in her and David's house and they had argued – the day that she had been forced to move out – had been playing heavily on her mind. She had been over it dozens of times, and one thing that David had said had stuck in her mind. "Take a long, hard look at yourself, Sondra."

She had thought that she knew herself. She could always count on herself and who she was. But he had implied that, if she really knew herself, she would not like what she saw. Sondra had always thought she'd liked herself, at least from the time she'd struck out independently. It wasn't something one thought about really. She had taken it for granted that the person she presented to the world, the person she was proud to be, was just fine. But since that night, she had been questioning everything she thought she knew. The discussion with Vicky only intensified this sense of not knowing. With all the time she had on her hands of late, all she could do was think things through and feel herself more acutely as that anchorless boat.

It was not yet light when she saw the Durban signs and lights. Sondra drove towards the beachfront. Everything was quiet. It felt like her hometown was holding its breath in anticipation of her return. She parked in the darkness between two light poles, hoping to blend into the landscape. There was no movement.

What? Did you expect Durban to rejoice because you had returned?

Sondra needed to stretch her stiff legs and warily stepped out of the car. It was chilly, and she reached back in for her jacket. She looked out towards the sea but could not see much of the water. The sound of the crashing waves was clear though. She looked away from the calling ocean and tried to orientate herself. It was a long time ago, but it felt familiar. Her mother had loved the sea and would take her for a swim almost every Sunday morning. But it had been many years since Sondra had taken a dip in the Indian Ocean.

It was not something the Carims enjoyed. They rarely went to the beach, and when they did, it was because their out-of-town family was visiting. The trips were always a production. Food was prepared the night before. Towels, hats, and sunblock were packed. Grass mats and umbrellas were invariably forgotten, and Abdul would purchase new ones from the vendors almost every time. The older sisters never went into the water, preferring to sit under umbrellas and broad-brimmed hats, fearing being burnt by the sun. They fiercely protected their fair looks. The younger ones would paddle along the shore, while their father watched them with his pants rolled up to his knees.

Sondra was easily able to slip away from the family. She would swim deep into the ocean's warm waters – beyond where the waves broke. The Durban beach is notorious for strong currents and waves that could toss a person around like a rag doll. If one wasn't careful, it could be lethal. Many families had stories of loved ones drowning.

Sondra would time her dives under the waves just as they broke and would wait to be swept towards the shore. Then she would swim back to catch the next round. Those waves she enjoyed; the emotional waves of anxiety, self-doubt, and uncertainty that were buffeting her around now, she did not.

Sondra leant against the bonnet of her car and imagined the warm, safe feel of the water. With her arms grabbing each other, she closed her eyes and listened to the sounds of the ocean, inhaling the salty air deep into her lungs. She silently and reverently acknowledged how much she had missed it.

Twice when Michael was little, David had planned trips to Durban. Both times, she had backed out at the last minute. Each time, she had persuaded David not to cancel or postpone. 'Your holiday shouldn't be spoilt because of my work,' she had told him. 'Go. Have fun with Michael.' She had sensed that David had wanted to probe into her reluctance to return to her hometown but had thought better of it.

In all the years that they had been together, she had never spoken of her childhood and had kept no contact with her family. Any attempts David had made to draw her out in the early years of their marriage had been thwarted. Eventually, he had stopped asking.

The first time that she had felt pressure from his probing had been before their wedding. Sondra had wanted it to be small. 'No, I won't be inviting any family. My mom died years ago. Things with my father were strained, and since he passed away, I've had no contact with that side of the family either.' David's parents had wanted a big celebration – he was their only son – and she had acquiesced. They had found it strange that she had had no one to stand up for her in the church, that she had no maid of honour, and that she had no one except a few work colleagues at the reception. Sondra had not entertained their questions either, and after a while, they had left it. David's mother had handled most of the arrangements, and that had suited Sondra just fine. David had made excuses for her. After a few weeks of his mother trying to involve Sondra, she too had given up.

It was gradually getting brighter, and she could see more of the ocean now. She felt a deep longing ... an ache. Was it for her mother, for David and Michael ... or was it for her childhood self? Sondra brushed tears away from her cheeks, cheeks that were sunken. She had lost weight in these past few months.

What did it help to relive the past? Why did she think that coming to Durban would help? She had alienated David, who was probably the only person apart from her mother who had loved her completely and unconditionally. From the outset of their relationship, she had kept him at arms' length. He must have found it frustrating but, being David, had complained little and had made the best of their life together. Poor David, long-suffering David. If she got a chance with him again, she vowed that she would do whatever it took to make it up to him. *I can be a loving wife. How hard can it be?*

Yet, in spite of her self-assurance, the truth was different. There she was, having consciously or unconsciously made the decision to drive to her hometown, a place she had sworn never to return to. Why? Maybe she subconsciously realised that she had to. She had no other choice.

Sondra's stomach growled, and she remembered that she had not eaten dinner the night before and had hardly had any lunch. Was there a twenty-four-hour place that served coffee? She didn't know any, she realised. The Durban beachfront had changed significantly. The long promenade seemed to stretch north and south as far as she could see. How safe was it to walk? She decided to wait until the sun rose and there was some movement.

She jerked up her windbreaker zip and winced as it caught the soft skin at the base of her throat. It was a sharp, cutting nip. She gingerly unhooked the skin and rubbed the burning spot. It forced awareness of her physical body. Every inch of her was sore from being held stiffly for hours, days, weeks. If only she could hold her mind and heart in as strong a vice. Her legs were weak as she trudged to the back of the car and leant heavily against it. Physical exhaustion overcame her. She fell onto the backseat, kicked off her shoes, locked the car, and fell into a heavy, dreamless escape.

When Sondra woke up, it was light. Her mouth was dry and stale. The water bottle was empty, and what was left of the coffee in the flask was cold. She choked and spat the small sip out. *Damn coffee grounds!* Sondra sucked in her lips and held them between her teeth. *Right. Get up and get moving. First things first: get some food.*

She grimaced as she passed a *McDonald's* drive-through. She wasn't that desperate. Fortunately, not too far beyond that, she found a half-decent coffee shop that was open and quiet. She ordered their "Country Breakfast" – eggs, macon, sausage, tomato, and toast – gulped down a glass of water, then went to find the bathroom. Ten minutes later, she surveyed her reflection and felt grimly satisfied. At least she didn't look like something the cat dragged in. It was amazing what a splash of water, a comb through her hair, and some lipstick could do.

She wolfed down her food, not differentiating the tastes. She should have a plan, she realised. She asked for a refill on the coffee and pulled out her notebook from her handbag. The last meeting noted in the red moleskin notebook recorded the date as two months before. She opened to a clean page and firmly rubbed her thumb along the inside spine. It lay open, but the pen clutched in her hand remained motionless. She needed a plan.

A plan? A hope? A prayer?

How do I start this? Or should the question be "where"? The obvious place was her last location before leaving Durban: her home from the age of thirteen to eighteen. Could she just arrive unannounced on the doorstep of the Carims? How would Sarah, her father's wife, react? Would she recognise her? She wondered if the other children still lived there.

It didn't matter. It didn't matter because her issues were not their fault. They were nobody's fault. She had to take responsibility for who she had become, who she had made herself into. She snapped the book closed and shoved it back into her bag. If she was going to visit her stepmother and half-siblings, she'd better clean up better and look more presentable. The confrontation would take all the courage that she could muster. Imagining critical eyes picking apart her appearance would only add to her distress.

Her phone had sufficient battery charge to go online. She searched for self-catering accommodation adverts and chose a B&B in Durban North that was small – only four rooms available. From the images, the rooms seemed private and were cut-off from each other and the main house to ensure privacy. She booked and requested an early check-in.

Sondra drove to a petrol station, filled up her car, and got it washed too. On route to Durban North, she stopped at a supermarket to buy rolls, milk, tea, biscuits, and chocolates. She surveyed the contents of her basket and was amazed at how unhealthy her choices were. Shrugging, Sondra paid and made her way back to her car.

'Please, *Aunty*. Help me, please. Just two rand.' A typical Durban Indian accent sounded behind her. It unnerved her but also welcomed her back home at the same time. It is really only in Durban where women, regardless of age, are referred to as "Aunty". She tossed the scruffy boy all the change she found and let him direct her out of the parking.

Her phone's navigation system indicated a thirteen-minute drive. Check-in was routine, well, routine for Durban. Of course, the *Aunty*, Mrs Simons, the owner of the well-maintained B&B, walked to Sondra's car when she rang the bell and was let in.

Mrs Simons was loquacious – Sondra had never met someone who fitted the description as perfectly. In the five minutes it took for Sondra to complete the paperwork and pay, she explained that she had turned the house into short-term rentals for extra income after her children had moved out. She wanted to know where Sondra was from, if she had family in Durban, how long she would stay, and if her family would be joining her. Mrs Simons looked Coloured but sounded and was as inquisitive as a typical Indian woman. Sondra did her best to evade the probing questions, still trying to figure all that out herself.

Mrs Simons offered to help her to the room. Sondra insisted that she would manage just fine but to no avail. The matronly woman grabbed the grocery packet and led the way to her room. It was through the well-tended garden behind the main house. Sondra was glad to see that the accommodation was neat and smelled of disinfectant and potpourri.

'The bathroom has a bath and a shower, and I put clean towels for you. You like that smell? It's *levennder*.'

Typical Durban Indian accent, Sondra thought. She smiled as she heard the old, familiar pronunciation.

'Oh, that's all you brought?' Mrs Simons was nosily peering into the bag that she had plopped onto the small eating table.

'I'll go shopping again. I wanted to check out the place first.'

'Kitchen is tip-top, Ma.' "Ma" – a term of endearment, another classic *Durbanism* – is used for any female, most often by older Indian women. 'Stove, oven, and micro. See?' Mrs Simons proceeded to fill the kettle and switched it on.

'Yes, thanks. Very nice.' *I'd better get rid of her now, otherwise, the woman will make tea and stay forever.* 'I'm going to be late. I have to shower and leave.'

'Where you going, Sandra?'

'It's Sondra.' She stepped towards the door and reached her arm out, hoping the woman would take a hint.

Mrs Simons sniffed. 'Okay, dearie. I'll leave you. Tell me if you need anything, okay? Don't worry, even if it's late. I'm up all the time. My landline and cell numbers.' She pointed to a laminated page with the numbers stuck on the kitchen wall above the microwave.

'Thanks, Missus Simons. I'm sure all will be okay, but I'll ask if I want anything.'

The older lady looked wistfully at Sondra, and with a pang of recognition, Sondra saw loneliness in her eyes. Did she see it in Sondra too?

Sondra collapsed onto the bed as soon as the door closed behind her landlady. When she dragged herself up after a short restless nap, she didn't feel revived. Sondra looked through her cabin-sized bag and chewed over what she had been thinking. In her haste to leave, she had packed a couple of three-quarter length running pants, a work suit and a couple of shirts, and sleepwear – nothing was casual. Maybe if she ironed a shirt, tied a scarf at her throat, and did not wear the jacket, it could pass.

Sondra found the iron and pressed out the shirt. She laid out toiletries in the bathroom and on the tiny dresser before taking a steaming shower. She was going to do this. Even if it killed her, she was going to confront her past.

16

GREETINGS AND TEA

It was early afternoon by the time Sondra left the B&B. She negotiated the drive to Asherville by memory. The road names had been changed, but the route was exactly the same. She was surprised at how much she still recognised, even though much of the landscape was different. There was a proliferation of restaurants and takeaway places. *Good.* She would buy and eat her meals there – it was close enough.

When she turned into Actum Avenue, she slowed down. The road seemed narrower than she remembered, but maybe it was her imagination. Or perhaps it was because of the trees and bushes on either side of the road that were badly overgrown. One would never have described them as pavements or sidewalks, even then, but the verge had been wide enough to allow for pedestrians. She had walked this road thrice a day when she was in her last few months of primary school – after school and then to and from *madressah* – and then once a day in high school. That had been during term times when she had moved there after Beryl had died. Now, walkers were forced onto the road.

A hooter blared behind her, jarring her to the present. She hadn't realised that she had slowed to a crawl. As she accelerated past the bend in the road, her old house came into view. She parked across the road because there was nowhere else. She switched off the car and regarded the house.

It was still the same, a tad more tired perhaps, as though it felt the weight of the years on its roofs and walls. The garden had never been much to speak of: a small patch of lawn that was more sand and dirt than grass and some bushes along the palisade fence. Sondra locked the car and instinctively tried the door to make sure; the habit of being wary of car jamming was ingrained. She crossed the narrow street and stood at the small gate for a quiet moment before pushing the bell.

'We don't need anything.' A voice came over the crackly intercom.

'Hello. Hello? Can you hear me?'

The woman's voice sounded agitated now. 'What you want?'

'I'm not selling anything. I'm here to see, uh ... Aunty Sarah.'

'Who? *Hayibo*. Wait. Wait. I'll call the *missies*.' Domestic helpers in Durban often referred to the lady of the house as "missies" and the man as "baas". She would have thought that custom would have changed by now. Apparently not, not in the Carim household for sure.

After a few minutes, when Sondra was just about to ring the bell again, the gate's mechanism buzzed, and she pushed the grey metal pedestrian gate open. The automation was some improvement, at least. Warily, she took a step into the yard but couldn't proceed further.

Sarah, her stepmother, stood at the open front door. She had aged. Had she shrunk too? She looked frail in a loose, flowing *abaya* with a scarf pulled low over her forehead and knotted at her chin. The creases alongside her mouth had deepened and made her mouth look like it was in parenthesis.

She leant against the security gate at the door and frowned. Then Sarah lifted her arm in a beckoning motion. 'Saadiyah? Saadiyah! Come. Come.'

Sondra had expected to explain herself. She didn't think she would have been recognised by anyone, least of all Sarah – the woman whose life she had thrown into turmoil when she was placed unceremoniously into her care.

'It's you! I knew it was you. The camera is not very good. It's black and white, but I could see from here. You still the same. The shape of your nose and your big forehead.' Sarah's hand moved to the top of her own face and stretched her fingers away from her thumb to indicate the height of Sondra's forehead. 'Come. Come inside.' She motioned with her arm, more urgently this time.

Sondra took a tentative step and then started walking along the paved but cracked pathway that led to the house.

'Close the gate.'

Sondra turned back and pushed it until it locked with a click.

Sarah stood aside to let Sondra in first, then shuffled past her, took her hand and led her down two small steps into the sunken lounge. Sondra was taken aback by her hand being held, but did not resist.

'Can't believe you came. I thought after Papa died, then you will come back home. So many years now.' Abdul was addressed as "Papa" by all his children and by his wife if she was speaking to them. Sarah turned to face Sondra, reached her hands onto Sondra's shoulders, pulled her face down, and gave her a small peck on the cheek. Sarah's lips were warm but dry. Sarah sat on a couch and motioned for Sondra to sit next to her.

Sondra's eyes adjusted to the dark room. The only window was covered with a blind, which let little light in. Not much had changed. The lounge suite, which had been really trendy thirty years before, had fitted in with the modern sunken lounge at the time. The gold, shaggy carpet had dulled and was now threadbare in patches. The solid TV-cabinet was still there but housed an assortment of mismatched ornaments where the TV used to be. A slim TV was now mounted on the wall next to it.

'So, tell me. How you, Saadiyah? Where you now? Still in Joburg?'

Sondra mumbled and nodded in response.

'Huh? What you said. You must speak louder. My hearing is bad these days.' She pushed the scarf back over her ears with her forefingers. 'How's the family? You got children? Haniefa's two daughters married, and her son is studying. IT. Luthfia, *bechaari*, her marriage broke. Her 'usband left her for another woman. Two small children she got. She stays in town in a flat and works in Papa's factory now.'

'Salma's okay? And AB?' The use of Abdullah's nickname came naturally. Sondra realised with an uncomfortable twinge that she'd hardly ever thought of them, yet they had been the ones who had been kindest to her.

'Salma is also married now. She's very lucky and very happy. Her children in school still. Big place her in-laws got in Umhlanga, four houses in one big garden, main house where the in-laws stay, and then the children all got their own houses. Very smart.' Sarah spoke quickly and comfortably. 'But, you, Saadiyah? How you? So long we never see you.'

'I'm okay, I'm okay. And you, are you okay?'

'Why you took so long to come see us? I missed you.'

Sondra was taken aback. She couldn't believe anyone in the house thought about her, forget missed her. 'I didn't know. I mean, I thought when I left for varsity, maybe it was better like that? Pa— ... uh, Papa didn't call or anything. And after he died, I didn't even know 'til the lawyer phoned weeks after it happened.' *Papa.* The word sounded strange in her mouth. Abdul had asked her to call him "Papa" while he had driven her to this house for the first time, but in the years that she had lived there, she had rarely addressed him directly.

'*Ja, ja*. I know. I told Haniefa to phone and tell you. Afterwards, she told me she didn't have your number, but she should have found it somehow ... somehow. She could have phoned the university or something. That time, we were so busy after the *mayyit* and the visitors.' Sarah sniffed loudly and looked contrite. 'But I can't blame her only. After my *iddat* finished, I made Luthfia also try and find you, but we couldn't. No one from university knew where you moved, and even the lawyer said he only had your bank account, not your telephone number.'

Sondra frowned, recalling having given clear instructions to her father's lawyer that she wanted no contact with the family, that he was not to share any details with them. It would seem that he had honoured that request.

'Oh, we must call Salma and tell her you here. I'll call everyone for lunch or supper one of the days, then we all can meet you again one time.'

'No, please. You mustn't worry about that. I'll meet them next time. How is Abdullah?'

'Aah, Abdullah. What I must tell you? He's here. I'll call him *just now*.'

'What's wrong? Is he okay?'

'He's okay. But he doesn't work, didn't study or anything. Very lazy, just spoilt by his father, and don't want to do nothing. He'll start going to factory for few days sometimes, but then he and Luthfia fight, so it's better he stays at home.' Sarah shook her head. 'I worry about him. When I die, I don't know what will happen. His sisters are fed up with him and his nonsense. Allah *jaane*.' *Allah knows.* That was Sarah's favourite expression, uttered in exasperation, or as an excuse, or if she had wanted to avoid addressing something. Allah knows so leave it in His hands.

Sondra was amazed by the news of her half-siblings but more at Sarah. She had probably said more words and shared more information with Sondra in the past twenty minutes than she ever had before. There was a lightness, an easiness that had never been there before as though she was finally free to express herself, her thoughts, her hopes, and her worries. Abdul's removed presence had revealed an open, relaxed, and even confident woman. Sondra half-listened as she was offered a general catch-up on some of the extended family too, people who had visited or stayed with them for holidays.

An image of Sarah tending over her fifteen-year-old self suddenly returned. Sondra had contracted chicken pox and had been confined to her room. Sarah had kept the room dark and had spread slinger berry leaves on her sheets and over her body. Their gardener had been sent to the house two roads away to fetch them where this tree grew.

'Don' scratch. Otherwise, it'll leave big-big marks on your 'ole body. Such a pretty face.' Sarah was pressing a wet, cold facecloth against Sondra's forehead in an effort to bring down her temperature. 'The slinger berry leaves will cool the scratchiness and dry up the pimples.' For two weeks, Sarah brought Sondra her meals, cleaned her room, removed and washed her clothes separately, helped with ablutions until Sondra could manage on her own, and vigilantly monitored her temperature. All the while, she had reminded Sondra not to scratch. Sondra remembered that she had wanted to stay ill forever just so that she could experience this tenderness freely. It made her miss her own mother even more, but it was also comforting.

Sondra started to say something and then realised that she had rarely addressed this woman directly before. If she spoke of her to others, she would use the address "Aunty Sarah". That's how Abdul had introduced her. Sondra had never been invited to call Sarah anything else, and the two females had not spoken much in the five or six years that she had lived at Abdul and Sarah's home.

Sondra swallowed hard and decided to speak her mind. 'Aunty Sarah, I can't believe this. You seem so different. You look and sound so ... so *happy*.'

Sarah laughed a loud, exuberant sound that stopped like it had started – with a sigh. 'Is true, Ma.' The term of endearment made it sound like Sarah had always considered Sondra as special. She let out another heavy sigh. 'Shame. Sorry, Saadiyah. That time, I didn't, I wasn't ... like I was so far-far from you. I didn't talk to you or worry 'bout you. I should have tried more, but I was ... I was scared for Abdul.' Sarah adjusted her scarf and retied the knot under her chin, then she pushed three fingers of each hand under the scarf on either side of her forehead to ensure that no loose tendrils were sticking out. 'Never mind now. You back now. You *came way* back home. I am happy, so happy.' A smile creased her features and made her look younger. 'You want tea, Saads?'

Saads? Only her two younger siblings had ever called her that. What a remarkable day – revealing and surprising!

Sondra pulled her sleeve up so that she could check her watch, then wondered why she had done so. She had nowhere to go, no one was waiting for her. Right now, Sarah was her only family, or her only family wanting to be with her. She pushed her head back and stretched her neck from one shoulder to the other. '*Jee*, Aunty Sarah, tea would be lovely.'

'Come. Come. Let's go in the kitchen, and we can carry on talking.'

As Sondra followed, she noticed that Sarah's gait had changed. She was still sure-footed but slower, and her body swayed from side to side like a metronome.

In the kitchen, Sarah pulled out a wicker chair and reached out a hand. Sondra clutched it, and the women stood like that, each looking at the other, saying so much without speaking. There was a silent understanding and acceptance of wishing things had been different but also an appreciation of this new opportunity to get to know one another, presented as a gift. The circumstances were now conducive for a real connection. Sondra was no longer viewed as the illegitimate daughter of her husband's mistress, and she was instantly cured of her historical resentment towards this woman.

This shift made her aware and relaxed her simultaneously. She sank low into the chair and dug her elbows on the sturdy wooden table, rested her chin in her cupped hands as she let Sarah fuss over her.

'I'll fry *samosas*. I made fruit cake also yesterday. You used to like my *ghess*?' Sarah asked, referring to the Indian dessert similar in texture to panna cotta but much softer, sweeter, and more fragrant. 'Let me make some. After supper, we can have.' Sarah took it as read that Sondra would stay for supper. It felt right for Sondra too. She was home after all.

* * *

Sondra was elated. Just one afternoon and evening of feeling like she belonged, like she was whole, like she was not alone had made her feel real again. Who would have thought that a human connection would have made such a big difference in such a short time? She and Sarah chatted happily, stories interspersed with laughter and even some teasing. The only interruption was when Sarah had excused herself for her *Asr* and *Maghrib salaah*.

It was dark when they sat down to eat. Abdullah joined them. He acknowledged and greeted Sondra cordially. He asked a few perfunctory questions, while answering hers, and encouraged her to take a second helping once. But she sensed a wariness in his demeanour. She shrugged it off. It was understandable. She had arrived unannounced on their doorstep after having dropped out of their lives years before. Sondra sniffed and licked her lips, enjoying the food lovingly prepared by Sarah.

'Is strong? Mmm, forgot how to eat chillies, heh?' Sarah teased Sondra and offered her a tissue from the box on the counter. 'Never mind. Just drink extra water and have some more.' She went ahead and dished up more chops chutney onto Sondra's plate.

'*Bus. Bus.*' They were all surprised when Sondra spoke the Indian word for "enough" or "stop".

Sarah laughed, shaking her head and wagging her finger. '*Achaaa?*' She drew the word out. 'So, you remembered something of Urdu. *Hoshiyaar.*'

Sondra felt herself blushing and tried to cover her embarrassment at enjoying the praise from her stepmother by raising her glass to her lips and sipping slowly.

'You must eat, Saadiyah. See how thin you are. Here, have more *roti.*'

After they had eaten, Abdullah excused himself, but Sondra and Sarah lingered at the table. Sarah asked about Sondra's family, but she must have sensed Sondra's reluctance to share, and let it go. Their conversation returned to safer topics. Sondra insisted on washing the dishes while Sarah cleared up.

'The taps are different!' Sondra noted excitedly. Apart from the TV and buzzer gate, it was the only other change that she had detected in the house.

'Uh-huh,' Sarah breathed with a nod. 'The old ones were always leaking, so we had to put the new one. Years now.'

At around nine o'clock, Sondra succumbed to the yawns she had been suppressing for the past thirty minutes. Turning down another offer to sleep over, Sondra announced that she was leaving.

'Promise you'll come back?' Sarah wrapped her in a close, warm embrace that Sondra luxuriated in. It felt good to be held, good to be heard. Touching another person and being touched in a pure, loving way was unusual for Sondra, but it felt right. It made Sondra feel accepted and loved – feelings she was not accustomed to. Why had she resisted touching like this?

When they pulled apart, Sarah placed her hand on Sondra's cheek. 'I'm so happy you came. So long I was thinking. I made *dua* by Allah that I see you again. Still so beautiful and clever.'

Sondra blinked rapidly as she felt overcome by simultaneous embarrassment and delight. She hadn't realised that she had needed acknowledgement or recognition. But from the way it made her feel, she must have. Before things got any more emotional, Sondra took her leave.

As she drove down the driveway at the B&B, she noticed that the curtain was pulled back at the front window of the main house. She wasn't annoyed, and that surprised her. Her irritation at Mrs Simons' inquisitiveness had dissipated. She would make an effort to be friendlier when she saw her next.

In her room, the silence reminded her that she was alone, although she no longer felt lonely. The quiet was welcomed and helped her reflect on the day's events. But almost as soon as she put on her pyjamas, she felt her fatigue. She pulled the duvet over her head and fell into a deep, long sleep.

* * *

It was the sound of a dog barking that roused Sondra the next day. There were sounds of children playing in the distance punctuated by chirping birds and traffic moving in the area. Her eyes opened, and she woke up in a space that felt oddly familiar. Sleepily, she stretched her body, wriggled her toes, and made small circles with her feet under the duvet.

She stepped out of bed. The tiled floor was cold beneath her bare feet. It felt familiar too, beckoning her to step further. She padded to the kitchenette and switched on the kettle. After using the toilet and brushing her teeth, she made a mug of steaming tea and went outside, still barefoot. The little table and bench were damp, the droplets glistening in the bright sunshine. She rubbed her soles on the cobbled ground and enjoyed the smooth, chilled feeling against her curved arch.

'*Shukar Alhamdulillah.*' Sondra verbalised the gratitude evocation that she remembered from years back, and it felt right to express the feeling she had woken up with.

The sound of her stomach growling forced her back into the unit. She opened the foil packages that Sarah had bundled for her – the leftover *samosas* from tea and the dry kebab in *pooree* that they'd started supper with. They weren't in the fridge, so she didn't bother with heating anything. She couldn't wait to eat anyway; she felt ravenous.

After such a hearty supper, how was it possible to feel so famished? The *azaan* sounded from one of the *mosques* in the area. It must be *Zuhr* time. No wonder she was hungry! She had slept right through breakfast, and it was now lunchtime. Almost fourteen hours of uninterrupted sleep. Sondra felt like she could conquer the world now that she'd had a full night's sleep and gotten some food into her belly.

She retrieved her phone from her bag so that she could charge it. On an impulse, she sent David a message.

I'm in Durban. Had leave due.

It was unlikely that he would respond, but it felt right to let him know where she was. They were still married after all. He was her husband, and she loved him. She had always loved him, in her own way of loving from afar, and it felt right that she start being more open with him.

She typed another message to David and pressed send before she changed her mind.

I miss you. I miss
Michael. I love you.

Sondra packed a bag for the beach and headed out for a swim in the Indian Ocean – her first in more than twenty-five years.

17

RELIEF AND REFRESHMENT

Sondra felt revived and upbeat. This impulsive trip to Durban had served her well. The last few days had flown by. She would spend mornings at the B&B or at the beach and evenings with her family. Mrs Simons would come to check on her and bring her breakfast at around eight in the morning, usually before Sondra went to the beach. Mrs Simons would stay and have a cup of tea while Sondra ate the freshly baked scones or muffins, eggs or waffles, pancakes or whatever other delicious treats she had prepared, and she devoured the conversations.

Sondra had learnt all about Mrs Simons children and grandchildren, and in return, Sondra shared bits of her life too and how she was in Durban to reconnect with her estranged family. She didn't mention how contrary this was to her normal behaviour. Sondra had always been fiercely private and had kept herself to herself. But in Mrs Simons, she found a willing, non-judgemental, and encouraging ear. Sondra found it was a blessing to be able to recount the previous day's events over breakfast. It gave her a chance to reflect and also see things from another's point of view.

After their talks were finished, Sondra would say her good-byes and take her leave. That bright and balmy Wednesday, Sondra declared, 'I'm going to go to the beach for a swim.'

The warm Indian Ocean – with its soothing, reassuring embrace – beckoned to her, and she answered its call. She swam deep in and let the waves toss her around for a long while before catching whitecaps and swimming back in with the current. Sondra inhaled the salty air and realised that she shouldn't overthink the past. It was over. It could not be changed, and the future would unfold as it wanted to. All she had was here and now.

Her body was tired, but her mind was energised as she drove back to her B&B. There was just enough time for a shower and change before she left to meet Salma. They had arranged to meet at a restaurant for a proper, private catch-up.

Salma and she arrived at the same time and kissed each other warmly before settling down and ordering drinks. After a few minutes of chit-chat, Salma's eyes misted over. She looked lovingly at Sondra.

'I'm so glad you're back. I've missed you, Saads. I need you, my sis.'

Sondra was taken aback at the sudden display of emotion. The sincerity and honesty in Salma's words reached Sondra in ways she was unable to pretend away. She felt the profound love in Salma's words, touch, and eyes which she felt grateful to receive.

She placed a hand on Salma's arm and squeezed. 'I'm back now.' Sondra smiled. 'You will always have me here if you need. I'm here for you.'

"I'm here for you." Simple words. The four words strung together when said from the heart and with sincerity brought moisture to Sondra's eyes too. Being needed by someone – simply because you were her sister and not for any specific reason, just to be able to share love and feel connected to – was a revelation. Sondra wanted to be there for Salma, loved being needed by someone, and realised that she needed her sister too. A sense of peace and acceptance embraced her. She felt warmed by its touch.

Sondra smiled and embraced the depth of her feelings. 'I'm grateful for so many things. So much has happened these past couple of weeks—months to bring me to this point. There are things that I would rather not have happened, sure, but there is a reason for everything, isn't there?'

'Yes.' Salma returned Sondra's smile widely. 'It's all part of Allah's plan, and we must learn to trust His will. Nothing ever happens without a reason.'

'I'm learning that the hard way.' Sondra sighed and leant back in her chair. 'Right, enough of all the serious talk. Let's lighten the mood. I must tell you about Missus Simons – such a lovely old lady. She owns the B&B where I'm staying. She is very sweet, but man, can she talk! ...'

When Salma mentioned her husband, Baboo, and their children, Maseeha and Uzair, Sondra thought about David and Michael. The openness and love in Salma's demeanour when she spoke about her own family lit a spark in Sondra's mind and in her heart. She had not allowed anyone too near, including her husband and son. She had used her self-involvement and infidelities to ensure that she was never consumed by any one person.

It was suddenly clear to her as she sat with her sister why she had done this, why she had kept people away. Her experience was that everyone that she loved had let her down: her mother when she died and left her alone; her father by never allowing himself to love her; her siblings because they had been jealous, intimidated, or resentful of her intrusion into their lives; ... and herself. Her experience of love was that it invariably led to heartbreak. She had felt unworthy of love, even from herself.

No more! She proclaimed the resolution strongly in her mind. *I will love fearlessly from now on. I will not care if the love is reciprocated. I will not care if it hurts me. I will not use love as a weapon or bargaining tool. Not anymore. Generous and loving Salma has shown me that. I can be different, and I must.*

The sisters talked animatedly about mundane, general things, but every now and then, they caught each other's eye, and a significant feeling passed between them – acknowledgement and recognition of a need and love for one another. It was the kind of feeling that Sondra would have previously thought would make her vulnerable. But not now. Now, she felt that nothing was more important for her than to be able to love and share this closeness with her sister. If she got nothing else from this trip, this was enough.

* * *

The next afternoon, Sondra was back at Sarah's house. Her stepmother was making *rotis*, and Sondra was helping by frying the rolled-out dough discs on a hot griddle – a *tawa*. The smell of the frying bread when she smeared *ghee* over was tantalising.

'I remember how Salma, AB, and I would come into the kitchen when you were frying *rotis*, Aunty Sarah. As soon as we got the smell, we would find our way into the kitchen from wherever we were.'

Sarah laughed. 'I remember. You three would take the fresh *rotis*, spread with butter and sugar, and roll them up, and eat them hot-hot.'

'I loved that. I loved all the food you made. I wish I'd been around long enough to learn more from you.'

Their reminiscing was interrupted by a hooter and a sound of a car driving up the driveway.

'That must be Salma,' Sarah said. 'You see how nice it is you here. Nowadays, I see Salma and her children more. Even Luthfia has visited a lot this week. They all want to know about you. Even if they don't ask, everyone's curious.'

On cue, Salma and her children burst in. The children greeted their granny enthusiastically and Sondra shyly.

Sondra felt an odd sensation warm her as she hugged Salma's children. Touching them with love, she understood about family, and how wonderful it was to be an aunt. She smiled coyly at the two and said, 'When we were children, your mother and uncle and I would love to eat *Naani*'s fresh *rotis* with butter and sugar. Would you guys like to try?'

The children looked timidly at their mother, who nodded silently. Sondra quickly made them each a buttered and sugared *roti*. Salma and the children sat down at the table. Sondra made tea while Sarah finished frying the last of the *rotis* she'd shaped with her wooden rolling pin.

Salma jumped up. 'This tea is too hot. I want to show you something. Come.'

Sondra, curious, followed her sister into the lounge. 'I pulled out this box from under Ma's bed. All the old photos of us when we were growing up. See?'

There were dozens, maybe hundreds, but Sondra was only in a few. If they were posed or standing in a row, she was always at one end.

'You were so beautiful, Saadiyah – prettier than all of us. Even though Haniefa and Luthfia were eye-catching, but your features! Stunning. Look. Even when you don't smile.'

Salma was right. Sondra peered at her younger self and recognised the features that were softer and finer but still her own. Her cheeks were fuller and had a healthy flush. Dark brown hair with a natural wave fell softly alongside a long face, ending in a pointy chin. Her chestnut brown eyes were big and framed by long, thick lashes – eyes that appeared hooded even though they were open in the photos like she was trying to hide something. Only in the spontaneous pictures that Abdul or someone must have shot when they were playing in the garden did Sondra look natural. Sondra liked this look. Maybe she would stop the Brazilian treatments that kept her hair super sleek and straight. The natural wave softened her look.

'Two years before Uzair was born, I had a miscarriage.'

Sondra looked up, surprised. Salma looked nostalgic but accepting. Sondra loved how easily Salma spoke to her, how the stories and conversations evolved naturally. Salma made Sondra feel like the years of separation meant nothing, like the hurt at missing her was long forgotten the moment that they reconnected. There was so much to be grateful for. Sondra looked at her younger sister and squeezed her arm. 'Sorry.'

'No, no. It's fine. The baby would not have survived, and it was the body's way of ... of ensuring that I only had perfect, healthy children. But after it happened, I was quiet and lost for a while. I guess maybe I was depressed. Ma came to stay with me for a few weeks that time, just to help with Maseeha – she was not even two. We had lots of time to talk, and it was the first time that she and I spoke about you, really.

'She was sad that she never showed you how much she cared about you. She never resented you, was not even jealous of your mother. Theirs was an arranged marriage that slowly grew to love, not passionate or all-consuming love, but a comfortable, solid basis for a relationship. Ma was a dutiful wife, and maybe deep love would have grown if Papa was more loving too. But I could see how he stifled her with his demands and expectations. The way he treated you was an indication of how he expected her to relate to you. She was not strong enough to resist him, and she regrets that.'

'I understand. I don't blame her or hold anything against her.' Sondra bit her lower lip and blinked rapidly. She was feeling emotional, but it had nothing to do with Ma or how she treated Sondra then. In fact, she was empathising with her stepmother. Muslim women, especially the older generation, would put up with a lot and never complain. *Ma.* In her head she'd started referring to Sarah as Ma, no longer Aunty Sarah.

Salma nodded thoughtfully. 'You made her very happy by coming home. She feels Allah gave her a second chance to make up for that sad time for you.'

Sondra nodded. There was nothing to say.

'I can't imagine how it must have felt when you were moved in. How old were you when your mother passed away?'

'Thirteen.'

'Shame, man, just a baby. Lost the only family and home you knew, then you had to come and live with strangers.'

Sondra shrugged. 'It was a long time ago, and I'm over it now.'

'Are you, Saads? Are you really over it?' Salma's forehead creased as she concentrated her steady gaze on Sondra.

Sondra smiled at Salma, a full smile that emanated light and love. 'I am *now*.' She laughed ruefully. 'Well, I'm getting there. For a long time though, I refused to think about it, pretended that I was okay, and that it didn't matter. So, I buried my feelings – not a healthy thing to do.'

'I'm glad you came back too. I'm happy for you that you are here, trying ... dealing with the past. If we don't resolve things, they linger and affect us more than we realise.'

Sondra slapped her sister on her arm playfully. 'Hey, enough of this morbid talk. Show me more pictures.'

Salma obliged, and Sondra pretended to give her sister her full attention, murmuring suitable responses and asking for help with faces or names she wasn't sure of. But her mind was miles away – six hundred kilometres away, actually, in Johannesburg.

That was the first time in her life, there with Salma on the worn carpet, that she had ever discussed their childhood so candidly. It made her feel light and unburdened. It made her aware that she—no, all people are more than just individuals existing in isolation. We are all connected, and this connection is what makes us whole human beings. She relaxed and her mind wandered over the recent past, in random images, like black and white movies of decades ago, framed and with rounded corners, images of David, Michael, her home, her office ... John, dear, sweet, besotted John.

She shut her eyes and the image of John was immediately replaced by that of his mother. The pain etched on Hannah's face, the heaviness of her body – the physical self that wore grief like a second skin – the hollow emptiness in the words she spoke, not because they were devoid of meaning but simply because the effort of being present and speaking was unbearable. In that instant, Sondra felt Hannah's pain as surely as if it was her own. Was this an extension of the spiritual connections she had become aware of, had decided she needed? Her eyes smarted, and she blinked rapidly. Fortunately, Salma was still peering at the photographs, engrossed in telling the stories behind each one.

Sondra had a sudden urge to unburden herself, to share her life with Salma – a life that she had single-handedly ruined. She knew she wouldn't though. It wouldn't matter how close they felt right now or how accepting and forgiving Salma was. She would not be able to conceal her feelings of judgement if Sondra told her about her affair with John, or how he had killed himself after she had spurned him. She wondered if seeing a therapist would help, but the idea of going to a stranger to reveal deep, dark secrets was unsettling.

It was David she wanted to talk to, to tell him that she was able to see herself as he saw her, to tell him that she was ready to accept responsibility for her actions. She wanted to ask for his forgiveness, beg for it if she had to, and plead for him to take her back.

She doubted that he would want to talk to her. Resolute, principled David had made up his mind to wash his hands of her and eject her from his life. Even if he did agree to see her again and she could confess all to him, he would probably still not forgive her. She played the scene in her mind, and she predicted that he would not be able to see past her part in the death of an innocent, young man. Yet she knew she had to try.

'Saads! Where're you lost?'

'Huh? Sorry, just daydreaming. Looking at old photos does that.'

'Thinking about Papa?'

'Papa? ... No.' She was slowly getting used to calling him "Papa". When he was alive, she'd never felt comfortable enough to call him that.

'He was very proud of you, you know?'

Sondra raised an eyebrow, then shrugged casually. 'Never said anything to me. Actually, he never really said much to me at all.'

Salma continued as though Sondra had said nothing. The words were measured as though she had thought about saying them for a while. 'When I started university, he used to say how proud he was that I followed in your footsteps. He would have wanted all of us to study and make careers for ourselves. Haniefa and Luthfia – well, at that time, they were never interested in anything other than shopping and holidays. And AB? I don't know. He's bright. If he wanted to, he could still do something.'

Sondra murmured noncommittally.

'I realised as I grew older how it must have been for you. And even Ma. Papa used to be affectionate towards us, his children. You and Ma must have felt left out. It was wrong. It must've been hard.'

Sondra turned her head to one side. 'You know – the years before I moved in, when I lived with my mom, he would visit every week, but he never bothered with me. So, it was normal for me ... how he treated me.'

'Did you feel like you weren't his child? Must have. I mean, he was kind to the rest of us.'

'It was weird. Sometimes, I would catch him looking at me, but as soon as he noticed, he'd look away.'

'I know. Well, I didn't really know, but I can guess. Things were awkward if you two were ever together in a room. At mealtimes, he ignored you. That was harsh.'

So, Salma did *notice. Obviously, then, the rest of the family did too.* Sondra pursed her lips together. *Whatever! It doesn't matter now. He is dead, and that story is over.*

'I'll tell you,' Salma continued, 'he was impressed and proud of how you handled yourself when you left home, taking part-time work and working over holidays.' Salma removed her glasses and peered at Sondra. 'It was pride. He was too proud and stubborn to show you. Why? Who knows? I think because the relationship you shared had started off the way it did. Maybe he was embarrassed by you, even though he fulfilled his responsibility to you and although it was common in those days for men to have affairs. You know how it is in our community – people talk.'

'What will people say?' Sondra's sarcasm was palpable.

'That's how it was in those days. Still, don't hold that against him. He loved you and was proud of you, even though he never showed it. He was impressed with your intelligence, your beauty, your grace.'

'You think? We'll never know, will we? I'm over it.'

'So you keep saying ... If you're here to reconnect with us and confront your past, you also have to move past this ... this—' Salma circled her hands and pointed to Sondra. '—this anger you feel towards him.'

Sondra kept herself deadly still, not letting any emotion show on her face. The mixed emotions that swirled inside of her were hard to ignore or pretend away. She felt sad at how her life had turned out from the day her mother died, but grateful too for the events that led to this point. Where she was now – physically, emotionally, spiritually – had evolved. On the one hand, she felt like a more complete person, but on the other, she still hankered for more.

The sisters were silent, an awkward silence that stretched between them. Salma moved to kneel on the floor next to Sondra and pulled her into a hug. The tenderness and love that radiated from the embrace was too much for Sondra. She, who had resisted unnecessary contact, relished her sister's touch. Without warning, she teared and, the next second, was sobbing softly onto Salma's shoulder. Salma held her and rocked her slowly while she rubbed her back soothingly. One gentle, loving touch from a sister was all it took to allow Sondra to release and breathe.

'It's okay, Saads. It's okay. Let it all out.'

This time, Sondra didn't stop herself. She succumbed to the overwhelming feelings of loss and sorrow. She was estranged from every significant man in her life – her dead father, her husband, her son. She'd been banished from her work, friendless and on her own.

Salma murmured things that she thought Sondra needed to hear, about their father and about the importance of forgiving and letting go.

When Sondra was able to pull herself together, she thanked Salma. 'You're right. I want to move on. I want to be able to preserve these memories – the happy ones *and* the sad ones. I know I won't forget, but it's important that I learn to accept them for what they are and how I've let them affect me. Only then will I be able to be whole and complete again.'

'I sense how you're holding yourself so tightly. You don't let people in too close because you're afraid of being hurt.'

The words rang true and resonated. A feeling of relief and release spread over her. Sondra pulled a funny face at her sister. 'Since when did you get so grown up and clever, my agony aunt?'

Salma smiled but then looked seriously at Sondra. 'If that's what you need, Saads, I want to help if I can. Even if you can't talk about it, you know that I'm here and will be making *dua* for you all the time, just like you asked.'

'Thank you, Salma. Yes, I know I can count on you.'

Together, they packed up the box. Sondra rose and stretched her body. 'Ooh, sitting like that was not fun. I feel like an old lady. I must get back to running and gym. Maybe I'll try yoga. Been so stressed recently that my routine has suffered. It's ironic, hey? You need exercise most when you have the least time or inclination to do it. It's been wonderful to go swimming in the ocean again though. Nothing tops Durban's beach.'

'Baboo and I take the kids to the beach on Sunday. He runs, and I watch them on their bikes. Come with us and you can run.'

'I won't be here on Sunday. I'm leaving on Saturday.'

'Oh? I thought you were here for a bit? Last time I asked, you were vague about your plans.'

That was true. Sondra had not decided until *just now* that she had to get back to Joburg. This trip to Durban had been the best idea she'd had in a long time. It had been good for her to come back and to confront old hurts and ghosts. But there were bigger issues to be dealt with back home.

'Sorry, Salma. I have to go. There are things I must attend to urgently. I would have left tomorrow, but Ma is cooking a big *Jummah* lunch and calling everyone. I can't disappoint her.'

Salma's eyes widened, and she stretched her neck forwards, moving her head towards Sondra like a peering bird.

'What?' Sondra enquired.

'I'm surprised ... surprised, and delighted. You called Ma "Ma", not "Aunty Sarah".'

Sondra grinned. 'Well, it's about time, don't you think?'

Their jovial laughter filled the whole house once more.

18

FROM PILLAR TO POST

Sondra timed it so that she arrived in Joburg on Saturday evening. Her plan had worked, and she was exhausted. Tossing her bags at the foot of her bed in her rented apartment, she changed out of her driving clothes and crashed onto the bed. She rose early on Sunday and got busy.

She thoroughly cleaned the apartment. Every nook and cranny that had been ignored since she had moved in was dusted, vacuumed, swept, and polished. She opened all the windows except one which was stuck – she hadn't even realised. She even switched off the fridge-freezer combo so that she could air it out and wipe it thoroughly.

As she worked, she kept adding to a shopping list, which was mostly cleaning equipment and detergents that she had not bothered stocking up on. This was definitely not going to be permanent accommodation, but she was going to make it as liveable as possible in the interim.

When she was done, she felt an immense sense of satisfaction. She took a few minutes to admire her handiwork, then sipped a cup of tea and watched the news. Her stomach growled loudly, reminding her that there was nothing in the fridge. Her next task was to grab a healthy lunch, do the shopping, and return in time for a run. She tossed back the last of her tea and hopped into the shower.

On Sunday evening, she switched off all the lights and got into bed with her laptop. She had been planning the e-mail all day and wanted to get it done and sent before she slept. It had been relatively easy to find an e-mail address for Hannah Bennett.

Dear Mrs Bennett

Hannah, I am very sorry for my behaviour when we last met. I have done much introspection and would appreciate an opportunity to meet with you again. My telephone number is in my signature below. Please contact me to arrange a day and time that suits you.

I hope to see you soon.

Best regards,

Sondra Carim-Edwards

Sondra resisted the temptation to log onto her work e-mail, realising that she didn't have the energy to worry about that. There were two weeks left before she had to return, and whatever was in her inbox could wait. Out-of-office messages would have redirected clients elsewhere in any case. She pushed her laptop under her bed and fell into a restless sleep.

* * *

She woke up twice during the night, once was to go to the bathroom, and the second time was because she was convinced that she heard someone calling her name. The dream was confusing and only snatches remained. She could not make sense of it nor could she recognise the voice she thought she had heard. Unsettled and weary, she eventually managed to drift back off to sleep. The next morning, her head was heavy, and she felt sluggish.

She wished she had slept longer. The day ahead seemed to stretch endlessly before her. She switched on the TV for some background noise so that she wouldn't feel so alone.

Sondra took her mug of tea and the newspaper she had bought the day before onto the balcony. Sandton traffic was at its Monday morning peak, but since she was quite high up and far back from the roads, it became white noise like the TV. She marvelled at the thousands of people all scurrying off to their schools and jobs, chasing their tails, getting to their destinations. She had been a part of that rat race and had revelled in it, but she had mixed feelings about it now.

She idly scrolled through her messages and saw a message from Vic, sent the day before. She'd missed it, somehow.

> Sondra, darling. It's done. I'm meeting Cravat on Thursday. I'll message you the time and place and then we can 'bump' into each other, just like you planned.

Sondra stared at her screen dispassionately. She didn't want to pursue this. Even though it would keep her busy and go a way towards getting her career back on track. She'd pass the lead on to one of the partners. If she didn't get Cravat's investments, the firm would still benefit. It would be a pity to miss the opportunity, but in the grand scheme of things, it didn't really matter.

Sondra laughed out loud. 'Look at you, Sondra Carim-Edwards,' she voiced the words in wonder. She couldn't believe her transformation. A few months before, she had sold her body to get this intro, and now, she had other priorities. Winning at work would take second place this time. She texted back.

I'm on leave. Thanks, but I
won't join you. I'll pass on
your details and one of the
partners will contact you.

Sondra ignored the surprised emoji Vic sent. He would get
the message soon enough.

Yet, Sondra knew she needed to feel busy again, but all
of the activities that she thought of were devices that she
had used in what she was now calling her "old life". She
wondered if that lifestyle – her "old lifestyle" – would fit
her now as well as she remembered it had. Did it ever suit
her? Was it a role she thought she had to play – a person
she had to be? The past week had given her some answers
but had left her with many more questions. There was a simultaneous need and reluctance to unravel herself. It would
happen, she felt. When the time was right, she would find
her real self, the one that had been hidden for reasons that
were complex and contradictory.

Maybe things did happen for a reason, just like Salma
had said. Although her life felt completely upside down, at
least she was not as distraught and distressed as she had
been when the proverbial shit had hit the fan and David
and Michael had found out about John. Thinking back on
her trip to Durban, she probably had subconsciously always
known that her attitude to people and life was rooted in her
childhood. But she'd never had a problem with her attitude
before, so she had never bothered to question it. It had never
occurred to her to do so. That realisation was hard to ignore
any longer. She hoped that this path she had begun on, that
started with a physical journey to Durban, was a way for her
to try and fix the mess she had made of her life.

A soft breeze blew over her, lifting her hair away from her neck momentarily. It made her feel vulnerable and exposed. Yet there was no one to see; she was alone. She ran her fingers through her hair – it was slowly returning to its natural wavy texture. She couldn't remember the last time she put a home treatment on her hair, and it had been months since she had a salon treatment.

Sondra needed to see David and Michael, but she knew that that was impossible now. Her other priority was to make amends with Hannah. When she had done what little she could to repair the damage she had wrought upon Hannah, would she feel prepared to approach Michael and David again?

Sondra could no longer put off the inevitable. She found her phone to check if Hannah had texted, convinced she would have. Sondra was right. The message was brief but not unfriendly.

> Hi Sondra. Thank you for your
> e-mail. I can meet after 5pm.

Sondra responded with confirmation and her address details. After a moment, she wondered if meeting on neutral ground would have been better. It didn't matter. Hannah's response confirming she would arrive by five-thirty meant that there was no turning back. Ready or not, she was going to take responsibility for her actions and apologise to Hannah Bennett.

19

THE EBB AND FLOW OF STRIFE

Hannah was let in at the security gate of Sondra's complex and shown where to park. The lift was silently efficient, and she was elevated to the fourth floor in seconds. She stood at Sondra Carim-Edward's door. Just before she knocked, she heard movement from within. Her knuckles landed on the painted wood in two sharp raps. The door opened, and the two women stared at each other, in recognition and shared uncertainty.

Sondra moved first. She reached out her hand. 'Hannah. Thank you for coming. Please, come in.'

Hannah's fingers brushed Sondra's in a weak grip. Sondra moved aside to allow her entry. Hannah shifted her weight from foot to foot, then she stepped over the threshold and tried to suppress the queasiness she felt. Why was *she* the one feeling awkward?

'I'm ... I'm glad that you're here, Hannah. I wanted to talk with you in person.' Sondra sat on a chair at the four-seater dining table and gestured towards the chair across from her in the compact living area.

Hannah did not move. Sondra hesitated a moment and then got up again. The women faced each other with just a metre between them.

'Thank you for coming to see me,' Sondra started again. 'The last time we met, I was ... my behaviour was appalling – unforgivable.' Sondra dropped her eyes twice as she spoke and then quickly returned her gaze to Hannah each time. Was she embarrassed? Ashamed? It was like Sondra had to force herself to look at her.

Hannah's eyes remained fixed on Sondra, who looked different. Without make-up, she looked younger but also vulnerable. 'Is this what this is about?' The harshness in Hannah's tone was foreign to her own ears. 'You needing to appease your conscience?'

'Yes—No! It's not like that. I don't want this to be about me. If you will allow it, I do want to apologise. My "sorry" cannot begin to excuse my actions or my behaviour, but I hope it's a start.' Sondra's hands fidgeted at nothing.

'I'm listening.' *That's why I'm here. Get on with it!*

Sondra's hands gripped each other – maybe she wanted them to stop their squirming. 'I was wrong. I wronged John. I wronged you and John. It's a terrible thing that happened. I used him, and when things became inconvenient for me, I moved on. I didn't care about him and barely bothered to explain or end things amicably. I hurt him terribly, and it's because of my ...' Sondra took a deep, quivering breath. '... callousness that he did what he did.'

The silence after Sondra's short speech attacked Hannah's steely resolve. She felt weak and dizzy, so she sat down hard on the chair that Sondra had offered earlier. She gripped the sides at her thighs fiercely, concentrating on the feel of the fabric under her palms. Her shoulders crept up to her ears, and she looked down at the carpet under her feet.

Sondra slowly sat down on the chair across from Hannah. She placed her elbows on the table and crossed her arms.

'Sorry.' Sondra's lids covered her eyes for a moment while she inhaled deeply. 'The word cannot begin to express how awful I feel for what I have done. I want you to know that I was wrong. Everything you said to me is true. I was selfish. I should have known better ... being so much older than him and supposedly wiser.'

Yes. If only you had realised that earlier. Hannah continued to observe the woman.

Sondra pulled herself upright in her chair, her arms and hands moved in a gesture of ... openness? Appeal? Her eyes were wide and clear, her lips parted. Two soft lines creased her forehead in the area above the nose – the beginnings of a frown – not in irritation or annoyance but rather in concentration. Hannah sensed that Sondra was being truthful. The sincerity in the even, quietly strong voice seemed genuine.

Hannah nodded slowly as her own hand reached for the side of her face. She rubbed her middle and ring finger along her upper lip, not sure how to respond. She had played this scene over and over in her mind, but in each replay, Sondra was the person that Hannah had met that first time. Nothing had prepared her for *this* Sondra. This person did not act, look, or behave like *that* monster. She was ... soft, cognisant, and ... humble.

'You don't have to say anything unless you want to. Your agreeing to see me, to come here, tells me that you *do* want to hear what I have to say.' Sondra rose carefully and pointed to a jug of water with lemon slices and mint leaves that sat on the kitchen counter. 'I'm having some. Shall I pour you a glass?'

Hannah nodded and watched Sondra's hands, hands that had caressed her son's body; noticed Sondra's hair as it fell forwards, hair that her son's hand had gripped in passion; surveyed the curve of her breasts under the soft grey T-shirt, breasts that her son's mouth had kissed; and acknowledged that the woman that her son had loved appeared strong but vulnerable too. This was the woman that John could not have considered his life without.

Sondra placed both glasses on the table and sat down facing Hannah again. Her body seemed less rigid. They both drank. Sondra sipped tentatively, but Hannah gulped down half the glass, steadying her resolve.

Hannah slowly put the glass down and asked, 'Tell me everything.'

'Everything? You're sure?'

'I am.' And Hannah was. 'Tell me.' *I have to know. Don't you realise that, Sondra Carim-Edwards? How else can I ever be able to understand what it was about you that John found so compelling?*

'Okay, I'll tell you ... If that's what you want, I will. If you want me to stop at any time ...' Sondra's shoulders slumped, and her chin dipped as she began. 'John was an incredible young man. He was charming without being overbearing, full of himself, or arrogant. Classy, but not in your face about it. Subtle. He gets that from you?' Sondra did not wait for a reply. 'Bright. Learnt quickly and was eager to help his colleagues. He was well-liked, had an easy-going way. People were drawn to him without being intimidated. He made everyone relax. It brought out the best in everyone. The team gelled well, and a big part of that was because of him.'

Hannah closed her eyes and saw her son the way Sondra had seen him, the way he was known and loved by all. Then she nodded at Sondra to indicate that she should continue.

'I was attracted to him immediately. His good looks, his cheerful attitude, his eagerness to please made me notice him. He had a presence that ... glowed. I didn't hide my infatuation. I didn't have to tell him I was attracted to him. He knew, and that made him bold. When he ... when he made a move—' *Is that your delicate way of describing it?* Hannah wondered. '—I ... I didn't discourage him.'

Sondra brought the jug to the table, topped up both their glasses, and swallowed a long, slow sip. 'One thing led to another. The liaison was all-consuming for John. I was taken in too. It felt good to have a years-younger, charming, handsome, intelligent man look at me the way that he did. I told myself I was in control ...' Sondra's eyebrows shot up. '... kept reminding him that I was married, that the affair meant nothing and would end. I wanted to believe that I was convincing. He was young, so young. I think it was the first time he had felt ... I think he thought he was truly in love.' The last two words were spoken a few decibels softer. Did Sondra feel undeserving of that love?

Hannah felt her throat tighten, and her eyes filled with burning liquid. The pain that was etched into her soul surfaced. She raged against the tears. She needed to hear everything.

'When I tried to break it off,' Sondra continued, 'he resisted. I cut him off.'

You cut him down. You felled him with one foul swoop.

'I didn't know what else to do. My only concern was for myself – *my* life, *my* family, *my* career, *my* reputation. I'm ashamed to say that I didn't care what he went through. I was heartless, and my actions ... they were ruthless. I never imagined that he would do something like kill ... something like that.' Sondra, who had up until then seemed calm, started crying. Her sobs were soft and punctuated by her sucking in deep gulps of air. 'I don't even have the right to ask for your forgiveness. But I'm sorry, Hannah, I'm so ... *so* sorry. If I could do things differently, if I could turn back the clock ...'

Hannah heard Sondra's voice drop to a whisper, so she leant forwards to try and hear Sondra better.

'Nothing will bring him back. He's gone. Your John is gone. I did that. I killed him. I killed him.' Sondra's head dropped onto her arms on the table, and her body racked with silent shudders.

Hannah stared at the top of Sondra's head and tried to comprehend her own feelings. She felt crestfallen; the chronic pain of loss was a dull ache. This was also quite an anti-climax; the release she thought she would feel at hearing Sondra confess did not come. Instead, she felt confused, confused at this woman who sat in front of her, begging for forgiveness; confused that hearing the explanation of her son's death was unfulfilling; confused that her instinct was to comfort Sondra, not lash out. Hannah didn't know what to do or say, so she sat still until Sondra's tears dried up and she made an effort to calm herself.

'I'm sorry. I didn't want to make this about me. I shouldn't have lost it like that. I ... I mean, I, uh ... do you ...?' She sucked in a breath between clenched teeth. The whistling sound did nothing to ease the tension. 'Do you have any questions?'

'Did you love him?' Hannah didn't think about the question and wasn't sure where the words came from, but as soon as she voiced the words, the urgency to know became paramount.

Sondra's widened eyes and her quickened breathing alerted Hannah that perhaps she hadn't anticipated the question either. Sondra's eyes darted to the corners of the room briefly.

'Are you thinking about your answer because you don't know or because you are deciding whether to tell the truth?'

'What?' Sondra sat straight up, and her eyes narrowed.

'Did you love my son?'

'No. No, I didn't love him.'

'You ... didn't ... love ... him.' The words were drawn out of Hannah excruciatingly.

'I was wrong not to – crazy even! He was worthy of love, of true, sincere feelings, because that's who he was: a loving and lovable person. But I didn't love him. I cannot ... I could not love anyone except myself. I didn't love anyone.'

'A classic case of "It's not you. It's me."?' Hannah realised that this uncharacteristic sarcasm and harshness was to cover up her own conflicting emotions, but she could not stop herself. On some level, she wanted to be cruel to Sondra.

Hannah wanted to hurt and punish her. She wondered what her perceptive therapist, Mary, would think of this ... or Pastor Benjamin. *How very unchristian of me.*

Sondra shook her head vigorously. 'No. It's not like that at all. You deserve the truth. I didn't love John. I was infatuated and lusted after him. I'm not the kind of person who loves easily. Even when I do, I always hold back, playing it safe. But even if I was different, I couldn't have loved John. I wouldn't have wanted to make a life with him. We're different people at different points in our lives. It would never have worked.'

'I see.' But Hannah didn't. *What hogwash are you trying to sell me?*

'I should have been kinder. I should have explained it to him. Maybe that would have helped. I don't know.' Sondra looked directly at Hannah. 'But I doubt it. He was convinced that it was *true* love – the real deal – and that we could've ridden off into the sunset and lived happily ever after. He thought I was pretending because I couldn't leave my family.'

What are you saying? That my boy was a fool? Naïve? Hannah challenged her silently. Out loud, she said, 'You could've tried to explain. You could've reached out to someone who could've gotten through to him – me, or anyone.' *Or you could've not started the affair at all!*

'You're right. I could have. I *should* have. That might have helped. If you knew, maybe you could've stopped him.'

'Are you blaming me?' Hannah bristled. She did not bother to stop her tears. They flowed unabated down her cheeks. Was it her fault? Did her love and protection smother him? Maybe he had not been allowed to grow up. Maybe he'd wanted to prove that he was a man. Hannah cringed. Her whole body pushed against the harsh questions and thoughts.

'No, Hannah.' Sondra's voice was gentle. 'That's not what I'm saying. Please know that I'm not blaming you. I ... I'm ... I want to take responsibility. I don't know how that works, but I know I have to start with trying to explain to you. It can't even begin to make amends, but I think ... I hope it can be a start.'

For a few minutes, the only sound was the humming of the fridge. Hannah watched Sondra surreptitiously through her tears. Sondra's eyes were hooded while she examined her fingers and nails.

Hannah's self-control was being tested. She wanted to physically lash out at Sondra but wanted to grieve her son more.

'I'm going to leave now.' Jerkily, she pushed her chair back, transferred her weight onto her hands on the table, and force her body to stand up. 'I have somewhere I need to be.' *Anywhere that's not here.*

Sondra covered the short distance between them in two steps. Her head tilted to one side, her eyes wearing a distant look. 'You're going? Will you be okay?'

Hannah didn't respond but gave Sondra an incredulous look. *I will never be okay thanks to you!*

'You ... you take care, Hannah. I ... I wish I could change things. Know that I'm sorry, and if I can ... if there's anything ...' Her words trailed off as though they realised their hopelessness.

Hannah turned her exhausted body away and shuffled to the door. Her body evidently did not understand the urgency she felt at needing to get away. She couldn't hear anymore, couldn't say anymore. A simple greeting was impossible. Her fingers fidgeted with the knob on the *Yale*-type lock. The door swung open. A cross breeze blew into the apartment. She wished it would whisk her up and blow her away ... far, far away.

* * *

The traffic was winding down while Hannah drove down Sandton Drive. For once, she would have preferred it to have been busier, which would have forced her to concentrate.

Her mind needed to be occupied, but memories of John refused to stay away.

When she stopped at the traffic light on William Nicol, she put "West Park Cemetery" into her phone's navigation. She knew the way but wanted to hear the directions in that clinical, computer-generated voice. She bought two bunches of flowers from a vendor along the way.

By the time she reached the cemetery, it was dark. John was buried next to his father. It was supposed to have been her plot. They had bought them when Eliot had turned forty. It had been a shock that Eliot had needed his in the year that followed. Things never go according to plan, do they? That was five years before, and yet, she felt the loss of her son more deeply and acutely than her husband's. Hannah placed one of the bunches of flowers on John's tombstone. It felt cold and smooth under her hand.

'I met her again, John. Sondra. She's sorry about what happened.' A weird, frightening sound escaped from her throat as the bitter laugh turned into an anguished cry. 'She's *sorry*. Here you lie, alone, cold, dead – and she's *sorry*.'

Hannah knelt to remove leaves, twigs, and a sweet wrapper that had blown onto the rectangular grassed area bordered by a neat row of white stones. She laid the second bunch of flowers as carefully as she would place a sleeping baby into his crib on the ground at the base of John's tombstone. She shifted her weight so that her bum settled onto her heels. The blades of grass felt sharp and cold through her pants.

It was deathly still, she noticed. There was no breeze and no sound apart from the annoying stridulating of the crickets.

'I miss you, John. I miss you every second of every day. I want to see you, touch you. Why did you do this?' Hannah squeezed her eyes closed and took a raspy breath. 'What is it about Sondra that captivated you? She's not even that beautiful.' *Okay, in her way, I guess she's striking.* 'As a person, she's nothing, John – cold, cruel, merciless. Even in her apologetic state, she's selfish and self-serving. Hah! She said she wanted the meeting to be for me, not about her. What did I get out of it? Nothing! More questions than answers, more anguish, not closure, not even some understanding.'

Hot tears spilt over her lids and dampened the skin on her cheeks. She felt the puffiness of her skin under the tissue when she pressed it against her eyes. Tears, endless tears, and a hollow emptiness stretched interminably before her – a life not worth the air it inhaled and exhaled ceaselessly, heartlessly.

The mental picture of John's body lying lifeless surfaced, his face set in a blank stare through slits of his unseeing eyes. She chased it away and tried to replace it with happier memories, images of John as a child, John looking up at her in adoration, touching a puppy in wonder, giggling as his father tossed him into the air, riding his bike up and down the park while she tried to keep up. Bittersweet memories that needed to be remembered and wanted to be forgotten. The images that scorned her with their malice wore her out and drained her. She was all talked out. But the questions in her mind were unforgiving.

Why didn't you talk to me, John? Why didn't you trust me enough? I would've understood. For your happiness, for your life, I could've listened and forgiven anything. Were you afraid of me? Afraid of how I might react? Afraid of hurting me? Disappointing me? You should've known that you ... you, John, you are my life, my oxygen. I can't live without you. I can't live knowing you did this. Why? Why? WHY? If only her thoughts could stop like her words did.

Hannah didn't know how long she sat like that, but when she tried to move, she struggled. Her body was stiff, and her legs were numb. She pushed herself onto her haunches first, and then onto unsteady feet, which arched and then relaxed in her shoes. As the blood flowed, feeling began to return to her legs. It was late and dark, but no one was waiting for her. She barely glanced at Eliot's grave and made no attempt to visit or talk with her mother. Slowly, she made her way to her car, using her cell phone torch.

Focus, Hannah. One step at a time. One moment at a time. Don't think about tomorrow or even the next minute, just this moment, just this here, just this now. Walk to the car. Lock yourself in. Switch it on. Put on the lights. Drive home.

20

DISQUIET TIME

For many hours after Hannah left, Sondra played their encounter over in her head. She considered other things that she could have said and wondered how things would have played out if she had. What had she hoped for? Definitely not liberation. That was not hers to have right now, nor was it Hannah's to give. Even if Hannah had accepted her apology and forgiven her, unlikely though that was, she had not forgiven *herself*.

David's words rang in her ears. "Take a long, hard look at yourself." Sondra had and had been brutally honest – she did not like herself at all. In fact, she was ashamed and aghast that this was who she had become. Forgiving herself was a long way off. For now, she had to learn to live with herself, just be able to tolerate her breathing, her existing, her living. But to what end?

The postulations of their encounter – it was much more than a meeting – kept her tossing and turning until she came to the realisation that she had to believe that this was the best possible outcome – that things turned out as well as they could have. Spent, she finally fell into a fitful sleep.

The next morning brought a fuzzy feeling – her head felt heavy, and her neck was stiff and sore. She felt the same kind of tension in her muscles as when she was stressed at work or had spent hours on her laptop.

She padded to the kitchen and switched on the kettle, then decided she should shower first. When she walked into the bathroom though, she walked out again. She pulled on *takkies* and decided to go for a run. It was early, before six, and the roads were quiet, apart from some minibus taxis and a few cars with early birds making their way to work.

She concentrated on the sound of her shoed feet hitting the ground. She had no set route; it was the first time that she had run since moving into the apartment after all. She thought it would be best to stay close though, so she circled her block several times. After thirty minutes, she felt winded. She had been running hard instead of varying her pace like she usually would.

She slowed down until she re-entered her apartment building and trudged up the four flights of stairs. Sondra took a long, hot shower and then made herself a quick breakfast of instant oats and toast. She looked at the clock above the microwave. It wasn't even seven-thirty.

The thought of the next two weeks, of just waiting for work to start, and wonderings about David, Michael, John and, moreover, Hannah, stressed her out. She needed a distraction or an activity she could focus on to keep herself occupied. Otherwise, she feared she would go crazy. She had to take action, had to feel like she was doing something to address her situation ... Her "situation", as though a change in environment could rectify the mess her life was in. If only she could make it all right again with a sweep of her hand ... but her hands only seemed to bring disaster to herself and those around her. She felt cursed and doomed to a life without being touched or loved ever again.

Sondra groaned out loud. She had to try and stop beating herself up. What was done, was done. Her intentions now were pure. She wanted to heal. How she was going to do that, she didn't know, but she felt satisfied that she had started the process. Now, she had to continue being honest with herself and hope for the best. She hugged herself and willed her touch to be nurturing – not harsh, not judgemental. If she wanted David, Michael and even Hannah to consider her differently, she would have to look at herself differently too. She made a silent and conscious intention to be gentle with herself.

Sondra considered her options. They were few, and none were appealing. Maybe, once she got back to work, really got back, that would give her a sense of purpose. Who was she kidding? Nothing would ever feel okay again unless she made an effort with Michael. If there was some way to connect with him on some level. Even if it was sitting with him and having him watch her with disappointed, judgemental eyes, it would be something, and even that would be better than this.

She was drawn to her computer. She wrote an e-mail to Michael, an impassioned plea, imploring him to consider seeing her, to let her explain where she was. She ended it by asking for "just twenty minutes. Please." She couldn't press send. She had to deliver this to him in person. She guessed there was a good chance he would delete the mail without opening or reading it, and not hearing back – not knowing – would be even worse.

She opened a new mail and addressed it to David. Her message was brief, bordering on professional.

Dear David

Please may we meet? I need to see you face to face.

Please David.

Thanks, Sondra

He responded while she was still online a few minutes later, saying he was glad to hear from her because he had wanted to discuss an equitable division of assets and other issues face to face as well.

Sondra felt relieved, but this was short-lived when she read further. He proposed meeting days later. The waiting would be torturous, but she quickly agreed, not wanting to sound pushy. The wait would have to be filled with reading, mindless movies, exercise, and whatever else she could think of to pass the hours in the days ahead.

She kicked off her shoes and crawled under the covers of her unmade bed. Maybe her exhausted body would catch up on the sleep she had missed out on and a few hours would pass. Thankfully, sleep did come.

Later that day, she saw a *WhatsApp* from Salma.

> *Slmz* Saads. How are you doing?
> All ok in Joburg? Why didn't you
> message when you arrived??

It would never have occurred to her to let anyone know, but that's what families do, right? Communicate.

> Sorry. *Maaf.* I was naughty.
> I will next time. How is
> Ma? And your kiddos? Give
> everyone my *salaams.*

> Everyone is ok. You give our
> regards to David and Mikey, ok?
> Miss you. Come back soon.

Sondra leant back in her chair and marvelled at how everything with her family was different now. That gave her hope. Maybe it foretold a change of heart from Michael and David too.

A message from the hair salon with a monthly promotion arrived too. She called to make an appointment for the next day. She may as well – it would kill a couple of hours.

* * *

The hair appointment did help, and she caught up on the celebrity gossip from the *Hello* and *You* magazines placed on the counter too. Angie was surprised she didn't want a Brazilian – just a trim and an oil treatment. The couple of hours passed quickly—too quickly. The route she took back to her apartment went past her offices. She drove in and parked in a visitor's bay.

What the hell was she thinking?

The security guard recognised her car and came to check why she wasn't going to her usual spot.

'I'm still on leave,' she explained. 'Just parking here 'cause I have an appointment in the area.'

He nodded and opened the small pedestrian gate to let her out onto the street. She realised she hardly ever walked the streets, although she was in the area every day for years, and decided to be a tourist in her own city. She would take in the sights. She revelled in the people-watching.

There were tourists, some with luggage, moving from or to the *Gautrain* station. She also passed dozens of labourers in overalls or similar outfits who looked like they belonged on construction sites. A few suit-and-tie types, looking foreign, walked alone or in groups of two or three. Men and women either in white-collar positions or possibly store assistants moved purposefully past, but none caught her eye. Everyone seemed to be preoccupied.

She found herself inadvertently tailing a family of holiday-makers – a middle-aged couple with three teenage boys in tow. They looked like they were her age or maybe a few years older. The family were wearing bright-coloured casual clothes with sunglasses and hats. They each had a backpack and were pulling suitcases on wheels behind them. It sounded like they were speaking Italian – Sondra caught a word or two of their loud conversation. They went into the *Gautrain* station, and she followed.

Her gold card for the train needed a cash top up. She sorted that out quickly and took the escalators deep into the bowels of the earth. As she stepped off the escalator, she watched as a train left the station, probably with the Italian family on board. The platform was deserted, apart from a few other passengers and security personnel. She amused herself by critiquing the adverts on the walls until the next coach arrived.

She hopped on without thinking. She jumped off at O. R. Tambo International Airport, browsed the stores, and had lunch at the food court. It was a pleasant enough time, and Sondra realised that as long as she did not have to stay in her oppressive apartment, the days would pass. So, she planned an outing a day until the day of her meeting with David. That was as far as she could think at that point.

21

IRRESOLUTE EMOTIONS

Hannah listened while the security guard buzzed the intercom in Sondra's apartment. 'Hi, madam. I have a Missus Hannah to see you.' A pause, then, 'Yes, okay.' He took the completed visitors' book from Hannah and said, 'Thank you very much, Miss. You can go up, fourth floor.' Hannah didn't need any reminding.

She saw Sondra waiting in the hall for her as she exited the elevator. The women looked at each other while Hannah walked the few metres to close the space between them. Sondra reached out a hand and warmly shook Hannah's. Hannah was sure her hand was limp and damp in Sondra's.

'Please, please come in. I wasn't expecting this,' Sondra said, closing the door behind them, 'but I'm so glad you're here, Hannah. I've just put the kettle on. Tea? Or would you prefer coffee?'

'Tea's fine, thanks.' Hannah seated herself on the same chair that she had sat on the last time and took a moment to take in the apartment. It was a stock-standard luxury apartment: small but tastefully and efficiently furnished to maximise the use of space. The fingertips of her middle and ring fingers rubbed at her temples in small circular movements.

'Are you okay? Headache?'

Hannah was surprised, touched even, to hear the sincere concern in Sondra's voice.

'No,' she replied, pulling her lips to one side in a rueful half-smile. 'Not now. But it seems like I've picked up this habit of late.' Her voice was raspy like she had a cold. She cleared her throat and rubbed her temples once more. 'Can't be good for wrinkles, hey?' Hannah was surprising herself today – first by coming here and now by her sudden capacity to make small talk.

Sondra shrugged. 'Tea, you said?' She busied herself with setting out mugs and teabags. 'I'm still on leave from work. I'll be getting back soon.' She poured the steaming water into the mugs, her back towards Hannah. She could have been anyone. 'Things at the office have been tough. There was an official warning. Anyway, what will be will be.' Sondra placed milk and sugar in front of Hannah, who stared at the white crockery. 'I heard about your mother. I'm sorry. I meant to say something the last time ... I guess I was ... it was ... My deepest sympathies.'

Hannah looked up sharply but saw only tenderness and maybe some apprehension in Sondra's gaze. 'Thank you,' Hannah eventually managed.

'My mother passed away when I was thirteen. Then I lived with my father and his family for a few years until I went to varsity.' An embarrassed laugh, then she added, 'I don't want to bore you with my life story. It ... it must've been awful to lose your mother so soon after John. But, I guess, there's never a good time.' Sondra sipped her tea.

'I'm not ...' Hannah took a breath. 'I'm not sure what I'm doing here, but I felt we needed to talk again. There's so much I want to ask, but I don't know where or how to begin.'

'Maybe I should.' Sondra inhaled deeply and sighed out her breath. 'I am truly, truly sorry about John. I can't even begin to imagine how you must feel. I know nothing I can ever say or do can bring him back or take away your pain, your loss.' Sondra's bottom lip quivered ever so slightly. She paused to sip her tea.

Hannah studied her mug. 'There was a time when all I wanted was to hear that, for you to acknowledge and take responsibility.' Hannah cringed. She couldn't believe she was talking normally and to Sondra of all people. 'It's not so great actually.' Hannah exhaled a short noisy burst of air.

Sondra nodded her head in acknowledgement. 'It's funny how we chase after something so desperately, thinking that's all we need, and once we get it, we think that everything will be perfect, only to find that it's all a bit of a let-down.'

Hannah wondered how this woman, who had everything, could possibly want more. 'You're missing work?'

'No, actually. Surprisingly! I thought I needed the cutthroat, fast-paced corporate game to make me who I am. It was always such a big part of me. Of late though, I've lost interest. *But*,' she paused to emphasise her point, 'I'm bored out of my mind!' Sondra's soft smile caressed her lips like she was amused and amazed at herself. That could not have been easy to admit.

Well, since Sondra was estranged from her family, and her work wasn't so great, her life wasn't so perfect after all. Hannah decided she could not be presumptuous to ask after her family or about her living situation. *What the hell, Hannah? Surely, the connection we have dissolves all other sensitivities.*

'You're living here? Moved out? When did that happen?'

'Months back. After David – my husband – found out about John.'

'Your son – Michael, is it? – how is he?'

Sondra's eyes clouded over, and she looked down at her hands before answering. 'I haven't seen Mikey since the day you came to my house. He refuses to see me, wants nothing to do with me anymore.'

'That's awful.' Hannah responded as any mother would. Losing a child was one thing – one had no choice but to accept that one would never see or speak to him again – but if the child was alive and chose not to see you, that was completely different.

Hannah felt torn. Her natural reaction would have been to reach over and cover Sondra's hands with her own in sympathy, in a shared understanding of what it was to lose a child. But some small part of her felt satisfied. It seemed right that Sondra should suffer the consequences of her actions, that her son cutting her out of his life was a fitting punishment. It was uncharacteristic for Hannah to be cruel or anything less than the loving, compassionate Christian she was, but – she had no qualms admitting to herself – it did feel good, even momentarily, to know that Sondra was in pain.

'It's my own doing. Guess I can't blame him. David says I have no choice but to accept the situation and be patient. Maybe things will get better in time.' Sondra didn't sound convinced or convincing.

'You must miss him?'

'I do.' The statement was emphatic. 'I really, really do.' Sondra's eyes drifted away again, a sudden longing appearing in her eyes. 'But he's always been his daddy's boy. We were never that close.'

'John and I were like two peas in a pod, inseparable and so similar.'

'Really? Wow! That must've been great.'

'It was. Eliot – my husband – well, he passed away a few years back, he used to joke that it was unhealthy for us to be so close. He said that if one of us went away, the other would never be able to cope.' Hannah tried to laugh, but it sounded forced and unfamiliar, so she stopped immediately. 'He was right. I'm barely getting through the day.'

There was a brief silence, but Hannah didn't feel that it was awkward or stilted.

'Let's not get sucked into morbid talk.' Hannah made an effort to change the subject and lighten things up. 'So, what are your plans for the rest of your break?'

'Oh, you know, the usual: movies, shopping. I was thinking of some touristy things just to kill the time. Being all alone in this apartment is depressing, so I've been trying to get out every day.'

Hannah nodded, not knowing what to say.

Sondra looked encouraged and chatted on. 'When the leave period started, I was dreading it. Having three weeks of leave was terrifying. So, I went to Durban for a while at the beginning.'

'Oh? That must have been nice. How was the weather?' *Really, Hannah? The weather? How clichéd.*

'Warm, mostly, rained on one day, but *ja*, it was good. I went to the beach a few times. It's been years since I swam in the ocean.' Sondra drained her mug.

'John and Eliot loved the beach. We spent almost every holiday at the coast – Durban, Margate, Southbroom, Ramsgate, Wild Coast, Cape Town too, although I refused to go into the water in Cape Town. It's freezing.'

Sondra laughed. 'I know. I completely agree. Cape Town is for the mountain and the scenery, the friendly people – not the beach. It's bloody miserable.'

'You grew up in Durban, right? Did you see any family?'

'I did.' Sondra leant forwards and looked straight into Hannah's eyes. 'It was quite a trip actually.'

'Oh?'

'Too many things happened.' Sondra's face scrunched up – not quite a grimace, not quite a smile. 'I don't want to bore you.'

'No, please, tell me. I'll stop you if it gets boring.' Hannah glanced at her watch. 'I'm not keeping you from something, am I?' Hannah thought that she owed Sondra the normal sensitivities expected among people – acquaintances – because she had just dropped in unannounced. It was *not* because they were friends though.

'Not at all. I would be flipping channels and deciding on whether to order some takeaways or pretend to cook myself some dinner.' Sondra cleared their tea things and walked to the kitchenette while she spoke and poured herself a glass of water. 'You want something?' Sondra tipped the glass in Hannah's direction.

Hannah shook her head.

'Sure? Okay, maybe later.' It seemed Sondra had decided that this was going to be a long visit. 'Are you okay here? I think we'd be more comfortable on the couch.' Sondra didn't wait for a response. She kicked off her shoes and settled on a two-seater in the living area.

Hannah hesitated. It would be more relaxed in the lounge area, instead of sitting upright on the dining room chair. She made a mental note to herself not to get too comfortable though. 'This is a rental, right? Fully furnished?'

'Yes, that's right. I wasn't going to bother about finding a place and then also furnishing it. This suits me just fine. I was hoping this would be a temporary measure, that I would move back home soon.' A frown creased her brow and made her eyes appear smaller. 'It's fine for now, close to work but damn expensive 'cause I've taken it on a month-to-month basis. Pretty soon, though, I guess I'll have to finalise this.'

'You and your husband? David ...?'

Sondra exhaled loudly. She sounded defeated. 'I've been hopeful. But I think the writing's on the wall. David has agreed to a meeting next week, but it's to talk civilly about the assets, he says ... you know, before the lawyers get us all worked up.'

'And he says it's because of your affair with John?'

Sondra nodded slowly, contemplatively. 'But more because he cannot live with the person I am. He doesn't like me, can't imagine how he ever loved me.' Hannah heard the anguish in Sondra's voice. It must have been hard for a woman like Sondra to be so brutally honest about herself, especially to an almost stranger. 'I've changed though.' The words were whispered but were firm. 'I'm not the same person. If only they could see that and give me another chance.'

'They?'

'I mean Mikey too. I think it was his reaction that sealed it for David. Otherwise, there might have been a chance that David would've forgiven me and taken me back.' Sondra groaned. 'I don't know. Maybe I'm being naïve.' She shifted on the couch. It looked like she couldn't find a comfortable spot.

'So, now what?' Hannah's eyes narrowed. She wondered why Sondra didn't see this as a way out. She was obviously unhappy in her marriage. Why else would she need to run around?

'I really want them to forgive and move on. I'm hopeful while being realistic. I know that it's an impossible situation for them – unforgivable. I want them to see me now and understand that I've changed.' Sondra ran her hands through her dark brown hair and roughly scratched at her scalp. The sound was loud enough for Hannah to hear. It must have thundered in Sondra's head. 'I'll try. There are very few things that I've set my mind to that I haven't achieved. I have to believe that it'll happen, maybe not now, maybe not soon. I'll just have to learn to be patient.' Sondra uttered a sound that was between a cynical laugh and sorrowful whimper.

Hannah stared open-mouthed, imagining the toll this brave front Sondra was presenting was taking on her. Should she say something? Offer encouragement or hope? Did she have it in her?

Hannah rose from her chair. 'Excuse me. I need the bathroom.'

Sondra indicated the way with her hand.

Hannah closed the door behind her and latched it. Her reflection in the mirror showed a woman torn between sympathy and anger, hate and compassion, empathy and feeling that Sondra's predicament was deserved. Hot tears rolled easily – tears that spoke of her confusion. *What am I doing here? Why am I listening to this woman who has caused me pain and a lifetime of sorrow?* Hannah could not answer herself.

She wanted to leave, to be away from this woman and her stories. She knew her as an emotionless, pitiless woman, merciless and self-serving. It was easier to hate her with that view. She dried her eyes and fixed her face as best she could. When she felt composed enough, she breezed back into the living room.

'Oh, my! I didn't realise the time,' Hannah announced cheerily. 'I've taken up enough of your time.' She picked up her phone and put it into her handbag.

'You're leaving?' The voice was puerile and forlorn.

'Yes. Loads to do. But I think traffic would have died down by now.'

'Oh. Okay. Will you ... uh, Hannah, I'd like to see you again.' Sondra shook her head rapidly; she could have been a bobble-head sitting on a car dashboard. 'Is that weird?'

Was it?

'I'll get going then. Sorry, it's quite late.' And without daring to answer the question, Hannah hurried out.

As she drove, she acknowledged her loss and her grief, as though seeing someone else in pain allowed her tears to flow unabated. It became difficult to see. After a few minutes, she turned into a shopping centre and parked. She needed a few minutes to pull herself together. She didn't want to let this woman who had caused her life to be destroyed have such a hold over her, but one doesn't always get what one wants or wishes. No one knew that better than Hannah.

She reached into her bag and pulled out the envelope that contained John's diary, like the coffin that contained John's body. She had been carrying it around with her since she had found it but never had the courage to look at it a second time. She held it up to her face and inhaled. It smelt of nothing.

When she opened it, she couldn't read much, so she put on the internal light. John's neat, child-like writing blurred in front of her eyes. She consciously stopped her tears. She didn't want them to ruin any of the words – the words that were heavy to read, the words that were all she had to try and understand John and his last few months.

John had written diaries before. There had been a teacher at school who'd recommended it. 'It'll help you deal with emotions and make sense of the scary thoughts you have.' When John had mentioned this to Hannah, she had brushed off the teacher's concerns – the teacher surely would not know her son better than she did. Now, though, she had to acknowledge, painful as it was, that she had not been able to see how her child struggled with his emotions or, even worse, had chosen not to see.

There had been times when John had felt anxious. At other times, he could be quiet, disappearing into his room for hours at a time. Nothing unusual there. As an only child, he'd learnt to enjoy his own company. Hannah had never thought to understand what caused this. The incidences weren't often and were over quickly enough. Was it easier for her to think that there was nothing wrong? Maybe because she wanted to believe that he was perfect, she was unable to see the truth. Would reading John's account of his last few months force her to be realistic? He was a good child, a great kid, but no one was perfect.

The pages were filled with descriptions of work and his obsession with Sondra. If the words were to be believed, she was a superwoman: the be-all and end-all of perfection, beautiful, clever, and charming. Everything about her, her professionalism and competence, her interactions with colleagues, her dress style, her feet – there was an entire page of John describing Sondra's feet – seemed larger than life. He didn't see her as ordinary in any way. John had built Sondra up to be the ideal person, the ultimate woman.

Was this love? Infatuation? Obsession? Maybe a combination of all of those. John must have been putty in her hands. There was a sticky note that had probably been attached to a file with hand-written instructions and signed with the initials "SC-E". Sondra Carim-Edwards.

Hannah felt anger boil up from deep inside her as she squashed the yellow gummed paper. There were some drawings interspersed with the narratives too. Flowers, elaborate hearts, suns, stars, and repeatedly, Sondra's name. The letters were drawn thick and coloured in with abstract designs within the borders. How much time must he have spent fantasising and imagining?

Towards the end, after the brutal description of her dismissal of him, there was a stick figure. It was suspended from a bar or rope, similar to the hangman game. As Hannah peered, she saw he had written notes, figures, and calculations alongside. 68 kgs. 3,5 m. Rope: 2m. Duration: 2-3 minutes. *What's this about?* Hannah wondered, and then, it struck her like a bolt of lightning through her heart.

A folded, printed A4 sheet slid out. It looked like a page printed off the internet. It was an article on suicide, specifically on hanging. Hannah vaguely recalled the paramedic asking her if John had tried to kill himself before, as well as his surprise at hearing that it had been his first attempt. As she read, it was clear that people often fail a few times before eventually getting it right. John had done his homework. John had made sure he would succeed.

Hannah used to tease John about his meticulousness. He was a perfectionist, even as a young child. This time, she loathed his pedantic nature. John was careful in his planning and execution of tasks and had applied this thoroughness to his final mission.

If he'd made a mistake, perhaps she could have saved him, and then, Hannah would have known. Had she known that he needed help, she would have moved heaven and earth to get it for him. But that was not to be. He'd researched, planned, and executed the perfect suicide.

Hannah bawled and smacked the book against the steering wheel hard, then harder, again and again. Maybe she should have prepared John for a more realistic world. Life was tough, and one had to be tougher to live it. Maybe if she had included some tough love in her parenting style, it would have helped him to grow strong. Then maybe, after one disappointment, the first time that something didn't work out perfectly, John wouldn't have killed himself. The realisation, like so many others from the past months, jarred Hannah's body and wracked it with silent sobs and regrets.

After a long while, she replaced the diary into the envelope and put it back into her handbag. She started the car and drove home.

22

CHANCES MISSED AND LOST

When the day finally arrived that she was to meet David, Sondra was a bundle of nerves. She changed clothes twice before reverting to the simple jeans and shirt she had put on initially. She read and reread her letter to Michael, tweaking a word or two, adding and then removing another impassioned plea. She printed it and placed it unsealed in an envelope before she changed anything else. *Less is more*, she reminded herself. Sincerity and simplicity felt authentic. She hoped Michael would feel that too when he read the letter.

David had texted the night before, confirming the appointment. She needed no reminders. She responded positively. So much depended on this. She would send only positive vibes out into the universe. *When did you become so spiritual, Sondra – you who believed that you were the mistress of your own destiny, you who believed that you could achieve anything on your own?*

Sondra felt queasy. The chicken and salad she had eaten earlier threatened to reappear. Slowly, she sipped a glass of chilled water and commanded herself to calm down. To get her mind off of things, she started singing songs that she remembered from the eighties and nineties, silently at first, then softly. When she got to her car, she tuned into a local music radio station. She recognised a number of songs and sang along, making up her own words when she didn't know the actual ones. That did the trick, and she arrived at the coffee shop in no time, feeling like her sanity had been restored somewhat.

She was a few minutes early, but David was already there. He stood up when he saw her, and she almost leant in for a hug. He pulled the chair out for her so that it stood firmly between them. They greeted each other convivially, then Sondra asked after Michael.

'He's well, just started exams.'

Sondra nodded. She hadn't even realised.

David's eyes narrowed while she seated herself. 'Something's different.'

Her back straightened. *What do you mean?*

'Aah, your hair. It's not straight!'

Sondra ran her hands over her hair self-consciously. 'Thought I'd give it a break from the chemicals.'

'Suits you. Makes you look younger.' David had always been observant and complimentary about her appearance, always the considerate husband. But she had not reciprocated much. She had convinced herself that she hadn't needed to follow any conventions or expectations as a wife. "We can make our own rules about what works for us," she had declared at the beginning of their life as a couple. That was a lifetime ago though, and so much had changed.

After they'd ordered, Sondra enquired about Michael's exams, then added, 'I hope the turmoil in his life – in our lives – isn't affecting him.'

'You know, I was worried about that too. But kids are resilient. I've been keeping a discreet eye. Don't want him to think I'm watching him. He seems to have put everything aside. I wondered if he was fooling himself, but I think he's good. I'm quietly optimistic.'

So, Michael hadn't missed her. She acknowledged her internal disappointment, trying to keep it off of her face. 'Good. I'm glad.'

'Things could have gone either way, I guess. But we're lucky with Mikey. He's a well-adjusted kid. What happened upset him – in fact, it tore him up – but he kept a brave front most of the time, always letting me know that he's fine, and I think he tried hard to ensure that he is, as if *he* doesn't want *me* to worry.'

'Or maybe I never really mattered anyway.' Sondra sounded and felt bitter, her anger directed at herself.

David's eyes narrowed. 'Where's that coming from? You can be a lot of things, Sondra, but I've never known you to be self-pitying.'

'You're right. Yes. I didn't mean that.' She wanted him to see the positive side of her, right? That remark was completely uncharacteristic for the old and new Sondra. *Where did it come from?*

'How've you been? Still on leave? How was Durban?' Thankfully, David was moving the conversation along.

'Durban was great. I didn't stay long. A week was enough. I didn't really have a plan when I got there, but well, things turned out well.'

'Oh?' He looked at her quizzically.

'It's a long story.'

He nodded but didn't push. She knew it was because he had long given up on her sharing stuff with him.

'There were some problems at work.' She gave a derisive laugh. 'Well, the problem will still be there when I return on Monday. Bet you would never guess in a hundred years.'

David cocked his head and fixed her with an inquisitorial look.

'I've been given an official warning. I messed up a couple of accounts.' Sondra gave a rueful smile.

'What? No way! You messed up? I don't believe it!' His laugh sounded incredulous. 'A warning?'

'Yep, an official one that'll go on my record. And they want me to go for counselling.'

David whistled in amazement.

'Yeah. I decided that I needed to address as much as I could personally—privately first. I've never been comfortable sharing with strangers.'

'Not only strangers.' David scrunched his mouth up. He wasn't being confrontational, just commenting fairly.

'You're right about that. I've always kept myself to myself, fiercely guarding myself from everyone – strangers and loved ones. You too. I'm sorry about that, David.'

David's face darkened for a moment. *Did he too wish that things could have been different?* 'It's done. It's over. Nothing we can do about it now.'

'Hmmm. If only we could change things.' Sondra's nostrils flared as she acknowledged the consequences of her behaviour and attitude with those that mattered: David and Mikey. 'I've had time to think. I've realised that this has ruined my relationships. It all relates to my past, my childhood. I had to confront it.'

He tilted his head to the side again, his brows pulling towards one another.

'Don't look so shocked. Is it that hard to believe?' Sondra's lips disappeared into her tightly shut mouth, and she bit down hard. 'I guess ...' She paused, then took David's silence as a cue to continue. '... I've done lots of reflecting the past couple of weeks. You were right – right about me and right to get me to do that.'

David watched her warily. 'Me?'

'When you said I should take a long, hard look at myself. I did, David, and I don't like what I see. I ... it doesn't matter now. I'm a different person. I've looked at myself critically, and I saw what Mikey sees, what you see. It's not pretty.' Sondra looked away from David as a harrowing memory surfaced. 'Mikey called me a ... he called me a whore! What kind of mother am I—what kind of person's own son swears at her like that?'

'Don't take that to heart. He was angry and upset that day.'

'I know, I know. But still, that's what he sees.' Sondra shuddered. 'I've really tried to see myself through your eyes and Mikey's. It's not been easy to admit, and it'll be a long time before I'm able to feel differently about myself.'

The waitress came over with their order balanced on a round black tray. Sondra watched David while he watched the waitress place a glass of water, his coffee, her tea, milk, and a glass cylinder containing sugar and sweetener sachets between them. *What will you make of this?* She was baring her soul, opening her heart to him. She was being more candid with him now than she had ever been. He would be interested, but would he care? And most importantly, would it make a difference?

Now that she had started, she felt compelled to continue. Even if he didn't change his mind about her, about their marriage, he should know this new her, the *real* Sondra.

'You were saying?' His eyes were concentrating on sweetening his coffee. That was encouraging. He wanted to hear more.

'I've changed, David. I have. I want to change more. I want to become the person I can be, the person I feel I am deep down, the real Sondra, not the one who was so careful about protecting herself, shielding herself from any chance of being hurt. Or the callous, cold-hearted bitch that uses and abuses people for her benefit.' She paused to sip some water. Her mouth felt dry. Voicing the words that she had been playing over in her head for weeks was difficult. It was strange to be sharing herself. It made her feel vulnerable and exposed. There was nothing else for it. She would have to finish what she started. 'At least I've taken the first step. I've realised that I've built up a wall around myself, that I didn't let anyone get too close, that I ... I only ever thought about myself and how I could use people to get what I wanted. That's going to change. It has already.'

'I'm ... I'm impressed.' David's eyes searched hers. 'Are you going to be all right? I'm no professional, but this sort of thing is serious. Are you sure this is what you want?'

'Yes, I'm sure.' She heard how categorical she sounded. 'It's not easy, but it's right. I feel it.'

'Why?'

Sondra shook her head and frowned at David, not following his question.

'I mean, why now? Are you doing this for yourself or because you think it'll change Mikey's mind?'

He had every reason to doubt her motives. She would explain and do whatever was necessary to convince him. He had to see how upfront and true she was being. He knew her better than anyone. If she was pretending, he would see through her. They both knew that.

'Of course, I hope that Mikey'll change his mind and give me another chance. But even if that doesn't happen—' Sondra squeezed her eyes shut as she contemplated that real, undesirable possibility. '—I need this. I need to do this if I have any chance of becoming a whole person.' She took another sip. She had become introspective and ... spiritual. She wanted David to see this and realise it was for real, but she also didn't want him to think she was trying too hard. *I mustn't overthink this. Just be frank and forthright, and David will hear me.* 'Fuck, I hope I'm not being dramatic. But you're so right, this *is* serious.'

David was still staring at her. She enjoyed having his attention. When did she stop appreciating that about him? Maybe she never really did appreciate him at all. Maybe she took it for granted like so many things about him ... and their marriage.

She continued. 'I've taken stock, looked at my life, looked at the person I am, the one I've become. Sure, maybe I wouldn't have done this if ... if John hadn't killed himself, or rather—I mean, this internal reflection wouldn't've happened if you and Mikey hadn't found out. I realise that. But it did happen. Then things were set in motion. I moved out. I lost you, lost Mikey, maybe forever. No. No! I mustn't think that. I have to believe that, in time, he will see me. When he sees I'm different, he may be able to forgive me, to let me back in his life.' Sondra's little speech was voiced vociferously but quietly. It should have exhausted her, but she felt strangely empowered ... until David spoke again.

He shook his head. 'I don't want to be negative, Sondra, but don't count on it. He's not in any space to think about that.'

Sondra's bottom lip quivered, and she pressed her fingers against it, willing it to stop. She stretched out her right hand, her palm facing up, and leaned over the table towards David. 'You're right. I shouldn't jump the gun. One step at a time. I'll be optimistic but realistic.' She sipped her tea. It was tepid. She topped it up from the white ceramic teapot and took another sip.

He leant back in his chair and interlaced his fingers behind his head. 'Well, this is quite something. I want you to be happy, Sonds. It'll be tough, like you say, but if anyone can do it, you can.'

Good old David, always her greatest support and cheerleader.

'Mmm, thanks.' The words were muffled. She wanted more than his support and encouragement ... so much more.

He continued looking at her, trying to understand, trying to know.

Did she have the courage to ask? 'Do you mean that? That you want me to be happy?'

'I do. You mean a lot to me, Sonds, and always will.'

Sondra moved the cups out of the way and again opened her hand to him on the table between them. 'I feel the same way, David. I love you. I realise now how much. Is there any chance, *any* chance at all for us?'

David looked at her hand but did not move to take it. 'No, Sondra. I'm sorry.'

'Oh.' It was not the answer she'd hoped for. The ground disappeared beneath her, and she was falling. She felt desperate. But he was still there, still listening, so there was still hope. She was not going to give up.

'I was telling you about Durban,' Sondra remarked. Would he think she was clutching at straws, trying to keep him interested, trying to get him to see her as she was now?

'Yes.' He nodded, bringing his hands to his lap. Sondra watched them disappear behind the table. It hurt that he moved his hands away from her touch. It wasn't fun to have the tables turned, to be on the receiving end of rejection.

'There's so much about me you don't know. I'll give you the short version.' Sondra summed up her early years with her mother and how her mother had died, how Abdul hadn't been there for her, and about the complications of her mother being Coloured and Christian and her father being Indian and Muslim.

David waved his hand dismissively. 'Religion never was an issue for me ... or you?'

'Right. That we agreed on, without ever having discussed it. I was raised Christian and Muslim but never really identified with either. I was never religious, but of late ...' Sondra laughed self-consciously. '... I've become spiritual.' Sondra's eyes locked onto David's. If she couldn't get through to him any other way, she'd use her eyes and her voice to do that. 'Even before my mother died, I was sent to *madressah*. My father, Abdul Carim, made sure of it. As a child, I would read the Quran and fast in *Ramadaan*. I was raised Christian too because my mom was. She was not overly devout, but we did go to church occasionally.'

'That must have been confusing?'

'No, not really. I guess, as kids, we're accepting without questioning. It was my normal. Then everything changed when I went to live with my father's family. The problem was that I never felt like I belonged. The two older kids made me feel like an outcast.'

'You have brothers and sisters?' David could not hide his surprise.

Sondra smiled outwardly but grimaced internally. David, her husband of twenty years, did not know this. How could she have possibly thought that keeping her secrets locked away would protect her? If anything, it had been to her detriment. She soldiered on. 'Three half-sisters and a half-brother. My younger siblings, Salma and Abdullah, were nice to me. Not so much the two older sisters.'

'And who else? Was there a stepmother?'

'Yes. Sarah, a quiet woman but strong in her own way.'

'Tell me more. Your sisters were ugly to you?'

'Not really, or not obviously. I guess they were warned by the parents. They ignored me, just sort of pretended I wasn't there. The older ones at least. Nothing was actually verbalised. It was all very subtle. But I was made to feel inferior because, well, I'm half-Coloured.'

'Couldn't have been easy or fun for you.'

Sondra shrugged. 'I don't want this to turn into a sob story. I was young and led a pretty normal but sheltered life until then. I had just lost my mother, and my whole life was turned upside down overnight. In the beginning, I hardly noticed anything. I was alone, confused, grieving my mother.'

'Your stepmother? How did she treat you?'

'Aunty Sarah? Ma. I call her "Ma" now.' Sondra smiled. The thought of Ma relaxed her. 'She was good to me but not very affectionate. It couldn't have been easy for her. She was forced to bring me up – the illegitimate child of her husband, living proof and a constant reminder of his infidelity.'

David's gaze was piercing. 'I hardly know you, Sondra Carim-Edwards. So much about you ... your past ... it's a mystery. How long did you live with them?'

She felt relieved. His questions meant that he was curious. She wanted to tell him everything so that he could understand and know her better. Maybe, just maybe, then there would be a chance.

'A few years. When I left for varsity after *matric*, I never returned. I pretended that I had no family. I was independent and needed no one.'

He raised his eyebrows and pulled his mouth in on itself. 'Yes, I found that out quickly, didn't I?'

'Yeah.' Sondra steeled herself against the discomfort of this new territory – opening up and sharing herself. She forged on. 'You and Michael suffered because of how I related to people based on the need to protect myself. To prevent myself from ever relying on others. I've changed, David. I'm trying really hard to be a more authentic person, more giving and more open to receiving love. If you guys give me a chance, you'll see.'

David put his arms on the table and interlaced his fingers. He looked down at his hands. What was he thinking? He would be sceptical. Of course, he would be.

'I want a chance to meet with Michael and tell him all this face to face. If he can see how I've changed, the effort I'm making, maybe he'll forgive me.'

'Sondra, that's up to him. I'm not getting between you two. He's almost an adult, sensible and mature, but he's grown up fast these past couple of months. He's become so responsible too.'

A shiver ran up Sondra's spine. Her boy was growing up. He was becoming a man, and she was missing it. 'I need my son, and he needs his mom too.' The voice was childlike in its need.

David sighed and folded his arms across his chest. He was done discussing this.

'Listen. I've written Mikey a letter. I can't send an e-mail because I think he's blocked me. My e-mails have been bouncing. Please, won't you give it to him?' Sondra produced the envelope from her handbag, the envelope that bore the weight of her aspirations, wishes, desires, and optimistic confidence. It felt warm in her hands like it was alive with a heart that beat in tune with her own.

David's eyes darted to it.

'You can read it if you're concerned. I don't mind. It's not sealed. If he gets it from you, he might be more inclined to read it.'

David leant forwards and placed his arms on the table. His eyes moved between the envelope and Sondra's face. She could tell that he was debating what he should do.

'I'll never give up on my son, never give up on us. Don't overthink this, please.'

David took the envelope, held it loosely in his right hand, and tapped it on his upturned left palm. 'Okay. I can't guarantee anything. He might not read it. He might just throw it out.'

Sondra closed her eyes briefly. The possibility had occurred to her too. 'I know, I know, but I'm trying to be positive.'

'Even if he does read it, he might be sceptical.'

And he'd have every right to be. Michael didn't like her. In fact, he hated her. Why would he trust her?

'Don't expect a miracle. We don't have magic wands that can make everything okay just like that.'

'No. No, we don't.'

Her stomach was tied up in knots. Her throat constricted. She had said all she could. A silence extended between them. Sondra felt exposed but, surprisingly, not weak. Revealing some of her past and her secrets felt right. Perhaps if she had shared more of herself, given and received more earlier in their lives, instead of trying to control everything and everyone, things would have turned out differently.

She stifled a sigh. It was pointless rehashing things in hindsight. Things were as they were. She had to think about the here and now.

'Sondra.' There was a heaviness in David's tone that made him sound serious and apprehensive.

'Yes?'

'There's something I wanted to talk to you about.'

'Yes. Yes, of course.' He had his agenda for the meeting too, and she had monopolised it. *Typical*, she chided herself silently. 'The divorce details.' She looked at him expectantly, but he said nothing. A glimmer of hope fluttered deep down. Maybe he was reconsidering. She sat dead still, but every fibre of her being was ignited in anticipation, arching towards him, reaching out and yearning for a reciprocal movement in her direction. It was an effort to keep still and quiet.

'Something's happened.'

The hairs on Sondra's arm stood up. The words were simple but loaded. She knew that she would not like what followed.

'I've met someone.'

Three simple words: "I've met someone".

You've met someone.

Once she got control of her mouth, she uttered, 'You've met someone?' The question drained out of her.

He nodded, and the force of emotions displayed on his face made her think he was struggling to keep her gaze.

'You've met someone.'

Who? When? How? Who? WHO? The silent questions raged in her head, screaming and banging against her denial, her hope, her prayer, banging until they burst through and erupted in a solitary tear that escaped the corner of her eye. She didn't move to wipe it away, but she didn't need to. It dried on her cheek.

The answers didn't matter. There was someone else for David, someone who deserved him, someone who would love him, cherish him, appreciate him, someone who would be loved in return, someone who would make him the centre of her universe. That someone was not Sondra. She saw herself in those waters again, in a stormy ocean, her body being thrown around by the fierce waves, the wind being knocked out of her, her being sucked under by the dark, swirling waves, enveloping her whole.

'I wanted to tell you in person.'

Considerate, noble David wanted to do right by her. He wanted to spare her the anguish of learning the news from someone else.

'I see.' That was all she could muster, so she repeated, 'I see.'

'I'm guessing you don't want to know details, but anyway, it's early days. It's only been a couple of weeks. It's too soon to tell. It may fizzle out or ... I don't know, develop.'

Where was the new Sondra – the one who would be able to take this news graciously, the one who would be selfless enough to wish him well, the one who loved him enough to put him first?

'Whatever happens, David, I hope it will be the right thing for you.' The words were strangled out of her.

David looked at her intently, probably wondering if she was being sincere. She wondered the same thing. It hurt, she admitted. It hurt to know that he could look at someone else. It hurt more because she knew that she had created this new reality. Suddenly, she realised how *he* must have felt in all the years that they were together and she had been unfaithful to him. She had hurt him, and it was only in this moment that she realised how much. She wanted to reach out and touch him, caress his arm with her hand, impart her new understanding of how he must have felt, apologise, beg for forgiveness ... She wanted to be there for him in ways that she never was before. She wanted to let him know she loved him.

Her hand reached over and lay on his arm. She let it rest a moment. He didn't move it or his arm away. He looked down at her hand, his eyes shielded from her view. She couldn't read him. After a long moment, she slowly pulled her hand back.

'I should go now. I will ... I'll wait.'

David raised a questioning eyebrow.

Sondra took a breath. 'I'll wait. Mikey will be in touch. I feel it.'

He nodded and smiled. At least he didn't discourage her or shatter her hopes.

'Take care of yourself. Thank you for taking care of Mikey too.' Sondra rose and pulled her bag onto her shoulder. 'You've always been there for him in more ways than I have ever been and now single-handedly. I know it and appreciate it.'

David rose too and came to stand close to her. He took both her hands in his and squeezed for a moment. 'Thanks for saying that.'

It looked like he was thinking of leaning in for a hug. Sondra found that she was torn. She so wanted to reach out to him and touch him in a way that would let him sense her as she was now. She wanted him to know her by touching her. Her skin, her breath, her blood, her cells would scream her sincerity. He would feel her truth. But if she hugged him, she was afraid that, in her vulnerable state, she might buckle. The tears threatening would spill over, and she would not be able to stop them.

'Goodbye, David,' she mumbled and shuffled out.

23

CHILDLESS MOTHERS

Hannah quickened her pace. How had she managed to run so late? She had wanted to be in control of this meeting. She was the one who had sent Sondra the venue and time, and she was the one who had carefully planned how she would approach Sondra. She guessed Sondra would have arrived on time fifteen minutes before. Hannah contemplated sending a message, cancelling or rescheduling, but knew that that would be a cop-out.

As she reached the end of the path and turned towards the rose gardens in the Botanical Gardens, she saw Sondra. She stopped running and paused for a moment to catch her breath. Sondra hadn't noticed her yet.

Sondra was leaning against a railing, looking at but not seeing the beds of beautifully coloured roses that stretched down in a stepped formation. Her red *takkies* seemed to shout merrily in contrast to the rest of her; she looked drab in all beige without make-up. She must have sensed being watched and turned. She waved at Hannah, then reached for her sunglasses that were perched on her head like an Alice band and placed them delicately on her nose.

They walked towards each other, neither moving fast nor slow.

Hannah spoke first. 'I'm sorry I'm late. Typical Joburg: two traffic lights out, and there's chaos!'

'It's no problem. I'm in no rush. How are you?'

'I'm ... I'm okay, I guess.'

Sondra nodded her head slowly and raised her eyebrows, crease lines appearing on her forehead.

Hannah swallowed. She wouldn't let Sondra unnerve her. 'No, that's not true. I'm terrible. My therapist suggests being honest about that. Acknowledging and admitting how I really feel to others forces me to be honest with myself as well.'

'Has it helped?'

Hannah laughed. 'No, not at all. I still feel terrible. The good thing is that at least I'm not pretending anymore. You try to present a picture of being strong. I don't know why.'

'Neither do I. Nobody really cares.'

Hannah was startled by the bitterness in Sondra's words. She wasn't sure how to respond.

'Oh shit! I didn't mean that. I did mean it, but I shouldn't be feeling sorry for myself, right? I only have myself to blame.' Sondra's tone dropped and softened. 'Let's start this again, shall we?'

'If you forgive my tardiness, sure.' Hannah recognised that they were speaking casually to one another. When did that happen?

'Hi, Hannah.' Sondra added what looked like a grateful smile.

Hannah returned the smile. 'Hi, Sondra.'

'It was a good idea to meet here. It's nice. People walking with their kids and dogs. I came early and walked around a bit. Wasn't sure I would find the spot, but you described it perfectly. You know this place well?'

'Yes. We've lived around here all our lives and would often come for walks.'

'You and your husband? With John?'

'Yes. And with my mother and Eliot's family too. We used to picnic here regularly, but not for a long time now.'

'Family was huge for you. I guess that's normal for most people. You must miss them – John, your husband, your mother. Life's a bitch, hey?' Sondra's eyes bulged, and she laughed to cover up her indelicate language. 'Sorry, I didn't mean to offend.'

Hannah laughed too. 'Don't worry about it.' Sondra was just being forthright and had spoken her mind. That was a good thing, right? She was not guarding her words. Hannah indicated a bench in the shade of a nearby tree. 'Shall we sit?'

She walked ahead and heard Sondra follow. When they sat, Hannah opened her bag and pulled out two bottles of water. She handed Sondra one and drank deeply from the other. 'I'm parched. Been sitting in traffic for almost an hour. Luckily, the ice cream vendors keep water.'

Sondra placed the bottle at her feet, propped her elbows on her thighs, and leant her chin on her fists. Hannah was able to observe her without being watched. Sondra looked sad and exhausted, maybe even defeated.

'Sondra, you're looking tired. Are you okay?'

'I'm okay. Got back to work this week. Just getting back into the routine again, I guess.'

'Yeah, I can relate. I don't particularly enjoy work, but it pays the bills. At least it keeps me occupied.'

'Yes, I agree. There's much to be said about making sure your mind has something to focus on. I'm glad you wanted to meet. I had something to look forward to since you called.'

The first time they met, Sondra refused to talk to her and threw her out. Now, that same woman was looking forward to seeing her! What a turnaround.

'My therapist, Mary, she's been helpful. It was her suggestion that I talk to you again. It's weird. She thinks that perhaps, if I reach out to you, it would be good for both of us.'

'She thinks I need help?' The retort sounded indignant. Then Sondra shrugged her shoulders and looked resigned. 'She's right. I *am* miserable.'

'Work?'

'Life! Everything's messed up. It's my doing – all my fault. Can't blame anyone but myself. Enough about me. The reason I wanted to see you is so that I can forget about all my own drama. Tell me, Hannah, how're you doing? Really.'

Hannah sighed. 'It's damn difficult. Impossible some days. I must admit, though, the impossible days are becoming more spread out. Now, most days are just terrible, and a few are bearable. I guess what they say about time is true. I'll never be the same or truly happy again. A part of me died when John did – a big part of me. I've changed fundamentally. When who you are or how you recognise yourself is related to another ... I know myself as John's mother. Without him, I've lost the most important part of me.'

Hannah took a deep breath. It felt weird to be talking about her grief to someone other than Mary – weird but not entirely undoable. She continued. 'I'm not complaining or feeling sorry for myself. Expressing the thoughts and emotions help. I realise that. For a long time, I kept it all bottled up, refused to talk about John. My mother – bless her – she tried to make me talk for months. Then she passed away before I learnt how to.'

'You miss her?'

'Very much, almost as much as I miss John. I'm grateful that she was with me in those last few months. She encouraged me, insisted I find out what happened, why John did what he did. I asked friends without much luck. Then I found the diary and spoke to one of his friends from work, a fellow intern.'

'You didn't give up. That's what's important.' Sondra's words sounded hollow.

'Talking to his friend at work, Samantha something – I can't remember the surname –Sam ... uh something with an "M". Sam and the diary led me to you.'

'Oh, and I was awful, wasn't I – when you called and were brave enough to come and confront me at my house?'

'Yeah. But it was a small miracle when you called me. In the beginning, though, I resented that too. I was wary of your motivation, unsure if you were only doing it to appease your conscience.'

'I don't blame you. The way I treated you, I would've been sceptical too.'

'After I left your apartment that first time, I was angry, didn't think straight. Then after a few days, I was able to think calmly. I accepted that you were being sincere. I knew you were struggling too and trying, trying to do the right thing and be better.'

'Yeah! Fat lot that's helped me!'

'What do you mean? You're a new Sondra. The Sondra I first met is worlds apart from who you are now. You're compassionate and empathetic and not in a pitying way. I appreciate that. Many people change around you after you've experienced a loss, treat you like you're glass, as though you'll break if they speak in anything louder than a whisper.' Hannah groaned. 'It's irritating. Then you start acting the way people think you should. You see yourself the way they see you, and it's a vicious cycle. Before you know it, you're at rock bottom: depressed because you've lost your child and depressed because that's what people expect you to be.'

'Sounds awful. Makes me realise how pathetic I am to feel sorry for myself. My situation is different. I brought this on myself, not consciously or wilfully. But my selfish, cruel actions have estranged me from my family.'

'No progress there?'

Sondra shook her head and then dropped it into her hands, covering her face. Her shoulders shook, and Hannah realised that she was silently sobbing. Hannah wasn't sure how to react. Should she try and comfort her? What would she say? After a minute, Sondra recovered. She wiped her eyes with a tissue she retrieved from her pocket. She grabbed the bottle at her feet, tipped it in Hannah's direction, said, 'Thanks,' then opened it.

'You okay?' Hannah placed a tentative hand on Sondra's shoulder.

'No, not really. After Durban, I was so positive. I thought facing my past and addressing my demons was enough to convince David and Michael that I'd changed. I thought ... I hoped that they would forgive me and take me back.' She started sobbing again. This time, she did not bother hiding it.

Hannah put her arm around Sondra and pulled her close. Sondra sobbed into her shoulder. Apart from a few handshakes, the two women had never touched each other before. Not in this way – in need, a need to comfort and be comforted. It was a wonder Sondra's touch didn't scald her, that her tears didn't burn her like acid. Hannah took a deep breath and allowed her true feelings to surface, her heartfelt words to be voiced.

'These things take time. It's only been a few weeks. They must learn to trust again. You'll have to be patient. It won't happen overnight.' Hannah had heard similar platitudes and hoped that she sounded sincere. The words didn't really help, but if they were said with feeling, they would be better received.

Sondra mumbled something between sobs.

'What? I can't hear you.'

But Sondra didn't speak again. After a couple of minutes, she stopped crying, and after a few more, she found her voice. 'This is ridiculous. I have wronged *you*, caused *you* such pain and sorrow in *your* life. And here you are, comforting *me*.' Sondra stood up and started pacing back and forth in front of the bench. 'Aargh! So much for having changed, hey? Still the typical, selfish Sondra.'

Hannah could see the irony of the situation. What surprised her more was her own response. Why did she not feel outraged by Sondra? Had she forgotten what this woman had caused? That John took his life because of her? Because she used and abused and tossed him aside when she had had her fill? Now though, she felt sympathy towards Sondra and wanted to comfort her.

Sondra stopped pacing. The women stared at each other, both gobsmacked and confused. Hannah was trying to make sense of things, and she was certain that Sondra was too. Did each see herself in the other?

Sondra found the bench again and sat down heavily next to Hannah. 'Please. I don't want to make this about me. I want to listen to you. I don't know if I can help. What you're going through ... I don't know. But I'm here. Tell me why you wanted to meet.'

Hannah was at a loss. The reasons for wanting to meet Sondra seemed insignificant now. She wanted to say all the things she had not said the first time they had met and had not been allowed to, all the things that she should have said the second time but had only thought about in retrospect. She had been persuaded by Mary that confronting Sondra and explaining her feelings may help her to move on, to get closure. Now, she wasn't so sure. She took a long, slow breath and tried.

'When I found out about you and John, I blamed you for everything. I wanted to hurt you. I felt that, if you saw me, recognised me as his mother, him as a young man, still just a child, you would feel guilt, remorse, shame – anything that would force you to take responsibility. I was distraught. I wanted to hurt you as you had hurt me and my baby.'

'You wanted revenge. I guess that's natural. Any person, any mother would feel that way. Punish me. I deserve it.'

'Punish you?' Hannah snorted. 'What should I do? Beat you? Swear at you? I don't think that would be satisfying or give me any relief whatsoever, not now anyway. I've come a long way too. I understand that every person is responsible for his or her own actions.' Hannah turned her head and looked towards the sound of the fountain that was just out of view. 'John's suicide may have been precipitated by the affair with you, but it can't be any one person's fault. I can't blame you.'

Hannah sensed Sondra moved, but she didn't look at her until she felt a gentle touch on her arm.

'Do you blame yourself, Hannah?'

She didn't meet Sondra's intent gaze.

'I can understand if you do. You need to make sense of it. The only way to do that is to have a reason. If you no longer blame me, and you don't blame John, you need something or someone to take responsibility.'

Hannah's eyes brimmed with tears until they spilt and silently rolled down her face.

'It's not your fault, Hannah.'

'Isn't it? Was I not a good enough mother? Why did he feel he couldn't come to me, talk to me, share his pain with me? Maybe I didn't make myself available to him. Maybe he thought I would judge him.' Hannah heard her loud voice quiver. 'Maybe he thought I would be disappointed. Maybe he felt ashamed or thought I'd be ashamed of him.' Hannah's breath tore at her throat as tears ran freely but quietly. 'If he knew how much I loved him – that my love was unconditional and pure – if he knew that, then he would've known that I'd forgive him anything and help him through anything.'

This time, Sondra's arm wrapped around Hannah's shoulder and gently pulled Hannah against her.

'If he doubted me, then that was my doing, then I didn't instil enough confidence in him. He wasn't able to trust me. He didn't trust me to tell me what was wrong. I wasn't worthy of his trust, his love. So, I got what I deserved.'

Sondra patted Hannah on the shoulder. 'You don't really believe that, do you? That's silly talk. He loved you, adored you. And he did trust you. I think ... he probably just decided. It wasn't like he was in a dilemma and wanted a sounding board. If anyone could've talked him out of it, it would've been you. He must've known that. He hid it from you because he was so determined to do it.'

'What? What are you saying?' Hannah pulled away, frowning and shaking her head.

'I'm sorry. I'm confusing you. Ignore that. Ignore me.' Sondra moved away and took a meticulous sip from her bottle. 'I do know he adored you, Hannah. When we first ... you know ... got together, he spoke about you often. It was clear that he adored you and that you were his hero. He admired and respected you. I remember feeling jealous. Michael and I have never been affectionate or close, ever. That's my fault.'

'What do you mean?'

'Motherhood isn't my strong suit. I kept him ... I mean, I ... I didn't let myself get too close to Michael, was never open or affectionate. He learnt early on, I suppose, that I would reject any attempts he made to hug or chat.'

'Why? You love Michael, right?'

'Of course!' Sondra's answer was instant and unequivocal. 'Loving him was not the problem. Showing him my love, allowing him to get close, to receive his love – that's what I'm no good at.'

'Oh.'

'That's me. Or rather, the person I made myself become.'

'You weren't always that way?'

'No. I grew up with a warm and tender mother. She showed me true, unconditional love. But as a child, she was my only family. I didn't know cousins, uncles, aunts. She wasn't close to her family. My father wasn't interested in knowing me, but I didn't mind, not really. I didn't know any different, so I wasn't aware that I was missing out. My mother, Beryl, was my whole world. I wanted for nothing or no one.'

'What changed? Why did you change?'

'That's a long, not-so-pretty story. I don't want to bore you.'

Hannah didn't push her, even though she was curious.

'If you want to talk about it ... I'm here to listen.'

'That's kind of you. I appreciate that. You, dear Hannah, have enough sorrow in your life. I don't want to burden you with mine.'

Hannah drank the last of her water.

'How're you feeling now?' Sondra asked softly.

'Okay. The old cliché, you know, about how a good cry helps? It does. At least, temporarily.'

'And otherwise? How's it been going?' Sondra tilted her head to the side. Hannah sensed that she cared.

'I'm, uh ... I don't want to pretend. I'm awful. Most days are a struggle. Getting through every day ...' The words got lost in her throat.

'I'm sorry.'

'It is what it is. The therapy has been helping. I don't go as often though. It's too much of the same thing now. It'll take a lifetime to accept. I can't rush or pretend. It'll happen as it should. I'm open to the healing. When the time is right, it'll naturally happen, I think, I hope. It doesn't matter when and how. I can't think about that, can't worry about tomorrow. Getting through each day is all I can cope with right now.'

'You're very strong and brave, Hannah. I admire you.'

Hannah half-grunted and half-groaned. She didn't feel brave or strong and certainly not worthy of admiration. 'I think we must start walking back. It'll be dark pretty soon. I'm exhausted all of a sudden.' Hannah could feel the tiredness creep over her from the tips of her toes to the ends of her hair.

Sondra nodded. 'Yes, okay.'

Hannah pushed her body off the bench. They walked in silence, unhurried, until they got to the car park.

'That's me.' Hannah pointed to her early model *Corolla*. 'Mom's taxi.' Then she laughed but not cynically. 'Mom! I'm no one's mom.'

'You are, Hannah. You will always be John's mom, just like I'll always be Michael's, even though he wants nothing to do with me.'

How similar we are now, Hannah thought, *both pining for sons who have disappeared from our lives.*

'Goodbye, Sondra.' Hannah got in, buckled up, and reversed out. She could still see Sondra in her rear-view mirror when she reached the stop sign. She raised her arm out of the window in a short wave and saw Sondra wave back. Then she turned into the road and drove away.

Back home, she fell into bed, and for the first time in a long time, she slept deeply and solidly through the night.

24

THE STRANGEST OF PLACES

In the days that followed, Sondra made herself focus on work, gym, basic cooking and cleaning and mindless entertainment like TV. The routine was good; it meant she didn't have to think, just do. Still she resisted doing more than was necessary – she simply did not feel it.

The days became weeks, and still, there was no news from Michael. A couple of times, she almost gave in to temptation and called David to ask him whether Mikey had read the note and what his reaction had been. But how would she talk to Michael? How could she ever again? She pushed the thoughts and questions out of her mind. She didn't want to know.

One thing that did come from the weeks that flowed endlessly before Sondra was regular get-togethers with Hannah, precipitated by their previous meeting in the rose garden. The more time they spent together, the more Sondra understood that having someone like Hannah in her life, someone that she could talk to and confide in, was what had been missing from her life.

They shared meals and time, talking about their pasts, their losses, the undeniable things that connected them. Sondra grew to realise how much talking with Hannah helped. Sharing her fears and doubts about work and the anxiety that she felt about Michael, verbalising these things made the world of difference to her.

There was one cool Saturday evening at Sondra's apartment where Hannah shared about herself. Sondra hadn't known that Hannah grew up on a farm and asked many questions about farm life. Hannah also told her about being young and in love with Eliot, how they married young and had John quickly. Went she first moved to Johannesburg for university, Hannah lived at a boarding house until she married Eliot.

Hannah seemed to come to a realisation in that moment. She stopped mid-sentence and smiled at Sondra. 'Your story, Sondra, has really helped me recognise how quick people are to judge one another without knowing the circumstances.'

Hannah also shared with Sondra that she had started talking with her mother in her head. It seemed to help Hannah more than her sessions with her therapist, so Sondra encouraged it. If she could have remembered what her own mother's voice sounded like, Sondra thought that she would find comfort in speaking to her too. Through this, and all of their interactions, Sondra learnt to appreciate Hannah as a friend, a guide, and someone to live up to.

Sondra rarely spoke about Michael, but when she did, it became very apparent to both her and Hannah how desperately Sondra wanted her son back. 'It's terrible, isn't it? Just missing and thinking and wishing?'

'It is, Sondra. It certainly is.' Hannah's misty eyes matched Sondra's.

* * *

It had been weeks since Sondra had met with David and had given him the letter for Michael. She had resisted the urge to follow up with him, but that morning, her anxiety at not knowing forced her into action. She sent David an e-mail.

> Dear David
>
> I had to e-mail you. Please tell me if you gave Michael my letter? What did he say?
>
> S

David's response was what she had feared.

> Hi Sondra
>
> Yes, I did give Michael the letter and he read it, but he didn't say anything.
>
> I know you were hoping for a more favourable outcome. Maybe later. Be patient.
>
> David

Sondra was distraught. She typed an impassioned e-mail to Michael, begging him to see her. She sent the e-mail but received a bounce-back immediately. Clearly, her address was still blocked. Sondra felt certain that if she left it at that, that the rift between them would never heal. The situation between them would linger and would become the norm. The longer she left it, the less chance she had at reconciliation.

Yet she was between a rock and a hard place. David's caring, cautionary words to be patient and to allow Michael time to deal with things in his own way echoed in her mind, but they didn't feel right. Should she trust her instinct and approach Michael? He would not be able to avoid a face-to-face confrontation. Or should she trust David's advice? David knew Michael better than anyone else after all.

The rest of her day was plagued by this internal conflict. To distract herself, she pulled out her laptop and went through her past week's labours. Work was necessary as a distraction – she would manage to get through the day somehow. Now that things were back on track in terms of her career, she didn't want to rock the boat. The appointment with Vicky the Friday before had gone well. There had been no mention of counselling as her performance had been on track.

She sent Hannah a message, asking if they could meet. She needed to talk to someone, and she instinctively thought of Hannah. Maybe her new friend would have a helpful suggestion. Sondra was hopeful that, by the time she returned from her run, Hannah would have responded. But it seemed that Hannah's phone was either off or was offline. Sondra's message had not been received.

She decided not to overthink anything. She would give it a couple of days before trying again. She had to focus on the new routine she had established. Now, she had the week ahead to look forward to, and she would focus her energies on that.

But Sondra was lonely, and she freely admitted that to herself. Sometimes, she felt depressed but was wary of letting that dark feeling overcome her. It wasn't an ideal situation, but it was all she could cope with at that time. Once she had spoken with Michael ... She couldn't complete the thought. Sondra didn't want to pre-empt or jinx anything.

On an impulse, she called Salma. She needed to hear a friendly voice. As expected, Salma was delighted to hear from her, and Sondra barely got a word in. Salma talked her ear off, filling her in about the weather, Ma's recent doctor's appointment, everyone in the family, and even updated Sondra on the latest shenanigans of the characters in her favourite soap opera. Sondra hadn't watched it ever but was entertained anyway. It helped to think of something else, to talk to someone who did not know the full story of her marriage and family situation.

'Baboo and I are taking the kids for *Umrah* and to Dubai at the end of the year. I'm really looking forward to a proper holiday – not the self-catering ones we usually go on where I have to prepare for days beforehand so that I'm exhausted when I get there and busy in the kitchen half the time.'

'Dubai and *Umrah*? Very nice. How long are you going for?' Salma's enthusiasm was contagious, and Sondra was genuinely interested.

'Three weeks! I'm so excited! Can't wait now. Just want it to be end of the year already.'

'Sounds lovely. I'm envious.'

'You have any plans? For the holidays, I mean?'

Sondra answered noncommittally and neatly changed the subject. Luckily, it was easy to distract Salma. Half an hour later, the sisters said their goodbyes. Sondra acknowledged and enjoyed the lightness she felt after the call. Chewing the fat with Salma was what the doctor ordered.

She kicked off her shoes, lay down on the couch, and rubbed her feet against each other. She decided to paint her toenails. The task would help her to focus on something else and maybe prolong the feeling Salma had spread over her. Taking one day at a time was what Hannah had recommended. She had internally scoffed at the advice at the time but then realised that it was the only way to continue. It was good advice. Put the past where it belonged – in the past – and deal with tomorrow when it presents itself.

It was easier said than done though, but it was what she had committed to, so she made an effort every day. She tried not to judge herself too harshly or to control things as much. She was more successful on some days than on others. She resisted the temptation to praise herself on good days or berate herself on bad ones. Overall, the strategy seemed to be working.

If only Michael would be open to seeing her, be open to forgive her, life would be perfect.

25

THE ANGUISH THAT TEARS

The rain wouldn't stop her. Even though it was pelting down by the time she got to the cemetery, Hannah forged ahead. Her raincoat and umbrella were always in the *boot* of her car, as were a pair of *takkies*, a cap, and a warm coat – the essentials that ensured she never missed a visit. She pulled on the coat and the raincoat over it.

She ran to the east side of West Park Cemetery where John was interred. Her mother's grave was in that area too about a dozen rows towards the fence. Her pace was quick but not because of the rain. She could not wait to talk to John. Once she had started having conversations with her mother in her mind, she started talking to John too. It was better than any therapy. Her daily visits to John's grave stopped being cryfests. Instead, she would tell him about her day, about how she missed him or about the little things that reminded her of him, and then there were the times, just sometimes, when she would sit quietly, content to just be there, content to just not be alone and lonely.

That wet Saturday was one of those days. There was so much swirling around in her head that she needed to be quiet and still.

The rain had stopped. She hadn't realised when. Hannah sat on her knees and looked at the grave. The storm hadn't lasted long but had been strong. There were bits of debris and rubbish lying everywhere. Her need to be still was over-powered by her need to clean the place where her son would forever be. She always had a pair of gloves and a small hand fork in the pockets of her coat. It took her twenty minutes to clear away the leaves and twigs from John's grave and the area around it, which included Eliot's grave alongside John's. She soaked up her beautiful son's presence while she worked, feeling him in her heart and in her mind, but no words were exchanged.

When she was done, she went to her mother's burial place. She placed her hand on her mother's tombstone. It was wet and cold. Hannah talked to Sylvia as she got busy.

'Sondra Carim-Edwards.' Hannah said the name solemnly, in acknowledgement of her changed opinion of the woman and in deference of John's feelings towards her.

'*I remember.*' Sylvia's dancing voice sprinkled light in Hannah's mind. '*You have mentioned her before.*'

'She's not anything I thought she was. My assumptions were wrong. Don't misunderstand, Mother, I'm not ready to forgive and forget. What she did was unjustifiable. Getting to know her a little though ... a lot actually, is ... it's making a difference. She's a complicated woman with a ... a colour-ful history.' Hannah laughed and whistled.

'*Such a departure from the previously harsh words you spoke about this woman,*' Sylvia declared.

'This is the reformed me, Mother. I'm trying not to be judgemental. It's bloody hard, I'll tell you. I want to honour you. I thought that the best way to do that is to try and em-ulate you, do what you would do.'

'*You make me blush.*' There was a giggle that played on the words.

'I told you about our meetings, me and Sondra? I can't believe it myself.' She patted the ground with the back of her hand fork. It helped that the ground was soft after the rain. 'We've spent time together. We talked and connected. I'm learning who she is, and I think she's getting to know me too. She likes me, thinks I'm some kind of hero. Can you imagine? Man, oh man! Me? Little ol' me. Your daughter! A hero.'

'*Of course, I can. You didn't get your wonderfulness only from your father, you know.*'

Hannah laughed at her mother's joke.

It took Hannah a while longer to clear the area around her mother's grave, and they talked all the while. When she was done, she surveyed her handiwork. She felt satisfied. She needed to be kept occupied with activities. Thoughts of John would not disappear, but at least they could be less poisonous.

Darkness was descending. With a hand on the tombstone, Hannah spoke softly. 'Goodbye, Mother. I'll come around more regularly from now on.'

'*So long, child.*' Sylvia's voice was strong and loaded with love. '*I'll see you soon.*'

Hannah gathered her things and left. When she got home, she was cold and tired. After a quick, hot shower, she made herself a hot chocolate and took it to her room. She had started to eat and drink the things that were John's favourites. It was another simple way to honour and remember him. The sweetness and warmth helped her relax, and within a few minutes, she fell into a turbulent sleep.

* * *

When Hannah rose the next morning, an incredible heaviness encased her. She pulled the covers over her head and tried to go back to sleep. Sleep was usually the only time she had that she did not think or feel. She didn't feel the anguish that tore at her insides; she didn't feel the loss that emptied her out until she was only a shell of nothingness; she didn't feel the anger that bubbled up within her like a boiling cauldron; she felt nothing. That's what she needed: oblivion. It was a pity her sleep was irregular and fitful. Snatches of dosing were welcome but not nearly enough.

Her body refused to oblige, and her helpless mind hurled heartbreak, misery, and rage that thrashed around her head like her body did until she sat bolt upright. The image that pierced her mind's eye was that of a smiling, relaxed Sondra.

The injustice!

Hannah pined for her dead son, and Sondra laughed. Sondra had moved on or was trying to, and there she was, stuck in a rut of torment. The longing for the image of John to appear was as real as her need for him to be alive. He could come breezing in, dive under the covers, and beg her not to tickle him when she knew all he wanted was for her to do just that. His morning smell would remind her of his boyish, fun-loving self, and they would giggle as she found his sensitive spots.

"You're too close to him, Hannah. That kind of love is one step away from obsession. It's dangerous." Eliot's words had proved true – too true. She was forced to admit that her feelings of "obsession" had grown since John had passed away. The circumstances of his death – the futility of the deed – enraged her further.

Sondra! Sondra was the cause. Why did she want to become *pals* with the woman she hated more than her own existence? Why would she help that woman, be compassionate towards *that* woman? What was she thinking?

She would stop this bizarre connection. She had to. She needed to hate and blame Sondra – otherwise, how else would she make sense of it? John's life and death would have no meaning, no reason. There was no room in her life for Sondra. Sondra hadn't needed her before, so she would manage just fine without her, without Hannah – the only person Sondra could call a friend. *Hah! That in itself is telling, isn't it?*

What was she doing anyway, making Sondra her friend? Sondra was the enemy – her mortal enemy. She could not kill her, or anyone for that matter, but in that moment, Hannah wanted her dead. *Why should Sondra be allowed to breathe and live and laugh and play when John cannot?*

She threw a pillow at the mirror. It bounced off and landed on the dresser, knocking bottles loudly to the floor. She walked over to straighten her mess. Everything on the dresser was dusty; they hadn't been used in months. Impulsively, she reached for the wicker basket bin that sat on the floor next to the dresser and swept the tubes and bottles into it. Declutter! Simplify!

Like an automaton, she began a huge clean. She dusted, polished, scrubbed, and vacuumed methodically, in each room and bathroom. Even John's room was turned over and cleaned out mechanically and coldly. After a few hours, she tackled the garden. It had been neglected for months. She cleaned and turned the beds, raked up the dead leaves, trimmed the overgrown bushes, and mowed the lawn.

By the time she was done, she had filled three bin bags with dirt, grass, cuttings, and other rubbish. There was no feeling of contentment or satisfaction in her work; she only felt frustration and anger. Thoughts of Sondra continued to consume her. Hannah's anger at her own weakness – her extending an olive branch to one whom she should only hate – surged through her in never-ending waves.

I should confront her, let her know that it's not okay. What she did to my boy is not okay. I do not forgive her. I will never forget.

Why am I so confused about this?

It should have been simple: there should be no relationship, no friendship, nothing between them. She didn't care about Sondra or her life. She knew what she had to do: cut off any and all contact. She would not call her, nor would she accept any of Sondra's calls. She didn't even have to explain anything; she owed Sondra nothing.

Stop this now, she commanded herself. Torturing herself with these thoughts was unnecessary. Hannah loaded the bags of garden refuse into her car and drove them to the dump. On her way back, she stopped at the car wash. While her car was being lavished upon, she bought a sandwich and a cup of tea from the garage shop. She did not taste the sandwich and struggled to swallow it. She gulped the tea to force it down.

On her way back home, she felt ill. Her tummy churned, forcing her to pull the car over. She threw up on the side of the road, her body retching, expelling bile and the half-digested sandwich and tea. She rinsed her mouth with water from a bottle that had been found by the car washer but was unable to get rid of the sour taste. She needed to get home.

She tore into her bathroom, brushed her teeth, then stripped. She stood under a hot shower and forcefully scrubbed her body as she cried her heart out. Her movements were harsh, and her skin burned red. She wanted some relief but knew that that was impossible, not now ... maybe never.

Witch, Not-witch

Dark, deadly, dangerous
Sunken yellow eyes
Sharp pointed fangs
Rank breath, musty clothes

Beware!

I turn to run
My body moves but my eyes are fixed
They stare into yellow orbs that
reflect pain, reflect terror

My terror, my pain

I run
I fall
Quicksand
I am disappearing

Help!

Dirt-crusted fingernails on the
fingers that pull me up
A rough hand soothes my brow
A crackly voice gentle as a breeze

I do not want to know
I do not want to see
Close my eyes
Stop my heart

When Hannah woke the next morning and read the scrawled writing, she couldn't remember penning the poem. Angry that she had spent so much time agonising over Sondra, she ripped it out of her notebook, crumpled it into a ball, and tossed it into the wicker bin. If only she could get her out of her mind as easily.

26

COFFEE AND COUNSEL

When the bell rang that fateful afternoon, Hannah was tempted to ignore it. She wasn't expecting anyone and was in no mood to see anyone. Maybe if she pretended not to hear it, the caller would go away.

It rang again. Irritated, Hannah strode to her front door and yanked it open. She hadn't even taken a second to check who it was. She was expecting a beggar or a vendor selling brooms door to door. But behind the gate stood Muriel, her neighbour. Hannah had been seen, so she had no option but to open the gate and wait as Muriel shuffled up the short path to her front door, carrying a small box. Her dark hair, speckled with grey, was neatly tied into her ponytail. It accentuated her plump cheeks.

'Hello, Hannah, how are you? I've been wanting to come chat to you for some time. So, here I am.'

Is that supposed to excuse you just arriving? Hannah silenced the internal snippy voice and spoke gently. 'I'm okay, Muriel. How are you?'

'Aah, you know how it goes, aches and pains – old body. But we must *maar* carry on.'

'You coming in? I have to leave soon. I have an appointment.' Hannah glanced at her arm, then realised she wasn't wearing a watch ... or any jewellery.

'Oh dear. Let's have a quick coffee, okay? I brought pastries.'

Hannah sighed, then led the way to the kitchen and put the kettle on.

Muriel placed the box on the table. '*Melktert* – my favourite.'

'I don't have much time, Muriel.' Hannah hoped she didn't sound ungracious.

'I'll get straight to it then,' Muriel said, making herself comfortable at the table in the middle of the small space. 'I'm worried about you. Your mother was too. I used to drop by to see her some afternoons. All she did was talk about you and John, hardly mentioning anything else. She was afraid you'd withdraw from the world. In fact, she said you already had, that you'd stopped living when John had. I tried to be encouraging, said it was a natural reaction for any parent, and that with time, things would get better.'

Hannah tried to appear nonchalant. 'I'm okay, Muriel. My mother was a worry-wart. Sugar?'

'One, please. She was, but with good reason. How are you coping? No, don't answer. I know what you will say. But saying it doesn't make it real.'

Hannah's irritation levels were peaking, but she bit her tongue. Muriel had been a good friend to her mother.

'I promised your mother I would look in on you. Will you talk to me? Try?'

'We're talking, aren't we?' This time, her impatience couldn't be hidden.

Muriel did not react to her abruptness. 'I understand your reluctance. Grief is a solitary thing. Sharing ... if you can talk to someone, it does help. Have you been going for your sessions?'

Hannah sighed again. She may as well play along. After a few minutes, she would excuse herself, she decided. 'I was seeing a counsellor, a therapist who specialises in the loss of loved ones – Mary. It helped.' *Up to a point*, but she kept that to herself.

'Good. That makes a huge difference in the beginning, even if only to realise that you're not the first person to have lost a loved one, nor will you be the last. It's the long-term that's daunting, isn't it?'

Hannah suddenly remembered that Muriel had lost her own daughter years back in an accident. The girl – Anna? Andrea? She couldn't place the name – had been a few years older than John. *Damn!* How could she have been so wrapped up in her own world of darkness that she'd forgotten simple human compassion?

'The accident! How long ago was it?' Hannah asked quietly, her hands no longer making the coffee. They just gripped the counter and held her up while she thought about Muriel's daughter. It had been awful. A drunk driver had mowed down the teenager right on their street. The whole neighbourhood had been in shock. They had mobilised themselves and had gotten the municipality to erect speed bumps.

'Eleven years.' This time, it was Muriel who sighed. She looked sad and accepting at the same time.

Eleven years. It's been just over a year since John's passing. The thought of surviving for so *many years* without him was unbearable. Her legs threatened to buckle under her. She pulled out a chair and collapsed into it.

'I wish I could tell you that you forget.' Muriel's voice took on a tone that Hannah had never heard before. It sounded sad but firm, compassionate but with true empathy. 'There isn't a day ... not one single day ... Every day, I miss my Angela, my angel. And for the rest of my life, I will continue to miss her. I don't want to lie to you, it's hard, bloody hard.' Hannah had never heard Muriel use anything less than lady-like language. This was new.

Muriel passed Hannah her coffee. She had made herself at home and done the necessary. Hannah watched as she peeled away the strip of clear tape and opened the box, extracted a tartlet, and pushed the box over to Hannah.

'There's no easy fix or miracle.' Muriel gave a simple matter-of-fact shrug. 'Rehana – a fellow teacher at school, a devout Muslim and a lovely lady – she told me that God does not give us trials we cannot bear. Mothers who lose children must be strong then, strong enough to bear that pain.'

Hannah sucked her top lip into her mouth and chewed on it hard. She didn't feel strong. She wished she didn't have to feel anything.

'There's a support group that meets at the church on Seventh Street on Tuesday evenings. It helped me. I was a regular until a few years ago. Every couple of months, I still drop in. Nowadays, I just listen mostly. Come with me next Tuesday. It starts at seven. We'd be home before nine. Think about it.'

Hannah had heard about the group. Mary had also suggested it.

The two women sat together in silence. Hannah was lost in her own thoughts. Muriel patiently sipping her coffee and chewing on her pastry. The silence was accentuated by the ticking of the wall clock above the stove.

Muriel cleared her throat. 'Forgiveness is tough. It's not like you can wake up one morning and all is over. The anger you feel, the blame you force on yourself, John, God ... the blame is also a constant. If only I hadn't let Angela walk home that day. If only ... If only the man had realised the dangers of driving drunk. If only traffic hadn't been so good that day and we were late getting home. The questions, the blame ... It's unrelenting ... Only the highly evolved can learn to make peace. It's a long, drawn-out affair and never absolute. At times, it may be easy to let go; at others, every fibre of your being will rally against the release that is inevitable. Our minds are complex, constantly in thought, looking and relooking, finding fault and acceptance simultaneously.'

Hannah impassively stared with eyes that looked but did not see, with ears that listened but did not hear, with a heart that beat but that remained shut.

'In the end, you'll find a way, after much stumbling, after stopping and restarting over and over again. I know this. I've known you for years, Hannah. But it was your mother's love for you that made me see you for who you are. When you learn to see yourself as that person again, as a child to a parent who loved you as much as you loved your own child ...'

Muriel's breathing had quickened. It was as though her heart and mind were at odds. Hannah recognised the struggle of grief ... the struggle of life. It was a reflection of her own tumult. The realisation swept over her, filling her up with more confusion, that hers was a never-ending road, tarred and smooth at some places, bumpy and narrow at others – a path that she could never avoid.

'It will not be over—never be over, but it *can* be okay. Not today, and not every day, but some days.' Muriel was at her side, her hand warm on Hannah's shoulder. Her touch was as gentle and calming as a breeze rolling over a still sea. 'Be gentle with yourself. As her child, you owe it to your mother; as his mother, you owe it to John.'

Hannah allowed her body to go limp and to rest against Muriel's generous one. She closed her eyes and remembered the comforting presence of Sylvia. She longed for that all-consuming, non-judgemental love, for that warmth that was a soothing salve to any hurt. That sanctuary from any storm was gone but not forgotten. She would not forget. She needed to clutch onto the remnants of all that would make her journey doable, that would make the path bearable.

'It's time for me to go.' Muriel took Hannah's hand, and they ambled along together. At the door, Muriel stretched up and kissed Hannah on both cheeks. 'I'm going, but I'm always here.' A smile lit up her wrinkled face but could not mask the sadness in her eyes. 'Goodbye, my dear.'

Hannah clicked the gate closed behind Muriel and watched as the woman put one foot in front of the other, walking her road. It was a road that they shared but a journey that they had to make alone. Hannah stumbled to the lounge and fell onto the couch. She allowed the tears to flow freely, praying for the oblivion that only came with sleep.

27

A SMALL CONCESSION

After not hearing back from Hannah for a few weeks, Sondra sent her another message. It was brief, and she hoped that it was considerate without being pushy.

> Been worried about you.
> Let me know if you're okay
> or if you want to meet.

Hannah read the *WhatsApp* and responded after a few hours.

> Hi Sondra. I did get your
> messages. It's been tough.
> Need some me time.

Sondra replied, wishing her strength with a hug emoji. Her guilt at her role in Hannah's situation was overshadowed by the sadness she felt for Hannah, a woman she had grown to know and love.

Love. The word came naturally to her now. She had read somewhere that love is always a verb, and now she understood that. Love needs to be given and received, actively performed and expressed. She wondered if she would be able to express love the way she felt it. Love was the overwhelming emotion she experienced: love for David, love for Michael, for Hannah, for her mother, her ... father. Anger, guilt, blame, concern, fear, these feelings were still there, still aimed at various people in varying degrees, but love trumped them all. She wanted to learn to express this love over and above all others emotions.

Sondra decided she would start right away. As she stood on her small patio at her apartment, she sent a silent message to Hannah.

I'm sending you love and light, Hannah.

She smiled at herself. This kind of spiritual response was still new for her. *Love and light.* Since when had she started believing in being able to reach people only through the power of feeling, through the power of the spirit? Previously, she would have scoffed at that kind of thing as hogwash.

I'm sending you love and light, Hannah.
I'm sending you love and light, David.
I'm sending you love and light, Michael.
I'm sending you love and light, John.
I'm sending you love and light, Sondra.

The love that she felt, the smile that danced on her lips, extended peacefully to the rest of her body, warming her from inside.

I love you, Sondra. You are worthy of my love. You are worthy of David's and Michael's love. You are even worthy of Hannah's love.

She prayed that Hannah would be able to forgive her, prayed that Hannah would let Sondra love her.

* * *

The next day, despite knowing that she should be focusing on work and the week ahead, Sondra felt confident enough to send a message to David.

> Sorry to bug. I want to see
> Michael. Can I come over?

David called her five minutes later, probably as soon as he had read the message.

When she answered, she heard fear and hope in her voice. 'David, hi.'

'Hello.' It was a curt response to her "hi". 'I thought we'd agreed that you'd wait. When Mikey is ready, he'll let you know.'

'It's been five months. I don't want to wait any longer. The way he feels, I'm afraid he'll never want to see me again. I can't blame him. But while I'm waiting, he'll get used to the status quo. He'll never make the first move. You know he can be as proud and as stubborn as me. Even then, if he does get over this, it might be too late.' Sondra prayed he would listen to her and try to understand where she was coming from. She was at the end of her tether, but she hoped that she didn't sound pathetic. Neither David nor Michael would respond positively to that – David because he didn't know a needy Sondra and would not know how to react, and Michael because, like herself – her old self, he saw neediness as a weakness.

David was quiet. She knew he was thinking about what she had said. She clutched the phone tightly, hoping against hope that he would consider her request.

'Okay. Let me talk to him. I'll ask him to consider meeting with you. Maybe on Saturday afternoon. He has plans on Friday night. I'll talk to him on Saturday morning and let you know.'

Sondra danced on the spot. She was overjoyed for the chance.

'That's great. I understand he doesn't want to have any-thing to do with me, and if he still doesn't want to after he hears me out ...' Sondra cut her sentence off. 'Please, just ask him for twenty minutes.'

'All right. I'm not promising anything, but I'll try.'

Sondra could ask for no more. 'Thanks, David. I appreciate it.'

'I'm doing this for Mikey. I don't want him growing up without every opportunity. And he needs his mother. Everyone does.'

Sondra was encouraged. If David's motivation was Mikey, then he would try his hardest.

'You're a good man, David.' She paused to reflect on her statement, not because she'd only just realised it but because she realised how seldomly she expressed her admiration of him to him. 'I think it's amazing that Mikey has grown up with you as a role model. Thank you ... for talking to Mikey on my behalf and for all that you do for him.'

David took a breath before responding. His voice was measured. 'Wow! That's nice to hear.'

'I should've expressed my appreciation for you more often ... and my feelings.' Silently, she laughed at herself, feeling a little foolish and self-conscious. *Why should it feel so strange to express yourself to your husband?* 'Better late than never, hey?'

David laughed, and she revelled in hearing it. She loved the sound of his laugh – she always had. He laughed a hearty, throaty, full-bodied laugh. This was another thing that she had never told him.

I love the sound of your laugh, David. She said the words in her mind and heart only, not wanting to embarrass either of them with uncharacteristic sentimentality. Sondra was surprised to feel moisture on her cheeks. *Oh, get a grip, girl. You had twenty years to whisper sweet nothings to him, and you didn't. Your timing sucks, Sondra!*

'It's okay, Sonds.' What was he reassuring her about? Did he hear her insecurities? Did he understand that she had never felt less confident but was still hopeful?

'Thanks, David. I'll leave it to you then. I'll wait to hear from you.' *It will be good news. Michael will agree to my request. He has to.*

* * *

Sondra paced the short length of her apartment. Ever since she had woken up – well technically, one only wakes up when one has slept – she had been a bundle of nerves, anxious and fidgety. She picked up her mug. The tea was cold, so she popped it into the microwave for thirty seconds.

For the umpteenth time, she checked her phone. Yes, it was still charged with full signal. Could the clock be right though? It had only been five minutes since the last time she had checked.

She aimlessly flicked through the TV channels. A snippet of an old Bollywood song that she recognised flashed momentarily on screen. She scrolled back. She had landed on an Indian channel. The Bollywood movie on screen was *Hum Aapke Hain Koun ..!*, which roughly translated means "Who am I to you?". It was hugely popular in the mid-nineties. The Carim family had owned the VHS – which Indian family didn't at the time? – and she had seen it a dozen times at least.

She surprised herself by remembering the words and singing along. This version had subtitles, but she didn't need to read them. She remembered the Hindi very well. She'd never spoken any Indian language but understood Hindi, primarily because of movie watching, and a fair amount of Urdu because that was the language the Carims spoke. Well, English was their primary language, but sometimes, Urdu words or phrases crept in.

The beautiful face of Madhuri Dixit, the undisputed Bollywood queen at the time, smiled coyly at the hero. Sondra settled down to watch the rest of the movie. At least it would allow an hour or two to pass. Another song started, and she remembered how Salma would dance along. There *were* happy times in the Carim household. She would just have to try harder to remember them.

She kicked off her shoes and lay down on the couch. Her sleep-deprived body took its cue, and she fell into a short but reviving sleep. The rest was a godsend in more ways than one. When she woke up, she saw a message from David.

> I've convinced Mikey to see you. It was not easy. Come by at 4 this afternoon.

Sondra literally jumped up with joy. A chance! A lifeline! She gave joyous thanks to David and to the universe. Surely this was a sign. Now, everything would fall into place. The sparsely stocked grocery cupboard did not encourage any baking, so she decided to buy a cake to take with as a kind of peace offering and as something to busy herself with to break the tension that she was sure to feel.

Please, she sent out a silent appeal to the universe, *let this work out. Let today be a success. Let it be the start of a new beginning for me and Mikey.*

She needed to share this with someone as though voicing the news out loud would solidify it and make it real. And if it was real, he could not change his mind.

She dialled Hannah's number, but it went to voicemail. 'Hi, Hannah. I just wanted to let you know that Michael has agreed to see me. Wish me luck!'

She had a couple of hours to kill before she would have to leave, so she decided to do some work. She switched on her laptop and focused. At around two-thirty, she switched off her laptop and prepared to leave. She went to a bakery in Illovo and chose a selection of Mikey's and David's favourite mini cakes.

She opened the electric gate – she still had the remote – and parked in the driveway. She thought it might be better to go in through the front door. David must have heard her car because he opened the door before she knocked.

'*Chateau Gateaux!*' David smiled when he saw the box she was carrying. 'Clever move.' He led the way to the kitchen. 'I'll make coffee. Tea for you?' He switched the kettle on.

She nodded. There was no sign of Michael.

'Will you get some plates and forks? I'll go find Michael.' David returned a minute later, chatting casually with Michael.

'Hi, Michael.' Sondra wondered if her voice was steady. She forced herself not to throw her arms around him and hug him.

Michael looked at his mother grudgingly, acknowledging her presence impassively.

I guess indifference is better than nothing. Sondra swallowed and busied herself with the cakes.

'What would you guys like?'

'Dibs on the black forest,' David replied quickly.

Michael solemnly pointed to the tiramisu. Sondra passed plates and made coffee for David and tea for herself.

'How's the holiday going, Michael?' Sondra didn't look directly at him, partly because the realisation of how he had changed in the past few months was difficult to acknowledge. She had missed out on that and felt a stab of responsibility. It was also partly because she would rather not see the poorly masked disdain in his eyes.

'Fine.'

'Make the most of the holidays. Next year will be busy-busy.'

Michael shrugged and focused on his cake. He didn't want to engage in any small talk. Sondra was at a loss – what else could she say?

'This was a good idea.' David, wonderful David broke the silence. 'We haven't had cake in forever. How's work going, Sondra?'

David and Sondra kept the conversation going, talking about work and the latest unfolding political drama.

Michael looked at his father, one eyebrow raised. He broke into their conversation abruptly. 'I'm not keen to have a pretend-fest like you two. We're *not* a family.' And with that, for the first time since he had walked into the kitchen, he looked directly at Sondra, a look of unveiled contempt.

Sondra wished the ground under her would open and swallow her whole. This was going to be harder than she had anticipated.

'*Miiiichael!*' David drew out the first syllable, an edge of one-part conciliation one-part warning to his voice.

Michael did not respond or react to David. He continued staring at Sondra and spoke in an even tone that belied his years. 'You have something to say, and because Dad asked, I'm here. I agreed to twenty minutes. You've already wasted ten. I don't think you want to waste anymore. Let's get on with it.'

Sondra looked at David, hoping for assistance. Flustered, she forgot her carefully thought-through and rehearsed speech. She took a conscious breath. *You can do this, Sondra. Speak from your heart. Mikey must believe you, must realise you're being real. That's the only chance you have.*

'Yes, okay. You're right. Let's not waste any more time.' She waited for David to gulp down the last of his coffee, deposit his mug into the sink, and excuse himself. 'Thanks for seeing me. I understand your anger towards me. It is justified. I'm not here to ask you to forgive me. I cannot make excuses. I live with the consequences of my behaviour every day. It was appalling. What I did was unconscionable.' She stopped to take a deep breath. When she started again, her voice had dropped. 'I caused the death of that young man, caused endless grief to his family ... ended a life without so much as a second thought ... I was awful. On top of that, I didn't take responsibility.'

'Is this a confession? I'm not the pope. I can't give you absolution.' His biting sarcasm, his steel-like demeanour, his cold, dark eyes aged him. He was a man – a bitter, angry man. She had robbed him of living his full childhood, delivering him to manhood too soon. Neither of them was ready.

'No, you can't. You can forgive if you want, but that's all. I don't deserve absolution. I live with the knowledge of John and the consequences of his death every day. But let me get to the point.' She must not get emotional. If there was any chance that he would listen, she had to remain focused. 'I am sorry for what I've done. You don't have to accept my apology. I want us to move past this and start again. I'm not asking you to forgive and forget, but I do want a chance to learn to be your mother. I won't pretend that everything is hunky-dory. I only want a chance, perhaps see you once in a while. I miss you, Mikey. I love you.'

Mikey let out an exasperated and irritated sigh.

She searched his eyes. She wanted to reach over and grab his hand but remained motionless. 'I never said that enough. Worse, I never showed you my love. I want you to see that I've changed. A lot has happened. I want you to have a mother. Mine died when I was thirteen. I've told you nothing about her or the rest of my family. I want you to have a chance at knowing who I am, to know my past, so that you will know yourself.'

'I don't care.' His words were flat, emotionless, unlike his eyes that glinted angrily. Sondra remembered how his moods could change in a second – like a typical teenager, she supposed. But this felt different. It was clear that it was deliberate and that he wanted to appear in control.

'You won't ... now. But you don't want to have regrets later on in your life like I do.' Sondra looked away, focusing on anything but the piercing brown eyes that stared accusingly. 'Believe me, I'm speaking from experience. When we're young, we think we have everything sorted out. Then life throws us curve balls, and we flounder. Stuff we think we knew, the stuff we had all figured out, was based on impressions in our head and not necessarily on reality.'

'Listen, if you going to get all philosophical, I'm not interested. I don't want to see you. I don't want to talk to you. I don't want to have anything to do with you – not now, not ever.'

'I know. A part of me knew it was unlikely that I would be able to change your mind. I had to try.'

'Right, then. I think we're done.' Michael pushed his plate away in a manner that was reminiscent of something ... someone?

Sondra reached over and held the hand that had pushed the plate. He flinched and pulled his hand away roughly.

'Don't,' he shouted.

Sondra was taken aback. She pulled her hand away too; guiltily. Her hands clasped each other, and she shivered. Did her touch really evoke such a passionate response from him?

His face suddenly masked, and she found his new expression unreadable. He had shut down. She was not going to get any further, not today. Sondra placed her tightly gripped hands on her lap. Hidden under the table, she clenched them into fists.

After a moment that stretched unnervingly for an age, Sondra took a steadying, calming breath and spoke. 'I'm not going to stop hoping for you to change your mind. If you ever do, you are welcome to get in touch. Maybe you want to say something later, even if it's just to shout at me. Whatever the reason, my door's always open.'

'Don't hold your breath.' His eyes flashed with an unforgiving rage that crushed her hopes.

No, stay positive. Never give up on him. 'I'm not going to give up either. I'll keep trying. Please unblock me from your phone, or at least your e-mail. Even if you don't respond ... there must be some way for you to reach me and for me to reach you. You're my son. Anything can happen to you or me. Or your dad. We must be realistic.'

'I can't imagine ever wanting anything to do with you *ever*, but fine, if it'll end this now, I'll unblock your e-mails.'

It was a small concession, but it was something. If that was all he was able to consider for now, it would have to do. *Baby steps, Sondra. Rome wasn't built in a day.*

Michael stood up.

'You've grown taller ... and more handsome.' She rose too and took a step towards him.

He ignored her comment. He stood rooted behind his chair, leaning his hands on its back.

She steeled herself and went to stand next to him. She placed a tentative hand on his arm. 'I love you, my boy. Take care of yourself.'

'Yeah, sure. Whatever.' He made a big show of shaking off her arm and walked out of the kitchen. But then he stopped and turned back. 'I'll walk you out.'

She picked up her bag and followed. 'Say goodbye to your dad for me. Tell him, "thanks".'

In the doorway, she took a long look at her son, committing his new visage to memory. Who knew when she would see him again? How much would he have changed by then? The thought scared her. She threw caution to the wind and her arms around his neck. It was a quick, tight hug before she stumbled away from him and briskly walked to her car.

She stopped herself from thinking or feeling anything. She didn't want anything to interrupt the image of her son's face as she drove. She just wanted to keep seeing him in her mind's eye.

28

THE VOICE OF WISDOM

Hannah had let Sondra's most recent call go to voicemail. She had decided not to take her calls or have anything to do with her. Sondra had sent a message or three and then this call. She figured Sondra would get the message after a while.

When she heard the voice message, she wanted to call back and wish her well with the visit to Michael. She knew that it was a big deal for Sondra. Then an internal voice questioned why Sondra should have a relationship with her son when she could never have one with her own son again. A feeling she recognised as selfish jealousy surrounded her, and she suppressed her urge to be caring. She pushed the thoughts of how the meeting would turn out aside ... or rather, she tried her best to.

Hannah tossed the phone on the kitchen counter, and it clattered in protest. She went outside. After an hour or two of tending to her garden, she gathered her things and got ready to go to the cemetery.

When she got to John's grave, she realised she had left her phone in the car and wondered if that had been a subconscious decision. If she didn't have her phone, she couldn't call Sondra. She admitted that she wanted to know what had happened with Michael but also that she shouldn't really care. Who was Sondra to her anyway? Only the woman who had caused her endless grief.

She spent a quiet hour sitting at John's grave and then walked slowly to her mother's. She heard her mother's voice greet her gaily, then upon getting no reply, her mother asked, '*Why the long face? Chin up, girl!*'

'Oh Mother, you're too much sometimes. It's easy to say that but extremely difficult to do. You think this is easy?' Hannah grumbled half-heartedly at the imagined voice of her mother.

'*Who promised you easy? If only, child. Tell me what's bothering you.*'

'You mean apart from being a childless mother? That my beautiful boy took his life and left me all alone. I'm all alone, Mother.'

'*You have people. There are friends who want to be there for you. Why don't you go to that support group with Muriel?*'

'Maybe. We'll see.'

'*What about Sondra? It sounded like you were getting close?*'

'That *is* bizarre, isn't it? Why should I become friends with *that* woman of all people?'

'*Things happen. We don't always know why, but there is surely some reason.*'

'Maybe I'm going crazy? What else is craziness if not total confusion. I want to call her, know about her, but I feel I should hate her.'

'*You can't force hate any more than you can force love, my child. It's silly to try.*'

'Silly ... or crazy?' A smile played on Hannah's lips. 'How did you do it, Mother? How did you always manage to make me feel better?'

'*That's my job, Hannah. I'm your mother.*'

'I'm a mother too. I was, but I couldn't do anything to help my son.'

'*You did everything a mother could have. You have to know that. What John did was his own decision. You can't blame anyone, not even Sondra or yourself. It might be easier to accept if you had someone to blame. It is what it is though, and you can't force it to make sense. All you can do is accept.*'

'And how do I do that?'

'*It will come. Things happen in their time. In the meantime, you just have to trust your instincts. If you feel like you want to call Sondra, then call her.*'

'I don't know, Mother.'

'*What's worrying you?*'

'It feels unnatural. How can I like this woman? I should hate her. It feels like I'm betraying myself.'

'*Hate is a draining emotion. It takes everything out of you and leaves a shell of a person behind. It's pointless and futile.*'

Hannah could not argue with that.

'*Don't waste your time here. Go to Sondra and talk with her. Talk to someone who is alive, someone who knows what you're going through.*'

'I don't need her.'

'*Maybe she needs you. Maybe you need each other in different ways. You can fulfil a need for each other.*'

'Oh, Mother. Stop being so clever and manipulative.'

'*Am I?*' The voice that Hannah heard in her head was amused. There was a hint of the tinkly laughter Hannah remembered and missed. '*Just answer me this: do you have anything to lose?*'

Hannah didn't respond immediately. She had been holding onto a need to hate Sondra for causing John's death. Was that all she had to lose? Hate? That couldn't be bad, could it? Loss of hatred could only lead to healing.

'Nothing, Mother.' Hannah groaned out loud. 'Urrgh! I hate it when you're right.'

'*Mmm, yes, child. I know. I suggest you get on with it. If you ponder over this too long, you'll probably talk yourself out of it again.*'

Hannah listened to her mother's voice and strode purposefully to the carpark. She got to her car, retrieved her phone, and texted Sondra.

> Just wanted to check how
> your meeting with Michael
> went. Do you want to meet?

Sondra's response was as expected, Hannah realised.

> I'm reserving judgement and
> trying to stay positive.

> Sure, let's meet when
> suits. I'm free today and
> tomorrow. Call me. S

Hannah dialled, and her call was answered even before it rang. Sondra sounded strained. 'Hi, Hannah. How're you?'

'I'm well. Just been visiting the cemetery but in no rush to get home. You?'

'I'm just at home, trying to pass the hours by not thinking about anything.' She laughed humourlessly. 'It's not easy or fun.'

'Tell me about it. So, what do you feel like? Shall we go somewhere for dinner?'

'I'm really not in the mood to go out. But I don't want to be alone either. Why don't you come to me? We can always order in later.'

'Okay, that sounds like a plan. I'll see you in thirty minutes or so.'

Hannah stopped at the entrance of West Park Cemetery. The flower sellers were packing up. She purchased two bunches of lilies. She would give one to Sondra, and she would take the other home. She hadn't had flowers at home in a long while ... not since her mother's funeral. It would be a nice change.

29

SHORT-LIVED DISTRACTIONS

Sondra sat on the little patio, waiting for Hannah. It was something different to think about and look forward to. She had tortured herself enough about the meeting with Michael. Him agreeing to unblock her e-mails *was* something though, and that's what she would remember. When she saw Hannah's car pull up at the security gate, she went inside her apartment and pulled her front door open. When Hannah came through a few minutes later with flowers, she was surprised and delighted.

'Wow! They're beautiful. For me? I don't even know if there is a vase in the kitchen. Come in, come in. Let me see what I can put these in.'

Sondra found a jug and arranged the flowers. 'I love lilies. They were my mom's favourite too. She always found enough money for flowers in the house. It was different when I moved in with my father's family. He was rich but stingy. He would have considered flowers a waste of time and money.' She was satisfied with the arrangement and decided to leave them on the kitchen counter.

Hannah had seated herself at her spot at the dining room table and watched as Sondra occupied herself with the task.

'You're quiet. Everything okay?' Sondra casually took the seat opposite Hannah.

'Yes, fine.'

'"*Yes, fine*",' Sondra teased. She grinned. *I've had a lot of those "whatever" answers today.*

'Uh, sorry. I *have* been quiet.' Hannah sighed. 'I was confused about what this meant, I suppose.'

'What do you mean?' Sondra leant on the table, consciously angling herself towards Hannah.

'You know ... us getting closer, becoming "friends".' She scratched at the air with both hands as she said the last word. 'Understandable, I suppose. You were supposed to be my mortal enemy. It felt weird.'

'Yeah, but what isn't weird these days?'

Hannah nodded and shrugged.

Sondra wanted to know, so she asked. 'You're here now. What changed your mind?'

'Lots of things. I don't know how this will end up, but let's just see how things go.' Hannah leant back in her chair, stretched her neck, and let her head drop back, staring at the ceiling. She raised her arms and rubbed the back of her neck as she straightened to look at Sondra again. 'Tell me, what happened with Michael?'

'It was ... it went okay. He still doesn't want to have anything to do with me, and he hasn't forgiven or forgotten. He only saw me because his father forced him to, I think.'

'Mmm.' Hannah clearly didn't know what else to say.

'I'll try again in a few weeks. I told him I would, and he didn't stop me. Maybe he just wants time to process everything, to get over the horror of it all.'

Sondra walked to the fridge and pulled out a rectangular carton of juice, which she proffered to Hannah. Hannah nodded, and Sondra poured two glasses.

As she brought them to the table, she asked, 'What's that saying? "You make your bed, now you must lie in it"? I have no one to blame but myself.' Sondra sighed and gulped down a sip of her juice. 'But I've got to be patient and remain positive.'

'Yes, I know the feeling. Try and be positive and carry on with life as though nothing has happened. Life's a bitch, isn't it?' Hannah laughed and sounded self-conscious.

Sondra couldn't remember ever having heard Hannah swear. 'Hannah Bennett! Good Christian-girl Hannah Bennett. You have a mouth on you!' She laughed too. Things lightened up, aided by the sound of laughter. 'I guess we can sit here feeling sorry for ourselves or do something.' Sondra announced. 'Would you like to watch a movie or something? I have *DSTV*, so there's always a movie on.'

'I don't mind. As long as it's nothing sad.'

'Agreed. A slapstick comedy is just what the doctor ordered. Speaking of, let's order something to eat too.' Sondra took out her phone and went to the *Mr D* app. She handed it to Hannah. 'Here, you choose. I don't mind what we get. I eat everything except pork.'

'You don't eat pork? Is that because of your religion?'

'No, not really. I'm not religious and never practised my faiths. I was trained as a Muslim – my father made sure of that – and when I lived with him and his family, I was brought up as a Muslim. But, no, that's not why. I just don't like the taste, even as a child on the odd occasion we had it in the house. Eventually, my mom stopped making it. It was easier to cook something we both ate, I guess.'

'When last did you have it?'

'What? pork? As a child, years before my mother passed away.' Sondra frowned as she tried to remember. 'A long time ago, and I haven't missed it.'

'Chicken okay? *Nando's*?' Hannah asked, looking up from the phone.

Sondra shrugged. 'Sure. Whatever you're getting, let's also order the spicy wedges. I love those.' Sondra went to stand next to Hannah so that they could both see her phone.

Forty minutes later, they were settled on the couch, eating and watching an old Eddie Murphy movie. They could have been best friends, enjoying a meal and each other's company, not really having to say much. Simply being together was enough.

When the movie ended, Sondra stretched and yawned. 'Mmm, that was fun. It got my mind off Mikey and all that drama.'

'Yes, same here.'

'Shall I make us some tea?'

'Yes, maybe a quick cup, and then I'll get going.' Hannah excused herself and went to the bathroom.

Sondra put the kettle on and cleared up the debris from the takeaways. She was humming a catchy tune from the movie. She turned and stopped abruptly. Hannah was watching her and smiling gleefully.

'Don't stop on my account. You have a good ear.'

'When I was younger, I used to sing all the time. My mom used to say she was going to enter me in competitions. She loved my voice, loved hearing me sing. If I ever felt that she was down or worried about anything, I would sing, and it would cheer her up immediately.'

'You stopped singing when you moved in with the Carims?'

'Yeah, now that I think about it. It was a strict household, or maybe a better word to describe it is "austere". Abdul ruled the house. He wouldn't have encouraged my singing. Can't really blame him only, though. I always tried to blend into the background, didn't want to be noticed, so I stopped singing.'

'I sang in the choir as a teenager. My Eliot was very good. We sang in the church choir. We did everything together, Eliot and me. We were inseparable.'

'His death must have been a terrible blow.'

'It was. But I pulled through. I focused everything on John; he became my world. Well, I guess John was always my world.'

'You probably didn't imagine your life like this ever? Without a husband, without John. You've never really spoken much about Eliot.'

'Eliot ... I wonder, if Eliot was still alive, would John have done what he did? He chose not to speak to me about his sorrows, ever. When something bothered or upset him, he wouldn't voice that to me or Eliot. Then why did I always think we were close? It doesn't make any sense.

'Eliot cautioned me sometimes, saying I overdid it with John. I didn't really think about it then, but what I think he meant was that he was afraid I ... I overwhelmed him.' Hannah's eyes unfocused as she stared at nothing. Was it the difficulty of remembering that pulled her whole body down? It appeared like she'd shrunk from the effort of understanding. 'He asked me one day if I thought I would live forever. I laughed at his silly question. He explained that, "If we want John to be okay after we are gone, we have to give him the tools to live his own life, to make his own decisions and live with the consequences of those decisions." I didn't give Eliot's words a second thought then, brushing them away as unnecessary or that they didn't apply to John and me. I believed John was perfect. I believed he could do no wrong. What a fool I was.'

A terrifying thought crossed Sondra's mind. *What if Mikey dies?* No! NO! Sondra realised that no matter how awful things were with Michael, she would feel a hundred times worse. She wished him a long, happy and successful life. That's what she wanted for him more than anything else. More than even a reconciliation, she wanted him to be okay. She wanted him to be a good person, a responsible and honourable man. She wished she could have a positive impact on him. But until he was ready to allow her closer, she would have to continue to only wish great things for him, eternal happiness and success. It was her greatest wish for him – a mother's *dua*.

Sondra didn't know what to say to Hannah. It could not have been easy for her to reveal herself and to Sondra of all people. All she could do was hold Hannah, so she did. She hoped that Hannah would sense love and kindness in her touch. She prayed that Hannah would recognise the feelings and accept them.

'Oh, Sondra! What did I do? Did I love my son too much?'

'No, that's silly. Mothers can never love too much. No one can.'

Hannah pulled away from the embrace and brushed the back of her hand across her cheeks. 'But what if I did everything wrong? Maybe I thought I knew what was best for him? As his mother, I ... I wronged him.'

'Stop this, Hannah. You are torturing yourself, agonising over what could have been, and it's pointless. We cannot change the past. We can only learn from it and try and be better.'

Hannah sighed, then groaned. 'You're right. I know you are. In theory, I know I should look forward and try and accept and move on, but it's fucking hard.'

'It is, Han.'

'FUUUCCCKK!' Hannah shouted.

Sondra raised an eyebrow and then grinned. 'FUUUCCCKK!' Sondra echoed Hannah's swearing.

Then almost as if they'd planned it, they simultaneously started shouting out swear words. In between fits of laughter, they competed to find the filthiest words they knew. After exhausting their nasty vocabulary, they ended up on the couch, laughing so hard that tears rolled down their cheeks. When they finally gathered themselves together, they looked at each other in bewilderment.

'Where did that come from?' Hannah's voice was incredulous.

'I don't know, but it felt good, didn't it? It was a release.'

'Yeah, it felt good. At least for a few moments we stopped being boring.'

Sondra laughed. 'Hmm. I guess so.'

'Listen, I'd better get going. I'd like to leave now before we get sucked into talking about how sorry we are for ourselves. Rain check on the tea, okay?' Hannah stood up and gathered her bag.

'Okay.' Sondra rose too and walked her to the door. With a firm hug, they said their goodbyes, and Hannah left.

30

GODSPEED

Hannah's steps away from Sondra's apartment, down the passage, and towards the elevator were sluggish. She'd finally voiced feelings that had been playing on her mind for a while. And to Sondra, whom she'd been avoiding for a few weeks. Hannah wondered if that was why she'd stayed away from her. Had she been avoiding this realisation? Had she hoped to keep pretending that she was the perfect mother, and that she had the perfect son? Admitting it had made her feel unburdened, yes, but there was still so much jumbled up. Her brain was running at a hundred and nineteen to the dozen.

The ambivalence she'd felt towards Sondra was further confounded. She liked Sondra. There was no avoiding that. As she got to know Sondra, the more she learnt about Sondra's past and present, the more Hannah wished her well. But it was more than that. Interacting with Sondra made her more aware of wanting to be a person who could be liked and trusted. Was Sondra making *her* a better person?

'You're one messed up girl, Hannah!'

'*Talking to yourself again, child.*' Her mother's teasing voice echoed in her head.

'Oh, Mother, stop it.'

'*Does talking to me make this a little creepy?*'

'It's not creepy if I know what's going on. I know I'm not actually talking to you. You're in my imagination. I mentioned this to Mary – you remember her? – and she didn't think it was creepy or crazy. She said to do whatever helps.'

'*I hope I do help.*'

'You do, Mother. You have no idea how much.'

'*And yet you still have mixed feelings about considering Sondra as a friend.*'

'Huh?'

'*Just forget all this angst you're putting yourself through. Just go with your gut. Your instincts are telling you to just let things happen. You get along with her, and you like her. That will develop into something solid, or it may just fizzle out. It happens. Some relationships last, some don't. Let this one run its natural course, whatever that is. Don't push Sondra away every chance you get.*'

Hannah stayed quiet. Her mother's voice – her inner voice – made sense.

'*Listen, child—*'

'You are on a roll, aren't you?'

'*—you don't have to decide anything now, and even when you do, you don't have to commit to anything. Just take it one day at a time, one interaction at a time. You don't have any friends anymore. You've cut yourself off from all of them. But you still need people. Otherwise, your loneliness is going to make you a bitter, cross old woman. It's all so unnecessary.*'

'But Sondra?'

'*Why not Sondra? I'll say it again: you have nothing to lose.*'

By the time Hannah got home, she thought it would be wise to have other people to talk to in her life. Right now, she only had John when she visited his grave, her mother, who often spoke with her in her mind, and Sondra.

She called Muriel, wanting to ask about the support group. Did Muriel's offer to accompany her still stand? It rang until it went to voicemail, so Hannah left a message.

Muriel called back later that evening, and the two women – bonded by a shared loss – chatted for an hour. Muriel talked more than Hannah did, but Hannah listened and was present.

Muriel talked a little about her day, the household chores, a nephew who was going to stay with her in the next year to study at the *University of Johannesburg* – everyday, mundane things.

Hannah enjoyed hearing normality, just plain, simple everyday things. Muriel had a charming telephone manner, and Hannah found herself laughing and responding with light-hearted retorts or comments more than once. It was good to feel connected to someone. Her mother was right ... again: people need people; people need connection with others. That's what life is all about.

After they said their goodbyes, a thought popped into Hannah's head, a memory from decades ago of the first time she had had a similar realisation. She was a teenager, growing up on the farm, footloose and fancy-free. She was well-liked and had many friends. Hannah loved being in company more than anything else. It was like she had figured out the meaning of life, that life was about connections, human connections, all those years ago. Somewhere along the way, she had forgotten that.

She rose from where she was sitting. Instantly, she knew that she was not going to do this to herself, that she wouldn't entertain the gloomy thoughts anymore. Her mood and spirit had been lifted, first by Sondra and then by Muriel. She was going to enjoy this good mood for a while longer. She would not dwell on her revealing conversation with Sondra. If she wanted to heal and move on, she could not blame herself. She could not blame John either, nor Sondra. The blame game had to stop.

Hannah found her notebook. She decided to write a poem but not one about Sondra. And this time, she wanted to be conscious and fully aware.

Dear John

All that is left for me is to cry
All that is left for me are memories

Memories of your bright blue eyes
Thoughts of your loving soul
Images of your smiling face
Visions of your tomorrows never realised

My knowledge is pure –
I could have done nothing more
Loved no harder
Cherished any more

All that is left for me is forgiveness
All that is left for me is acceptance

Goodbye, dear John
Godspeed

31

IMPORTANT CONNECTIONS

Sondra was cautiously optimistic about the way that things were working out. Over the last couple of months, she had settled into a comfortable routine. Work was going well. She was exercising regularly but not excessively. She had even started cooking properly, not just heating up premade supermarket meals or takeaways. Sondra was also in contact with Salma. They had regular calls and *WhatsApp* communication, and through Salma, Sondra had contact with the rest of the family in Durban too. But the best of all was that, since she and Hannah had become friends, she was not so lonely.

They saw each other about once a week and were in regular communication for the rest of the time. Sondra had even encouraged Hannah to go to one of the support group meetings that Hannah had told her about. After some feeble resistance, mostly because Hannah had already made tentative arrangements with Muriel to go, Hannah had agreed.

Since Sondra had started cooking, and because Hannah disliked cooking for herself, Hannah would frequently join Sondra at her apartment for dinners. Sondra told Hannah how she had learnt to cook from Sarah and how her own mother, Beryl, had not been a good cook. Sondra shared that she regretted not learning more from her stepmother while she had had the chance. Carim family life revolved around food, often being generous and welcoming with the extended family, especially when it came to providing and sharing meals.

'How was that for you? Was it an adjustment?' Hannah asked, taking a sip of her juice.

'Yes. But I quite liked it. With other people around, it was easier for me to blend into the background. I observed and didn't have to actively participate. *Urrgh*, but there was one family that I didn't like. Not the whole family, mind you, just the aunty – *Bibi Chachi*. She was married to Abdul's cousin. She was snide about me being illegitimate and having a Coloured mother. Then I learnt later that *her* mother was a second wife and that *she* was a revert – that's the politically correct Islamic way to say it now. "Revert." Before, they would say "convert" – anyway, with all her airs and graces, it was because she was embarrassed by her own mother. At least I was not ashamed of who I was. In fact, I was proud of my identity.'

'Must have been tough.'

Sondra thoughtfully dried her hands on a tea towel then rubbed her fingers along her palm in a massaging motion. 'It was. Then one day, I overheard Ma telling her to stop. She was quite upset and said she didn't like how *Bibi Chachi* spoke to me. She implied that if she didn't stop, she wouldn't be welcome in the house anymore.'

'Would have loved to have been a fly on that wall.'

'That was me! Eavesdropping. I was surprised. I didn't think Ma had it in her. She appeared meek and compliant. But I realised then that she's strong, that she was just doing what she had to, to make the household run smoothly. And she did. Five kids, constant entertaining, with an old-school Muslim husband – he didn't do anything to help out at home.'

As always, as they ate their shared meal, they would talk more. They talked about their families, their shared experiences of being what the other kids called "bookworms" at school, and all manner of topics that came to either's mind. But there was one topic that they always circled back to: their sons.

Sondra mentioned her pampered youngest sibling, Abdullah, and how he was spoiled by Abdul. 'Even the elder sisters and Ma doted on AB, so he took it all for granted. Boys were the heroes, and the world revolves around them.'

'Aah, mothers and their sons.' Hannah shrugged listlessly.

Sondra's face fell. 'Well, most mothers … I did a lousy job. I never expressed my love freely, always keeping Michael at bay.'

'He'll come around. You have to keep trying and stay positive.' Hannah gave a smile that warmed Sondra with its admiration but did not make her feel better.

'Mmm. I'll keep trying to remember that.' Sondra sighed audibly. 'What if he never comes around?'

'You think that might happen?'

'My fear is that he'll get so used to being on his own with his father that he'll never need me.'

'What is it you're always telling me? "Don't overthink it." "Live in the moment." All that mindfulness stuff.'

'I know. Okay, yes, you're right.'

Hannah said no more. Sondra noticed a faraway look in her eyes. This happened often enough. Sondra had realised that the look was brought on by a sudden thought of John that would dance through her mind. She would escape into another world for a second or two while she revelled in the memory. It was similar to the way that Sondra would find herself thinking about Mikey, where he was at that moment, what he was doing, who he was with, if he was happy.

And much as they needed to remember their boys, talking about John and Mikey would bring them down – Sondra because hers didn't want to see her, and Hannah because hers couldn't want to do anything anymore. The realisation would instantly crash any happiness that had been conjured by their time together, but it wasn't as simple as that.

The topic would recur frequently because the hurt each felt never went away – "unescapable" was how Hannah had described it once. They could not escape the reality that was their new lives, the reality that neither had their son. They would remind each other to be positive though, trying to bring the other back to a good, constructive emotional plane again.

* * *

One Saturday morning, Sondra woke up, feeling refreshed and raring to go. It wasn't often that she felt this energetic. She decided it was a good sign and sent Michael an e-mail.

> Dear Mikey
>
> I'm sure you are okay, and things are fine at school? I'm okay too - same old, same old.
>
> I had a guest yesterday and it was good to have company. Then my sister from Durban, your Aunty Salma, called. Maybe one day you will meet them. She was very curious about you.
>
> I miss you loads, my boy, and I pray and hope that we see each other soon.
>
> Love, Mom

She didn't get a bounce-back and was overjoyed. That confirmed that he had unblocked her address. He might not respond or even read it, but at least it would be received. That was progress.

* * *

The next Saturday, Sondra surveyed her sparse wardrobe. She wanted to look smart but casual like a woman out for a spot of shopping. Apart from work- and gym-wear, there wasn't much else to choose from. She would have to go and collect some more things from her house ... David's house ... it was still theirs. There was no point in putting it off any longer.

She called David. He answered with a dejected tone. 'Sorry, Sondra. I'll send some pictures of Michael in a bit. I saw your message, but I guess, I forgot.' Sondra had messaged him in the week asking for some current pictures of Michael. Salma had asked again.

'Okay, great. That's fine. I was actually calling because I wanted to arrange a time for me to come and fetch some of my things. It's getting warmer now.' *What if my stuff is getting in his way?* Sondra thought ruefully.

'Yeah, sure. If you can come during the week, mornings are fine. Mikey and I are not around, so you can do your thing in peace.'

'Thanks, David. I'll check my schedule and see which day is good.'

'Just let me know the day before. I'll tell Cynthia to expect you.'

The call ended, and within a few minutes, David had sent about a dozen pictures: Michael at home, lounging around, at school, with buddies, at soccer or cricket, and a couple of selfies with David and him together. She stared at each one in turn, marvelling at how handsome and grown up her son was. He was a man now. She searched Michael's face for subtle changes and familiar features until the images became blurred by tears. She allowed herself a cry.

As though thinking of Salma conjured her up, a *WhatsApp* message arrived from her.

Aslmkm. How are you, sis?

I'm well. Before you nag
again, I remembered.
Here's pics of Michael.

She chose six of the best from the selection that David had sent and forwarded them to Salma.

She'd never felt like she had needed friends or sisters before, but now it felt natural.

Another thing you were way off on, Sondra. It's quite a thing, living your life based on certain beliefs, and then discovering you're wrong on so many counts. It forces a girl to take a long, hard look at herself. Sondra lowered her gaze and realised that at least she was aware, and for that, she was grateful.

Nowadays, Sondra was mindful of things and made a concerted effort to always be grateful. It was not always easy to find something to be grateful for. So she chose to appreciate the simple things, things that she would previously have taken for granted or never really noticed like the weather or fresh food. She wasn't sure how and when this change had happened. It was probably a natural extension of her learning to be mindful and conscious. No matter why or when, it was good, making her generally feel more positive or, rather, that the times she felt down were shorter and less frequent.

When Sondra got home, she saw a missed call from Salma and returned her call.

Salma dove straight in, ignoring Sondra's hello. 'Your Michael, the pictures you sent, I can't get over it! He looks like Papa.'

'What?' Sondra shook her head. 'He looks like David. Everyone says so, ever since he was born.'

'No ways! He doesn't look like David at all. That picture you sent with them standing together, they are quite different.' Salma sighed to convey her exasperation. 'How can you not see it? He's the spitting image of Papa. Look at Mikey's nose: strong and long and slightly flared. And the top part of his cheek, the angle of the cheekbone, it's exactly like Papa.'

Sondra screwed her eyes in concentration. She put the phone on speaker and carried on chatting as she scrolled to the images. Now that Salma had pointed it out, she could see it clearly. Looking at the screen, she could imagine her father's face superimposed. They were so similar. 'How did I miss that?' Michael was fairer, he had a broader forehead, but even the bottom part of his face was similar in shape and symmetry to her father's.

'Wait! I'm going to send you something. It's a picture of Papa and Ma on their wedding day. Phone me back after you get it.' And with that, Salma disconnected. A moment later, the picture she promised pinged on Sondra's cell phone. Abdul and Sarah were young and made a striking couple as they smiled at the camera. Salma was right! It was like looking at Michael in a bygone era.

Sondra was surprised but also a little excited – it was another connection between the past and present. She spoke out loud to herself. 'Huh! My son looks like my father, and I didn't even realise.'

32

THE SEEDS ARE PLANTED

Once home from a dismal visit with Sondra, one where Sondra's self-doubt and anxiety about Michael had re-surfaced, Hannah automatically went through her pre-sleep routine before falling into bed, exhausted. That was one thing she could give herself and Sondra credit for – since the two had started spending time with each other, she slept much better. It took less time for her to fall asleep, and if she woke up during the night, she was able to doze off again quickly and only woke properly when her alarm went off.

Not that night though. Hannah's mind was abuzz. Thoughts of Sondra and Sondra's worry that Michael would never rec-oncile with her whirled around endlessly. The more Hannah tried to push the thoughts away, the more she couldn't.

How would I have felt if John had done this to me, cut me off without any hope of him ever talking to me again? Isn't that what John did by killing himself?

Was this not a case of just desserts for Sondra? The image of Sondra – sad but courageous, terrified but hopeful, facing an unthinkable possibility but trying to remain positive in the face of it all – played over in Hannah's memory.

It's not fair. She's trying so hard. Sondra is doing everything she can to make amends. She's confronted her past, she's reconciled with her estranged family, she's admitted her mistakes, she's begged me for forgiveness, made efforts to get David to forgive her and take her back, and yet Michael, who she loves as much as any mother can love her child, refuses to forgive and forget.

Her mother's voice tinkled in her ear. '*Gosh, child, look at you! You've come full circle, haven't you? From hating the woman – blaming her for all the pain and suffering you've felt, making her responsible for John's death – to now caring for her, feeling her pain, and actually wanting the best for her.*'

A case of Dr Jekyll and Ms Hyde indeed. But Hannah knew that that wasn't really the case. She knew that she was still the same person and that it was in her to be compassionate and forgiving.

Even in her darkest moments, when she had wanted to kill Sondra, she had remained the good person she had always been, the person that her mother had raised her to be, the person that God loved. That innate quality – that which makes us human, that which draws us to one another, that which ensures that we seek a connection with others – was never lost. It had just been hidden. In the confusion of dealing with her pain and loss, it had gotten buried for a time. As she learnt to forgive and accept, she had found that part of herself again, that essential part that made her who she was. She was Hannah Bennett, daughter of Sylvia and Frank Gardner, wife of Eliot, mother of John, all of whom had shaped her and who, in turn, she had shaped.

That was what being human was all about, making the connections to those near and dear to you. It became clear to Hannah why things had happened the way that they had between her and Sondra, the way that the relationship had developed, and the way that it would continue to evolve.

Just like life was unknown and unforeseeable, just like death was unpredictable and unstoppable, so too the act of living was a constant struggle. One never has it all figured out. It is a constant learning curve of messing up and trying again. We never figure it out completely. We constantly get it wrong, learn, correct, realign, and then do it all over again. The one constant, the one thing that ensures that we are whole is the connections that we make with others, the simple act of being there for one another.

Hannah was glad that she had allowed herself to be there for Sondra. Hannah had found a role that she could fulfil in Sondra's life: she would help Sondra. In so doing, Hannah would find peace and relief in her own life again. Realising her new-found purpose, Hannah eventually drifted off to sleep.

* * *

The next Sunday, Hannah sent Sondra a text.

> Hi Sondra. How are you? Are you busy this afternoon?

> Would you like to join me on my cemetery visit?

It was a few minutes before Sondra responded.

> Okay. What time?

> Two o'clock. Meet me at the entrance to West Park Cemetery.

Now that that was decided, Hannah felt uncertain. Was her motivation pure? Did she want to make Sondra feel guilty? What she wanted to propose to her friend, she could have done anywhere. Was it macabre to do this in the presence of her dead son?

No point in rethinking it now. The wheels were in motion, and she would just have to follow through. She arrived an hour earlier and went to visit her mother's and her son's graves. She went to John's first where she sat quietly, allowing herself to feel the pain of her loss. A feeling of peace and acceptance invariably followed. Fifteen minutes before Sondra was due to arrive, she walked slowly to her mother's grave.

'Mother, I'm bringing a visitor. You won't believe—actually, you will. Maybe you'll even feel a little smug. You want to guess who?'

'*Sondra? About time too. What's your plan?*' Her mother's voice was upbeat. '*Okay. Don't tell me. Let it be a surprise.*'

'Hah! Like I can ever surprise you. You probably knew this was going to happen. Probably planted the idea in my head.'

'*You give me too much credit, child. This ... your journey, how far you've come ... how you have dealt with tragedy, it's all you. I wish I could say I had more to do with it. I've watched and worried, then realised you would have to walk your own path. You have grieved, and you have grown. I respect and admire you. Whatever you're going to do, trust yourself. Your intentions are pure, and that's all that matters. The outcome will be good. I'm sure of it.*'

'Thanks, Mother. I needed to hear that.'

'*I love you, Hannah, and I'm proud of you.*'

Hannah's phone beeped. It was a message from Sondra.

> I'm here. See your car.
> Where are you?

> Wait there. I'll come get you.

Sondra's face appeared drawn, probably masking her feelings. That was understandable. She must have been nervous but also curious.

Hannah gave what she hoped was a reassuring smile. 'Thanks for meeting me here, Sondra. Come, I want you to meet my mother. Oh, that sounds weird. I should say, "I'd like for you to come visit her grave."'

They walked side by side, Hannah gently guiding. 'She's an amazing woman. Even in death, she's managed to give me the soundest advice.'

'She's *your* mother. I wouldn't expect anything less than miraculous.'

Hannah shook her head. 'Miraculous, maybe. Kind and knowledgeable too. Today, she's sounding quite smug. But don't worry, now that you've arrived, she'll be on her best behaviour, right, Mother?' They had arrived. 'Please meet Sondra. Sondra, my mother, Sylvia.'

Sondra looked a little awkward.

'Don't worry. I'm not expecting you to be as crazy as I am and actually *talk* to her. It's helped me though. A lot. I know what you're thinking. It's all in my mind, and yes, you're right. I think it was just a way for me to deal with my emotions. To deal with them, one has to express them, even if only to oneself through an imagined ghost.

'We were close. I was her only child, and she was an adoring, doting mother. My only regret was that ... I shut her out ... I closed off completely to everyone after John died, including her. I could see how it hurt her. She was dealing with his loss too, and we could've been there for each other. She just wanted to help me, and it pained her that I didn't let her.'

'She would've understood. You were going through the worst thing that could ever happen to a mother.'

'I know. She was the one who got me to try and find out what happened. If she hadn't insisted, I would never have started looking. It was only after I found the diary and then spoke to Sam that things fell into place. She helped me understand.'

'Tell me more about your mother.' Sondra inclined her head.

'She was an incredible woman: selfless, loving. She was a housewife who made time for everyone. She was involved in the church and was loved by all.'

'Thank you, Hannah. Thanks for inviting me here, sharing your mother, letting me in and letting me close. I'm overwhelmed.' Sondra sat on the ground and rested her cheek on her knees. 'This is a beautiful spot, isn't it?'

Hannah knew the view well. She too sat down. If one looked upwards, one would not notice the gravestones; they were just out of sight from that angle. All one saw was greenery against the blue and white sky.

'I try to be grateful, and this gesture of yours is truly something to be grateful for.'

Hannah raised an eyebrow.

'I mean, you inviting me here and sharing this with me.'

Hannah nodded, and they fell quiet.

It was Sondra who broke the silence. 'It's so peaceful and calming. I appreciate the quiet.' Sondra exhaled. 'Even though I try, I can still hear all the noise.'

'The noise?'

'My own voice – accusing, blaming, wishing for different decisions, different outcomes, bargaining for a do-over, a chance. Here, I feel I can close my eyes and let it all go.'

Hannah placed an arm over Sondra's shoulders, and Sondra propped herself against Hannah. Hannah stroked Sondra's hair and back. A few minutes later, Hannah realised that Sondra was asleep. Hannah shut her eyes too and adjusted her breath to follow Sondra's rhythm. She wished Sondra and herself peace and love.

A time later, Sondra stirred. 'Hannah? Han?'

'I thought you were asleep.'

'Maybe I am. It feels like I'm in a dream ... The smell... what is that? Something fruity.'

'A lemon-drop sweet.'

'It reminds me of my mother. She always had sweets in her handbag and pockets.'

'A good memory?'

'Mmm.' Sondra nodded.

'You've never shown me a picture of her.'

'I don't have any. It was pre-cell phones, and my mom didn't own a camera. It never occurred to her, I guess. I had some of her when I was a child and a few that other people took, some school ones. When I left with Abdul, I didn't know what to pack or think about what to look for, what to keep.'

'What happened to your stuff?'

'I don't know. My father sold the house and contents, I guess.'

'That's a shame.' The sympathy was sincere.

'It is what it is. And the hardest thing was ... after a few years, I started forgetting what she looked like, not completely, but the image became fuzzy. *But* I've never forgotten her smell. I can close my eyes and inhale and sense it in my pores.' Sondra straightened and looked directly at Hannah. 'You're lucky. You have your mother's image, her words, her voice with you. You carry her in your heart.'

'That's beautiful, Sondra.' Hannah raised her head and beamed at Sondra. Even in the dazzling afternoon light, her brown eyes shone brightly. 'It's as important to be carried in someone's heart as it is to carry people in your own.' Hannah sounded wistful. She repositioned herself so that she was facing Sondra. 'I wanted to talk to you about something. The other reason I called you here was to introduce you to my mother. The main reason is to tell you my idea.'

'There's more?'

'It's about Michael.'

Sondra stiffened and tilted her head. 'Michael?'

'How much have you told him about you and me?'

'Nothing.'

'You've told him you've changed, but why should he believe it?'

'That's true. I've given him no reason to trust me. And he does not see me, so he can't see for himself.'

'Yes. The only way you can rebuild his trust, rebuild your relationship, is if you show him how you've changed.'

'How do I do that? He won't let me see him. I can only hope he reads my mails.'

'Even if he reads them, they're just words. He has to *see* the change.'

'What are you getting at?' Sondra seemed to study Hannah through slightly narrowed eyes, her nose scrunching in on itself ever so slightly.

Here we go! Hannah reassured herself. Then she took a deep breath and Sondra's hand in her own. 'If you'll let me, I'd like to talk to him.'

'Michael? You want to talk to Michael?'

'If he'll let me, yes, I'd like to try.'

Sondra sat bolt upright. 'You'd do that? For me?'

Hannah nodded and smiled. The surprise that she heard in Sondra's voice was heartening.

Sondra's eyes filled with tears. 'Really? That is so, so kind, so generous. How could I ever thank you?' She squeezed Hannah's hand.

'Let's not jump the gun. We don't know if he'll even agree.'

'He might. If David ... I think you may have to meet David first. If he believes you, believes I've changed, he may be able to talk to Mikey.' Sondra jumped up and started pacing. 'It could work. It must work. I'll give you David's number. If he'll agree to meet you, if you can explain about us, maybe ... just maybe ...'

'You're getting ahead of yourself, Sondra. It's just an idea. Sondra, please stand still. You're making me dizzy.' Hannah reached for Sondra's hand and pulled until she was sitting on the ground next to her again.

'When shall we do this?' Sondra clearly hadn't heard what Hannah had said, hadn't even felt the ground below her. 'Today ... um ... it's Sunday. Yeah, maybe. Maybe now. I wonder what he's up to today. No, we can't just call him out of the blue. Okay, maybe an e-mail rather, an introduction, and then we see.'

Hannah smiled. 'Sondra, take a deep breath.' Hannah laughed and playfully nudged Sondra with her elbow like they were sharing a joke.

'Huh?' Sondra looked at Hannah properly for the first time since this conversation had started. 'Oh, you're right. I shouldn't get my hopes up. All right, okay. Let's just take a second and calmly think this through.'

'I think you should leave it to me. You're too vested in this. It's too close to you.'

'Okay, okay. Yeah, okay, I'll shut up now.' Sondra put her index finger on her lips to indicate that she would be quiet. She took a deep breath, placed her hands on the ground behind her, leant backwards, and stretched. She straightened up again and took Hannah's hands. 'Thank you, Hannah. If it doesn't work or whatever ...' Sondra shook her head '... but you're willing to do this ... for me! I can't believe how amazing you are, how good you are to me.'

'Let's just sleep on it and discuss it tomorrow, okay?'

Sondra groaned. 'I don't know if I'll be able to sleep.'

They walked together towards the car park in companionable silence, each lost in her own thoughts but glad to be with the other.

33

HONESTY MOVES US FORWARDS

Hannah reread her e-mail to David. It was brief, business-like, but not cold. She thought she had struck the right balance.

> David,
>
> My name is Hannah. We have never met, but you know of me. I'm John Bennett's mother. I met your wife again a few months back, and we have become friends.
>
> I have a request to make. I would like to meet you and Michael. I think you and I should meet first and then I can explain. I'm sure you are surprised to receive this message, but I'll explain and answer all your questions when we meet. My contact details are below. I look forward to hearing from you.
>
> Kind regards,
>
> Hannah Bennett

David responded a day later. His e-mail was just as courteous and brief.

> Good day Hannah
>
> Thanks for your message. We can meet on Thursday at
> 5.30pm. Rosebank or anywhere around there will suit me.
> Please confirm the venue. My cell phone number is below.
>
> Regards,
>
> David

Hannah didn't delay in responding and secured a date and venue. She decided to wait until after she had met with David to tell Sondra. When Sondra got in touch, she was vague, saying that she was busy clearing out some of her mother's things and that they would catch up over the weekend.

When Hannah arrived at *The Peech Hotel* in Melrose, she walked through the small reception space and out to the open area by the pool where they had agreed to meet. She recognised David immediately from the pictures she had seen. He was seated at a round table on the deck by the pool.

David was even more good-looking in person. His dark curly hair framed his strong face. His brown eyes were kind, and the soft laugh lines that creased the edges around them complemented the high forehead and dimpled cheeks. The beard concealed the dimples, but Hannah knew from Sondra that they were there. He would age very well, she thought. Another thought immediately popped up: he was a perfect match to Sondra's looks. They would make a striking couple. She took a deep breath and prayed for a miracle.

'David, hello. I'm Hannah.'

He stood up and warmly shook the hand she offered. They sat and made small talk as the waiter took their orders and returned with her tea and his coffee. Hannah was surprised that they were naturally comfortable with each other. *I do know him*, she thought. *Sondra has told me so much over the past few months that he feels like an old friend, someone not seen in a while but not forgotten.*

David held her gaze. 'I'm so sorry about your son. My deepest sympathies. How long has it been?'

'Thirteen months.'

'That long? Yes ... I guess I only heard about it a few months after it happened.'

'Sometimes, I feel it must be longer, and at other times, I feel like it was only yesterday.'

'I'm sure it feels unreal still.' David shook his head. 'I can't imagine how I would've coped. If it was Mikey ...'

Hannah squeezed her eyes shut. 'No, don't say that. I wouldn't wish these feelings on my worst enemy.' Hannah laughed. 'No, I don't mean that you're my enemy or anything like that.'

David laughed too, and then they fell quiet, each sipping their hot beverages.

Hannah decided that she should get to the point. All that could be said in pleasantries had been said. 'Sondra and I have gotten to know each other these past couple of months.'

'You said so. I must say, I'm surprised. How did that happen?'

'She got in touch with me. She wanted to apologise. She felt awful for what had happened, her part in it, and she also wanted to apologise for her behaviour that first time we met.'

'Yes, I heard about that, got a blow by blow from Mikey. He heard the whole thing. It was quite an altercation, according to him.'

'It wasn't pleasant, but I guess that was the start of the ... the journey that Sondra and I have been on together. I don't know how else to describe it. It started when she got in touch with me. She had just returned from Durban—she told you about her trip?'

David nodded, his eyes open, his body straining towards her without actually moving.

'She reconnected with her family and her past. She dealt with the difficult issues of rejection and loss, and the confusion—the bewilderment of being suddenly taken away from the only life she knew.' Hannah noticed how David seemed to be holding his breath. 'Sondra said she shared very little with you.'

'That's true, I knew very little of her past while we were married.' His hand stroked his neat beard thoughtfully. 'I thought there was something awful or shameful, like maybe her father was in prison for killing her mother or something crazy like that, like she ran away from something horrible, and that's why she never wanted to go back to Durban.' David grinned.

Hannah half-smiled. Without much information, it seemed natural that David imagined just about every scenario. 'It was sad, but nothing quite so dramatic.'

'She did tell me a little bit recently though, so I have some idea now. I realised that I really didn't know her when we were together.' David sipped his coffee and then placed his hands on the table between them, his fingers interlaced. He was obviously waiting for more.

Hannah continued. 'With that knowledge about her family situation, I think it helps one to understand her and why she tried to keep people away. It was to protect herself from further hurt and disappointment that she built those walls around herself. She let no one in. She didn't allow anyone to love her. You and Michael suffered the fallout of that.' Hannah stopped and sipped her tea. The effort of sharing what was not really hers to share had dried her throat.

When David did not speak, and feeling somewhat recouped, Hannah added, 'I guess your imagined scenarios of her past are not that far-fetched. It makes sense that there must've been trauma, the kind that one wants to forget completely.'

'She pretended very well. She always appeared strong and determined, like she could accomplish anything. It was awesome to watch.' David did not keep the admiration he had for his wife from his voice.

'She *is* strong. She couldn't have come this far if she wasn't. The hardest part must've been to look at herself now and be critical. She acknowledges that she doesn't like what she sees, who she has made herself into. But there is positivity. She wants to change and is trying very hard to.'

'I've noticed subtle changes, even in the last few times I've seen her. She's softer, she listens more, is more approachable.'

'Yes. Yes.' Hannah sat up straight and clasped her hands together in her lap, heartened by David's understanding. 'It's all positive. She knows she has a way to go and keeps saying it's a process. One morning, she'll be upbeat and be so secure in what she's decided, and the next, she'll be a bundle of insecurities, unsure if things will ever get better, second-guessing herself, and undoing the good steps she's taken.'

'I feel for her.' David leant his head forwards and stroked the sides of his forehead.

'She's been through a tough time. She's amazing though. She doesn't allow herself to feel sorry for herself anymore. She's focusing on her work, her exercise, herself, and me too.'

David smiled. 'That's good. I'm really glad for her. I only want the best for her.'

That was her cue. She swallowed a lump that suddenly appeared in her throat. She felt she was as invested in the outcome as Sondra was. 'That could be, if we could get Michael to consider a reconciliation. She's not expecting an overnight miracle, but if he could at least give her chance ... How could he know how she's changed, that she's become the person who is worthy of being his mother, if he can't see the changes in her?'

'Every child needs his mother. I know that.'

'I was thinking—hoping that maybe my talking to him would make a difference. If he hears it from me – the person who he thinks should hate her the most ...'

David stopped his fidgeting and trained his eyes on Hannah. He was clearly thinking hard.

'By the way,' Hannah added, 'this was my idea. I asked Sondra to let me try and help. I told her that we could only hope that it would make a difference. I asked her for your e-mail address and haven't discussed it with her any further. I haven't even told her that we're meeting today.'

'She doesn't know?'

'Not about today. So, there's no pressure. You can think about it. If you feel it's the right time, talk to Michael and see if he'd be interested in meeting me.'

'I don't know. He's closed up on the subject of his mother.'

'*But* he unblocked her e-mail.'

'Really? I didn't know that.'

Hannah nodded enthusiastically. 'Yes. That means there's hope, right?'

'Mmm.' David's eyes darted around, unfocused on anything they landed on. 'I can see you're sincere, Hannah, and Mikey would too. Thanks for that. Thanks for being brave enough to do this. I'm sure it took a lot of courage.'

Hannah's lips disappeared into her closed mouth. Then she acknowledged the compliment with a shy smile.

'Thanks for being there for Sondra too. She really didn't have any friends, no one that she's close to. I'm sure your being there for her has made a huge difference to her.'

'Yes. It's been mutual. She's helped me too, in more ways than I can explain.'

'That's marvellous. She always tried to hide her soft side, but I saw it come through every now and then.'

'You're right. She actually is quite a softie. It would be a shame if Michael wasn't able to see that for himself, be able to experience her love now that she wants to express it.'

David's eyes creased as he examined Hannah's face. 'I can see why she took to you. You're an incredible person.'

Hannah flushed at the unexpected praise. 'Thank you. Sondra is too,' she said, trying to deflect the attention away from herself. 'Michael needs to see that and experience it. It'll make the world of difference to him.'

'You've convinced me. Okay, Hannah. I'll wait for the right moment and broach it with him.'

'Fantastic. Thank you.'

There was nothing more to say. Hannah thanked David again for meeting her and was about to take her leave.

'I know what we should do!' David's outburst was sudden, almost boyish in its enthusiasm.

Hannah stopped abruptly and turned to face him, looking at him quizzically. David had a mischievous expression dancing in the corners of his impish smile.

'You said you didn't tell Sondra about us meeting?'

'No, I didn't tell her,' Hannah replied. 'I didn't want her to get her hopes up or be nervous the whole time, wondering what we were saying.'

'Okay, great. Good. Let's walk a bit.'

34

HONESTY BRINGS US CLOSE

Sondra was surprised to see David's face light up her cell phone screen. He hardly ever called her these days. She put the magazine she had been reading onto her lap while she sat up straight on the couch in her apartment.

Frowning, Sondra answered hesitantly. 'Hello, David. Is everything okay? Mikey ...?'

'Hi, Sondra. Everything's fine. I just wanted to talk to you.'

And I've been longing to hear your voice all day ... 'Oh, okay. Yes. Lovely. How are you? How's Mikey?'

'He's very well. I'm good too. I've ... uh ... I'm just here with ... Okay, hold on.' There was a cacophony of sounds that came through the phone, then they went still.

'Hello?' It was Hannah's voice, sounding tentative.

'Hannah?' Sondra could not hide the confusion in her voice.

'Yes. Hi, it's me. Hello.'

'Where are you? David's with you?'

'Yes. We arranged to meet. I didn't want to tell you before because I didn't want you to, you know, unnecessarily worry.'

'Oh?'

'We've had a good chat. I've told David that we've become friends and explained how hard you've been working to improve yourself.'

'Is that a good thing?' Sondra sounded hesitant and unsure.

'I think it's great. David's heard me out. It's too soon to say much, but he's said he'll talk to Michael.'

'Really?' A note of hope crept into the voice.

'Here, talk to him.'

David came back on the line. 'Sondra, I think it's great what you've done. I'm happy for you: going back to Durban, meeting your family, trying to repair relationships. That's very brave of you.'

And bloody hard, Sondra thought. 'I ... uh ... Thanks, David. It's been quite a journey, and there's still a long way to go.'

'Yeah, I'm sure. But you've started. Hannah explained that you've been making an effort to grow and that you're trying. That's amazing.'

'Hannah's been a big help. I couldn't have done any of this without her.' Sondra shut her eyes and breathed in slowly. 'I so want Mikey to know this me.'

'Yes, I think that's important too.' David's voice was firm and confident. It made Sondra bolder.

'If he does and still wants nothing to do with me, I'd have to accept that, I guess. But he needs his mother, and I need my son – my family.' There, she said it. She wanted him to know her too. Again. Now. Properly.

'I'm going to talk to Michael the first chance I can get.'

'You will?' Sondra couldn't believe what she was hearing.

'Yes. If he'll consider it, I'm going to get him to meet Hannah. She'll be able to convince him, I'm sure. She convinced me.'

'She's an amazing person.'

David laughed, the sound warming her. 'Isn't she though?' Sondra imagined that David was looking at Hannah and smiling as she looked back in confusion. 'You're very lucky to have Hannah.'

'I know.' The words were enthusiastic.

'Hold on a sec.' She heard David saying goodbye to Hannah and thanking her.

'Okay, I'm back. Hannah just left.'

'If only I could have met her under different circumstances. Our connection is .... If it wasn't for me causing her pain, causing her to lose her son, I would never have met her. How weird is that?'

'Ironic, hey? But that's life. Things don't work out neatly, but there's always a reason. Things happen as they're supposed to.'

Sondra's heart fell. If only there was hope for Hannah too. But death is final and uncompromising. John was gone, and she, Sondra, had had her role in that. When she spoke again, her voice was thick with emotion. 'Can you imagine another woman as selfless and as giving as Hannah? If only ... If I hadn't done what I did ... treated John the way I did, things could have been so different.'

'It's done. There's no point in torturing yourself over the past. What you're doing now, being a friend to her, helping her heal, that's what matters.'

Was that what she was doing, helping Hannah heal?

'I'm not going to rush things with Michael. He's still fragile. He tries to appear strong and blasé, more for me, I think. But this whole thing *has* affected him. He's mostly at home. He goes out with his friends but not as much. None of them come over anymore.'

Sondra could guess why. Mikey didn't want to have to explain why his mother was not around.

'It may take a couple of days to talk to him and then weeks before he thinks about meeting Hannah. I won't force him. I may just wait until the idea is his.' That had always been David's way of persuading Michael, suggesting and encouraging only. He had told her once that, for a person to commit to something, it was best that they arrive at the decision themselves and not by being forced into it.

'Sondra?'

'Yes, I'm still here. Just trying to take all this in.'

David laughed. He sounded relaxed like he'd released the breath he'd been holding onto for so long – anxiously watching Michael, worried for him and about him, wondering if he was doing the best thing for his son. If that was the case, he should never doubt himself. David had always put Michael first. 'It's been quite a year, hasn't it?'

Sondra laughed too, not an amused laugh but a sound of happiness. Even if Michael didn't come around, at least David had made some steps to understand and maybe eventually forgive her. 'It's hard to believe sometimes. So much has happened in such a short time. I'm just grateful: grateful for every moment, grateful that I've learnt to appreciate the little things. It's made my life ... meaningful. Strange, isn't it? I thought my life was fine, close to perfect – great job, great house, handsome husband, bright kid. I thought I wanted for nothing. It's only when you lose everything that you realise ...'

They became quiet briefly.

'Guess what, Sondra?'

'What, David?'

'I think that this must be the longest telephone conversation we've ever had in our whole lives.'

'You're right.' Sondra laughed, but she didn't feel joyful. It was a pretty miserable realisation. 'Trust me to get it all confused. It was when we were together that we should've been speaking like this, being open and sharing with each other. I kept you at arm's length, and I'm sorry about that. I thought that that was what I needed to do to protect myself. And from what? From you? My husband? If only I'd known then, realised earlier.'

'It can't all be your fault. It takes two to make a marriage work just like it takes two to destroy it.' David sighed. 'I could've tried harder too. It was easy to just go along with the way things were. I didn't want to rock the boat, I suppose.'

'We should've done things differently. But, like you said, there's no point in rehashing the past now.'

'Mmm. It's over.'

Is it, David? Is there no chance for us? 'I wish things could've been different. I wish I'd realised what my pushing you guys away meant. Not letting you in too close caused this. I was so internally focused. It was all about me then. Maybe now – maybe because of Hannah, we can have a chance to get to know each other again.'

'Hannah might be the catalyst, but you should take the credit too. It couldn't've been easy.' He paused for a millisecond. 'I'm proud of you, Sonds.'

Sondra couldn't believe she'd heard those words. She couldn't stop her tears and soft sobs.

'Hey, are you crying? Sondra Carim-Edwards, are you crying?'

'Don't be silly.' But she didn't really expect him to believe the lie. 'All right, all right. Yes, I'm overwhelmed. I can't help myself. I'm sorry.'

'You've apologised so many times this past year, but this is one time that you don't have to. There's no need for apologies for crying. It means you're being real. If you'd felt like that more in our marriage, felt like you could share your feelings with me instead of hiding them ...'

Sondra sobbed harder, the magazine sliding off her lap and landing forgotten on the floor at her feet. 'I'll regret it forever.'

'No. You'll get over it. You're a strong woman. You'll learn from it. At least you won't make the same mistake again.'

What did that mean? Was David saying that there was a chance for them to try again, or did he mean in new relationships ... like he was in? 'David?'

'Yes?'

'Can I ask? ... The pers—the woman you've met. Who is she?'

'Kate?' There was a pause and the slightest intake of breath before he continued. 'Katherine Reardon. We met at one of Mikey's cricket games. Her son goes to *Hyde Park High*.'

'Is it serious?'

'It's early days yet. I don't know. We'll see.'

She could tell that he didn't want to discuss it. She couldn't let it go though. 'Has Michael met her?'

'Of course. I've met her son too.'

'Oh?' So, things must have been moving along then – their kids knew.

'We don't have to get into that now.'

So ... is this what it feels like to be shut out? Sondra acquiesced with a sigh. 'Yes, you're right. I'm sorry. I was just thinking ... maybe hoping ... you know ...'

'No, Sondra. Please don't misread this. I'm really glad that you're doing better. I only want the best for you. We may not be together, but you'll always be an important part of my life, and you're still the mother of my child. I don't hate you. And I really want you and Michael to reconcile, for his sake especially.'

'Thank you. With your support, I'm sure it'll be a matter of time before he ... well, he'll think about it at least.'

'Yes. Let's stay positive. If he'll meet Hannah, hear from her, he may be more open to a reunion. It'll be a long road though, so be aware.'

'I know. I'm prepared to be patient. I'll do what it takes. Right now, I'm hoping and praying and leaving it to you. You'll know when the time is right, and you'll do the right thing, I know.'

'Right. Okay, then.'

'Okay.'

He spoke slowly. 'This has been good, Sonds.'

'It has. Thanks again, David.'

'Thank yourself too. Goodbye.'

'Goodbye. I love you.' They were three simple words that were more real now, three simple words that she hadn't said nearly as often or as sincerely as she should have before. This time, she said them with intention, fully aware.

He didn't reciprocate, and he probably didn't want to hear them, but she needed to tell him.

'I love you,' she said again, then ended the call.

Sondra let the tears and sobbing that had started during their conversation flow freely – tears of sadness, relief, hope, and release.

35

TOO MUCH TOO FAST

Hannah's stomach was tied in knots as it had been since she had received the call from David. So much depended on the meeting with Michael going well – for Sondra and, by extension, for herself. She knew that, if she was able to assist Sondra in reconciling with Michael, it would somehow help her in dealing with her own loss. It was strange reasoning, and she wasn't sure how she had reached the conclusion, but this was the only reality for her now.

As soon as she had heard from David, she called Sondra instantly instead of waiting until after the fact like when she had first met David. When they spoke, it was Sondra who was cool and calm, contrary to Hannah's own anxiety.

'Things'll work out the way they're supposed to, Hannah.' Sondra repeated. 'We can't pre-empt anything. All we can do is be grateful for the chance.'

Hannah knew that she would have to be up-front and sincere with Michael. He would see through anything less than that. Michael needed to believe that she was doing this for her own sake, not only for Sondra. Just because she had learnt to forgive Sondra did not mean that Michael would.

He was entitled to his bitterness and anger. She decided that she would speak only of Sondra and what she had witnessed over the past couple of months. He didn't know this new Sondra and never would, not unless he interacted with her himself. If she could get him to at least consider that, she would have done well.

* * *

The next Saturday, Hannah drove into the driveway of David's house. She recalled the many times that she had driven that route, when she had sat in her car and watched the house, glimpsing the small family while she waited for something to happen, being too inert to do anything. Only on that one day had she finally found the courage to walk in and confront Sondra. That had been the starting point of the breakdown in the relationship between Michael and Sondra. Maybe this, her second visit to the property, would start the healing for them. She could only hope for that.

David was standing at the front door, waiting to welcome her in. She opened her car door and trudged up the path. He was striking, framed in the doorway. He was one of those men whose personality positively influenced people's reaction to them. He had an open, warm way about him, and people would be naturally attracted to that.

'Hello, Hannah. Welcome.' He reached his hand out and guided her into the hallway. When she saw of the hallway and the lounge that David led her into, she was struck by how well Sondra had described it. In terms of space and light, it was as different as it could be to Sondra's current apartment. No wonder she missed her home, as well as the family and life she had lived here.

'You have a lovely home.' Her nervousness made her voice tremble like an uncertain little girl. She cleared her throat.

'How're you doing?' David gestured to the couch.

'Well, thanks. Where's Michael?'

'He's upstairs. He's expecting you, and I'm sure he heard you drive in. I said I'd call him.'

Hannah's eyes darted around the lounge, seeing but not really taking in the décor or furnishings. She rummaged in her bag and found a tissue, which she dabbed under her nose. She didn't really need to.

'How's Sondra?'

'She's well.' Hannah's head vibrated for a second, and she inhaled deeply. Maybe that would help still the butterflies playing havoc with her tummy. 'Much calmer than I am.'

'Oh?'

'She says I mustn't stress about ... today, about meeting Michael. "What will be will be," she says.'

'I think it's amazing that you're doing this.'

'You think it'll help? Will it make a difference to Michael?'

'Maybe. But you shouldn't let that worry you now. We can only hope and see.'

'You'll stay?'

'Yes. Michael has asked me to.'

'Good.' Hannah's fingers tapped her handbag that she placed on her lap as she sat on a couch.

'Are you okay? Comfortable?'

'Yes, thanks. Can I have a glass of water?'

'Of course. Where are my manners?' David smiled and shook his head. 'Guess I'm nervous too. Just water? Tea?'

'No, thank you. Just water for now.'

'All right. I'll call Mikey.'

As David disappeared through the door they had come through, Hannah was left alone in the lounge. She placed her handbag next to her on the couch and looked around vaguely. As she heard David call Michael's name, she sat up straighter and tried to roll the tension out of her shoulders.

A minute later, David walked back with a glass of water and placed it on a coaster on the dark wood coffee table in front of her. Michael walked in a few steps behind him. She immediately recognised him from the photos that Sondra had shown her. He looked as hesitant as she felt.

Hannah stood up and took a step in his direction. 'Hello, Michael.'

'Hi.' He smiled – a typical teenage boy, awkward at meeting someone new ... or maybe it was just the circumstances. She couldn't tell.

'I'm Hannah, your mother's friend.' She hadn't planned on saying that, but it felt right. She was there to talk about Sondra after all. Hannah wanted him to see her as anyone other than the mother of the boy his mother had had an affair with.

'I wish I could say I'm happy to meet you.' His words weren't harsh or cynical. That was good. He was being direct, which was a sound beginning.

'Yes. If circumstances were different, maybe.' Hannah sat down again and sipped her water. It was chilled and refreshing. 'I'm grateful that you've agreed to meet me. This was my idea.'

Michael's head snapped back, his eyes narrowing.

'*I* asked your mother to introduce me to your father in the hope that you and I could get a chance to talk.'

'Why?' It was a direct question. He was obviously wary of her motives.

'I've gotten to know your mother these past couple of months, and we've become good friends.'

'Really?' He raised an eyebrow in her direction. His mouth was open. He crossed his arms over his chest and stood up straighter. His scepticism was etched into his face and in his demeanour. She had prepared herself for a cynical reception. He hadn't disappointed so far.

'An unlikely alliance, but yes, that's what has developed between Sondra and me. She came to me a few months back. She feels terrible about what she did and what that resulted in.'

'She should. She's disgusting.' The last word was spat out. It was judgemental but belied feelings of hurt, disappointment, and anger. It was much easier for a parent to get over their disappointment in a child than the other way around. Parents, especially mothers, are supposed to be faultless.

'You're angry, and I can understand why. I'm not here to change your mind. I simply want to tell you that your mother has changed. She feels deep remorse. She's asked me to forgive her.'

'How's that working out for you?' Michael wasn't pulling any punches. His feelings towards his mother were influencing how he was reacting to her. She felt sure of that.

'It was the most difficult thing I've ever done.' Hannah paused, choosing her next words carefully. 'I have though. I've learnt to forgive her. That's not to say that I don't sometimes blame her or get angry at the situation. But since I've gotten to know her, I can see that she *is* sincere. She wants to make amends and be a better person. I didn't want to believe her at first, but she showed me with her words and in her actions.'

'Michael, why don't you sit down?' David pointed to the armchair that Sondra had told Hannah was his favourite spot in the lounge.

Michael glared at his father, then threw himself into the chair. He cracked the knuckles of his hand as he watched his father and Hannah with long eyelashes veiling his eyes.

'Your mother has been on a journey of self-discovery. What she saw in herself, she did not like. She is doing everything she can to make changes to become a better person in her own eyes and for herself. It takes great courage to do that.'

'I've noticed the change too.' David nodded at Hannah.

'Yes. It's clear to everyone. It started when she went to Durban and reconnected with her family there.'

'Her family? She doesn't have any family. I've never heard about any family.' Michael's hands stopped their merciless attack on his fingers.

'She does, but she cut herself off from them years back. That is a story I think you should hear from her. She had her reasons for doing what she did. Now, she realises ... I mean, she sees things differently. She knows that she can't undo her past, but she has made attempts to reconnect with them again.'

Michael was still, his expression set.

David nodded at Hannah, grinning. 'Yep, it's pretty incredible, isn't it?'

The queasiness in her stomach she had felt as soon as she'd walked in was settling. 'There's so much you don't know. Your mother was wrong not to tell you about her history. It's important for you to know so that you can understand who you are.'

'Well, she's not a model mother. I'm not surprised.'

'True. No mother is perfect. We try our best but still make mistakes along the way.'

'Mistakes? Mistakes! What she did ... carrying on with a man young enough to be her son, while she was married! I'd say that was one *biiiig* mistake.'

Hannah pulled her mouth to one side and frowned. She was glad that she was the one hearing this and not Sondra; it would have been difficult for Sondra to hear. 'Sondra knows she cannot undo what has happened and is prepared to do whatever it takes to win back your trust. But that's between you and her, when you decide, when you feel ready. Coming to terms with all that, that's a long way in the future.' Hannah finished her water.

David rose. 'Top up?'

'No, thanks, but maybe I'll have that tea now.' Hannah offered him a smile as he walked past her.

David shuffled out of the lounge.

She focused on Michael again. 'Michael, I'm here because I want the best for you. You may think you have things all figured out. That's how it is when you're young. You're so sure about everything. But every child needs their mother. I know, I lost mine not too long ago.'

'Sorry to hear that.' Even under the strange circumstances, he was a well-mannered and well-raised young man. The response was automatic but not insincere.

'It's been a crazy year, but here I am. I've lived to tell the tale. If it wasn't for your mother's help and friendship, I would *not* have come this far.'

'My mother helped you?'

'Yes, in many ways.'

'It's her fault though, what she did to you, your son.'

'As I've said, I used to blame her too.' Hannah took a deep breath. 'John ... John was a beautiful boy – sensitive, caring, loving. But he did what he did on his own. He could've asked me for help, reached out to someone else, but he chose not to. After what happened between him and your mother ... after it ended, that was what *he* chose.'

David appeared with two steaming mugs. 'It's been very difficult for you.' He'd obviously caught the last of her words to Michael.

'Yes, it was. I tried to talk to him before, when I could see that something was wrong, but I couldn't reach him. I think he didn't want to let me. I didn't see it then, but in retrospect, I realise he was depressed.' Hannah's eyes were locked onto David's. He looked at her with compassion. She sensed his sincerity, him trying to understand and empathise.

'Does my mother know this?' For the first time since the conversation started, Michael sounded interested in knowing the answer to his question.

Hannah nodded. 'She knows. But what he did, that was *his* decision. I know that now. No one forced him to do it.' Hannah shuddered – she could not help herself. It was not easy to talk about John and his death. She steeled herself to be strong. 'It was John's decision. We all have our role in it, but no matter who we assign blame to, it was his choice to end his life. It was final – there's no chance for any attempts to undo it. I've been trying to let go of judgements, but I ... it was wrong and stupid. *But* it was still his decision.'

'If it wasn't for my mother, it wouldn't have happened.'

Was there a hint of sympathy in his voice? For her? 'Yes, she had her role to play, just as I did as his mother. We all influenced him as a person.'

'You can't think it's your fault?'

'No. No, I don't. That's my point. It's no one's *fault*.' Hannah's heart was pounding loud against her ribcage, and she took a few slow, long breaths. She needed to keep it together just for a little while longer. 'It is what it is. All we can do is learn to accept and move on.'

'Have you accepted?'

She hadn't expected this kind of interrogation. Maybe that had been foolish of her. It would not have been possible to keep the focus solely on Sondra. 'I have. In my own way, I have. I've had to, for the sake of ... of my sanity.' Hannah lifted the mug David had placed in front of her, but she didn't sip. 'I still rage against it sometimes, still get furious, still miss him terribly ... But I've accepted it in the sense that I can't pretend he is alive anymore, that he is still with me.'

'I see.' Michael sounded wary.

Hannah knew she had to convince him that she wasn't lying. 'No, I don't think you do.' Hannah forced her face to relax as she looked up at Michael. 'That's my cross to bear. I won't have a single day when I'm won't miss my son.' She placed the still unsipped tea back on the table. She balled her hands into fists and then forced herself to relax again. 'I want to tell you, though ... I hope to help you realise that you have a mother and that you need her. The older you get, the more you will realise this. You don't want to wake up one day when it's too late.'

'That's true, Michael. Listen to what Hannah is saying. Try and understand how difficult things are for her. But she is here because she cares about you *and* your mother. She has no ulterior motives.' David nodded towards Hannah, indicating that she should continue.

'What I'm saying, Michael—what I'm asking is for you to just give her a chance. Hear her out. Get to know her. Don't forgive her if you feel you can't. But you'll never know if you can if you don't give her a chance. You should do this for yourself. By cutting her off like this, you're only hurting yourself. You want to punish her, but the reality is that you're punishing yourself in the process.'

Michael stuck his chin out and clenched his hands into fists. Maybe Hannah had gone too far.

'I'm sorry if I've offended you. I care about you, and I just want you to know that.'

'Why?' Michael shouted, jumping to his feet, his fists becoming hard balls of anger. 'How can you feel anything but hate towards her, jealousy that I'm alive and your son's *dead*? I don't understand.' His face contorted as he spoke.

'It's crazy, I know.' Hannah calmly sipped her tea, then placed the mug gingerly back onto the table. She knew how teenage anger flared and raged and performed, and she knew that being cool, calm, and collected was the only way to meet it. 'I know that if *I* don't let things go, if *I* remain angry and keep blaming Sondra or myself or anyone else, that *I* will never be able to move on. If I don't release this, I'll become a bitter, hateful person. I'll be miserable and make everyone around me miserable too. The biggest victim will be myself.'

David moved to stand beside Michael. He placed a hand on Michael's shoulder. 'You know me, Mikey. You know I would only do what's best for you. You're everything to me. I know what Hannah is saying sounds ridiculous, but I believe it's true. If you don't try and understand your mother's point of view, even if you don't agree with it—but if you don't at least try to hear her out, see your mom, really see the—this new person she's become, it will be your loss.

'At the end of the day, you're *her* child. And, much as you may think it's impossible to imagine, you need your mother. You always will. She is not perfect, and she's admitted that. She's understood what her actions have meant. She's taken responsibility, and she *is* doing what she can to right her wrongs.'

Michael turned to his father. 'You want me to do this? You want me to pretend it's okay how she's hurt you. She betrayed you, humiliated you, disrespected you. I can't forget that!' Michael choked on his words. He threw off his father's hand and stepped back abruptly, breathing hard and loud. 'I just can't, okay?' And then Michael stormed out of the lounge and thundered his way up the stairs, slamming his door loudly behind him so that the whole house seemed to quiver.

David looked at Hannah with appealing eyes. 'I guess we'll stop here then. It's a lot for him to absorb.'

'Yes, I see that. It's all right. I'll take my leave.' Hannah gulped down the remains of her mug. She followed David to the front door and found that she needed to ask, 'Will he be okay?'

'Yeah, he'll be okay. He's strong ... like his mother. I think it's just all a bit too much to take in all at once.'

'You're right. Please let me know, okay?' Hannah's eyes searched David's.

'I will. Thanks for coming. It's quite something, you doing this for Mikey ... and Sonds.'

Hannah smiled when she noticed the glint in his eyes as he said Sondra's nickname. 'It's fine. I wish I ... I just wish I could make all his pain go away.'

'We'll work it out.' David looked upwards. She knew that he wanted to get back to his son as soon as possible.

'Goodbye, David. Good luck.'

By the time she'd climbed in her car, he had opened the gate to let her out.

36

REASSURANCE IS A TWO-WAY STREET

Sondra had her cell phone in her hand, looking at a message, when she let an agitated Hannah into her apartment.

'I've been going through everything over and over in my head. I don't know what to think.'

'Hello, Hannah.' Sondra cheerily derided. 'Yes, by all means, come in.' Sondra knew exactly why Hannah was there and the reason for Hannah's mood, but there was still an element of amusement that Sondra could not resist.

Sondra closed the door and watched as Hannah dropped her bag onto the couch and began pacing the length of the small area. She doubted that Hannah had even heard her teasing.

'I'm sorry,' Hannah rambled on, 'but I tried my best. I tried to get him to understand. I thought that he would at least agree to see you.'

'Slow down, Hannah.' Sondra placed herself in Hannah's path and took hold of her hands. 'Why don't you start by telling me what happened. It couldn't have been that bad.'

'I upset him. Oh man, I messed up. I just wanted him to give you a chance. Maybe I pushed him too much.'

Sondra gave Hannah's hands the slightest of tugs. 'Here, come sit down. Take a deep breath, and tell me what happened.'

Hannah sat down and buried her face in her hands. She groaned behind her fingers, then raked her hair backwards over her head and sat up. After a deep, calming breath, she breathed, 'Okay.' Hannah proceeded to give a blow-by-blow account of her meeting with Michael and David. By the time she'd finished, she appeared and sounded less agitated.

'It sounds like it went well, Hannah. He listened. He asked questions. And David was encouraging too.'

'He was. David was great, actually – very helpful and positive.'

'I don't doubt that. He's very level-headed and will do anything for his family.'

'I'll call him. I'll ask him how Mikey is doing.' Hannah fidgeted with her bag.

'You don't have to. He's sent me a message just before you got here. He reckoned that it went really well and said that he and Michael had a good chat after you left.'

'Really? Why didn't you lead with that?'

'You didn't give me a chance to, Han!' Sondra laughed, hoping that the sound would further relax her dear friend.

'Yes, of course.' Hannah sighed again. 'I'm sorry. Do you know what they discussed?'

'No, he didn't go into the details, but he seemed positive.'

'Oh.' Hannah didn't appear convinced.

'I think you're overreacting and overthinking. Didn't you hear your own account *just now*?'

Hannah blinked rapidly, her forehead creasing.

'I'll read you David's message. Hold on.' Sondra pulled her phone from her pocket and unlocked it. It was still open on her *WhatsApp* chat with David.

> Hannah has just left. Michael heard her out and listened and talked with me after she left. I think he's ready to listen to her suggestions. Let's keep 🤞 and hope for the best.

'Let me see.' Hannah unceremoniously grabbed Sondra's phone and read the message.

'See my response below, thanking him?' Sondra leant closer and pointed down the chat. 'And there's his next message, asking me to thank you. I'm sure he'll call you himself in a day or two and thank you personally.'

Hannah's finger moved up and down the screen as she read and reread the messages. 'So, Michael's okay?'

'Yeah, sounds like all is fine.'

'But he was so upset when I left …'

'I'm sure he was. But isn't that what we hoped to do? To get his attention? To get him to show how he's feeling? He's been pretending to be all blasé about what's happened when he isn't. He's my son, and I know him. He *is* upset, hurt, disappointed, et cetera. Meeting you forced him to face those emotions. He couldn't pretend that he's okay anymore.'

Hannah handed Sondra her phone back and stared pensively at the floor.

'Did you expect that it would all be sorted after one meeting?' Sondra frowned and tilted her head.

Hannah's mouth pinched to the one side as she raised her eyes to meet Sondra's.

'It's going to take time, Hannah.' Sondra tried to make her voice sound as reassuring as possible. 'I'm prepared to wait however long it takes. I think he *will* agree to see me, maybe not soon, but eventually, and David sounds confident of that too. So, the truth is: you did it, Hannah! You managed to get through to him.'

'But when I left, he was so upset. David looked worried too.'

Sondra nodded knowingly. 'Yes, I'm sure that was the case. It must've been a lot for Mikey to digest – meeting you, knowing the circumstances, getting to grips with you knowing me, you speaking on my behalf, everything that you said about me. It was never going to be a walk in the park.'

'I guess ...' Hannah's mouth pulled to the side again.

Sondra touched the side of Hannah's face and gently stroked her cheek. 'Hey, relax now, okay? What's done is done, and what'll happen will happen. I'm leaving it to the universe.'

Hannah giggled and then exhaled loudly. 'You've become very spiritual.'

'Nah, not at all. I'm just saying that. Hey, are you hungry? I haven't really eaten today. Join me? You in any hurry to be anywhere else?'

'No, no rush. Yes, I could eat. What have you cooked?'

37

THE TRUTH IN SINCERITY

Some weeks after Hannah and Michael had met, Sondra finally succeeded in pushing any expectations of the meeting out of her head. During that time, she spoke to David regularly. They slipped into a kind of rhythm of weekly calls to check in on Michael. It was only in the last call that Sondra had not asked if there was any change in his attitude, if there was a chance that he would want to see her.

Sondra also went back to the cemetery with Hannah one Sunday, and that time, she visited John's grave too. They were quiet, both contemplative, neither saying much, hands linked in their connectedness, hearts joined by their solitude.

Hannah thanked her afterwards. 'It was good to have someone with me again. But don't feel obliged to come, not unless you really want to.'

Sondra nodded but did not respond. She had wondered if visiting John's grave was indeed the thing to do. She didn't want to intrude on Hannah's alone time with him. Hannah had told her a few times that it was the only place where she felt a sense of peace and comfort. Hannah had thought about going back to church too but confessed that she didn't feel ready. She had started praying again though. Hannah told Sondra that while it was still a struggle, prayer helped. She was angry at God and she raged that He could have allowed this to happen. "But at least I'm talking to Him. My conversations with God are changed now. But that's okay. No point in pretending about my true feelings. He would know what's in my heart." Sondra nodded but said little, except to encourage where she could.

Attending the support group of other parents who had lost children was "okay" – Hannah went mostly to appease Muriel, and her therapy with Mary had stopped long ago. Sondra knew that Hannah's cemetery visits were still her greatest and strongest lifeline to her past, her present, and her future.

'It's up to me now,' Hannah had said. 'If I want to feel better, it doesn't really depend on anyone but me. Sure, I got tools from the therapy to deal better, and the group made me realise that I am not alone, that there are others who have gone through what I have. There are some people who are there every week and participate every week, others who are regulars but who just listen. I think I'll become a regular, like every couple of weeks, and maybe, one day, I'll really open up. But for now, this is all I need.'

Sondra was glad that Hannah was sounding positive. It made Sondra feel grateful for the reprieve Hannah felt at the grave. Although, she wondered if giving thanks that you had a *graveside* to sit at, to feel less lonely at, and to wait for a peace to descend and settle was something to be thankful for. It must be. Whatever helped Hannah – no matter how arbitrary, small, or bizarre – was to be acknowledged and celebrated.

* * *

The two women, the most improbable of compatriots, had gotten closer. They spent time together, seeing each other over weekends and sometimes in the week too. Sondra had started attending evening talks and events – it was a way to keep busy in the evenings and over weekends – and sometimes, Hannah would join her if it was something she fancied. It was the unlikeliest of alliances, borne out of a connection that, if either was being truthful, they would rather not have had happened, but it was what it was. Neither questioned it, and in their own ways, they were glad for the friendship.

During breakfast at Sondra's apartment one cool and rainy Saturday, Sondra let out a mildly exasperated huff. 'One day, I'm going to get you to come with me to gym.' Sondra was tired of listening to Hannah complain about her weight.

'Never. That's not for me. We can keep walking though.'

'If you're really keen on losing weight, you should eat regular, healthy meals. The takeaways are not good.'

'I know, but it's too much of an effort to cook for one person. You know that.'

'I do, but *you* know that I do it.' In recent months, Sondra's cooking had become adventurous, and almost all her meals were Indian. She visited the Fordsburg area once a month and stocked up. It became a part of her new and ever-evolving routine.

'You know,' Hannah said as she scrunched up her nose, 'it was only after Eliot passed that I started cooking. Towards the end, John had lost his appetite, so I cooked less. Then when my mother moved in and couldn't do anything for herself, it all started up again. But after *she* passed, there was no reason to. One day, I walked into the house, and there was an awful stench. I had to toss everything from the fridge and most things from the pantry. I realised that it had been *weeks* since I'd even opened the fridge.'

'Sounds hairy.' Sondra inadvertently shuddered.

'It was. But I'm much better now. I don't have stuff in the house that's going to spoil.' She grinned cockily. 'I enjoy *your* cooking and am happy to buy ready-prepared meals for the most part.'

'You're just lazy. *Tsk-tsk.*' Sondra shook her head.

'Can't argue with that.'

Sondra's phoned beeped, announcing the arrival of an e-mail. Normally, she would ignore e-mails until she was at her laptop. This time, she checked the notification and saw that it was a mail from Michael. She couldn't believe it.

'What?' Hannah must have been watching her and noticed her reaction.

'It's a mail from Mikey.'

'Really? What does he say?'

'Don't know. I haven't opened it yet.'

Hannah came to stand next to her. 'Go on then. It must be good news. I feel it.'

Sondra hesitated.

'Do you need me to go? Do you want to do this alone?' Hannah's tone softened.

'No, it's fine.' But still, Sondra stared immobile.

'*Soooo*ndra.'

'Uh, yes. Yes. But I'm going to look at it on my laptop.'

She leapt from the table, grabbed her laptop from its case just inside her bedroom door, and returned before Hannah had taken her seat again. Sondra switched it on and opened her e-mails. Sondra felt Hannah watching her as her eyes danced over the screen. She closed her laptop.

'Well ...?' Hannah pushed. 'What does he say?' When there was no reply, Hannah waved a hand in front of Sondra's face. 'Hello! Earth to Sondra.'

'Sorry. Sorry. It's just so much to take in at once.'

'What do you mean? He's still angry? Is he angry at me for talking to him?'

'No, it's good really. For weeks now, I've been waiting and hoping, and only recently have I been able to push this out of my mind. Then this comes.' She shook her head and smiled sagely. 'That's life, isn't it?'

'So?' Hannah's patience was clearly running thin.

'It's good news. He says David has managed to persuade him to give me a chance. He says he just wants to talk via e-mail for now and see where that leads. He's warned me to not to be too hopeful. He's not convinced that things will change between us.'

'Smart boy. I knew he'd come around.'

'Yes, you were right, Han. *And* you had lots to do with his change of heart too. Thank you.'

Hannah laughed. 'It's my pleasure. This really *is* great news, Sondra. I'm happy for you.' Hannah reached her hand out, placed it on Sondra's arm, and squeezed. 'I am truly happy for you. It's a definite step in the right direction.'

'Yes, it is.' Sondra only managed a half smile. *Is this too good to be true?*

'Are you going to respond?'

'Yes, but later. I'll say thanks and that I'm looking forward to it or something like that. Maybe I'll start telling him about my childhood too.'

Hannah nodded her agreement. 'Excellent plan.'

'Yeah, that's what I thought. I don't want to be too pushy. *Just now* I say the wrong thing or say something too soon, and then everything blows up again. At least with e-mails, I have a chance to read everything before I send it.'

'Yes, that'll help. Just don't overthink it. Be yourself. Don't pretend to be anything other than you are. He responds to that.'

Sondra nodded and stared out of the glass doors that led to the patio. The rain had slowed to a soft patter and wafted the scent of freshness into the room.

'Okay, I'm going to get going. Thanks again for the wonderful breakfast.' Hannah raised her arms over her head and stretched.

'Are you sure?'

'You're too distracted to be any decent kind of company right now anyway.' Hannah crinkled her nose and gave a soft snorting laugh.

The two cleared up and slowly made their way to the door. Hannah gave Sondra a light hug, a reassuring smile, and left.

Immediately, Sondra got started on her response to Michael. She wanted to sound genuine but light in her response. She had to be wary of getting too emotionally heavy. She decided that it was a good thing that she had a story to narrate – that of her childhood – and focused on that. She didn't want it to necessarily be chronological, more snapshots of her experiences with her mother and then when she moved in with the Carims. It was easy, easier than she'd expected it to be.

After thirty minutes, she read over what she'd written and shortened it a bit. She figured one page would be enough to start with. The last thing she needed was for Michael not to read her messages because they were too long or, even worse, boring.

Later that evening, she received a short reply from Michael.

> There's so much about you I don't know. At least you're sharing.

Sondra was delighted at the acknowledgement. It was a start.

* * *

This became the pattern of renewed contact with Michael. She would tell him about an incident at the office or about something that reminded her of another incident. He seemed to lap everything up, often asking a question for clarity. She would also send one or two photos: old and current images of the family that she had gotten from Salma. Michael responded positively to being told about Abdul.

> ...
>
> My father was larger than life to me. From not knowing him at all to suddenly having to live with him and learn about him... I went from 0-100 in a few short weeks. He was powerful, and I was quite intimidated. If I have any regret, it's that I didn't allow myself a chance to get to know him. Once I left home, I never looked back.
>
> ...

Michael responded, saying he couldn't imagine being afraid of one's father. Of course, he couldn't; the experience with his own father was so different.

> I never saw it before, or maybe I chose not to, but the attached photo from your Aunt Salma made me aware of how much you look like him.

She attached pictures of her father to the e-mail.

> I see it, Mom! He was a looker!

Sondra cried when she read the short reply. It was two sentences – less than ten words, yet he addressed her as "Mom" and had made a joke. That was a definite sign of the thawing between them. She rejoiced. Gratitude, that was what she felt, immense gratitude for the unexpected boon.

'Alhamdulillah.'

She was surprised when she heard herself utter the Arabic word, the Muslim way of praising and expressing thanks to Allah. She repeated it, feeling the syllables in her mouth. 'Alhamdulillah. Shukar Alhamdulillah.' The words did not feel strange, even though it had been years since she'd uttered them. It occurred to her that it was perhaps the first time that she had expressed them without being prompted. It was a natural response with the purest motivation. *I wonder if I remember any other* duas *and words?*

She started reciting the *kalimas* and was delighted that she remembered most of the five verses. She forgot the ending of the third one but remembered the others quite well. Sondra felt a sudden urge to hear Arabic, specifically words and verses from the Quran. After a quick search on the internet, she found an audio clip of *Surah Yaseen.* The familiar-sounding words were read beautifully, and they lifted her spirits even more.

A celebration was definitely in order. She decided to call and invite Hannah to dinner. 'Let's go to a fancy restaurant.'

'Are we celebrating something special?'

'Yes. I'll tell you all about it at dinner.'

'Oh, great! I can't wait.'

* * *

At dinner that warm Friday evening, Sondra breezed through the pleasantries, practically bursting to share her news. 'It's happening, Han. What I've been hoping and praying for! Mikey's coming around.'

'Really? That's ... good. Terrific! Details, give me the de-tails.'

'He called me "Mom".'

'Oh?' Hannah's smile didn't quite reach her eyes.

Sondra didn't notice and nattered on. 'I've told him about my mother and father and the rest of the family, that I've finally reconnected with them. He's curious, been asking loads of questions. I mentioned about Salma and how she made me aware that Mikey looks like his grandfather. I sent pics too. The resemblance was clear to him. Apparently, he even showed it to David.'

'Really?'

'Yes. David sent a *WhatsApp*, saying that Mikey had shown him the photo. David is also amazed at the likeness.'

'Indeed?' If Sondra had been paying attention, she would have noticed the pursing of Hannah's lips, how her eyelids drew down, and how her chewing slowed.

'I'm so happy. I'm so grateful. It's all your doing, Hannah! You've been a dear friend, and I can't thank you enough.

'Good. That's really good.' Hannah drank from her wine glass and choked. She coughed and spluttered into the linen napkin.

'You okay?' Sondra reached over and patted Hannah on the back.

'Silly me. Went down the wrong pipe.' She picked up her glass of water instead, though unsteadily. This time, she sipped slowly.

Sondra waited until Hannah nodded her head, indicating that she was all right.

'That's good, about Mikey. You have your son back.' The last sentence sounded guttural and raw.

Sondra looked up sharply. 'Hannah?'

Hannah coughed and cleared her throat again. 'That's better. Sorry. You were saying?' Hannah looked past Sondra like she was looking into the past for something long coveted. There was an urgency in the look too – a searching, a long-ing, a need.

'Hannah, are you okay?'

'Yes.' Hannah's gaze returned to Sondra, and she at-tempted a smile. 'I'm happy for you. I'm glad you've gotten your son back.'

And then the penny dropped. It must have stung that Sondra was getting her son back – her life back.

'Not yet.' Sondra's words were carefully considered. 'It's too soon to tell if it will really lead to anything. His reaction may just be excitement at, you know, realising that he has his grandfather's face.'

'I'm sure it made the stories real for him.'

'I think so. Probably, up until now, it was all just stories for him – interesting but without any real connection.'

'And now he can see himself as a part of that story. It's become a reality.' Hannah nodded as she spoke.

Sondra felt encouraged. 'That's it! That's right. You're so clever, Han. He can identify with my past in some way. Because of his likeness to my father, he has a connection to my long-lost and recently found family.' Sondra couldn't contain her excitement. Was that selfish? 'Hannah ... I ... are you ...?'

'What?' Hannah's shoulders crept up to her ears.

'Is this hard for you?' Sondra leant forwards.

Hannah's eyes did not meet Sondra's.

'It must be,' Sondra breathed. '*It is.*' The last two words were said with a finality, an awareness of what Hannah felt.

Hannah eventually met Sondra's eyes. 'Is it wrong of me to feel like this? I'm happy for you. Truly, I am. I wish you all the best. You know that.'

Sondra nodded. 'I do know that. You've been in my corner all along. If it wasn't for you, this wouldn't have happened. It's not wrong for you to feel this way. You've lost John. He's gone forever. Now, this happens, and even though you've been hoping and praying for it, you can't help but wish that you could have it too. I get it. I should've realised ... should've been more sensitive. I'm sorry.'

'You didn't do anything wrong, Sonds. I'm glad you told me, glad you feel you can share this with me. Don't stop doing that, okay? I don't want you to change how you relate to me, not now that we've come this far.'

'Okay, that's fair. You too. You must promise me something: please, you must tell me how you feel. Don't hide if you're upset for any reason. Our relationship, this friendship has grown and developed because of truth. It's based on us being able to be our authentic selves with each other.'

Hannah tilted her head to one side and gave a sort of smile. 'My friend has grown from an acorn into a mighty oak, hasn't she?'

'Don't be silly. Are you trying to say I'm being corny or sentimental?'

'Not sentimental, and definitely not corny. But you've become more ... what's the word you used? – authentic, and even more spiritual.'

'Uh, I guess so. But, no, not in a religious way.' Sondra didn't mention that she had started listening to Quranic verses. It wasn't religious, she realised. It was an extension of the feeling of reconnecting with her family and her past.

'No, not like that. I'm sure you've noticed how you've become more aware of others and your space though. It's like you're more in tune with things on emotional and spiritual planes, not purely physical or mental.'

Sondra laughed self-consciously. Since she had become more truthful with herself, yes, she had noticed. The transition to where she was now had been slow and long in the making, but it was surely there. 'You're right, Hannah. But you're not allowed to gloat about this, okay?'

They laughed heartily at each other and at themselves.

'Right! Enough of this deep stuff. I'm hungry. Why's our food taking so long?'

And right on cue, the waiter arrived with their main courses. They each ordered another round of drinks as well. The rest of the evening was delightful. Their food was delicious, and the company was even better. They laughed and chatted and teased each other as friends do.

By the time the waiter cleared their empty plates away and brought the dessert menu, they were stuffed and declined anything more, except for tea.

38

THE TIES WE SEVER

Sondra and David sat in the reception area of his attorney's offices in Rosebank. They were there to finalise the settlement agreement. It was more of a formality than anything else. They had amicably agreed on a neat division of assets, no alimony either way, and that they would share Michael's expenses equally. Thereafter, they would be divorced. Sondra still hoped for a change of heart from David but knew that, if she fought this, she would alienate him further.

They were discussing Michael; he was now a safe topic. After a few weeks of regular e-mailing between her and Michael every two or three days, Michael had asked all he had wanted to know about her Durban family. Then he had started a new topic: her time studying in Cape Town. He was curious about where she had stayed, who she had stayed with, where she had hung out, her job, and also about her chosen courses. When his initial casual enquiries became more probing, it became easy to guess where this was going.

When she mentioned this to David, he explained that Michael was considering options for his tertiary studies and that he was quite keen on a Business Science degree at the *University of Cape Town*. This confirmed Sondra's suspicions. Her brow furrowed as she wondered if there was an opportunity in Michael's questioning.

David watched her closely, then asked, 'What's going on in that little head of yours?'

'You think he might consider visiting Cape Town with me?'

'Michael?' David's eyes bulged in his head.

'Too soon? I just thought ... maybe you're right. He hasn't even seen me face to face yet. A trip would be premature. I actually did want to ask him if he would come with me to Durban to meet my family, but that would only be at the end of June, depending on how things develop between us of course.'

David sighed and crossed his arms.

Sondra panicked and back-tracked quickly. 'I'm just smoking my socks. I shouldn't jump the gun. It can happen, just not so soon. I'll have to practise patience.'

The receptionist came over and asked that they follow her. David jumped up. He was clearly relieved that the conversation had come to an end. They were shown to a boardroom where their attorneys were already seated.

In less than an hour, the documents were signed, the rest of the process was decided, and it would be a matter of weeks before their marriage would be over. Sondra felt sad but refused to let the feeling be visible.

'If only all clients were so agreeable, our jobs would be smooth.' Sondra's attorney, Madeline du Toit, shook her hand firmly as they walked to the elevator. She was a middle-aged attractive woman with dark hair in a pixie cut.

David took the elevator with them. 'Surely you'd be out of business then?' David smiled at Madeline, who grinned back.

Sondra watched and realised, not for the first time, that David was a consummate charmer. It wasn't intentional; it just came so naturally to him, being warm and friendly. People, especially women, responded to that. He was good-looking and as he matured, became even more so, adding to his natural charisma. No wonder he was able to feel ready to be in a new relationship so soon. Women were attracted to him and felt comfortable and confident to approach him. People like David needed to feel loved and affirmed. Well, she acknowledged ruefully, it wasn't only people like David, it was all people, including herself. It was only after she had lost everything that mattered that she had realised that.

David got her attention by lightly patting her arm. 'Sonds, you okay?'

She nodded, not trusting herself to speak.

They reached the ground floor, and Madeline shook their hands again, said her goodbyes, and walked to her car.

'I'll walk you.' David took Sondra's elbow lightly, and they walked towards the other end of the carpark. It was the most natural thing for him to do. He sensed she was upset and was concerned. His touch may have been light, but it conveyed understanding ... maybe even love. 'It'll be okay,' David assured. 'You're strong. We'll get through this.'

Sondra was touched by the concern in his eyes and voice. Again, all she could do was nod.

'I hope you won't be alone. Make plans with Hannah or something.'

His care and worry for her well-being had been constant. Even when he had been at his angriest and most bitter, he had always wanted what was best for her. How could she not have loved him as selflessly and unconditionally in return?

Sondra's instinct and only need at that moment was to throw her arms around David and hold on tight and forever. She blinked rapidly and fumbled with her key as she hoarsely uttered, 'I'll be okay.'

She got into her car and opened her window. He leant down, resting his hands on the door through the window. She squeezed his hand. He turned his hand over, held hers and squeezed back.

'Thanks, David. Thanks for caring. Thanks for always being here for me. Goodbye.'

He stood up, took a step back, and waved his farewell.

39

A TURN AND A SWIRL

Sondra was at work when Michael called, and she was totally unprepared. Even though it was all she'd been wishing for, it was a surprise to see his face flash on her phone screen, especially on a school day.

'Hello? Michael?' It could have been a mistake. Maybe he had butt-dialled her without even realising it.

'Yes, it's me. How're you?'

'Michael,' she repeated. Being caught unawares made her lose her normal civilities. The micro-moment of hesitation on her part could have made things awkward. She responded automatically. 'I'm well, thanks. And you? How're you doing?'

'I'm okay.'

'Good, good. School? How's school?' She took a deep breath.

'It's fine. You know, same old, same old.'

Sondra laughed. 'Great. I must say you caught me off guard. I wasn't expecting this.'

'Shall I call when you're not busy?' She could tell that he enjoyed his joke.

'Of course not, Mikey. I'm thrilled you called. It's what I've been wishing for, for months.'

'Mmm.'

'Does Dad know you're calling me?'

'No, I didn't tell him. He won't be surprised, I don't think. I've been dropping not-so-subtle hints recently.'

'Really?'

'Yeah. I've been sharing stuff with him about you that neither of us knew. Even showed him the pictures of your dad and the others.' He giggled mischievously. 'It's so obvious. He had to admit that I look more like my grandfather than I do him.'

'I'm sure that didn't go down too well.'

'Oh, you know Dad. He didn't really mind too much.' She did know David. He would have taken it all in his stride. 'You mentioned that you want to introduce me to the Durban family?'

'Yes. They're keen to meet you. I've shown Ma – that's my stepmother, Sarah – and Salma your pictures. When you're ready, we'll see.'

'That's the reason for my call actually. I'm going for a weekend to KZN with the school for a cricket tournament.'

'When?'

'Next weekend. We'll be staying at *Hilton College*. It's close to 'Maritzburg, I think, but also close to Durban.'

'*Ja*, I know that area. It's not far at all.' Sondra sounded like she was back in Durban. *How did that happen?*

'Anyway, we'll be busy most of the time, but on Saturday night, we can do our own thing, and I was thinking I could go visit them.'

It was a good thing that Sondra was sitting down, otherwise, she would have fallen over. 'Really? Wow, that would be great.'

'You'll arrange it?'

'Sure. I'm sure they'll be thrilled. They're all very excited to meet you.'

'Okay, cool. Then, uh, yeah. I'll send you the dates and where I'm staying and whatever. I guess the best thing would be to give them my number and let them call me?'

'Yes, okay. I'll call Aunty Salma and send her everything.' *You'll meet my family.* They'll *get to spend time with you.* Sondra couldn't help herself from feeling a pang of jealousy. 'I was thinking uh ... Mikey, I thought I'd be the one to take you to meet them when the time was right.'

'Yeah, uh ... I guess that could work too. If you're not busy the weekend? Some of the parents will be going with to watch the matches and stuff.'

Sondra couldn't believe what he was saying. Was he really suggesting she go to Durban too? 'I can come? You'd be okay with that?' she blurted out without thinking.

'Yeah, why not? If you're not busy?'

'I'm not. Okay, that's perfect then.'

'I'll e-mail you the schedule and the venues and stuff, and we can finalise next week or whenever?'

Sondra jumped up, her office chair rolling wildly towards the wall behind her, and did a little jig on the spot. Then she forced calm into her voice. 'Perfect. Yes, I'll sort out my flights and accommodation. I'll look out for your e-mail.' Sondra's heart was soaring, and her whole body was quivering as the warmth for this turn of events spread through her. She was being given another chance. She didn't dwell on the reasons or whether it was deserved or not. She was simply grateful. 'Thank you, Mikey.'

'Huh? Yeah, okay, okay. No big deal.' Obviously, he wanted to play it cool too.

It was probably the right way. There was no point in building up her hopes for a happily ever after. She had to take this for what it was: an opportunity to be there for her son. The rest would work out as it would. Sondra would have to keep her enthusiasm in check.

'*Gotta* go, Mom. Later.' And he was gone. But Sondra stood in that attitude for a frozen minute longer. He had addressed her as "Mom" again! That was too good to be true.

'Bye, my boy.' It didn't matter that he had already cut the call. She could call him her boy, her son, even if he didn't hear it. That door that had been so solidly shut and securely locked had been unlocked and opened a crack. It was a start, and she couldn't have asked for more than that.

Sondra dropped her cell phone onto her desk and walked towards the door of her office. She changed her mind and went to the large window that overlooked Johannesburg from far above. She pressed her hands and cheek against the cool glass and let the sensation still her as her rhythmic breath frosted the glass. All she focused on was the sound of her breath whistling out of her and the mistiness in her eyes.

Then the view of Johannesburg flitted into focus, and she marvelled at the green of the trees, the blue of the sky, the network of roads, and the surrounding structures. From as high up as she was in her office, she could not hear the traffic at all. She needed to share this deep sense of appreciation that filled her with someone.

Not Hannah, she realised. *David maybe?* She walked back to her desk, found her phone, and dialled without questioning her intentions. David answered on the second ring.

'Hi, David. How are you?' Sondra wanted the pleasantries out of the way.

'Hi, Sondra. I'm good, thanks, and you?'

'Michael called.'

'Mikey called? You?'

'Uh, duh! Yes, me.' Sondra's excitement was reflected in her high-pitched voice.

'Really? Wow! That's great.'

'Yeah. It was a great call, actually. Couldn't have worked out better.'

'Oh? Well, don't keep me in suspense any longer.'

Sondra noticed her fingers were gripping her phone very tightly, so she forced them and herself to relax. 'It was unexpected, just out of the blue.' She recounted the first part of their conversation to her now ex-husband.

'Mmm ... I'm not surprised. He's been quite into learning about your family.'

'But that's not the best part.'

'There's more?'

'*Yeeees*. I said I'd sort it with Salma and then mentioned that I had always hoped to be the one to take him and introduce him personally. So ... he suggested I come too!'

'What? I don't believe it. You're going? To an out-of-town school cricket thing? That's a first.' David was teasing ... mostly. She could tell from the humorous note in his voice.

'There's a first time for everything, right? Now's as good a time as any.'

'Uh-huh. Considering there's only months left of school for Mikey, it *is* about time you made your presence felt.'

'Oh, stop it, David. I'm not going to let myself feel guilty about the past. What's done is done. I'm going to try and be the best mother I can be *now*.'

'Hey, cool it. I'm just teasing.'

Sondra giggled. 'I know. It's all good.' He didn't know just *how* good though.

'Things have really worked out well, hey? Good for you, Sonds. Your patience worked out.' He laughed. 'Your tactics too.'

'My tactics?'

'Getting him hooked on your past. Clever strategy.' Was he needling her?

'It wasn't like that, and you know it. I do want him to know my family, if only to get to know me better. I'm grateful it worked out well though. Up until he called *just now*, I never let myself believe it was possible. I kept reigning in my enthusiasm because I didn't want to jinx anything.'

'I'm glad, Sonds, for both you and Mikey. I'm very happy that it's all worked out all right.'

'Yeah. I must make sure the weekend goes off smoothly.'

'It'll be okay. Normally, they're quite busy with matches, so there's no alone time. There's just the one evening that they leave free for the kids who want to do their own thing.'

'Mmm, okay. ... David?'

'Hmm?'

'What do I do there? Will I be expected to make nice with other parents?'

'There'll be lots of curious eyes for sure. Some of those mothers ...' David whistled softly under his breath. '... can be hectic.'

'Don't make me nervous.'

'No, it's not like that. I'm joking. Don't stress. Just be friendly. Introduce yourself first, chat a bit, and then keep your head down, and pretend like you've been to these things before. There's not much expected of the parents except to watch the matches and cheer, not just for your own child or his school, hey?'

'Yeah, okay. I guess I can do that.'

'You'll be fine. Just follow their lead.'

'Right. Okay, got it.'

'You're a funny girl sometimes, hey.' He chuckled to emphasise his point. 'Can command respect in the corporate world and handle millions of rands but can get intimidated by other parents.'

'Some of those mothers can get scary.'

'Some, sure. But most are just normal, regular people like you and me. You'll find someone who'll take you under their wing and try and include you. Before the weekend is over, you might actually have made a couple of new friends too.'

'Yeah, right!' Sondra snorted.

'Hey, don't scoff. Everyone needs friends.'

I have Hannah. 'Yes, I know that now. No harm in getting into the school spirit.'

'You may be surprised. The socials and things can be quite a bit of fun actually. Listen, it's been great chatting, but I have to go.'

'Sorry. Didn't mean to keep you. Bye-bye.'

'Just one more thing,' David quickly added. And in spite of what he had said about being busy, David chatted on, giving her other information about the cricket and the outings and catching Sondra up on how Mikey had been playing. She asked loads of questions.

When the call did end, she noticed they'd been on the phone for almost twenty minutes. These long phone conversations were getting quite customary. How strange was that?

40

A PARENT'S LOVE

ondra didn't know how she made it through the nine days until she met Michael, but she did. She pulled her cabin baggage behind her, with her backpack-style handbag slung over her shoulders and walked to the pick-up area.

Salma was waiting to fetch her. She was standing next to her car wearing large sunglasses and a scarf securely tied over her head. Salma waved enthusiastically when she caught sight of Sondra. Sondra quickened her pace as soon as she saw her sister.

They embraced and greeted each other warmly. Salma had refused to let Sondra hire a car or take an *Uber*. When she couldn't persuade Sondra to stay with her, Salma had suggested a B&B close to her home. Sondra didn't like disappointing her sister, but if there was even a small chance that Michael would stay over that evening, then they would need their own space. David had mentioned that the kids could stay overnight with parents, provided that they were in time for the Sunday match. Sondra hadn't mentioned her thought to David or Michael but hoped anyway.

Salma chatted away, and Sondra sent *WhatsApps* to Michael, David, and Hannah, letting them know that she'd arrived.

'Once you check in, I'll take you home. After a cup of tea, you can take the car.' It warmed Sondra's heart that Salma had offered to lend her the car.

'You sure, Salma? You won't be stuck without it?'

'It'll be fine. Over weekends, Baboo is around, and he takes me wherever I have to go. This weekend, we're just at home. Don't worry, okay? How do you like the new airport? It's a little bit far for Ma and them, but for us in Umhlanga, it's easy. You remember when we had that house in Tinley Manor? It's close from here.'

'Had? What happened?'

'Papa sold it about a year before he died. We'd stopped going anyway.'

'Oh?'

'He got a good price. Remember how we enjoyed our time on the beach there? You must take Michael to the beach if you can. You were always a strong, natural swimmer. I'm sure Michael is too.'

'I don't know if there'll be a chance. By the time we come to Durban later, it'll be time for the *braai*.'

'Next time then. I'm very excited about the *braai* tonight. Everyone is coming.'

'Don't make such a big deal. We don't want to overwhelm him.' Sondra laughed and decided being tactful with her sister would not cut it. 'Just dealing with you and your non-stop chatter and questions will be enough to keep him busy.'

'Don't worry, Saads. We're his family. You'll see. It'll all work out. He'll fit right in.'

Sondra wasn't as sure but realised it was too late to change things now.

'What? You don't trust me?' Salma gave her sister a cheeky grin. 'It's just Haniefa's and Luthfia's families ... and Ma, of course. AB will bring her.'

Salma was organised, and things worked out as well as she had planned. Sondra got to the cricket grounds to watch the first match just as the captains were calling the toss to decide which team would bat first.

The rest of the day went almost exactly the way that David had predicted. The other parents were friendly and welcoming. She didn't have to try too hard to relax and enjoy herself. There was only one chance to chat to Michael though, when he was with some of his teammates in between matches.

'You're really good with the bat,' Sondra declared, beaming at her son. Michael had scored fifty-two off sixty-four balls before being bowled out. His tally had helped the school win that match.

Michael flushed and grinned. 'Thanks, Mom.'

After the last match, there was a generous tea spread out for the parents of sandwiches, muffins, fruit, as well as several types of juice and hot beverages. Michael showered and changed in that time, and they left soon after.

'The car's a hire?' Michael asked.

'It's Salma's.'

'Salma? Right. I know. First Aunty Haniefa, then Aunty Luthfia, you, Aunty Salma, and then my only uncle, Abdullah.'

Sondra laughed. 'Spot on. You've been studying. Let's see ... do you remember Ma's name?'

'Sarah. What do I call her?'

'Ma. "Ma" is fine. I hope you're hungry. Knowing Aunty Salma, she's pulled out all the stops.'

'I'm ravenous ... and tired. How long to their house?'

Sondra glanced at the clock on the dashboard. 'An hour or so. Aunty Salma lives in Umhlanga.'

'Is it okay if I catch a quick nap?'

Sondra nodded. *Good*, she thought to herself, *he'll be well-rested.* He bunched up his jacket as a cushion, and in a minute, she heard his even breathing and knew he was out.

He got that trait from his father. David could also sleep as soon as his head touched a pillow.

She eased onto the freeway. There was a fair amount of traffic, and she had to concentrate. That made the trip feel quicker. Every now and then, her eyes would flit to Michael's face. He looked so peaceful. He was a good-looking boy, with a strong jawline and an aristocratic nose – a mini Abdul Carim from this angle. How had she not seen it all these years? Sondra offered a silent prayer to the universe. *Please, let him learn to accept and forgive. I need my son back, and he needs me.*

The drive went quickly, and before she realised, they had arrived. She shook Michael awake gently. 'Wake up, sleepy head,' she prompted and handed him a bottle of water.

He yawned and stretched, his long frame straining against the leather-covered seat. Michael drained the bottle in two long sips.

'Ready?' she asked.

'Yep. Let's do this.' He jumped out and surveyed his surroundings. 'Nice. Big property.'

'It's a couple of families – Uncle Baboo's family.'

'I know, Aunty Salma's husband.' He pretended to shoot her with his cocked hand and blew on his index finger. 'I got this.'

'It's not a test.'

'Pity. I would have aced it.'

The front door burst open, and Salma rushed out. Her arms were outstretched as she half walked, half ran and wrapped Michael in a bear hug. Sondra grinned at her sister's similarity to Sarah, who had greeted Sondra as heartily a few short, long months back.

'Michael! Mikey! So tall. So handsome.' Salma grinned at Sondra over Michael's shoulder. 'I can't believe it. You're here. We're all dying to meet you. Come in.'

She ushered them both into the house. There was a hubbub of excitement as adults introduced themselves and shook hands with Michael and kids stared open-mouthed at the handsome young man that they could claim as their own now.

Somebody pushed a drink into Sondra's hand. She sipped and grimaced. It was too sweet. Michael raised an eyebrow at her. She grinned as she mouthed the word "sweet" and pointed to her glass. He was as observant as ever.

She remembered how, as a child, he had always been in tune with her. If she was stressed or worried, he would imme-diately notice. His powers of observation had not lessened over the years, but their closeness had. *Never mind*, Sondra thought. *There's hope that things will change for the better.*

It was a balmy Durban evening. People were everywhere, relaxed, chatting, and eating. Kids were playing and running around as moms chased them down to feed them or wipe noses. There was a variety of salads, meats, and seafood.

Baboo came around with prawns he had just taken off the coals. 'Saadiyah, try these. My cousin lives in Mozambique and brought them fresh to me yesterday.' He generously dished a couple onto her already full plate.

She smiled, knowing that it was futile to resist. She sam-pled one as he watched her. 'Oh, very tasty, Baboo,' Sondra praised. 'You *braaied* them well.'

Salma sampled her own prawns. She turned to Sondra. 'You remember that restaurant where Papa used to fetch that yummy prawn curry whenever we used to stay in Tinley Manor? What was the name? Sea Breeze? No. Uh ... *Seabelle*.'

'I remember the curry but not the restaurant. We never ate there.'

'No, but he used to take us to go fetch the food. Me and you and AB.'

'No, Salma. I never went with. I remember that Ma used to give Papa the empty pot to fetch the food, and he'd call you and AB. We'd be doing things together, and he'd know that, but I guess that's how it was. Didn't want to be seen with a

Coloured child.' Sondra shrugged her shoulders, appearing quite nonchalant, almost blasé.

'Hmm. You never came with us? You're sure?'

Sondra shook her head slowly and focused again on her prawns.

'That was a silly thing to do to a child. Papa was so clever but clueless about some things.' Salma grimaced. 'Can't blame him. You know how it was in the old days? Even in our own family, people would talk.'

'I don't blame him. Actually, I don't ever think about that time or hadn't for a long while. I remember some nasty comments being passed. "*Bushie*" was a favourite. I was just a child. How silly can some people be?'

'Don't blame Papa. That was just how he was.'

'You know, Salma, I don't. I'm over it. It's over.'

Salma nodded gravely. 'Still couldn't've been easy. I wish I'd known then or realised.'

'What could you have done? It wasn't your fault or your place to do or say anything. You were just a kid too.'

Salma sighed. 'I'm sorry, Saadiyah. We were sisters. We should've been treated the same. But I can see how different things must have been for you.'

Sondra shrugged. 'It's over now. And tonight is a party – a celebration! Let's not talk about it now, okay?'

'Okay, agreed.' Salma squeezed Sondra's arm and then walked around, checking on her guests.

Sondra felt eyes intently on her and looked up to see Sarah watching her with a strange expression.

'Ma?' Sondra asked pointedly.

Sarah blinked rapidly. 'You got everything, Saadiyah? You tried the chicken sosaties?'

Sondra nodded and tried to hold Sarah's gaze. Sarah's eyes darted away, then came to rest on her again with a sad look.

Sondra rose and went to sit next to Sarah. She offered her stepmother a drink, but Sarah declined.

'I heard what you said now.'

'*Jee*, Ma?' Sondra wasn't sure what Sarah was referring to.

'About Abdul. About how he was with you. You feel he wasn't close to you.'

'Oh? It was a long time ago, Ma. It's over now.'

'Good. You mustn't feel bad, you know. It wasn't because of being Coloured or anything like that. He loved you and was proud of you.'

'Hmmm.' What else could Sondra say?

'You reminded him of your mother. You look exactly like her. When they got together, it was hard for me to accept. Then I could see how much he loved her. I knew her little bit. She was a good person. She loved him too. She was younger, but they had love and respect for each other.'

Sondra was curious. She would never have asked how Sarah had reacted to the "other woman", so Sondra was glad that the information was being volunteered.

'Abdul was going to marry her. Well, he wanted to, but she was stubborn. She didn't want to become a Muslim.'

'Oh? I didn't know that.'

'He would have married her still. This was even before she got pregnant. He wanted to have a proper marriage and everything. You know, Muslim men, they can have more than one wife. In the beginning, the first wives are not happy, but eventually, they have to accept and agree.'

Nothing new there, Sondra thought. 'You would have agreed to that, Ma?'

'We can't say no. And it was better than if my husband was making *gunah*.' To commit sin.

'He should've married her then.'

'He wanted to. Then she said, if he was going to marry her, he would have to divorce me, and you know Abdul. He wouldn't have done that. He was happy with me. We made our life, and we had two children by then. He would have had two wives, two houses. It would have worked out like that. But Beryl, she was a good person, but she was stubborn like that.'

'I didn't know.'

'You know we had an arranged marriage, but Allah puts love in your heart.' Sarah lightly tapped her chest with her flattened hand. 'But with Beryl ... so young, so beautiful, so full of life, so modern ...' Sarah sighed loudly.

'This must be hard for you, Ma. We don't have to talk about it if you don't want to.' What was the use of dredging up old wounds? Was the pain of retelling this worth it?

'No, I don't mind. I want you to know. You will under-stand better. When Beryl died, he was finished.'

'What?' Sondra's heart beat faster. She never realised that he had been in mourning too.

'Oh, *ja*. He cried for many nights, made *dua* for her also. He was cross, said she didn't want him to buy her a car. He never liked her to take taxis and buses, but your mother was a proud one. I think she didn't want people to think she was with your father for his money. She worked and paid her own way. Only after you were born did she accept money from him.'

'I wish I'd known that.'

'In the end, he became cross, then he would only go see her once a week. Only because of you. He was always hoping she would change her mind and marry him. He even said she didn't have to become Muslim as long as you were.'

'But why he didn't show me how he felt?' Sondra heard how she mimicked Sarah's accent. It wasn't mocking. She was only trying to identify with her second mother.

'It was complicated. They were both stubborn and proud. But when you came to live with us, it was very hard for him. He was missing her a lot. And every time he saw you ... you look just like her.' Sarah gracefully cupped Sondra's chin as though seeing her face properly for the first time. 'It was too painful for him. So, he kept you far. He didn't want you to see him cry.'

Sondra's mouth gaped. No matter what she had expected from the weekend, this wasn't it. She couldn't believe what she was hearing. Abdul had kept his distance because she was a reminder of his dead love. Sondra felt tears well up in her eyes, and she dabbed at them with the serviette that had been held under her plate.

Sarah covered Sondra's hand with her own. 'No. Now you mustn't be sad. I wanted to tell you but not to make you sad. Now you can understand him better and forgive him.'

Sondra turned her hand in Sarah's and gripped tightly. 'Oh, Ma. I was silly. I thought he didn't care about me, thought that, because I was from his Coloured girlfriend, his side-piece, he was ashamed or embarrassed of me.' Sondra shuddered and caught her breath. She didn't want everyone to see she was crying. Her voice dropped a couple of decibels. 'He loved me. He was proud of me. He just couldn't show it.'

'Men are like that, especially at that time. They don't like to show their emotions, want to be strong. But they are the same as us. Their hearts bleed and cry just like us.'

Wise words, Sondra thought reverently, *if only you'd shared them with me sooner.*

'Not only men, Ma. I'm like that too. I *was* like that. I pushed everyone away because I didn't want them to think that I was weak. I did the same thing to my son what Papa did to me.' Sondra laughed and openly wiped her eyes. 'Isn't that funny, Ma – the cycle? We make the same mistakes as our parents.'

'No, *beti*. Don't say that. Your son and you are together. You are close. Look! Look how he watches us. He is worried. He wants to come and check on you, but he is waiting, knows we ladies are talking and gives us our chance to finish up nicely.'

Sondra followed Sarah's eyeline to Michael who was indeed watching her with concern and confusion. She put her plate on the chair she was sitting on and walked over to him. He was standing around the *braai* with Baboo and some of the older cousins.

He took a step or two in her direction. 'You okay, Mom?'

'I'm fine, Mikey. I'm just fine.' She reached for him and wrapped him in a warm embrace. He didn't pull away, and after a moment's hesitation, he hugged her back. She was warmed and touched by his reciprocation. 'Okay, I'm sure we're attracting enough attention.' She gave a hard squeeze before letting go.

Salma appeared at her side. 'Saads? Everything okay?'

'All fine. Ma ... she's something else, isn't she?' Sondra looked in Sarah's direction. The woman was sunk low in a camping chair, but she was larger than life in Sondra's eyes. Sondra saw more clearly now than ever before the strong, quiet woman that Sarah was, the selfless kind who always put family first. If only Sondra had learnt from Sarah when she had had the chance. If only the two of them could have connected then. 'I love Ma. I wish I'd realised that when I was growing up.'

Salma also looked at her mother. 'Allah grant her long life and good health. She's our rock. She keeps this family together.'

'Oh, you'll turn out just like her, Salma. I don't doubt it for a moment.'

Salma grinned with pleasure. 'Inshallah.'

* * *

Sondra and Michael were quiet while she drove him back to *Hilton College*. He hadn't brought his things with him, so if he had stayed over, it would have meant that they would have had to get back to Hilton too early the next morning. Sondra was disappointed but decided that perhaps it was a good thing after all: they could each independently reflect on the past couple of hours.

As they turned into the school grounds, Michael turned to Sondra. She was glad it was dark. She felt uncertain under his intense gaze.

'What happened at the *braai*? What did Ma say to upset you like that?'

'I wasn't upset. ... Well, maybe a little. It was something I didn't know – or didn't understand – when I was growing up. It came as a shock.' Sondra tried to concentrate on the hand signals Michael was giving her to get to the dorm where he would sleep that night.

'You're okay?'

'I am. Better now that I know this. I'll tell you all about it one day.'

'When you're ready.' Michael nodded as though accepting the inevitable.

When did you grow up so much? she wondered. It's probably true what they say: growth and development only come from being tested. He'd had a tough year, but this new Michael that had emerged was a caring, considerate person.

'It's here, Mom. Turn right at that tree there.'

'Michael, I can't begin to tell you how much this weekend has meant to me. It's been amazing getting to know you again. You've changed, grown, for the better. I'm so proud of you, my boy.'

'Okay, don't get soppy on me now. One emotional gush a night is enough.' His eyes twinkled in the light coming from a street pole where they had stopped.

She knew he was teasing her. She punched him lightly on his arm. 'Can I get a hug at least?'

They pulled closer over the centre console and rested their heads on each other's shoulders. Sondra clung to him in the confined space before letting go.

'I'll see you tomorrow at the match. I may bring Uzair with, Aunty Salma's son, if he gets up in time. They were exhausted from all the running around.'

'Right. Night, Mom.' He bounded up the stairs and was gone before the sound of the car door closing registered.

'Night, Mikey.'

As she drove back to her B&B, thoughts of her father, her presumptions about him, and how those had determined who she'd become whirled in her head. How different things would have been if she'd known. It couldn't have been her fault. She was a child. The adults – her father, her mother, her stepmother – should have told her, or at the very least, they should have been gentler and more forthcoming with her.

Anyway, it was what it was. She couldn't change the past, but she could learn from it. *I know now at least. I never thought to question Papa's reasons or motivations for keeping me at bay. Would it have made a difference? Perhaps, but it doesn't matter now. It's in the past, and I can look to the future now.*

Sondra sighed loudly. What an eventful weekend! A good weekend, a great weekend – quality time and real connection with Michael *and* a better understanding of her parents.

'Enough surprises to last me a lifetime!' she voiced aloud in the dark car.

41

THE MIRACLE OF RELEASE

The trip to Durban was a cherished memory. It was the first of a few outings that Sondra and Michael shared. They were doing things together, little things that had a great and positive impact, but there was something that didn't sit right with Sondra.

A few days after returning from Durban, she'd stumbled on the box with the chain that John had gifted her. She had been looking for something in her desk drawer, had felt the square box with the ribbon, and had realised immediately what it was. Seeing the delicate chain and remembering his excitement at giving it to her unsettled her. John's smiling face when they were together, his distraught face when she dumped him merged with Hannah's. Sondra could not shake this and was unable to fully appreciate her renewed relationship with Michael.

After finishing late at work one evening, Sondra drove to Hannah's house. Sondra needed to talk to her friend about the turmoil that was rushing around in her head.

'It's a miracle,' Sondra verbalised for the first time, 'this new and improved relationship that I have with Michael.

And it's all thanks to you. But I don't know if it's one that I deserved.' She didn't add that it was her resurfacing guilt over John's death that had made her question if she had a right to reconnect with her son when Hannah could not.

'Oh, don't be like that.' Hannah sounded exasperated and stirred their teas a little more vigorously than necessary. 'Like I keep reminding you, Sonds, enjoy these developments with Michael. Celebrate them. It's been a tough journey for you. You've gotten a second chance. Don't blow it because your brain is overreacting. What is it that you're always encouraging me to do? "Live in the moment"?'

'I want you to be okay. No, more than okay. I want you to be happy too.'

'Why would you think I'm not happy?' Hannah raised her hands to prevent Sondra from speaking. 'I know what you're going to say, so don't. Obviously, I would be happier if John was alive. Where I am now is a safe, contented place. Listen, Sondra, and listen to me carefully.

'I do *not* hold you responsible. I cannot hold you or John responsible for me. My life is my own. I make my own happiness or sadness. John is gone, and I'll never stop loving him. I am his mother. That will never change.' Hannah paused and brought their teas to the table. When she sat, Sondra saw that her eyes were glassy, but there was an attempt at a smile too. 'But everyone's happiness – or unhappiness – is their own responsibility. I realise that now. John's ... his living ... his life and death is no longer the be-all and end-all of my life or my happiness.'

Sondra sunk deeper into her chair and dropped her head into her hands. 'How? How do you do it? How do you carry on? John ... he kil—I mean ... I don't know what I mean. Tell me.' Her voice was muffled through her hands.

She heard Hannah come stand next to her and felt a comforting arm embrace her around her shoulders.

'You know what would make me happy? If you could just put all these nonsensical ideas out of your head. If you stop feeling guilty, then I'll be at ease too. Sometimes, I stop my-self from talking about John to you. I want to share things with you, but I'm worried that you'll start all this again.'

Sondra lifted her head and leant against Hannah, wrap-ping her arms around Hannah's waist. She was glad Hannah could not see her face. *If she wants to share with me, surely she should feel free to do that? Is this guilt I feel restricting Hannah's interaction with me?*

'Sondra, you've become a dear and close friend.' Hannah spoke softly, almost inaudibly, but her words carried the warmth of a hundred suns. 'I know we're not the kind of friends who're always hugging or expressing our feelings in words, but ... I ... I ... I love you. Nothing would make me happier than to see you happy, *truly* happy.'

Sondra heard and slowly began to understand. Hannah was right. 'Okay. Okay. I appreciate that, Han. I feel the same about you. I've never had any close friends. Acquaintances and colleagues only, but that's changed. I have you and sisters now. But you ... you've become my best friend. I love you too.'

'I'll always be here for you as I know that you're here for me.'

They remained like that for a few minutes, Sondra leaning against Hannah, and Hannah holding her lightly but warmly. After drawing in Hannah's warmth, Sondra let go of Hannah and leant back in her chair. Hannah reached for Sondra's tea mug and held her hand on it for a second.

'Tea's gone cold. Shall I make you another?' Hannah asked, rubbing Sondra's back with her free hand. Sondra nodded and excused herself to go to the bathroom.

The reflection that stared back at Sondra certainly needed some water, which she splashed on three times like she remembered from making *wudhu* as a young Muslim girl. She pumped some hand soap from the dispenser on the sink and washed her face thoroughly. The face without make-up was surprisingly youthful but somewhat perplexed.

She fixed her eyes on her reflection and thought hard. She thought about what Hannah had said, and it made sense. John was young and naïve, but still, he had made his awful decision on his own, the consequences of which Hannah had to bear. Hannah had come through it and survived. So, Hannah was right, and Sondra had to accept that. She took a deep breath and let herself believe – believe in acceptance, forgiveness, love, and ... hope. It was not going to be easy to remember and celebrate those feelings all the time, but she could try and hoped to.

On top of that acceptance, she rejoiced for herself too that she and Michael had reunited. Sure, things between Michael and her were still a bit tenuous, but they were on the right path at least. It was only a matter of time before the relationship would be better than ever before. She hoped. No, she *knew* with every fibre of her being and would continue to work at the relationship. All she needed to do was let things run their course and not try to control everything, only herself. If she just let things be, she could be whole again.

Her body shuddered, and she knew she had to believe in herself first and foremost. She had to learn to trust herself, and she would work at that every day.

Sondra's eyes unfocused as she stared in the mirror. Another face appeared superimposed on her own. It was similar to her, but while it was a softer familiar face, it was unknown. Unknown? No! She knew this face; she knew this woman staring back at her. It was the face of her own mother – Beryl Jobman. Sondra blinked and looked again, and her own face came back into view.

Sondra closed her eyes and rejoiced at finally being able to conjure up the face of her mother. *Mom? Mom! It is you!* The shape of the face was the same as hers – broad across the middle and then tapered towards a pointed chin. The long nose slightly flared at the nostrils. The dark eyes were the same colour, but Beryl's eyes didn't turn up at the outer corners. Beryl's eyes were straighter and level, whereas Sondra's eyes were almond-shaped.

Sondra kept her eyes closed and allowed the feeling of seeing her mother in her mind's eye to wash over her. After years of not being able to remember what Beryl looked like, Sondra was able to see her. The visage that was reflected was clear and undoubtedly her mother as she had known her. Sondra didn't need to question why this happened now. It didn't matter.

I love you, Mom.

I miss you, Mom.

I understand, Mom.

I forgive you, Mom.

She smiled at her mother's face, and her mother's face smiled back at her, radiating love and joy. The feeling of release that she needed to acknowledge spread over her, and she remembered her father too.

I love you, Papa.

I forgive you, Papa.

When Sondra opened her eyes, the reflection that stared back at her was recognisably her own, yet there was a definite but subtle difference. Sondra appeared more beautiful, and she realised it was because she recognised her own inner beauty.

Sondra identified a complete person who was as different from the Sondra of a year ago as could be. This was a Sondra who was loving and caring, who introspected and made conscious decisions and actions to be a better person – one who would be a credit to herself, her son, and to her family. She had many to thank for this including David, Hannah, Michael, her family in Durban, and even John. Many people had been instrumental in her rebirth.

First and foremost, though, she thanked herself, Sondra Carim-Edwards.

I love you, Sondra.

I forgive you, Sondra.

She touched the side of her face, first with one hand, then the other. Sondra's hands and fingers ran along the contours of her face, touching but feeling more than her warm skin under her fingertips. She felt love, hope, and forgiveness. The emotions were overwhelming but simultaneously liberating. Sondra knew that she had been healed, that she had started the process many months back when she had been forced to take a long, hard, and honest look at herself, and that the process would continue.

The awareness of acceptance and gratitude surfaced and surpassed all other emotions. That is what she held on to, and that was how she was going to live her life from that moment on. Sondra had learnt to accept herself, her past, and her present, and was looking forward to her future. She hugged herself tightly and rubbed her hands over her arms warming them up. Her touch was loving and pure.

With a spring in her step and a song in her heart, Sondra stepped out of the bathroom and into the rest of her life.

GLOSSARY

Arabic / Urdu terms

abaya – long, loose dress, most often black, worn over clothes for modesty and as part of Islamic discipline of covering the female body

acha – good

Alhamdulillah – 'Praise God'

Asr or **Asr salaah** – the third daily prayer, prayed in the afternoon

Assalamu-a-laikum – 'Peace be upon you'; formal Islamic greeting (sometimes abbreviated to 'Aslmkm')

azaan – Muslim call to prayer

bechaari – person to be pitied (female)

beti – daughter

Bibi – lady; aunt (respectful)

bushie – abbreviation of the word, "Bushman", a derogatory word for Coloured people

Chachi – the wife of your paternal uncle

dua – prayer; request for needs from Allah

ghee – clarified butter

ghess – fragrant Indian dessert made with milk and china grass; similar to panna cotta

gunah – sin

hoshiyaar – clever; prudent

iddat – the four-and-a-half-month period after a divorce or a woman's husband passes away and she becomes a widow. Strict rules govern this period, including not leaving the house after hours and then only to work to sustain herself and her family

jaane – knows

jee – yes (respectful)

Jummah – a congregational prayer that Muslims hold every Friday around noontime

kalimas – short prayer, explaining and declaring the five pillars of Islam, read daily before bed

maaf – forgiveness; to request forgiveness and to forgive

madressah – daily religious instruction school for Muslim children

Maghrib or **Maghrib salaah** – the fourth daily prayer, prayed just after sunset

maulana – learned Muslim scholar

mayyit – funeral

mosque – a Muslim place of public worship; Muslim temple

Naani – maternal grandmother

pooree – deep fried bread made from flour

Ramadaan – the ninth month of the Islamic calendar, when Muslims fast from sunrise to sunset. Considered the holiest of all twelve months

roti – round, flat unleavened bread made with flour and *ghee*

salaam – 'peace'; abbreviated Islamic greeting

samosa – traditional Indian savoury pastry, filled and fried

shukar – thanks

Shukar Alhamdulillah – 'thanks to God'

Surah Yaseen – thirty-sixth verse of the Quran; considered the heart of the Quran

tawa – flat frying pan, similar to a skillet or griddle usually used for frying *rotis*

Umrah – the non-mandatory lesser pilgrimage made by Muslims to Mecca, which may be performed at any time of the year

wudhu – ritual washing before prayer

Zuhr or **Zuhr salaah** – the second daily prayer, prayed after midday

South African Terms

boot – the trunk of a car

braai – barbecue; to barbecue

Durbanism – indicating behaviour, characteristic or linguistic term that is associated with Durban

hayibo – exclamation of surprise, traditionally used by Africans but widely adopted by all race groups

ja – yes

just now – indicating something will happen soon but not a determined time

maar – but

matric – Grade 12; common term used to refer to the last year of high school

melktert – a popular South African dessert with a sweet pastry crust and a custard filling

sjoe – exclamation of surprise or exhaustion

ABOUT THE AUTHOR

 Raashida "Raashi" Khan is a 50-something South African Indian Muslim woman, living in Johannesburg. She is married and has two sons, fresh out of school. As a caring, compassionate, and empathetic person who loves observing people and life, she is a storyteller of note. She would like to be remembered as being 'never boring.'

A content creator, copywriter, editor, and proofreader by day, she is as passionate about being an author, poet, wife, mother, and friend − a unicorn that does exist. Raashida also facilitates workshops on writing prose, poetry, and her passions − the themes which are reflected in her writing.

Her short story "Your Voice, My Strength" was selected as the winning entry for the 2017 South African Muslim Women's Short Story Competition by Irtiqa Magazine. Raashida was on the judging panel for the same competition held in 2019. Another short story, "It's Not Funny", appears in the *Happy Holidays: Anthology of short stories* by Andrew Christie. Her contribution, "Hungry, darling?", appears in *Saffron: A Collection of Personal Narratives by Muslim Women* (launched 8 April 2018). Another of her stories appears in The Durban Review's *Drumbeats From Africa, Writings From Women Of Africa. Womandla!* (a collection of women's short stories, essays, and poetry), launched in Durban in 2019, features her short story *"A Hundred Times Over"*.

Raashida's first novel, *Mirror Cracked,* won the Minara Aziz Hassim Literary Award (Debut category, 2017) and was serialised into a radio drama by Lotus FM in 2019. *Fragrance of Forgiveness,* the sequel, was launched in March 2019, to much acclaim. She has also published an anthology of poetry, *Happy Birthday, Raashi,* and another of short stories: *Your Voice, My Strength and Other Stories.* In the meanwhile, she continues penning emotional, emotive poetry, and the occasional social commentary blog.

Read independent reviews of her work here:

www.goodreads.com/book/show/38641943-happy-birthday-raashi
www.goodreads.com/book/show/40853776-mirror-cracked
www.goodreads.com/book/show/44013884-fragrance-of-forgiveness

Contact details and social media links

🌐 www.raashisreflections.com
www.facebook.com/raashisreflections
🐦 @Raashisreflect
📷 @Raashisreflect

www.ingramcontent.com/pod-product-compliance
Lightning Source LLC
Chambersburg PA
CBHW032137190626
46814CB00005BA/1726